Praise
Novels of the F

Skykeep

"An exciting, romantic, and imaginative tale, *Skykeepers* is guaranteed to keep readers entertained and turning the pages." —Romance Reviews Today

"*Skykeepers* will knock you off your feet, keep you on the edge of your seat and totally captivated from beginning to end." —Romance Junkies

"Jessica Andersen's *Skykeepers* is a gripping story that pull[s] this reader right into her Final Prophecy series. I have not read *Nightkeepers* or *Dawnkeepers* yet, but after reading *Skykeepers*, they are both on my must-read list!" —Romance Reader at Heart (top pick)

"The Final Prophecy is a well-written series that is as intricate as it is entertaining!"
—The Romance Readers Connection (4½ stars)

"The world of the Nightkeepers is wonderful, and I love visiting it. It is intricate, magical, and absolutely fascinating. . . . Step inside the Nightkeeper world and prepare to be swept away!" —Joyfully Reviewed

"If you're looking for a book to read, one that has an intricate, inventive, and well-researched world with characters that are fully realized, might I suggest *Skykeepers*?" —Romance Novel TV

continued . . .

Dawnkeepers

"Prophecy, passion, and powerful emotions—*Dawnkeepers* will keep you on the edge of your seat begging for more!"
                                        —Wild on Books

"This strong new series will appeal to fantasy and paranormal fans with its refreshing blend of Mayan and Egyptian mythologies, plus a suitably complex story line and plenty of antagonists."
                                        —Monsters and Critics

"This exhilarating urban romantic fantasy saga is constructed around modernizing Mayan mythology. . . . The story line is fast-paced and filled with action as the overarching Andersen mythology is wonderfully embellished with this engaging entry."
                                        —Genre Go Round Reviews

"Using the Mayan doomsday prophecy, Andersen continues to add complexity to her characters and her increasingly dense mythos. This intense brand of storytelling is a most welcome addition to the genre."
                                        —*Romantic Times*

"Action packed with skillfully written and astounding fight scenes . . . will keep you on the edge of your seat begging for more."   —Romance Junkies

Nightkeepers

"Raw passion, dark romance, and seat-of-your-pants suspense—I swear ancient Mayan gods and demons walk the modern earth!"
          —*New York Times* bestselling author J. R. Ward

DEMON KEEPERS

A NOVEL OF THE FINAL PROPHECY

JESSICA ANDERSEN

A SIGNET ECLIPSE BOOK

SIGNET ECLIPSE
Published by New American Library, a division of
Penguin Group (USA) Inc., 375 Hudson Street,
New York, New York 10014, USA
Penguin Group (Canada), 90 Eglinton Avenue East, Suite 700, Toronto,
Ontario M4P 2Y3, Canada (a division of Pearson Penguin Canada Inc.)
Penguin Books Ltd., 80 Strand, London WC2R 0RL, England
Penguin Ireland, 25 St. Stephen's Green, Dublin 2,
Ireland (a division of Penguin Books Ltd.)
Penguin Group (Australia), 250 Camberwell Road, Camberwell, Victoria 3124,
Australia (a division of Pearson Australia Group Pty. Ltd.)
Penguin Books India Pvt. Ltd., 11 Community Centre, Panchsheel Park,
New Delhi - 110 017, India
Penguin Group (NZ), 67 Apollo Drive, Rosedale, North Shore 0632,
New Zealand (a division of Pearson New Zealand Ltd.)
Penguin Books (South Africa) (Pty.) Ltd., 24 Sturdee Avenue,
Rosebank, Johannesburg 2196, South Africa

Penguin Books Ltd., Registered Offices:
80 Strand, London WC2R 0RL, England

First published by Signet Eclipse, an imprint of New American Library,
a division of Penguin Group (USA) Inc.

First Printing, April 2010
10 9 8 7 6 5 4 3 2 1

*In loving memory of my grandmother Marian Woodard,
who was never without a book close at hand.*

ACKNOWLEDGMENTS

The Nightkeepers' world is well hidden within our own; bringing it to light isn't always an easy process. My heartfelt thanks go to Deidre Knight, Kara Cesare, Claire Zion, Kara Welsh, and Kerry Donovan for helping me take these books from a dream to a reality; to J. R. Ward for her unswerving support; to Suz Brockmann for being a mentor and an inspiration; to Nancy N. and Julie C. for being rock-star beta readers; to Liz F. for taking over the Keepers' message board; to my many other e-friends for always being there for a laugh or cyberhug; to Sally Hinkle Russell for keeping me sane; and to Brian Hogan for too many things to name in this small space.

What has come before . . .

Two years ago, a reluctant king stepped up to rule the scant dozen surviving Nightkeepers and their winikin protectors. Bound by blood and magic, this small band of saviors must protect mankind from the rise of terrible demons on December 21, 2012, as prophesied by the calendar of the ancient Maya. In order to reach their full powers, the magi must find and bond with their gods-destined mates . . . who aren't always who or what they seem.

With their numbers decimated by demon slaughter and their information stores destroyed by religious cleansing, the Nightkeepers fight a rearguard action against not only the dark lords of demonkind, the Banol Kax, but also against their earthly enemies, the magic-wielding members of the Order of Xibalba, who seek to preempt the end-time for their own purposes. Badly in need of new spells and prophecies in the final three years before the end-time, the Nightkeepers must gain access to their ancestors' library, which is hidden in the barrier of psi energy that gives them their mage powers. *Their only hope for this lies in the scarred hands of a formerly demon-possessed human who now harbors the powers of a Prophet but can't figure out how to use the magic to save his own life . . . or that of the woman he once loved.*

PART I

✴

SUNRISE

The beginning of a new day

CHAPTER ONE

June 12, New Moon
Two years, six months, and nine days to the zero date
University of Texas, Austin

"I just got the booty call," Jade announced as she let herself into Anna's office, which could've doubled as the set for a movie of the archaeologist-slash-adventurer-saves-the-day variety, with artifact-crammed shelves and framed photographs of rain forests and ruins. After closing the door to make sure nobody out in the cool, faintly damp halls of the art history building could overhear unless they made a real effort, Jade dropped into the empty chair opposite her friend's desk and let out a frustrated sigh. "Thing is, it wasn't the booty-er calling. It was your brother."

Anna winced. "Ew."

"No kidding, huh?" Not that Jade thought Anna's brother was an "ew"—far from it. Strike was massive, raven haired, and seriously drool-worthy, but he was also thoroughly mated, and the fact that he was the Nightkeepers' king had added to the squick factor, taking the uncomfortable phone call from "gee, it'd be nice if you and Lucius hooked back up" into royal-decree territory. Granted, Jade had volunteered for booty duty, and the sexual mores of a mage were way more liberal than human norm, but still.

Propping her feet on a cracked, knee-high clay pot that showed a sacrificial scene of a victim's beating heart being ripped out, and which currently served as Anna's trash can, Jade slumped down and let her long, straight hair fall forward around her face. It obscured her view of the trim jeans and upscale, low-heeled sandals that would've looked casually elegant on Anna, but on her just blended. As she slouched, she swore she heard Shandi's voice in her head, chiding, *Sit up straight, Jade. The members of the harvester bloodline are always dutiful, diligent, and decorous.* The three "D"s. Even before she'd known she was a Nightkeeper, or that her last name of Farmer was a modern take on her bloodline, she'd been hearing about duty, diligence, and decorum, along with the familiar remonstrations: Walk, don't run; listen, don't talk; speak, don't shout; follow, don't lead; blend, don't stand out.

Gack.

Tucking her hair behind her ears and straightening her spine—because she wanted to, not because of her *winikin*'s remembered chidings, dang it—Jade glanced at the black, tattoolike bloodline glyph she wore on her inner forearm, along with the scribe's talent mark that tagged her as little more than a glorified librarian. Bared by the soft white button-down sleeves she'd rolled up past her elbows, the marks stood out in sharp relief against her pale skin, which refused to tan despite her otherwise dark coloring of sable hair and light green, almost sea-foam eyes. *Ten bucks says Shandi never expected that the "duty" part of the three "D"s would come down to something like this,* she thought snidely. Really, though, she had zero problem with what she was being asked to do. Her problem was that Strike had been the one doing the asking. *Damn it, Lucius.*

"You could bail." Anna leaned back in her desk chair, toying with the thin metal chain that disappeared at her neckline. The king's sister was a striking woman in her late thirties, wearing a moss-colored lightweight sweater that counterpointed her dark, russet-highlighted hair and the piercing cobalt eyes she and Strike had both inherited from their father, King Scarred-Jaguar. Despite her heritage, though, Anna had recently stepped up to head the human university's ancient civilizations department. Of the scant dozen Nightkeepers still living, she was the only one who had refused to take up residence at Skywatch and commit to the Nightkeepers' war against the *Banol Kax* and the fast-approaching zero date. Although Jade knew that Anna's decision had caused—was still causing—problems back at Skywatch, she considered herself lucky that the other woman had stuck to her guns, not just because the university connection gave the Nightkeepers access to high-level information on the ancient Maya and the world at large, but because the campus itself had turned into a landing spot for magi looking to get away from Skywatch without being totally out of the loop . . . like Rabbit, who'd needed to escape the compound's isolation and memories of his borderline sociopathic father, and Jade, who'd needed . . . Hell, she didn't know what she'd needed. Space, maybe. Perspective. A cooling-off period, and some new skills that didn't rely on magic.

Now, though, she was being called back to Skywatch. Back to duty. And back to a man who . . . *Shit*.

Jade took a deep breath. "Sure, I could back out." As she turned her palms up, her forearm marks flashed a stark reminder of duty. "But then what? We need access to the library; Lucius isn't getting it done on his own, and the others haven't managed to trigger his powers using rituals and blood. Besides, we've got plenty of proof that sex magic trumps blood sacrifice. Strike and Leah used it to drive the *Banol Kax* back to the underworld; Nate and Alexis used it to repair a breach in the barrier; and Michael and Sasha used it to defeat Iago and his Xibalbans." Although that last point was somewhat debatable.

Sure, the Nightkeepers' earthly enemies, the members of the Order of Xibalba, had been quiet since the winter solstice, but the last time the Nightkeepers had laid eyes on the Xibalbans' leader, Iago, he had been in the process of summoning the soul of the long-dead—and seriously bloodthirsty—Aztec god-king, Moctezuma. Iago had been trying to create an *ajaw-makol*: a powerful human-demon hybrid that retained its human characteristics in direct proportion to the degree of evil in the host's soul. But the transition spell had been interrupted when the Nightkeepers had breached Iago's mountain lair, making the outcome far less clear. The few hints Jade had found in the Nightkeepers' archive suggested that an interrupted *makol* transition could go one of two ways. Most often, the human host-to-be slid into a comalike stasis for weeks or months while the demon spirit fought to integrate itself—or not—with the host's brain. Which was what the Nightkeepers suspected was happening with Iago. Less often, both the demon and human consciousnesses could coexist while the host remained conscious, with the two souls fighting for dominance . . . which was what had happened to Lucius. The Nightkeepers had eventually managed to rescue him and banish the *makol*, but that hadn't actually been their goal. What they'd really done was offer his soul to the in-between in an effort to turn him into the Prophet: an incarnate conduit capable of channeling badly needed intel from the metaphysical plane. Lucius's exorcism and survival had been a side benefit, which galled Jade at the same time that it forced her gratitude.

Now she tried not to notice how Anna was just sitting there looking at her, the way she did with her Intro to Mayan Studies students. *Keep going*, the look said. *You'll see where you went wrong in a minute.* "Three times now," Jade continued doggedly, "sex magic has turned out to be the key to unlocking the larger powers necessary for successful high-level magic: Godkeeper magic in Leah's and Alexis's cases, the Volatile's shapeshifting ability for Nate, and the balanced matter and antimatter of Michael's and Sasha's talents. So it seems logical that sex magic could be the key that triggers the Prophet's power in Lucius."

Granted, he wasn't a Nightkeeper. But despite the ongoing debate among the Nightkeepers, particularly the members of the royal council, Jade didn't think the problem was his humanity, his former demonic connection, or the fact that he'd retained his soul when the library spell had called for its sacrifice. Her instincts said he just needed a jump start, with an emphasis on the "jump" part—as in, he needed to get himself jumped. And if that was bound to make things complicated between them, so be it. She'd made herself scarce for the past five-plus months since his return to Skywatch; she could leave again afterward if she had to. It wasn't like anyone was begging her to come back. And didn't that just suck?

"There's one big difference between your situation and the other cases you're talking about." Anna raised an eyebrow. "Unless there isn't?"

And there was the crux of another major debate. Was it the sex magic itself that unlocked the bigger powers, or was the emotional pair-bonding of a mated couple the key, with sex magic as a collateral bonus? *Hello, chicken and egg.* Of the three couples Jade had named, in the aftermath of the big battles they'd been instrumental in winning, two had gained the *jun tan* marks signifying them as mated, soul-bound pairs. And although Michael's connection to death magic prevented him from forming the *jun tan*, he and Sasha had gotten engaged human-style, diamond ring and all. Which suggested it wasn't just the sex magic that was important; it was the emotions too.

Jade had heard the argument before—ad nauseam—

but it pinched harder coming from Anna, who had become a good friend in the months since Jade had fled from Skywatch to the university for a crash course in Mayan epigraphy and some breathing room . . . And Anna's relationship with Lucius went a good six years farther back than that—she'd been his boss, his mentor, and briefly his bond-master under Nightkeeper law.

"I don't think it's a question of love," Jade said, glancing past Anna's shoulder to the shelf beyond, where a crudely faked statuette of Flower Quetzal, the Aztec goddess of love and female sexuality, seemed to be smirking at her. Doggedly, she continued: "I think in each of the prior cases, the couples were struggling with identity issues, trying not to lose their senses of self to the magic or their feelings for each other. That won't be a problem for Lucius and me. I don't have much in the way of magic, and we're not . . . Well, we had sex once; that was it." And oh, holy shit, had that been a disaster. Not the sex, but the way she'd flubbed the aftermath. "We're just friends now," she finished. *Sort of.*

"The *jun tan* the others earned through sex magic doesn't symbolize friendship . . . and neither does what Strike wants you to do."

"It's just sex." Jade glanced at her friend as a new reason for the cross-examination occurred. "Unless you think he's still too fragile?" Even with his grisly wounds on the mend, thanks to Sasha's healing magic, Lucius had been badly depleted in the weeks following his return to the Nightkeepers. He'd been disconnected and clumsy, as though, even with the *makol* gone from his head, he wasn't at home inside his own body. More, he'd been deeply ashamed of the weakness, thanks to a childhood spent as the weakling nerd in a family of hard-core jocks. Had his condition deteriorated?

"Fragile is *not* the word that comes to mind." There was an odd note in Anna's voice.

"Then what's with the 'don't do it' vibes?"

"I think . . ." Anna trailed off, then shook her head. "You know? Forget I said anything. It's not fair for me to say on one hand that I want Strike to deal me out of the hierarchy, then on the other go running around trying to subvert the royal council's plan."

Jade winced at learning the should-Jade-jump-Lucius discussion hadn't just been a three-way of her, Strike, and Anna, as she'd thought, but had also included the other members of the royal council: Leah, Jox, Nate, and Alexis. Michael had probably been involved too, as he was practically a council member; and if he knew what was going on, then so did Sasha. Shandi had also likely been in on the conversation, though the *winikin* probably hadn't added much beyond, "Whatever you think is best, sire." Jade was determined not to let any of that matter, though. For once, she was the one taking action while the others hung back and played supporting roles. The harvester bloodline might have traditionally produced shield bearers rather than fighters, and she might be the only living Nightkeeper aside from Anna who didn't wear the warrior's talent mark, but this time she was on the front lines, ready to take one for the team.

So to speak.

Anna touched her chain again. Though Jade couldn't see the heavy pendant it held, she could easily picture the yellow crystal skull. Handed down through the maternal lineage, the quartz effigy was the focus of an *itza'at* seer's visionary gift. Normally Anna blocked her talent, which was glitchy at best, but Jade thought she caught a faint hum of power in the air as Anna said, "I'm not sure. . . ." She trailed off, eyes dark and distant.

Jade straightened. "Are you seeing something?"

"Gods, no." Anna self-consciously dropped her hand from her throat, pressing her palm to the solid wood of the desk. "It's just a feeling, probably coming from the fact that I care deeply about both of you, and hate that I can't be there for Lucius without breaking promises that I've made to people here."

Jade didn't bother pointing out that vows made to humans were pretty far down in the writs when it came to the list of a mage's priorities. Anna was forging her own path, which wasn't necessarily the same one set down by the First Father and the generations of magi since. "Will it help if I promise to be gentle?"

Anna made a face. "Again. Ew."

Jade laughed, but the humor was strictly on the surface. Underneath it all, she wanted to press further—about whether Anna was having visions, about how Lucius had looked when she'd last seen him . . . and whether he'd asked about her. But, just as Jade had cut off Strike and Anna whenever they had tried to tell her about Lucius's progress before, she didn't ask now. In the end, what mattered most were the results. Besides, she'd given her word to her king, and according to the writs, a vow made to him was second only to a promise made to the gods. Since the gods were currently incommunicado, thanks to Iago's destruction of the skyroad . . .

She had a booty call to answer.

CHAPTER TWO

Skywatch
Near Chaco Canyon, New Mexico

The strange orange sun was slipping toward the horizon as Strike and Jade materialized, not in the great room, where the teleporter king usually landed his homeward bounds, but out behind the big mansion that formed the heart of Skywatch. Jade appreciated his discretion; she wasn't exactly jonesing to endure a round of "Hi, how are you?" pleasantries while everyone tried not to say anything about what she was there to do. Except Sven, who was perpetually seventeen, and would probably do a wink-wink-nudge-nudge routine.

Yeah, she'd skip that, thanks.

She and Strike had zapped in beneath the big ceiba tree that stretched over the picnic area out behind the mansion and pool. There, cacao saplings grew beneath the rain forest giant, the out-of-place tropical plants flourishing in the arid New Mexican landscape thanks to Sasha's lifegiving *ch'ul* magic and her affinity for plants. Nearby, the steel building that served as the Nightkeepers' training hall was a dark silhouette of deepening shadows.

The scenery was all very familiar to Jade. The atmosphere, though, wasn't.

Stepping away from the big, black-haired king, who was wearing his usual nonregalia of jeans, T-shirt, and sandals, with his right sleeve just brushing across the *hunab ku* mark that denoted his gods-validated kingship, Jade filled her lungs with moisture-laden air that seemed more appropriate to the lowlands of the Yucatan than a box canyon in New Mex. The air smelled faintly wrong, though she couldn't immediately place the odor, which clung to her nasal passages and made her want to sneeze. She glanced at Strike, who was a dark shadow in the rapidly dimming light. "Did you guys install a giant Glade air nonfreshener while I was gone?"

"I wish. At least then we'd know what we're dealing with . . . and it'd presumably come with an 'off' button." His deep voice was edged with frustration. "We seem to be going from desert to tropics, and it's not just the ceiba tree growing out of place now, or even the cacao. There are patches of slimy green crap—like dry-land algae or something—growing all over the area, though it's worse down here. Sasha says it's only partly her talent that's promoting the growth; mostly it's the funky sun."

Jade glanced at the horizon just as the last sliver of orange light disappeared. The gas giant had been off-

color worldwide since the previous fall, when humanity had awakened one day to a sun that had turned
from white light to blood-tinged orange overnight.

The amount of solar energy reaching the earth had
dropped precipitously even though the earth's atmosphere was its same ragged, ozone-depleted self. Scien-
tists worldwide had various theories—no big surprise
there—but the consensus seemed to be: *Beats the living
hell out of us.* The astrophysicists were testing whether
a cosmic dust cloud or something was blocking things
between the earth and sun; the ecologists were freaking about issues of climate change, crop losses, and
killer red tides; and the threat of mob stampede was
growing as food prices skyrocketed and microclimates
shifted over the course of weeks or even days. And all
the while, people were asking, *Why is this happening?
How?*

Unbeknownst to most of humanity, the answers that
came the closest to reality were those of the supposed
crackpots who blamed it on aliens . . . or, rather, demons
and the approach of a doomsday predicted by the calendar of the ancient Maya. In depicting the end-date,
the Dresden Codex, one of only four Mayan codices to
survive the conquistadors' book burnings of the fifteen
hundreds, showed a terrible horned god standing in
the sky, tipping a jug that poured fire onto the earth. Although most human scholars assumed that meant the
Maya believed that the world would be demolished by
a fiery apocalypse, Jade had dug up information from
the archive suggesting that the solar fire would be part
of the gods' efforts to *help* the Nightkeepers during the

final battle, which was good news. . . . Or it had been until the sun got sick.

Unfortunately, in the absence of a reliable oracle—aka the Prophet—there was no way for the Nightkeepers to ask what the hell was going on or how to fix it.

Shivering, Jade scrubbed at sudden gooseflesh. "Maybe there'll be something in the library," she said, voicing the sentiment that had grown to a refrain over the past six months. "Which is my cue to get down to business."

But when she turned toward the mansion, which was a darkly solid, reassuring silhouette in the gathering dusk, Strike caught her arm and one-eightied her in the direction of a nearly invisible path leading away from the main house. "Lucius moved into one of the cottages a few months back. Said the mansion made him feel claustrophobic after being trapped inside his own head for so long."

"Oh." She tried not to let the change unsettle her, though when she'd pictured the pending booty duty, she and Lucius had always been in his suite, which was a few doors down from her own and nearly identical in floor plan and bland decor. *Not a big deal*, she told herself. *It's just a shift of scenery.* Experience had taught her that people didn't fundamentally change; only peripherals did. Human, Nightkeeper, it didn't matter. Some people were good, some bad, most a mixture of the two. She trusted Lucius despite knowing that he harbored a deep darkness that had attracted the *makol* and allowed it to gain a foothold within his soul. But he also had a strong core of innate goodness; that was what had kept the demon from possessing him fully, setting up the internal tug-of-war he'd suffered through for more than a year.

"Is that a problem?" Strike asked. The deepening dusk made his voice seem to come from the humid air around her rather than from the man himself.

"Which cottage?" she said, ducking the question because she knew it would take far more than a change of scenery to scare off a warrior, and she was determined not to let herself be anything less.

"The one farthest from the mansion; you'll see the lights. He sleeps with them on. Or else he doesn't sleep at all; we're not sure." The king paused. "Nate and Alexis are spending the night in the main house rather than their cottage. With Rabbit and Myrinne at school, you'll have privacy." Closing the distance between them, he pressed something into her hand. "Take this."

Feeling the outlines of one of the earpiece–throat mike combos the warriors used to stay in contact during ops, she didn't ask why. "Who's going to be on the other end?" Even knowing that the mike would transmit only if she keyed it on, she couldn't help picturing a voyeuristic tableau in the great room.

"Either me or Jox. Unless you'd prefer Leah."

He was doing his best, she realized, to maintain the illusion of privacy while keeping her safe, letting her know the warriors stood ready to come to her defense if the sex magic went awry and Lucius once again drew the attention of the underworld lords of the *Banol Kax*. Which had been only one of the numerous daunting possibilities that had been thrown around over the past few weeks.

"Whatever you think is best," Jade said, just barely managing not to tack on "sire" at the end, as her *winikin*'s voice echoed in her head, reminding her of the three "D"s. *I'm not following orders this time. This was my idea. My choice.* Raising her chin, she said, "Lucius won't hurt me." No, she'd manage that part on her own. Always had.

"He's not the guy you used to know. Becoming the Prophet has changed him."

"He's not the Prophet yet. If he were, you wouldn't need me."

Strike didn't have anything to say to that, which pinched somewhere in the region of Jade's heart. Given her inability to tap her scribe's talent for the spell crafter's gift it was supposed to convey, she didn't bring much in the way of a unique skill set to the Nightkeepers . . . except in the matter at hand. She was the only female mage who remained yet unmated, and she and Lucius had—briefly, at least—shared a sexual connection. More, in the wake of her and Michael's failed affair, back when they'd all first come to Skywatch and gotten their bloodline marks, she'd proven that she could be sexually involved with a man and not lose her heart. While that was more innate practicality than skill, she knew the royal council saw it as a plus. Lucius wasn't one of them, with or without the Prophet's powers.

Realizing that Strike was waiting for her to make her move, she took a deep breath. "Okay. Wish me luck."

She halfway expected him to come back with something about getting lucky. Instead, he said, "I want you to remember one thing: You can call it off at any point. This was your idea. I wouldn't have summoned you today if you hadn't volunteered. So promise me that you'll stop if it doesn't feel right."

She frowned at the sudden one-eighty. "But the writs say—"

"Fuck the writs," he interrupted succinctly. "Which probably isn't what you expected—or wanted—your king to say, but there you have it. Over the past two years we've proved that the writs aren't perfect or immutable. So now I'm telling you—hell, I'm *ordering* you, if that makes it better—to make your own decision on this one. Take me out of it. Take the others out of it. This is between you and Lucius. Sleep with him or don't, your call."

Jade drew breath to whatever-you-say-sire him, but then stopped herself. After a moment's pause, she said, "I get where you're coming from, but with all due respect, it's bullshit. I'm here because we're out of other options. If we don't get our hands on the library soon, the earth might not even make it to the zero date. Between whatever's going on with the sun, and the threat that Moctezuma could come through into Iago any day now, we might be looking at going into full-on war with the Xibalbans long before the barrier falls in 2012. Sorry, but you don't get to tell me to take all that out of the equation just so you can feel better about making the call. If it doesn't bother me to offer myself to Lucius this way, under these circumstances, then it shouldn't bother you. And if it does, that's not my problem."

There was a moment of startled silence. Then Strike said, "Huh."

Jade didn't know if that meant he was offended, taken aback, or what, but told herself she didn't care, three "D"s or no three "D"s. "What? You didn't know I have a spine?"

"I knew you had one. I just wasn't sure you'd figured it out." He made a move like he was going to touch her, but instead let his hand fall to the warrior's knife he wore at his belt. "Good luck, then. And remember that we'll be monitoring the radio in case . . . well, just in case."

Without another word, he spun up the red-gold magic of a Nightkeeper warrior-mage and disappeared in a pop of collapsing air, leaving her standing there thinking that the 'port talent was a hell of a way to get the last word in an argument. Not that they had been arguing, really, because they were both right: She couldn't separate the act from the situation, but at the same time, the act itself *was* her choice. Strike had called only to tell her that the other magi and the *winikin* were out of ideas, and they were up against the new moon, which was the last day of any real astrological significance—and hence increased barrier activity—before the summer solstice that would mark the two-and-a-half-year threshold. Her response to the information was her responsibility, just as the suggestion had been hers in the first place.

"So why are you still standing here?" she asked herself aloud.

"Maybe because you're not sure this is such a good

idea after all," a stranger's voice rasped from the darkness.

Adrenaline shot through Jade, making her skin prickle with sudden awareness. "Who's there?" But even as she asked the question, she realized that the voice hadn't been entirely that of a stranger. The whispery tone wasn't familiar, but she knew the cadence and faint Midwest accent. Knew them well, in fact. Swallowing to wet her suddenly dry mouth, she said, "Eavesdropping, Lucius? That's not like you. And why are you whispering? Trying to creep me out? Well, congrats. You succeeded."

The shadows near the training hall moved and she heard the faint hiss of denim, the pad of sandals on the steps leading down to the packed dust of the canyon floor. That same voice responded, "I'm not trying to do anything. But considering that you've been discussing my sex life, or lack thereof, with the royal council, do you really want to complain about my listening in on your conversation?"

He wasn't whispering, she realized belatedly. Six months earlier, Iago had nearly hacked his head off—which, along with ritual disembowelment and performance of the banishment spell on a cardinal day, was what it took to kill an *ajaw-makol*, as Lucius had been back then. Although his possessing demon had kept him alive and Sasha's magic had later knit his flesh, the grievous injury to his throat had made it difficult for him to speak in the immediate aftermath. Jade had assumed that would improve with time. Apparently not. *Your poor voice*, she wanted to say, but didn't. Regret pierced her for the loss of his lovely storyteller's tenor, even as the change sent a fine shiver racing along the back of her neck and down her spine.

It's just Lucius, she told herself, as she'd been doing ever since she'd first broached the sex-magic idea to the king. Now, though, she wondered whether she'd sold herself on a lie. Granted, she'd learned early and often that human beings didn't fundamentally change, not at their core. But what if the human being in question might not be entirely human anymore? He had been an *ajaw-makol*. He'd survived the Prophet's spell. Was she trapping herself in her own logic by applying human rules to him on the one hand while on the other arguing that he could be susceptible to sex magic?

She took a deep breath that didn't do much to settle the sudden churn of nerves. "I guess your eavesdropping makes us even, then. And it saves me from explaining why I'm here . . . though I doubt you're surprised. You had to figure something like this was coming."

His gritty tone darkened. "Given the choice of sex versus ritual sacrifice, I vote for sex."

She didn't even try to pretend that execution wasn't another of the options that had been discussed. The Prophet's spell called for the sacrifice of a magic user's soul, assuming that the sacrificial victim would have just one soul in residence, and would therefore yield an empty golem through which the Prophet's power would speak, answering the Nightkeepers' questions from the information contained within the library of their ancient ancestors, which had long ago been hidden within the barrier to keep it safe from their enemies. In Lucius's case, though, the *makol*'s soul had been sacrificed, leaving his human consciousness behind. It wasn't clear whether his failure to access the library had come from the retention of his soul, the fact that he wasn't a true magic user, the thick mental defenses he'd built up over more than a year of sharing head space with the *makol*, or what. But it wasn't much of a stretch to think that the only way to get a fully functional Prophet might be by emptying Lucius's body of its remaining soul through another sacrifice. To be fair, Strike was holding that out as the absolute last option—the Nightkeepers practiced largely self-sacrifice, helping separate them from the Xibalbans and their dark, bloodthirsty magic. But at the same time, the Nightkeepers' king would do whatever was necessary to protect the magi and their ability to combat the Xibalbans and *Banol Kax*. That was his responsibility, his duty. But what was hers in this case? She wasn't sure, and nobody seemed to have an answer for her.

She had lobbied the royal council on Lucius's behalf just as vehemently as she'd begged the warriors to search for him after he'd gone *makol*. Now, as then, the answer was a maddening, *We'll do our best, but he's not our priority.* She knew what it felt like not to be a priority, which had only made her fight harder on his behalf . . . earning the victory that had her standing there in the darkness, suddenly wondering if she was making a Big Freaking Mistake.

It's Lucius, she reminded herself again. *You're not afraid of him.*

"So . . . does this make *you* the sacrificial victim?"

A spurt of irritation had her snapping, "I'm not the loser's forfeit in one of your brothers' drinking games, Lucius. I'm not offering you a pity fuck, and I don't need to sleep my way to a better grade in Intro to Mayan Studies. I'm—" She broke off, swearing to herself. *Great seduction technique, genius. Remind him of all the embarrassing stuff he's ever told you. While you're at it, why not call him "Runt Hunt" like his old man used to?* She had to remember that the past wasn't important just then. What mattered was what happened—or didn't—next. At the thought of that *next*, heat skimmed through her, brought by the memory of a sexual encounter that had registered Richter high. Leveling her tone so it wouldn't betray the sudden *thudda-thump* of her heart, she said, "I'm just trying to help. If you want to turn me down because of what happened before, then do it. But don't try to make me into the bad guy because I'm offering."

There was a long beat of silence before he exhaled. When he spoke again, his rasping voice sounded more like that of the man she'd known, or else she was getting used to the change. "I don't want to turn you down. And I don't think badly of you. I couldn't. You're the only person here that I—" Now it was his turn to break off.

The only person that I . . . what? Jade skimmed through possibilities to settle on "trust." Despite what had happened, she trusted him. That might work both ways. Given that he knew she'd been discussing his potential for sex magic with Strike and the others, he probably also knew she was the closest thing he had to an ally within Skywatch. "Then why the hell wouldn't you *talk* to me?" The question was out before she could stop it, despite her plan to stop bringing up the past. But it had hurt when he'd refused to let her help him deal with the shock of the exorcism and the memories of what he'd done—or rather, what his body had done—while under the *makol's* control. She'd been overjoyed by his rescue, had wanted to do everything and anything in her power to bring him back to the man he'd once been, the friend she'd once treasured.

"Because I was a godsdamned mess," he said. "I didn't want you to see me that way."

Jade wished she could see his eyes, wished the darkness didn't leave her trying to interpret his feelings from a few clipped words in a stranger's voice. Before, his lovely tenor had painted the old legends of the Nightkeepers into word pictures for her as they'd worked side by side. Though he was only human, he'd taught her about her own ancestors in a way Shandi had never managed, making it less about duty and more about adventure and glory, and the joy of doing something because you *could*. Now, though, each word sounded like an effort, each sentence a study in pain. The change made her ache from knowing she'd promised her king results in a situation complicated by human factors. "I was only trying to help you back then," she said softly. "The same as I am now."

He shifted in the darkness, though he didn't come any closer. "I didn't want you to fix me. I wanted you to go away and give me room to fix myself. . . . I don't want your pity, and I'm not one of your patients, damn it."

Ice splashed in her veins, chill and uncomfortable. "I never said I pitied them."

"If there's one thing I'm good at, it's reading between the lines."

Refusing to go there, she said, "Of course you're not a patient. Nobody said you were."

"Yet you came back to fix me."

No, she thought in a frustrated knee-jerk, *I came back to fuck you.* She didn't say that, though, because while she considered sex more entertainment than a religious experience, she didn't like reducing it to that level. She didn't know whether it was the innate cool reserve of the harvester bloodline, the wisdom that had come from her own experiences, or what, but romantic love wasn't her thing. Too often in her practice, she'd seen otherwise high-functioning women lose their dreams to love, or because of its loss. The things that love and heartbreak did to otherwise normal people most definitely did *not* fall within the three "D"s.

Still, as she and Lucius faced off in the darkness, the air thickened with the memory of sex, the anticipation of it.

Blowing out a slow, settling breath, she said, "I came back because you haven't been able to get into the library, and we're running out of time and options." She paused, peering into the darkness and seeing nothing but the shadows. "It's not your fault. It's a power incompatibility, that's all." He might have spent years collecting the Nightkeepers' legends and reconstructing their elusive history, despite the derision the hobby had earned in academic circles, but that didn't make him a mage. Whereas genetics and magic meant that the Nightkeepers were big, strong, and charismatic, Lucius was more angles than muscle. He was human, blood and bone. And the sooner he came around to accepting that the limitations of that had nothing to do with him being Runt Hunt, the better off he'd be . . . and, she suspected, the closer he'd get to gaining control of the Prophet's magic. She hoped.

"Whose idea was it for you to come?" he asked. He remained hidden in the shadows, but his voice shifted with a thread of what she thought might be acceptance.

"Mine, start to finish." New heat furled across her skin as the anticipation built.

Their one spontaneous, somewhat rushed coupling in the archive had lit her up like nothing had done before, not even being with the far more polished Michael when the two of them had both been running hot with transitional hormones and their first tastes of sex magic. Where Michael had been skilled and considerate, Lucius had been raw, teetering on the borderline of control. Where Michael had held a portion of himself apart—out of necessity, as they had later learned—Lucius had been entirely *there* with her, making her feel like he didn't see her as support staff, a backup, or a fill-in for what he'd really wanted. Unfortunately, that very openness, combined with a Xibalban attack on the antimagic wards surrounding Skywatch, had allowed the *makol* to briefly emerge from its hiding place and take over Lucius's consciousness in the aftermath, leading to the near destruction of the archive and beginning Lucius's downward spiral to *makol* possession. Despite that terrifying ordeal, though, and the strained "I don't do love; I do friends with benefits" conversation she'd been forced to lay on him when he'd tried to make their lovemaking into more than she'd ever intended, she wanted this. She wanted *him*, though that hadn't been the argument she'd used on the others. She hadn't dared.

"Are you doing this because it's your best chance to finally be on the front lines, finally make a difference in the war?"

"Do you blame me?" It wasn't really an answer, but she didn't want him to know that somewhere along the line, duty and desire had gotten mixed together inside her. She wanted to fix him, to help him gain the magic he'd sacrificed for. At the same time, she wanted what they had found together in the archive, when nothing had mattered but the slap of flesh, the rake of nails, the clash of lips and tongues. She missed that, wanted it. It wasn't magic, wasn't love, but it was a power she could summon, something she was good at.

"I don't blame you," he answered, rasping voice going soft, "but I need you to understand what you're getting into."

The night had gone fully dark, and the pinpoint stars did little to lighten the blackness of the new moon. The pool deck at the back of the mansion was unlit; the only real illumination came from a few gleaming windows up at the mansion, and the lights coming from a single cottage off in the middle distance. The darkness meant she felt and heard rather than saw when he moved toward her, closing the distance between them until she could feel the heat from his body, the stir of his breath. Desire tightened her inner muscles and made her acutely conscious of her own breathing, her own actions, as she wetted her lips with her tongue.

"Light a foxfire," he said. "Just a small one."

It was one of the few weak spells she could muster, one that had delighted him when they'd first been getting to know each other. His eyes had gleamed with gratifying awe when she'd sent the foxfire dancing from her hand to his and back again, though even that small spell had taxed her.

Thinking that was what he wanted, that this was foreplay of a sort, she turned one palm up and called the magic with a single word in the language of the ancients. "*Lak'in.*" It meant "east," the direction of the rising sun.

A tiny light kindled, starting pinpoint small and then expanding outward to a ball of cool blue flame that shed light on the two of them. She looked up at him, smiling, expecting to see his joy in the minor spell, a small connection to better days between them. Instead, familiar hazel eyes looked at her out of a stranger's face.

"*Gods!*" Jade jolted as shock hammered through her, sending her back a step. "Who . . . What the . . ." She faltered to silence as reality and unreality collided and she recognized the man standing opposite her. Sort of.

It was Lucius, but he wasn't for an instant the man

she'd known. Instead, he was what Lucius would have been if he'd gotten the "big and burly" genes of his massive linebacker brothers and father along with the "tall and borderline willowy" genes he'd inherited from his mother's side. The combination had yielded a frame that was only maybe an inch taller than that of the man she'd known, but carried twice the muscle, layered onto bone and sinew as though sculpted there. He was wearing new-looking jeans; she honestly doubted his thighs would've fit in the old ones. The bar-logo T-shirt was familiar, but there was nothing familiar about the way it stretched across his chest and arms, and hinted at a ripple of muscle along his flat abs. Above the shirt's neckline, a thin white scar spoke of the attack that had cost him his voice, nearly his life. And his face . . . gods, his face. Features that had been pleasantly regular before were sharper and broader now; his jaw was aggressively square, his formerly overlarge nose was brought into perfect proportion, and his newly high cheekbones and broad brows framed hazel eyes that she knew, yet didn't know.

Watching her with an unfamiliar level of intensity, he held out his hands and turned his palms up, so the foxfire lit the lifeline scars and the dual marks on his right forearm: the black slave mark that bound him to Anna and the Nightkeepers, and the red quatrefoil hellmark his demon-possessed self had accepted from Iago. Jade had seen the scars and marks before, of course, but back then they had seemed entirely out of place, magic unwittingly imposed on a human, drawing him into a place where he didn't belong.

Now, though, they looked . . . right. Like they belonged. She didn't know why the sight chilled her, or how that fear could exist alongside and within the churning sexual heat that somehow flared higher rather than died when she realized this wasn't the man she'd come to seduce. Not by a long shot.

"Well?" he asked.

"You look . . ." She trailed off, not sure he'd be flattered by her first few responses, which involved steroids and testosterone poisoning, clear evidence that her normally hidden wise-ass side was kicking in, trying to buffer the shock. Nor did she go with the calm, analytical response brought by her cool counselor's reserve, which often came to the fore when Jade-the-person didn't know how to respond to something. But he had called her on both of those knee-jerk defenses in the past, so she paused, trying to find the words. In the end, all she came up with was a lame, ". . . different."

In fact, he looked amazing, reminding her of the long lunches she'd spent at the Met during her student days, wandering through the Greek and Roman art galleries, and imagining that the carved marble statues and bronze castings could come to life. He was that perfectly imperfect, human, yet something more now. And that "more" had new heat skimming beneath her suddenly too-sensitive skin, making her acutely aware of her own body, and his.

It's just Lucius, she told herself. Only it wasn't. This was a new, different Lucius, one who had broken the rule that said people didn't fundamentally change. Because it wasn't just the voice and the body that had changed; *he* had changed. Gone was the endearingly awkward geek who'd made her feel comfortable with herself. In his place was two hundred pounds of raw, potent male sexuality regarding her with hot hunter's eyes. And—oh, gods—she'd offered herself to him. More, she'd fought long-distance for the opportunity, and she'd ignored Strike and Anna when they had tried to tell her that he was different now, that the Prophet's spell had done something to him. In her rush to finally break free from her backup role, she'd thrown herself headlong at . . . what? What was he now? He couldn't access the library, yet there was clearly magic at work within him. How else could she explain the added bulk and muscle, and the gut-punch of pheromone-laden charisma he'd lacked before, but now wore as though born with it?

"Not exactly what you were expecting when you volunteered for sex-magic duty, was it?" he asked, his eyes going hooded in intimate challenge.

Heat touched the air between them, thickening her breath in her lungs.

"I . . ." She trailed off. What was wrong with her? Where had her words gone? She was the one with the answers, the cool-blooded harvester who didn't get rattled. But right now her body was saying one thing, her spinning brain another, and her verbal skills had gotten lost in the cross fire.

His not-quite-familiar mouth curved in a humorless smile. "That's about what I figured. I wish they had warned you."

That, at least, she could respond to. "They tried. I

wasn't listening. But . . . you could've called me, or e-mailed." She'd posted her contact info in the mansion's kitchen, just in case. "I hate thinking of you going through all this alone."

"I haven't been in the mood for company."

It was easier not to look at him as she said, "What *are* you in the mood for?"

"That, dear Jade, is entirely up to you."

The way he said her name reminded her of the man who had been her friend. But the unease that coiled through her warned that he wasn't the man she'd known, wasn't the man she'd volunteered to be with. He was suddenly so much more. "I . . . don't know what to say."

"That's a first." There was a little sting in his words, though. How could there be?

She wouldn't have, *couldn't* have known to brace herself for this. Anna had said he'd gained weight, that he'd been working out, but this bulk hadn't come from protein shakes and free weights. "Magic." The word escaped her on a sigh.

Lucius spread hands that seemed wider than they had been before, their tapering fingers stronger. "That's the current theory, that either I retained something of the *makol*, or I've gotten something of the Prophet. Either way, I'm a new man."

Not only that, she realized, he'd become the man his family had expected him to be, the one he'd always wanted to be. Satisfaction gleamed in his eyes as he took in her response, the heat of attraction she didn't bother trying to mask. But also the nerves. "I don't . . ."

She trailed off, blew out a breath. "I'm rattled. When I imagined how this was going to go, we were always in your suite in the main house, and you were, well, *you*." She'd known what to expect, or so she'd thought.

He covered the last half step separating them, so the tips of her outstretched fingers brushed the taut fabric of his tee. The foxfire that still glowed in her hand lit the shirt's logo silver-blue. "Tell me what else you imagined," he ordered, the words thrumming with sensual meaning.

Feeling the small magic begin to drain her shallow power reserves, she let the foxfire go out, plunging them back into a darkness that shouldn't have been as much of a relief as it was. But she didn't drop her hand as the light faded. Instead, she flattened her palm against his torso, feeling the faint hollow beneath his sternum, along with firm flesh and a thick layer of muscle that hadn't been there before. Heat traveled up her arm and across her body; her nipples tightened and her core was washed with a sudden tingling anticipation, like the moment before an orgasm. He was warm and solid, and the strong, steady beat of his heart pulsed beneath her fingertips. She was acutely aware of the press of her clothing against her skin, and the warmth of him, the scent of him, more potent than before, more masculine. "What I pictured was nothing like this," she whispered, as much to herself as to him.

"I imagined how it would be too, each day the *makol* held me trapped in the in-between. I imagined what I would say to you if I ever made it back, what I would do to you, *with* you."

The humid air went suddenly thin in Jade's lungs, even though she had imagined the same things, only to have the reality fall far short, as it always did. "It's only natural to lock onto some sort of goal," she said, falling back into quasi-therapist mode when all her other options were too complicated, too revealing. "You needed to feel like you had something to come back to, something more personal than the war and the magi."

"Maybe." Something hard and hot flashed in his eyes. "And you don't need to worry about me getting clingy this time. I know this isn't about a relationship, or love, or anything beyond expediency."

"It's not . . ." she began, but then trailed off as he leaned in and her brain shut down: click, gone. One heartbeat she was thinking, and then the next, cognition disappeared and she became a creature of pure sensation. She felt the steady thud of his heartbeat beneath her scarred palm, along with the warm strength of his chest and the play of strong muscle, and she suddenly *wanted*, with a pure intensity of being that she didn't remember ever experiencing before. She wanted his body against hers, wanted them both naked and straining together, finding the power of flesh and fire. And in that moment, what had started as duty morphed to pure desire.

His words feathered across her lips as he said, "Expediency or not, there's no reason we can't enjoy ourselves. Which brings me back to those fantasies I was talking about. They all started something like this."

He closed the last few inches separating them. And kissed her.

Jade was dimly aware that a small sound escaped her, part surprise, part invitation. Whereas the old Lucius might have paused a moment, as if questioning whether it was really what she wanted, this new version of him bypassed the niceties and went in deep, long and wet, kicking the heat inside her even higher and sparking an inner moment of *holy shit* as she was assaulted by a barrage of sensations, both familiar and unfamiliar.

A stranger's muscular arms banded around her, pressing her to a stranger's wide, hard chest. But although the angles and pressures were different, and the smell and very *energy* of him were more potently masculine than before, she recognized the man she'd known in the earnestness of his kiss, his sense of focus. For a fleeting second, she thought this was what it must be like to kiss a first lover years later, after he'd matured. It was as if the old Lucius had been her high school sweetheart, not yet grown into his body, whereas the man who slid his hand up to her nape, gathered a handful of her hair, and used it to change the angle of their kiss, bringing it deeper and wetter—that man was the fully grown version of him, the fulfillment of the young man's promise. Except that the Lucius she had known had been a man already, full-grown and genius-smart. Which meant . . . what? Who was holding her now?

That thought brought a kick of nervous heat. Or maybe—probably—the heat came from the way his lips slanted across hers, the way his tongue touched hers, stroking, bringing sensations that were familiar, yet not. His bulk and strength both excited and intimidated her as he caught her up against his body, their clothing creating crazy-hot friction as he lifted her to her toes, letting her feel every muscled inch of him. She felt the hard ridge of his erection straining behind the fly of his jeans, and a spurt of hot, heady desire pounded through her at the thought of straddling that place, riding it, taking him within her. This was about the two of them now, about the pleasure they could give each other without expectations, hurt feelings, or recriminations. Heat flared in her bloodstream; she poured herself into the kiss as energy coursed through her—maybe magic, maybe pure lust; she wasn't sure she knew the difference anymore, wasn't sure she cared.

On one level, she remained dimly aware that she was there for a reason, that the kiss was about far more than two people—former lovers, former friends—turning each other on. Yet at the same time it was just the two of them. Friction was a delicious incitement as he got a hand between their bodies and cupped one of her breasts, rubbing the nipple to a point while kissing her with the same raw intensity she remembered from before, yet bringing a response that was so much more than it had been. His new bulk made her feel small and delicate, while the focus of his concentration made her feel that she was, at that moment, the center of his universe.

Yes, she thought as a moan hummed in her throat. *Yes, there.*

She wasn't thinking of the Nightkeepers now, wasn't

pursuing her promise to her king or her opportunity to be on the front lines of the war. Her whole world had coalesced to the sensation of his body against hers, the drag of his hands down her ribs and back up again, and the hard press of his mouth as they twined together and kissed, hot, wet, and deep. Her response spiraled higher; she fisted her hands in his hair, trying to get closer to him, plaster herself against him, hell, get inside the jeans and tee that barred her hands from the body she felt beneath. *More,* she thought. *I want more.* Or maybe she said it aloud, whispering it in one of the brief interludes when their lips parted for a breath. She must have, because moments later he broke the kiss and eased away.

She was breathing hard, her heart pounding a mad race in her chest. He was breathing fast too—she could hear it, practically feel it even though they weren't pressed together anymore. Peripherals returned; she could hear the faint rustle of leaves around them, feel the hint of coolness as the too-humid air brushed along her overheated skin. She felt more than saw when he held out a hand to her. "Come back to the cottage with me," he said, the words seeming more a command than a question.

A greedy knot of excitement lodged in her core as she ignored the faint warning still chiming deep within, and instead reached for his hand, twining her fingers through his. "Let's go."

CHAPTER THREE

Anticipation vibrated through Lucius as he guided Jade along the packed-dirt path to the cottages. Clustered together, the cabins formed what he thought of as a mage motel, relatively private, but cookie-cutter generic. Just now, the other cottages were empty. He'd noticed it as the dusk fell on the night of the new moon, and had guessed what the Nightkeepers were up to, and why. The knowledge had sent him out into the night to wait for Jade, because he'd wanted to approach her on his terms this time. Before, he'd fallen too hard, too fast, making the mistake of thinking yet again that the woman he was panting after was on the same page as him, relationship-wise.

Not this time, though. This new and improved version of him wouldn't make the mistakes of his other, weaker incarnation.

He glanced over as they walked. In the dim light coming from his cottage, her face was a pale oval of smooth, pearlescent skin and features so perfect they could have come from a Victorian cameo. The darkness robbed her eyes of color, but his mind filled in the delicate sea-foam green that matched so well with the sacred stone she was named after. She was Nightkeeper-tall, only a few inches shorter than the six-four he'd recently attained. But where Alexis, Patience, and Sasha often moved with aggressive swaggers, Jade always seemed to glide, serene and elegant and wholly feminine. Maybe it was because she, like Anna, commanded a talent more cerebral than the warrior's magic, but the comparison ended there. Where Anna was reserved, Jade was open and giving; where Anna wanted to escape her duty and destiny, Jade wanted to be more than her bloodline role. And where Anna stayed away, Jade had come back when the magi needed her. When *he* needed her, though he hadn't wanted to admit it, or make the call.

Her straight, dark hair was longer than it had been before, an empirical reminder of the five, almost six months that had elapsed since he'd last seen her. But he had needed the time to put himself back together on his own terms. He hadn't wanted to be her patient, didn't want her to see him the way she did her old clients, with a mixture of empathy and secret inner horror. He'd wanted to be stronger than that, tougher. He'd worked out, hour after hour, forcing himself through increasingly punishing routines as he fought to reclaim his body from the weakness that had plagued him in the wake of the *makol*'s exorcism. In doing so, it seemed that he'd triggered something else, something that had made him progressively bigger and stronger.

Magic, she'd said, and she was probably right; he'd discussed that possibility with Strike and the others as they had tried to figure out how to unlock the Prophet's powers. But the question remained: If he'd internalized a connection to the psi barrier that powered the Nightkeepers' magic, thereby gaining some of their physical traits, why the hell couldn't he connect to the damned library? He was perfect for the job; what Mayanist wouldn't give his right nut to get his hands on an artifact cache of the library's reputed scope? More, he knew how to read the glyphs and interpret the inscriptions, knew what the Nightkeepers needed. He just had to get into the pocket of the barrier where the library had been hidden . . . but so far that had been a big-ass fail.

He'd shed blood onto the Nightkeepers' sacred altar and the First Father's tomb. He'd prayed to gods deafened by the skyroad's destruction. He'd attempted to uplink with Strike and the others during the spring equinox. Hell, he'd even whacked off onto the damned altar—all that had gained him was an unceremonial mess. It didn't take a rocket scientist to figure that the next step was Jade. He'd been making plans to go after her, but the royal council had beaten him to it. And as he'd stood in the shadows, eavesdropping, he'd known he wasn't going to turn her away. He was going to love her as he should have done before—with pleasure and without strings. And, gods willing, he'd find his way to the magic that had become his through accident rather than bloodline destiny.

The man he'd been before would've paused at the

cottage door to make sure she hadn't changed her mind on the short walk. The man he'd become shouldered the door open, tugged her through, and kicked the panel closed behind them.

His living space began with a small kitchen that was neat and organized-looking, more because he ate up at the mansion than because he was either neat or organized. Not pausing there, he led her to the room beyond: a decent-size TV room that was more his style—or lack thereof. The upholstered sofa and chairs, the glossy coffee and end tables, and the kitschy retro Western lamps had been there when he moved in, and were hell and gone more upscale than the hand-me-downs and garage-sale specials of his shared student apartment back at UT. But the leaning piles of books, the drifts of note-scribbled printouts, and the oversize flat-screen jacked into a high-powered laptop were all reminiscent of his student days. So, too, was the image showing on-screen: an enlarged photo of a Late Classic–period Mayan painting. Glorious and vivid, it caught Jade's attention immediately.

"Wow." She let go of him, moved to the TV, and raised a hand to trace the stylized figures of six men arranged in an asymmetrical pattern, two on the left, four on the right. All done in profile, as was the Mayan tradition, they faced a dark sphere that was set off center on the panel. The man closest to it was kneeling in supplication, while four of the others stood near him in postures of protection, or maybe aggression. Those five wore elaborate, feather-worked headdresses made from the skulls of jaguars and coyotes, along with protective shielding that covered only one side of their bodies. There was even more asymmetry in the painting itself, created by the sixth figure, who stood at the far right, apart from the others. Wearing a musician's loincloth and lacking a headdress, he held a conch shell to his lips. Glyphs emerged from the crude instrument as though they were musical notes, though no such scheme had been identified for the ancient Maya—or, for that matter, the ancient Nightkeepers. The paint colors ranged from pale mauve through rusty red to charcoal black. The earthy hues reflected on Jade's face as she frowned at the text, trying to parse out the glyphs.

Lucius shook his head. "Don't bother; the writing doesn't make any sense. The current theory is that the artist was illiterate, and just copied a bunch of cool-looking glyphs off nearby inscriptions or whatever else he had on hand. It's just gibberish." He didn't say why he'd been studying the painting, why it was important to him.

Under other circumstances, with another woman, talking translation would've spoiled the mood. With Jade, though, it served only to heighten the sense of intimacy provided by the small, quiet cottage and the rust red light. They shared a love of language, and although he couldn't honestly say he was more attracted to her brains than her body, the two together had made a hell of an impression when he'd first met her. Or rather, once he'd gotten past her habitual reserve, which came across as shyness, but he'd learned was her way of hiding in plain sight. He'd long ago realized that they each suffered from their own cultural conditioning, though hers had come from a too-demanding *winikin* and a set of writs rather than family dysfunction.

"There's something . . ." She trailed off, still frowning at the glyphs, but then she shook her head and turned back to him, her expression going from intrigue to warmth with a hint of nerves. "Never mind. That's not what we're here for."

"True enough," Lucius agreed, trying to keep it casual, because she'd made it clear that was what she wanted. But at the same time this wasn't just about sex for either of them. There was a far larger goal, one that hung over them, weighing on him as it had for nearly half a year now, though now edged with a sharp sense of anticipation. Determination. He was getting his ass into the library, whatever it took. And if that meant that the Nightkeepers' needs and his own desire to be part of things wound up getting mixed together with the desire he felt for Jade—had felt for her from the first day they'd worked together—then that was part of the Nightkeepers' culture, wasn't it? Sex was magic, magic was power, and power could save the world.

Reaching out to Jade, he recaptured her hand. Satisfaction kicked through him as his fingers enfolded hers, locking on with easy strength. Rather than growing awkward as his body had increased in size and mass, he'd lost the sprawling clumsiness that had plagued him his entire life. It was as though his brain and synapses had been designed all along for this larger body, and hadn't known how to tone it down for the scrawny, too-tall beanpole he'd been. Tightening his fingers on hers, he tipped his head toward the other side of the TV room, where a short hallway branched off. "The bedroom's this way."

But she tugged him back toward her, lips curving when their bodies bumped. "Let's stay right here." She nodded to the screen. "I want it to be like it was before, only better."

In a flash, he remembered being with her in the inner, most secure room of the three-room archive buried deep within the mansion. He remembered kissing her almost desperately, thrusting into her against the backdrop of the ancient writs, which were displayed in flat cases on three sides of the tiny room, with their elaborate glyphwork and painted illuminations highlighted by museum-quality lighting. Back then, he'd been fighting time, fighting the lure of the *makol* and the song of dark magic in the air. Now he was fighting to gain the power that was his by right of spell and sacrifice. In that, he realized, the ancient backdrop was a fitting one. "Right here," he agreed, drawing her into him.

She looped her arms around his neck, using the leverage to draw herself up his body, onto her tiptoes. "Right now," she whispered against his mouth.

He kissed her, feeling the play of lips and tongues in a way he never had before, as though his neurons had changed along with the rest of him, becoming more sensitive, more ready to fire the signals of sex. Heat arced across the point of contact with an almost physical force, jolting through him, lighting him up. He'd been hard since before they'd even kissed out by the training hall, but now he filled to bursting, straining uncomfortably in his jeans. He slid his arms around her, caught her up against his body, and was acutely aware that she might be tall, but she was delicate and fine boned, and so much smaller than he'd become. Fierce protectiveness welled up inside him, an unexpected surge of emotion he squelched before it could begin, reminding himself of the rules she'd set before, the ones he needed now.

Jade broke the kiss, breathing lightly, her body seeming to vibrate against his. "Do you feel that? Do you feel the magic?"

"Maybe." He wasn't sure he'd recognize Nightkeeper power if it ran him over doing eighty-five in a forty zone. He'd heard the thoughts of the demon that had possessed him, the one he'd named Cizin. *Flatulent one.* The *makol's* foul, angry temper had echoed inside him, becoming his own. Marking him. He knew he would instantly recognize the awful pressure of possession if the *Banol Kax* ever sought him again. But he wasn't sure he'd ever felt true magic, not the way the Nightkeepers meant it. Even when he had lain on the floor of Iago's giant volcanic cave, bleeding out onto the stone while the Nightkeepers crowded around him and enacted the Prophet's spell, he couldn't say he'd felt the magic. He'd felt inner chaos and the soul-deep agony of Cizin being ripped out of him, but he couldn't have pointed to any part of the spell casting and said, *That's magic.* He was only human, after all.

"There's magic here," Jade whispered against his lips. "Trust me."

In answer, he kissed her again. He didn't want to think about trust or power, not really; he wanted to think about the woman in his arms, who would be his first lover in this new body. He wanted to touch her, shape her with hands that spread wider than they had before, registering the soft curves with fingers that seemed to have gotten exponentially more sensitive as the other parts of him had grown and changed. He kissed her, caressed her, learning her body and letting her get used to his, even as *he* was getting used to the newly acute bite of heat, the powerful thunder of the blood surging through his veins, impelled by the beat of a heart he instinctively knew was stronger than before.

Murmuring appreciation, Jade slipped her delicately capable hands beneath his tee and ran them up his back, skin-on-skin with an inciting scrape of fingernail. He groaned as an answering avalanche of lust swept into his system, bringing an unexpected and unwanted slash of raw aggression. In the next instant, nothing existed but his need to take her, to wrap her around him, to put her up against the nearest wall and pound into her, lose himself in her. *Mine*, the heat said, branding the possessive howl across his consciousness.

His mind jerked back but his body leaned in instead, inviting her maddening touch. Unnerved to be suddenly teetering at the edge of his hard-won control, he broke the kiss and smoothed his hands down her body and back up again, soothing himself more than her. *Hold it together*, he told himself. *Don't lose your shit*. Before, he'd let himself be taken over, used. He didn't intend to let that happen again, whether by *makol*, desire, or power. Not ever.

Needing a moment, he released her to turn and snag the quilt he'd left tossed over the back of the couch, having dragged it in from the bedroom one night when he'd been working on a series of translations, unable to sleep. Done in masculine shades of rust, brown, and cream, the quilt's color scheme mimicked the hues on the TV screen. Shoving aside the coffee table with his foot, he spread the comforter on the thick carpeting and swept a bunch of pillows off the sofa onto the quilt, creating a layer softer even than the padded wall-to-wall carpeting beneath, a comfortable nest in the wide-open space of the floor rather than the close confines of a too-soft couch that occasionally made him feel trapped even when he was sitting there alone.

Unable to bear the constricting chafe of his tee, he shucked off his shirt over his head and tossed it aside. He was acutely aware of Jade watching him, taking in the sight of muscles where there hadn't been any before. He was grateful that she didn't seem to linger on the heavy, gnarled scar that ran across his stomach, just below his ribs. Maybe, like him, she didn't care to remember the day he'd almost died . . . and had been reborn instead. He'd taken the pain and the smell of his own blood pumping from his slashed throat, the grotesque panic of seeing his heart on the outside of his chest cavity, connected to him by a few thin threads of vessel and fascia—and he'd locked those memories deep inside, away from the things that mattered. He hoped she could do the same, hoped she already had. And yes, he hoped she cared enough to need to lock those things away. Just because they were distilling sex to mutual pleasure didn't mean he didn't care deeply for her. It was just that he'd finally grown up—and out—to the point that he got what she'd been trying to explain before: that not every sexual relationship had to be aiming for more. Sometimes it was just about friendship and sex. And in this case, there were also the issues of their summoning sex magic and getting his ass into the library. Gods willing.

Blood humming, feeling back in control, he toed off his sandals, dropped to the makeshift bed, and stretched out on his side, head propped up on one hand. Looking up at her, he patted the wide empty space beside him. "You want to at least get horizontal this time?"

He meant as opposed to their rushed coupling in the archive, when they'd stayed partially dressed and gone at it hard, starting up against the wall and finishing on one of the study tables in the inner sanctum. But they both knew that he was also saying, *Last chance . . . you going to go through with this or not?*

Jade stared at the bare skin of Lucius's torso, where hard muscles glowed with burnished highlights in the reddish brown light. Shirtless and barefoot, wearing only his jeans and an I-dare-you gleam in his eyes, he looked like something out of the pages of *Cosmo*.

His caption might have read, *Ways to let him please you*, or some such nonsense that implied the article was aimed at female self-actualization, but the subheading would've been a thin lipstick gloss over the simple fact that sex sells, the hotter, the better. *Hell, yes, I'm going through with it*, she thought, wetting her lips and seeing his eyes darken in the rusty light. Dipping into the pocket of her jeans, she touched the earpiece Strike had given her, partly to make sure it was toggled off, partly to reassure herself it was there, just in case. Because even if Lucius couldn't feel the magic, it crowded thick and warm around her, seeming expectant, the calm before the storm.

Yes, there was magic in the air. She only hoped her reserves would be enough to jump-start the Prophet's powers. But if Lucius could grow into the jock's body he'd always wanted, then she should be able to grow into the power she craved. And if that wish bumped up against the knowledge that people didn't really change, she ignored the disparity to focus on the moment, and the man watching her with an intensity that brought heat to her skin and tension coiling deep inside her.

Entirely conscious of his eyes on her, imagining herself silhouetted against the fiercely elegant painting projected on the big screen behind her, she caught the hem of her floaty green shirt in both hands, gave a little shimmy as she skimmed it up and over her head, then stretched sinuously to let the garment fall beside his discarded tee. Leaving her soft, lace-edged bra—the same jewel green as the shirt—in place because it made her feel wholly feminine, she toed off her sneakers and socks into a small pile. The cool air tightened her skin, though the blood pumping through her veins still sizzled with desire.

He was wholly focused on her, hot for her. The knowledge added an extra wiggle to her walk as she crossed the short distance to where he lay waiting for her. She lowered herself to the comforter, coming down on her knees with the thought of touching him, enticing him, letting the hum of magic lead the way. The moment she knelt, though, he reached out and snagged her wrist, overbalancing her and then rising up to cover her body with his own. She gasped, her senses revving to flash point as he pressed into her, the sensation of skin on skin heightened by the chafe of their remaining clothes. He caught her other wrist, bracketing her hands together in one of his, holding them captive above her head in the pillows. Nearly helpless in the face of the heat that speared to her core at the move, Jade gave herself up to his kiss.

She was peripherally aware that the bedding carried his scent, bringing some of the intimacy she'd hoped to avoid by keeping them out in the main room, with its glowing scene of ritual and magic as a pointed reminder of their goal. But she wasn't thinking of ritual or magic as she dragged her fingernails lightly down his sides, then stroked his ass, his hips, and the long columns of the thighs that lay alongside hers, slightly bent to take some of his weight. As she did so, he shifted, moving the line of his kisses from her mouth to her jaw, her throat, all the while touching her breasts through the thin fabric of her bra, stroking her, bringing her nipples to twin peaks beneath the lace, then popping the clasp of the bra and tugging the wisp of fabric away, baring her breasts. She arched into him on a gasp when he touched her next; she wasn't heavily endowed, but she was exquisitely sensitive there.

As though her soft cry had broken through whatever small restraint had kept him in check up to that point, he growled something in his new, rasping voice, and plunged into the next kiss, letting go of her wrists and dragging his hands down her body in a rough, inciting stroke. He used his tongue; teeth, and hands on her with ruthless intent and an edge of anger that demanded a response. Barely breaking the kiss, he stripped her out of the rest of her clothes with impatient movements, then came back to cover her naked body with his own, his jeans making an arousing contrast against her skin.

Lust slammed through Jade, revving her system from zero to *holy shit* in two seconds flat. *Gods*, she thought, latching her fingernails onto the solid muscle on either side of his spine as he rolled fully atop her and pressed her into the piled bedding, making her even more aware of the feel of him, the scent and taste of him, the *fact* of him. Moaning as the world went white-hot behind her eyelids, she clung, knowing that this was what she'd wanted, what she'd come back for. Not just the chance to make a difference, but to feel the burn of lust and chemical combustion she'd found with him before. More, this time there was no *makol*, no one-sided hopes or expectations of more than she was willing to give; there was only the plunge and surge of raw, unabashed sex, and the buzzing hum of magic. The heady flow of power swirled around them, inside her. Urgent yet formless, the energy made her feel that her low-level skills were straining toward an unknown destination . . . and falling short.

A hollow kick of disappointment threatened to break through the sensual spell when she realized it wasn't working, that she was too weak—or Lucius too human—to force the gathered magic to detonate. But then he slid a hand between them to touch the place where their thighs twined together, and the sensation of his strong fingers rhythmically stroking her core blotted out all other thought or logic.

Arching into his touch, she grazed his earlobe with her teeth, making him groan, then whispered hot incitements until he shuddered against her. Her inner muscles locked around the long fingers he slid inside her; she surged against him as he set a hard, fast rhythm, then mimicked it in a deep kiss until an orgasm rolled through her, shattering her remaining thoughts in a wash of sensation. She came hard and fast, fisting around him with a long, wordless cry as the whiplash pressure released only to quickly recoil within her, tightening her to a waiting, wanting knot that demanded more than his fingers and his kiss.

Gods, she thought. *Just . . . gods*.

Growling something under his breath, Lucius rolled aside. She heard the slide of cloth as he shucked off his jeans and briefs in a single impatient yank. Before she could gather herself to look at him, fully naked in the reflected light, he rolled back to her, covered her with his body, and kissed her long and hard. Between the disease resistance inherent to the magi and the fact that they were all using contraceptive spells now, this close to the end-time, there was no need for a condom, and skin on skin was glorious contact, an erotic contrast between his skin and hers, his body and hers. When she wrapped her legs around him wantonly, wonderfully, he reached to position his hard cock at her opening . . . and slid home.

Jade's vision dimmed as all of her senses turned suddenly inward, concentrating on the feelings that sparked as he stretched her, filled her, invaded her, possessed her. His first thrust set off a chain reaction within her; heat slammed into greed, which banged up against a kernel of fear, not of him, but of being weak, of failing. She didn't even know anymore what she was afraid of failing at, knew only that she existed to hold on to him as he surged into her on powerful thrusts that he counteracted with the iron grip he kept on her body, holding her in place as he took her with more lust than finesse, seeming driven beyond himself, beyond them both, by the chemistry they'd shared from the first.

Heat rocketed through her as she clung to him, dug into him, and tried to give as good as she was getting, counterpointing his movements with her own to create heady, insane friction. Air hissed between his teeth in a word that might have been a curse, might have been her name, as he drove into her again and again. Jade forced herself to keep breathing, but oxygen did little to cut the spinning that swept her up and threatened to take her over before she was ready to go. Fighting the raw, edgy pleasure that seemed certain to push her over to the other side of an orgasm that loomed large on the horizon of her senses, she bit his sweat-dampened shoulder. When he groaned harshly at the back of his throat, she turned her head to whisper in his ear: "Come with me. I don't want to leave you behind this time."

"*Fuck.*" He turned his head, blindly sought her lips with his, and locked them together in a hard, deep kiss as he surged against her, swelled within her.

The added pressure—and the raw intensity of the kiss—drove her over whether she was ready or not. Her muscles clamped and pulsed, milked and demanded. He made it two more thrusts, then came, his body shuddering as he heaved into her and stilled, rigor-locked with the force of his orgasm. A long, low groan resonated from his chest as he broke the kiss to press his cheek to hers, holding on to her as the pulses of pleasure went from her to him and back again. Caught in her own ecstasy, Jade could do little more than cling and gasp while the full-body throb went on and on, seeming to cycle up instead of down. Heat poured through her, not an afterglow, but more an extension of the orgasm, a new level of passion and energy that seemed to travel through the point where their bodies merged, becoming something more than sexual gratification, until it felt almost like—

Magic, she realized, her eyes flying open to find that the sepia tones in the room had gone to red-gold.

Nightkeeper magic limned their bodies, making it impossible to tell where his skin stopped and hers began. His face was very close to hers, his eyes locked on hers as the red-gold light intensified, becoming a prickling heat that seemed to come from the last ripples of pleasure within her, centered at the point where his flesh still joined with hers.

Again, the panic of impending failure flared; the power running through her was stronger than she'd ever felt before, but she didn't know what to *do* with it. Was there a spell? A gesture? What?

"Jade, I—" Lucius began, but then his face changed, his eyes going blank and wide as the magic changed its pitch and swirled around him in tightening spirals. "I see it!" He rolled off her without ceremony and scrabbled into his clothes. "Get dressed!"

Jade wasn't supposed to enter the library with him, but the magic was wrapping around her too. Heart hammering, she yanked on her own clothes, knowing that whatever a mage was holding or wearing typically made it into the barrier, and they didn't want to wind up transitioning bare-assed naked. *But I'm not supposed to go anywhere!*

A sharp pain pierced her forearm, a voice—maybe a woman's voice, maybe her imagination?—whispered, "*Beware*," and the world suddenly jolted and spun. She felt the familiar ripping sensation of her spiritual self leaving her physical body, but she wasn't being pulled sideways into the gray-green flow of the barrier. She was being pulled *down*. She screamed and tried to block the magic, but it was too late. She heard Lucius bellow, saw him reach for her as their physical bodies collapsed to the floor. She lunged her metaphysical self toward him; their hands caught and held, feeling solid and real as the world blurred around them. And disappeared.

CHAPTER FOUR

Kaleidoscope images flashed across Jade's perceptions: She saw a vibrant green rain forest cloaked in gray fog; a screaming skull carved into the base of a mountain, its gaping mouth forming the opening of a dark, forbidding cave. To one side of the cave mouth, a picked-clean skeleton was spiked to the cave wall, incongruously wearing tattered purple velour. Then darkness whipped again, a shock wave detonated, there was a sense of wrenching disorientation, and she was slammed flat onto a gritty surface that drove the breath from her lungs. Heat slapped at her first, then a bright, searing light that radiated through her lids and made her squint even with her eyes already shut.

Gods! She rolled onto her side, curling partway fetal as she fought to get air into her chest, then coughed when hot, dry air rushed in, starkly contrasting with the cooler moisture of the earth plane.

Heart hammering, she rolled onto her back, con-

scious of the way the surface beneath her yielded and
crunched, sandlike in its texture. She cracked her eyelids and blinked until the light resolved itself into a
pale reddish brown overhead that shone brighter than
the dull orange days she'd gotten used to on earth.
The span was cloudless and sunless, radiating a uni-
form wash of light and heat; she wasn't sure if it was
a strange sky, or a ceiling far above them. There was
no breeze, no sound, and the dry air smelled faintly of
foreign spices, or maybe overdone barbecue. Wherever
they were, it wasn't the barrier.

The realization brought a tremor of fear, but she
squelched it as best she could. *You wanted to be involved?
Here's your chance.*

"Are you hurt?" Lucius's face crossed her field of vision, his head casting a shadow over her. His eyes held
concern, but behind that was a layer of reserve, of battle readiness. The old Lucius would've been jittering
with a combination of fear and exhilaration, resolved
to do his best but not sure it would be good enough.
The man he'd become seemed to be waiting for additional intel before panicking, or else he'd gotten better
at hiding his feelings. Maybe both.

Either way, it was comforting solidity, especially
given that neither of them had the warriors' skills of
shield or fireball magic, and they didn't wear warriors'
knives or automatic weapons loaded with jade-tips.
With them unarmed, she could only hope that wherever they were, it was safe. Considering that Lucius
hadn't taken one look around them, grabbed her,
tossed her over his newly massive shoulder, and taken

off at a dead run, she was hopeful. For the moment, at least.

"I'm okay." As the churn of the strange barrier crossing subsided, she found it was true. She felt fine. Better than fine, actually; despite the mad rush to yank on their clothes as they'd been vacuumed into the magic, her body still hummed with deep satisfaction. Her skin was acutely sensitive, open-pored and prickling in the heat, giving off the faint, shared scent of sex. Some of that realization must have shown in her face, because his eyes suddenly locked onto her with new intensity, bringing a heightened curl of sensual awareness, an added kick that notched her temp up even further. In an instant, she wanted him inside her, though he'd been there only minutes before. Or maybe that was why the desire was so much more acute now; she knew what it could be like, how his big body felt against hers, inside hers.

She had reached for him before she was aware of moving, cupping his angled jaw in her palm, then sliding her hand around to the softer skin at his nape, up into the thickness of hair that had gone from unruly to luxurious with the magic-wrought changes that had taken him from the man she had known as a friend and pleasant diversion, to one who compelled her, fascinated her. She wanted to strip him naked and stare at him, wanted his solid weight pressing into her, grounding her. Pounding into her. Caught in a spell of heat and sensation, she levered herself up as he leaned down. Her heart raced; her eyelids eased shut even as her lips parted on a low moan of anticipation.

The sound emerged very loud in the strange silence around them, shattering the moment. Jade froze, and felt Lucius's neck go tense and tight beneath her caressing hand. When she opened her eyes, she found him staring back at her, his expression mirroring her own inner shout of, *What the hell are we doing?*

They were in a completely unknown situation, brought there by a type of barrier magic she'd never experienced before. Gods, she hadn't even looked around. One glance at Lucius, one touch, and she'd lost all sense of rationality and self-protection. *Love isn't a miracle*, she remembered writing once in a patient's notes; *it's a damned mental illness.* Here was her proof, and this wasn't even love. It was just good sex.

Okay, really, *really* good sex. But still.

Lucius's face went shuttered, but one corner of his mouth kicked up. "I think I'm starting to understand why sex magic is such a driving force for you Nightkeepers. If that's what this is, it's powerful stuff." He eased away from her, shaking his head. "Somebody should've warned me it's like hammering a double Red Bull with a Viagra chaser." He cut her a look. "Not that I've ever tried that, mind you. I'm just saying."

Jade didn't say anything; she wasn't sure she could've managed to meet his wit, given the sudden hollowness that had opened up inside her. It wasn't that she minded his attributing the intensity of what had happened between them to sex magic—she was relieved by the explanation, though a little embarrassed that she hadn't figured it out first. No, what had her breathing deeply to fill the emptiness was the knowledge that she'd bought into it so quickly, so thoroughly. And that she'd been helpless in its throes, vulnerable in his arms, without the slightest thought for safety or the job at hand. For all that she had bragged inwardly about not losing herself to the sex magic before, she had come damned close this time.

You're a mage, she reminded herself. *Use the magic. Don't let it use you.* But deep down inside, she couldn't escape the fact that she wasn't much of a mage, and didn't know bupkes about using the magic, not really. *Shit.*

"Well," she said, blowing out a breath that did little to settle the churning in her stomach, "the magic got us here. Let's see where 'here' is." Though even as she straightened to look around, she remembered the strange downward lurch of the magic. Had it been her imagination, or had someone really whispered, "Beware"? And if so, who? The only true occupants of the barrier were the *nahwal*, a group of strangely withered ancestral ghosts that spoke with many voices all in synchrony. This had been a single female voice. At least, she thought it had.

Then she got a look around herself, and she stopped thinking about the voice, about the magic, and even about the man beside her, because all she could do was stare as her mouth fell open.

They were . . . Dear gods, she didn't know where they were. They had materialized roughly in the center of a long, perfectly rectangular canyon—or maybe a pit? an enclosure?—that was a mile or so long, a quarter mile wide, and open to the mauve sky. Red rock walls rose up around them, sheer and unbroken, stretching several stories high before ending in perfectly straight lines. The sand underfoot was a gritty version of the same reddish stone, with something else that sparkled faintly in the unchanging light. Huge, unadorned columns sprouted from the sand, one right beside where Jade and Lucius had landed. More important, several hundred yards away from where she and Lucius crouched, in what looked like the exact center of the enclosure, sat a huge four-sided pyramid made of three tiers that descended in size from bottom to top, forming god-size steps leading upward. At each corner was carved a humanoid head, easily ten feet tall, with a fiercely scowling face that was surrounded by a halo of radiating lines. She couldn't immediately place the image, but thought it was familiar. Each tier was painted a different color: red at the bottom, black in the middle, white at the top. As was the case with many Mayan pyramids, human-size staircases ran down the center of each of the four sides, with rectangular doorways set on either side of the staircases on the upper and lower tiers. Practically every available surface was worked with intricate glyph carvings that were the traditional blend of art and language. Unlike the other pyramids she'd seen in person or studied at UT, though, this one didn't culminate in a ceremonial platform, or with a boxy temple built at the top. Instead, the center of the pyramid was an open, empty space crowned by a series of stone archways running parallel to one another, looking like some ancient

creature had died atop the temple and gone to fossil
with its rib bones bared to the bright, sunless sky.

Wonder shimmered through Jade. Though vaguely
bunkerlike, it was elegant in its own way. More, it
wasn't a restored ruin of a bygone era or a computer-
generated rendering of what an ancient Mayan temple might have looked like. This was the real thing.
Somehow.

"Do you think that's the library?" she asked softly.
During its tenure on earth, the library had been hidden in a subterranean cavern that could be accessed
only by a series of water-filled, booby-trapped tunnels.
The natural cavern, embellished with carved scenes
and ancient spells, had been empty when Nate and
Alexis discovered it. Since then, the Nightkeepers had
assumed—or at least Jade had—that when their ancestors had cast the powerful magic needed to hide the
library within the barrier and create the Prophet's spell
to retrieve the information it contained, they would
have replicated the stone-carved cavern within the barrier's gray-green, foggy milieu. But this was no stone
cavern, and that hadn't been any ordinary barrier transition. Not to mention that the Prophet's spell hadn't
said anything about the Prophet entering the barrier or
traveling to the library itself; the magic was supposed
to connect Lucius with the information, allowing him
to channel it while he stayed on the earthly plane.

Instead, he—a human who wasn't quite a Prophet—
and she—a mage who barely rated the title—had somehow been sucked . . . where?

When he didn't answer her question, it was an answer nonetheless. She blew out a breath. "You saw the hellmouth too." The image of the cave mouth overlain with a carving of a screaming skull was burned into her retinas. Iago might've locked and hidden the earthly entrance to Xibalba, but somehow they had gotten through.

Lucius nodded. "Yeah. I saw it." He glanced upward. "And damned if that doesn't look like the sky from the in-between, only way brighter." The in-between was the limbo plane where his consciousness had been trapped while the *makol* demon had been in full control of his body. In it was the dusty road leading to the river-crossing entrance to Xibalba.

"The library is hidden in the barrier," Jade pointed out. "If it had been in the underworld already, the *Banol Kax* wouldn't have needed to infiltrate Iago's camp to ensure that his people didn't gain access." Yet they had, through Lucius's *makol*. Which suggested the library wasn't in Xibalba. But if that was the case, why were *they* there? "Do you think someone—or some*thing*— pulled us here?"

"More things are possible in heaven and earth," he misquoted, expression grim, but she also heard an undertone of suppressed excitement. He caught her hands and pulled her to her feet, so they stood facing each other in the lee of the big stone column, hands linked. "But given where we've ended up, I don't like the idea of who might've been doing the pulling." He glanced past the concealing pillar toward the pyramid, then looked sidelong at her. "We should go back and get weapons, maybe reinforcements."

"You're assuming the *way* spell is going to work." The homing spell that was supposed to return an out-of-body mage to his or her body was notoriously fickle. "And that we'll be able to get back here afterward." What was more, the same skitter of excitement she saw on his face was running through her veins, urging her onward. "Let's check out the pyramid." The suggestion came partly from duty, partly from her growing need to *do* something . . . and also from her growing suspicion that whoever had brought them there would have to be the one to send them back. The day of the new moon wasn't one of barrier flux, which meant she and Lucius shouldn't have been able to enter the barrier, never mind get all the way through the hellmouth.

Beware.

"We're unarmed. Shit, we don't even have a pocketknife to blood our palms." But he wanted to do it. She saw the building excitement in his face, felt it race in her own system, as though they were daring each other without saying the words.

"We're just going to go look around." But he had a point; stupidity didn't favor survival of the fittest. So she took a deep breath. "I'll shield us." At his sharp look, she shook her head. "I know it's a warrior's spell, but there's something—" *In the air*, she started to say, but broke off because that wasn't it, precisely. The faint glitter of red-gold magic and the hum of Nightkeeper power were right there in front of her, misting the air between her and Lucius, close enough that she thought she could reach out and grab the power if she was brave enough. *Do it*, her instincts said. She didn't know if it was the residual vulnerability from the sex magic, the barrier crossing, or something about the strange canyon, but the magic suddenly felt as if it were a part of her, in a way that was both foreign and compelling.

Acting on instinct, her body moving without her conscious volition, she bit down sharply on her own tongue, drawing blood. Letting go of Lucius's hands, she stepped back and spit onto the sparkling, red-tinged sand, offering a sacrifice of both blood and water to the gods. The red-gold coalesced around her, then around Lucius, as it had done before, when they had been lying together in the aftermath. Magic spurted through her like lust, hot and hard. It caught her up, spun through her, making her want to scream with the mad glory of it.

Lucius said something, but she barely heard him over the hum of magic that gathered around her, inside her.

"I can do this," she said, or maybe she only thought it. Either way, the certainty coiled hard and hot inside her, and the shimmering magic that hovered in front of her coalesced into . . . what? She could almost see shapes in the sparkles as she reached out to the magic, touched it. A soundless detonation ripped through her, a rush of power that strained toward something that stayed just out of reach. If she could just—

"*Jade!*" Lucius's shout broke through, shattering her concentration. He had her by the arms and was shaking her, his eyes hard. "Pull it back, *now!*"

The magic snapped out of existence in an instant, without her volition. The loss of that vital energy sapped her, had her sagging against him. Her head spun, but his urgency penetrated. "What? What's wrong?"

Then she heard it: a dog's mournful howl coming from the other side of their concealing pillar. Lucius crowded her closer to the column, pressing her flat against it with his body. Against her temple, he whispered, "There's something going on in the pyramid."

The carved stone was warm and rough where Jade's fingers clutched at the grooved surface, grounding her even as her mind spun with the power of the magic she'd just touched on, and the sharp grief that she'd been unable to do a damned thing with it. Her heart banged against her ribs as she and Lucius eased around the edge to take a look.

"Oh, shit." She wasn't sure which one of them said it. Maybe they both had.

Whereas before the pyramid had seemed deserted, now a man stood on the first of the three big, god-size steps. He was wearing a simple white loincloth and had dark hair and strangely gray-cast skin, and after a moment of standing motionless, he raised a carved conch shell to his mouth and blew a shrill note. Moments later the call was answered by movement at the darkened doorways on the lower tier; then five more men emerged, but these guys were wearing ceremonial regalia and full-face masks carved to look like various creatures: a snake, an antelope, a white jaguar, a bird of prey, and a wolf. The masks were topped with elaborate feather-and-bone headdresses that created colorful halos, and the men's bodies were asymmetrically shielded on their left sides, leaving their right arms free to wield the short-handled clubs they wore at their belts.

Jade just stared, stunned. The skin of the men's arms and legs was gray-cast in places, missing in others, peeled away to show reddish meat, even down to glimpses of stained bone. Worse, the animal shapes weren't masks; those were the actual heads of the man-beasts who had come from the pyramid. For a second, denying the horror of it all, her brain locked on the image: five armored men and one musician against a background of rusty hues. It was just like the painting that'd been showing on Lucius's flat-screen. But why? How? What did it mean?

"They sensed the magic," she said, forcing the words. What had she been thinking, trying to wield a warrior's spell? Worse, she'd let the magic take over, let it use her—or at least attempt to use her.

"I think so." But he squeezed her shoulder in silent support. "Now the question is whether that's a good thing."

Jade held her breath, though it wasn't as if that was going to change anything.

Without hesitation or consultation, the five armored men—demons? what *were* they?—headed straight for their hiding spot, with Jaguar-head in the lead and the others grouped behind him. He pulled the short club from his belt, held it out to the side, and uttered a sharp command. The weapon shimmered momentarily and a malicious rattle skidded through the air as the short club elongated to become a long, deadly looking shaft with a wickedly barbed spike at one end and a bulbous knob at the other. The blunt end roiled greasy brown.

Dark magic!

A cry caught in Jade's throat. She locked eyes with Lucius as their question was answered all too clearly. "Not good!" they said in unison.

CHAPTER FIVE

"Come on!" Lucius grabbed Jade's hand and dragged her to a skidding run that churned up the sparkling sand and pebbles underfoot. He kept his body between her and their pursuers, impelled by a vicious, blood-thirsty sort of protectiveness he'd never felt before. For all that he respected the hell out of the Nightkeepers' egalitarian use of both men and women in the warrior caste and on the front lines, this was a different situation, a different woman. She shouldn't even *be* there, damn it. Neither of them should.

As they burst from cover, the jaguar-masked warrior shouted something that probably translated to "Halt, intruder!" or the equivalent, though Lucius didn't know what language they were using. It wasn't Mayan; at least, not any version of it he'd ever studied or heard.

From within the stone enclosure, the dog stopped howling and started barking, and was soon joined by a second set of snarling barks, feral-sounding and mean.

Then, half a heartbeat later, the barks were drowned out by a roar that wasn't made by anything so mundane as a canine. The noise shook the canyon floor and made the arched top of the temple start to seem less like an artistic flourish and more like the top of a cage.

Lucius glanced over his shoulder. Their pursuers were gaining fast, in a blur of ceremonial armor, ragged flesh, and flashing fangs. And what the hell were they? Animal-headed zombies didn't feature in the Nightkeepers' legends, at least, not that he knew. A connection nudged at him, but he couldn't think about that right now. They needed to find a way out of the strange canyon, which was starting to feel too much like a gladiatorial pit. Gods knew *that* concept wasn't outside the legends.

"Look!" Jade pointed toward one of the corners where the canyon ended—only it wasn't a corner anymore. As they drew nearer, the optical illusion of a dead end gave way, showing where their canyon made a T intersection with another running at right angles. Maybe that was a way out!

They tore around the corner, hand in hand. Twenty feet into the narrower canyon, they slammed into an invisible, unyielding surface stretched across the opening. Lucius's breath exploded from him on an "oof" that became a howl when unseen coils snapped tight around them both, jerking them off their feet to dangle in midair.

"*Fuck!*" He struggled to get to Jade, to free himself, to do something, anything. A harsh rattling noise surrounded them, marking the invisible force as the dark magic wielded by the denizens of the underworld. He had a nauseating image of him and Jade being caught in a huge, invisible spiderweb, with something terrible and eight-legged advancing intangibly toward them.

If you're ever going to connect to the magic, now would be a good fucking time, he thought, and bit down viciously on his tongue. Pain flared and blood welled in his mouth, but that was it. No magic. No power. No nothing.

"Lucius!"

Jade's shout was scant warning as Jaguar-head grabbed Lucius's ankles and yanked, pulling him free of the web magic. Lucius hit the ground hard and let himself go limp, though his heart hammered in his chest, impelled by rage and the pounding need to get to Jade, to protect her, to somehow get her back to safety, though he wasn't the mage she needed him to be.

Then Snake-head leaned over him, hissing in satisfaction. Revulsion lent added force as Lucius lunged to his feet, kicking hard at the demon warrior's kneecap. He hit his target, felt a hell of an impact, and heard the sick pop of bone and cartilage. Snake-head howled and went down. Lucius kicked him in the face, connecting with a watermelon crunch that was disgustingly satisfying.

Blood pounding, he scrambled up and spun—straight into the stubby end of Jaguar-head's spear. The weapon rattled and belched greasy brown smoke, which whipped around Lucius, immobilizing him in the same invisible coils as before. Then Wolf-head stepped up and smashed Lucius in the temple with his short club. The impact thudded through him and the world spun as he dropped with the grace of a corpse. Jade screamed, but her cry cut off midway, choking to silence. Lucius roared in answer, struggling against the unyielding bonds. "Jade. *Jade!*"

As the world faded around him, he tried to fight his way back to full consciousness, all the while praying, *Gods, don't let it end like this!*

It didn't. When he came to a short time later, he was being carried head and foot between two of the animal-headed warriors. Beside him strode Jaguar-head, who carried Jade over his shoulder; she lay still, but her eyes were open and reflected her relief when Lucius sent her a wink. He didn't dare do more, though. Not until he better understood what the hell was going on . . . and what they could do about it.

He couldn't see who had shoulders, but Snake-head was at his feet, not even limping. *The damn things have healing magic,* he realized. But what the hell were they? Not *Banol Kax* or *makol,* he knew. The dark lords of the underworld were huge and inhuman, and the archive said the demon souls of the *makol* took on a shadowy, green-eyed form when they weren't possessing human hosts. So what other classes of badasses existed within Xibalba, and how could they be taken down for good? Unfortunately, that was yet another example of the Nightkeepers' critical need to fill in the gaps. Someone, at some point in the past, must've known what these things were, and how to kill them. But that knowledge, like so much else, had been lost.

So think it through, he told himself. *There's got to be*

something *we can do here.* But unfortunately, the whole "everything happens for a reason" religious tenet of the magi had a major flaw in this case: With the sky-road destroyed and the gods unable to communicate with the Nightkeepers or directly influence things on the earthly plane, logic said that it hadn't been a god that had brought them to the canyon. More likely, one of the *Banol Kax* or a powerful demon underling had detected the sex magic and the stirring of the Proph-et's powers and usurped the energy flows somehow. Which would suggest that he and Jade didn't have a destined role to play in the underworld; the dark lords were just looking to cut down on their enemies.

Okay, so maybe thinking it through hadn't been such a great idea.

Try the homing spell, he mouthed to Jade, chancing the communication. When she got a mulish *I'm not go-ing without you* look on her face, he added, *If you can get back, you can bring help.*

Maybe. Maybe not, but at least she'd be safe.

The small party passed through the stone pillars, clearly heading for the pyramid and whatever had made that terrible noise earlier. They were running out of time. "Do it!" he hissed.

Eyes bleak, Jade nodded. But when she whispered the ritual word, nothing happened. Not one freaking thing.

Lucius cursed inwardly as that brief hope guttered and died. He had no illusion that he could summon the power on his own, and he doubted sex magic would be an option anytime soon. So what the hell else could he do? There had to be *something*, damn it. Problem was, he knew that was a self-serving lie. Sometimes life just wasn't fucking fair.

The group came within view of the pyramid, which loomed ever larger in Lucius's limited field of vision, bringing a mixture of awe and dread. Awe because he'd spent a third of his lifetime studying a dead culture suddenly coming alive in front of him. Dread because . . . well, he wasn't an idiot. But that didn't mean he was giving up, either.

The whistle-blower wasn't on the ramparts anymore, and the dogs—and whatever else was inside— had gone ominously quiet as the procession stopped short of the temple structure. Lucius's captors unceremoniously dumped him facedown in the scuffed dirt. He landed cursing, and rolled onto his side as Jade thumped down on her butt next to him. She cried out when she hit, but then snapped her mouth shut and glared instead.

Good girl, Lucius thought. He didn't get a chance to do more than lock eyes with her before Snake-head and Pig-head moved in and dragged him to his feet. Still bound in the relentless yet invisible shield magic, he had zero choice in the matter. He hung between his captors, glaring when two of the others hauled Jade to her feet, so the captives and their animal-headed guards stood facing one of the low-linteled doorways that led into the pyramid's lower tier.

Brain racing in search of a clue, explanation, or escape route, Lucius scanned the intricate Mayan glyphwork carved into the surrounding stones, automatically starting to arrange the phonemes into words and meanings. But before he'd gotten beyond, "On this cardinal day of . . ." there was movement within the temple and four newcomers emerged. They looked like men—in that they had all their flesh and normal human faces—and they wore elaborate cloaks over jewel-encrusted armor plates and armbands. But, incongruously, the armor wasn't made of wood, leather, and stone, as were the traditional trappings worn by the animal-heads. Instead, it was made of burnished metal: copper, or maybe gold. Which didn't make sense, because the Maya hadn't been metalworkers, and the Mayan paradigm prevailed in Xibalba.

At least, he thought it did. But the more he looked at the metal-armored men, the more he became convinced that they were outfitted like pharaohs' guards, pure Egyptian from their kohl-lined eyes to the rayed-sun symbols on their cloaks. Before he could do the necessary brain shift to figure out what the hell it meant, there was another stir of movement from within the temple, followed by a glint of luminous green that obliterated every other thought inside Lucius's skull. Rage and revulsion surged to tunnel his vision as a smoky shadow emerged, becoming a dark, man-shaped ghost with glowing green eyes. *Makol!*

The demon soul drifted across the ground, moving toward him. The air went cold and Lucius's bones ached with death and damnation, and the things he'd sworn he would never be, ever again. Clamping his teeth against a stream of foul curses, he strained against the unyielding shield magic. As the *makol* drew nearer, the shifting shadow morphed and solidified, becoming almost a man, one that wore a tall diadem marked with the sun symbol that had been in use for only a single Egyptian dynasty, that of the pharaoh who had converted the empire to monotheistic sun worship, largely by killing off anyone who preferred the polytheistic religion that had been entrenched for thousands of years.

Gut tightening further with the ID, Lucius bared his teeth. "I thought you'd had yourself declared a god. Is this your idea of a deity's fitting reward . . . Akhenaton?" Although the pharaoh's animal-headed minions—which he belatedly recognized as perverted versions of the Egyptian pantheon Akhenaton had outlawed—might still speak their native tongue, he had no doubt the *makol* understood him. The damn things could see straight inside a man.

"*Akhenaton*." Jade spat the name of one of the Nightkeepers' most ancient enemies: the pharaoh who had been responsible for the first of the three massacres that had driven the Nightkeepers nearly to extinction.

At her gasp, the demon spirit turned. Started drifting toward her.

"Stay the hell away from her," Lucius snarled. The demon's dark presence scraped along his nerve endings; worse, he could feel its interest in Jade, its dismissal of him. What *makol* would want a human when a Nightkeeper was available? The thought of Jade going through the transition sickened him beyond reason, past caution. "I said, *hands off*!" Deep within, the rage spun higher, becoming a strange, edgy energy that buzzed through him, coalescing at the places where the shield magic held him fast.

From within the temple, the dogs suddenly started barking again, their cries sharp and frenzied. Excited.

Akhenaton hesitated at the sound, and Lucius thought he caught a thread of satisfaction coming from the damned soul. Some message must have passed, because the four pharaoh's guards broke from their positions and closed on Jade.

"Lucius!" She craned her head, looking back at him as the guards started dragging her into the fortress. The dogs went nuts, barking and howling, sounding almost human in their cries.

"Jade!" Anguish hammered through Lucius, catching him up and taking him someplace within himself, someplace he hadn't been before. Pain ripped through him, his vision washed red-gold, and pressure detonated inside his head. Liquid flame poured through his veins, bringing a burning agony that he latched onto, instinctively sending it toward the places where the shield magic held him immobile.

A terrible roar of rage split the air; for a second he thought it had come from him. Then the air went instantaneously from cool to blistering hot, huge feathered wings boomed in the air, and a red-orange specter rose into sight, lifting from behind the step-sided wall, flapping hard to stay aloft on ragged, bleeding wings. The sky lit supernova bright in an instant, driving back those standing below on the sand.

Squinting into the flare, Lucius couldn't pinpoint the thing's image: One second it seemed a terrible winged and feathered demon with curling horns and fangs, its outline wreathed in fire; then in the next it shifted, seeming to flash the image of a huge figure, that of a masked man, his face obscured behind the symbols of a god. More important, Lucius knew the symbols. Was he really seeing what he thought he was seeing, or was this another of Akhenaton's creations?

He didn't know, but he had to chance it. Throwing back his head, he shouted, "Kinich Ahau!"

The horned Mayan firebird, one aspect of the great sun god itself, roared in answer, beating its wings against the stone bars that held it contained. Flames poured from its beak and eyes, licking along the bars and turning them gradually molten. And, as Lucius squinted against the blazing light, he remembered having seen this before.

Or rather, *he* hadn't seen it . . . but Cizin had. His demon possessor had been a double agent, planted within the Order of Xibalba to keep Iago in check when the dark lords began to worry that their earthly namesakes were getting above themselves. The *Banol Kax* didn't want Iago to ally with Moctezuma's demon soul, not just because the bloodthirsty Aztec king had once led powerful armies and plotted his own version of the end-time, but also because he'd elevated himself to the status of a god, one affiliated with the sun itself . . . and the *Banol Kax* didn't want that to happen because they already had plans to put in place a sun god of their own choosing: the sun king Akhenaton.

They had captured the true sun god, Kinich Ahau, along with his canine companions. When the barrier's activity peaked during the summer solstice of the first triad year—aka in nine fucking days—the dark lords were going to sacrifice the true sun god and elevate Akhenaton in his place.

And oh, holy fuck, that couldn't be allowed to happen.

Snarling, Akhenaton turned on the firebird, lifted shadowy arms, and chanted a spell. In an instant, a chill wind blew, the air cooled, and the molten stone bars turned solid; they were slightly deformed, but not by enough to free the god. But that hadn't been the firebird's aim, Lucius realized seconds later, when two dark blurs hurtled through the widened openings between two pairs of archways: pony-size black dogs with sharp white teeth and red eyes.

The companions!

One of the dogs went for Jade's captors, the other for Lucius's. Dark blood sprayed as the ravening canine ripped out Snake-head's throat; the man-beast went down and stayed down. When it did, the shield magic surrounding Lucius disappeared.

The old Lucius wanted to stand and gape at legends come to life. The better man he was becoming landed running. He lunged for Jade; three of the pharaoh's guards were using their elongated pikes to keep the big black dogs at bay while the fourth force-marched her toward the fortress, following the demon shadow as it disappeared into the darkness within. Inside the pyramid, the sun god shrieked in rage and pain.

"No!" Lucius bolted after them, catching up with the rearmost guard just outside the temple. The guard spun and leveled his pike, his eyes lighting with battle glee as dark magic rattled. Seconds later, though, they flattened to terror, and a dark blur flashed past Lucius and hit the guard in the chest, sending the bastard down and away from Jade. Blood sprayed and vertebrae crunched. Lucius charged forward and grabbed Jade, who stood where the guard had left her, blank eyed and shocky-looking. The magic that had been holding her fast was gone.

"Lucius!" She sagged into him, grabbed onto him. She might've said something else, but he couldn't hear her over the tidal roar that was rising within him. His body heated to flash point and beyond; he was burning without flames, writhing in agony without screams. The world closed in on him from all sides until he could feel only hot agony and the press of Jade's body. A howling scream slammed through him, out of him.

He felt that same slipping, sliding sensation from before, only this time it was sucking him *up*, not down. There was a jolt of movement; he heard the *makol's* screech of anger, Kinich Ahau's roar of satisfaction, the companions' howls . . . and then it was all gone. The world whipped past him; he caught a glimpse of the hellmouth, the cloud forest, and what he thought might be the barrier, followed by the outlines of his cottage at Skywatch. Then there was a dizzying jolt and he was back in his body, sprawled inelegantly on the living room floor.

Home.

He lay still for a moment, blinking as his body came back online. When a few of his larger muscle groups checked in, he used them to roll over and stretch out a hand to where Jade lay, an arm's length away. Her eyes were open, though blurred with disorientation. She was there, though. She was okay. *Thank you, gods*, he thought, but then jolted as the rest of it returned. "The firebird! We have to"—*go back and rescue the sun god*, he started to say, but couldn't get the words past a sudden rushing noise in his head. His vision blurred. He heard her call his name, felt her grab his hand, but those inputs seemed very far away, and so much less important than the powerful surge that caught him up, feeling very different from the magic that had yanked the two of them to Xibalba. He saw her worried eyes through the whirling tunnel of power as he was yanked back into the magic . . . this time alone.

"Lucius!" Jade screamed his name, even though deep down inside, she knew he was already gone. His eyes were rolled back in his head; his body had gone limp. She told herself not to freak, that it was normal for that to happen when a mage entered the barrier. Except that he wasn't a mage . . . and the magic had already gone very wrong once tonight. Which meant . . . what? What should she do now?

Her hands were shaking; her whole body was trembling. But strangely, the memories of what she'd just been through seemed oddly blunted, allowing her to think and react rather than just freaking the hell out. She'd heard the others talk about the preternatural focus conferred by the warrior's talent, and how it helped them function under terrifying conditions. She thought she might be experiencing something like that now, only coming from shock rather than innate talent.

Pushing to her feet, she reached for her pocket, intending to call Strike, both to report in and to get help with Lucius. She didn't know where he'd gone, hadn't even felt the magic that had taken him, and that worried her. If their shared magic had dumped them in Xibalba, where would he wind up now that he was flying solo? If they were lucky, he'd make it to the library . . . but it wasn't as if luck had been with them so far.

She had the earpiece partway to her ear when a whispery word echoed through the room: "*Jade.*"

It was a woman's voice. The same one she'd heard just before being yanked into Xibalba.

Freezing, she looked around. "Who is that? Where are you?"

"*I'm here. Come to me.*" The world wavered. Red-gold magic flared, surrounding Jade unbidden.

This time, the power jolted her in the familiar sidelong direction of the barrier, but she hadn't performed any transition spell, hadn't called the magic. Lifting the earpiece, she screamed, "*Help me!*"

But as Lucius's cottage shimmered and disappeared, she realized she'd forgotten to turn the damned earpiece on. The others wouldn't know there was a problem for hours, maybe longer. And by then it might be too late.

CHAPTER SIX

Lucius materialized in a long, narrow stone chamber that was lit by a row of burning torches running down either side. He'd zapped into a relatively open space at one end of the room; the other end was lost in the distance, obscured by countless rows of racked objects that blurred one into the next in the dim torchlight.

Exhilaration slammed through him. *The library!*

Then gravity caught up with him and he fell a good three feet to land face-first on the chamber floor. His chin cracked against granite and the breath left him with a hiss of pain as he pancaked it hard. He was also unexpectedly naked, which made the pancake thing suck more than it would have otherwise. Stone slapped his belly and mashed his 'nads, and he let out a grunt as he hit. But the pain didn't last long in the face of the crazy-making wonder that surrounded him.

He rolled onto his back, laughing and gasping for air. "I did it. I fucking *did it*!" Granted, the Prophet wasn't supposed to physically—or metaphysically, for that matter—travel to the library, but maybe that was the sacrifice required for his having kept his soul intact. *If so, that's not going to be much of a sacrifice at all*, he thought. Aloud, he crowed, "What glyph geek *wouldn't* want access to a place like this?"

The walls were carved in the Classical Mayan style, with figures turned in profile as they bent over codices, holding quill pens and feather-and-fur paintbrushes, or hammering away at chisels, carving stories into stone. And if those walls pressed too close, sparking a hint of the suffocating claustrophobia that had plagued him for the past half year, he'd learned to shove the weakness aside and focus on the things that mattered. Like the library.

He'd finally gained access to the knowledge the Nightkeepers needed. *Deaf gods be praised*. More, there was a new and oh-holy-fuck problem facing them: namely that the *Banol Kax* had stolen the sun god and were planning on making a switcheroo in nine days. And although the information surrounding him dated only up to the fifteen hundreds, when the conquistadors' pillaging of the so-called New World had prompted the surviving magi to hide the library and create the Prophet's spell, the Nightkeepers were hoping—praying— that the cache would contain additional prophecies dealing with the end-time . . . including the role the sun god was supposed to play.

"So all I've got to do is find those prophecies . . . or better yet, a spellbook entitled, *How to Put the Sun Back into the Sky*." But, standing naked in the room he'd spent the past six months trying to find, and a decade prior to that dreaming of, even when he hadn't known precisely what he'd dreamed, he looked around the narrow, jam-packed arcade . . . and realized that he didn't have the faintest clue where to start. It wasn't like there was a computerized, searchable cross-ref system already in place.

The memory of putting together just such a system for the Nightkeepers' archive caught him hard, bringing a blast of the mingled desire and frustration that had ridden him as he and Jade had worked together day after day. Back then he'd done his damnedest to get her to notice him as more than just a friend, only to find that, when he thought he'd gotten past the friends zone, it was only to friends with benefits. At the time, that wasn't what he'd wanted or needed. And now . . .

"It's not important," he said aloud, though that wasn't entirely true. Jade was very, very important to him, whether as a friend or as . . . whatever they were now. But at the same time, he couldn't focus on her, or on trying to figure out what sort of relationship they were going to have going forward. He was in the *library*.

Reminding himself to breathe, he took a long look around.

He was standing in a relatively open space at one end of the narrow room. There was a study area nearby with a low stone table and a couple of fixed benches. Three intricately carved stones were set into the floor beside the table, and several wall hooks held lush-looking woven green robes worked with brilliant yellow at their edges. In one corner, a deep wooden rack contained an assortment of quills, tools, fig-bark strips, limestone wash, and all the other necessities for making the ancient, accordion-folded codices of the Mayan-era Nightkeepers. There was a jaguar statue in the opposite corner; he thought it might have been a fountain at one point. It looked as though water would have emerged from a tiny spout halfway up the wall, then dropped into the open mouth of the snarling stone jaguar. The animal's lower jaw formed a bowl that would have drained down the back of the creature's throat, presumably to recirculate.

A second bowl rested between the recumbent jaguar's paws; it was marked with a looping glyph that resembled a thumbs-up gesture made by a stubby-fingered hand. The glyph, which translated to "*sa*," represented corn or corn gruel, but was more generally taken to mean "food."

Okay. Food and water. He got that. If he was lucky— or as smart as he liked to think he was—he'd be able to figure out how the rest of the place worked.

He prowled the study area, trying to get a mental picture of the magi who had set it up. If he could understand how they ordered their workspace, maybe he could guess at how they had organized the contents of the shelves. He badly wanted to dive right into the stacks, but held himself back, knowing his own ability to hyperfocus and lose track of things. Odds were that unless he went in there with a plan, he'd get sucked in by the first codex he laid hands on, regardless of its contents. So he behaved, staying in what passed for his analytical brain.

Everything was bright and new, dust free and fresh seeming. *Magic*, he thought, knowing that also accounted for the torches that burned steadily without emitting smoke or noticeably impacting the oxygen level in the room. Almost as an afterthought, he snagged one of the robes and shrugged it on; it proved to be a loose-fitting ceremonial garment worked with quills and feathers down the back, in the geometric pattern of repeating "G" characters that was often associated with the gods, or places of sacred thought. The realization humbled him with the reminder that he wasn't just a guy on a mission; he was the latest in a long line of scholars who had served the library. He might not be a mage, but he'd kick the shit out of anyone who tried to take the title of "scholar" away from him. He'd damn well earned it.

"And now it's time to earn it all over again," he said, staring at row upon row of racked artifacts and codices and noting the total lack of distinguishing marks on any of the shelves. "But I've gotta ask: Is there any way to find what I'm looking for without cataloging every bloody artifact myself?"

With a sudden lurch, his body seesawed into motion without his volition, walking him stiff-legged to an open space near the stone table. Shocked, Lucius cursed under his breath and tried to stop moving but couldn't, tried to change direction, but couldn't do that, either. He flashed back hard on the memory of his body doing things his mind couldn't control. *Godsdamn it!* But before either panic or rage could fully form, the compulsion drained away and he found himself standing beside the study table, near where the three carved stones were set into the floor.

Magic, he thought, wonder shimmering through the loathing that came with being controlled, compelled. "Don't do that again," he warned, though he wasn't sure whether he was talking to his own body or whatever force had briefly animated it, divorcing his flesh from his soul. Gods, what was it about him? Was he so loosely connected to himself that it was *easy* to pull that shit? One of these days, would his consciousness take a walk without his corpse, and that'd be the end of things?

Okay, now he was freaking himself out. *Focus, moron.* Forcing himself back on task, he studied the carved stones. There were three of them arranged in a triangle, all engraved with familiar glyphs. His bare toes were touching the left-bottom stone of the two-dimensional pyramid. The stone at the apex was carved with the so-called "snaggle-toothed dragon" glyph, that of gaping jaws framing an open space. It was one of several glyphs for *way*.

"Now we're getting somewhere. That could be how I get out of here." It might be as simple as standing on the stone and saying the word, or it might involve a blood sacrifice. He wasn't ready to leave yet, but it was good to have a starting point when the time came.

He stared down at the two other carved insets. The one on the left, the one he'd first stood on, was an intricate glyph: a large, rounded square flanked with two rounded rectangles, one ending in a fanlike shape. Each of the main shapes had shapes within shapes, curling and looping back on one another in the Mayan tradition, which was as much about beauty as writing. "*Yilaj*," he said softly, translating the three phonetic symbols spelling out *yi-la-ji*. It meant "was seen." The other stone bore a stylistic reptile's face in profile, with a closed eye and an appended symbol for a second syllable, written phonetically. *Ma ilaj*. "Was not seen."

Ohhh-kay, he thought, trying to parse it out. He had *was seen* and *was not seen*. Positive and negative. Or . . . yes and no.

Lucius's breath shuddered out of him as he remembered the last thing he'd said before his body walked him over to the "yes" glyph. He tried it again. "Is there a trick to help me find what I'm looking for in here?"

His body jerked and he took a step forward. *Yilaj*. Yes.

Oh, holy flying fuck. He was in the middle of a Nightkeeper Ouija board, and he was the damned planchette.

Pulse racing, he stepped off the carved stone and tried another question. "Is Jade safe?" He hadn't meant to ask that, really. But he needed to know. His body jerked and he found himself standing on *ma ilaj*. No, she wasn't okay. *Shit*. "Is she in danger?" he demanded quickly. Nothing happened. Realizing he hadn't stepped off the indicator stone, he jumped to neutral ground and repeated the question. He found himself standing back on the "no" stone, which didn't make any sense. How could she be unsafe, but not in danger?

She couldn't be. Which meant he'd screwed up the translation, or its intent.

He looked back down at the glyphs for a moment, then got it. Stepping to neutral ground, he said, "Does *ma ilaj* mean you can't answer the question?" *Yilaj*. Okay, at least he'd cleared that up. The library's magic—or was this the Prophet's magic itself?—not only had its limitations, it knew what they were. *Cool*, he thought, pulse starting to skim faster now, not from his dislike of his body being used this way, with or without his permission—though there was some of that—but with the sort of academic anticipation he hadn't felt in a long, long time. Back at UT, when the most important thing in his life had been finishing up his thesis, he'd felt the buzz every time he made even infinitesimal progress in finding the elusive screaming-skull glyph that was rumored to mark Nightkeepers' involvement in the end-time. At Skywatch, he'd felt the buzz nearly every damned day at first, when he'd suddenly found himself surrounded by the people of legend and been given access to archived codices and artifacts that were purely unknown in the outside world. Since his return, though, there hadn't been any buzz. There had been only failure and frustration. He might have grown into himself physically, but in doing so, he'd lost part of that other side of himself without even really realizing it.

Now, standing in the library of the ancients, finally in a position to do something to help the Nightkeepers rather than hurt them, he felt the buzz. And he fucking loved it.

Grinning, he stepped off the stone. He didn't let himself ask again about Jade. She was safely back at Sky-watch. And besides, the library didn't know her status. Which brought up an interesting point, come to think. "Are you unable to answer because the question relates to current events rather than something contained specifically within this library?" *Yilaj.* He was getting the hang of this, he thought. But when he stepped off the "yes" stone again, he stumbled. As though it had been hovering at the periphery of his consciousness, waiting for him to notice it, dizzying exhaustion suddenly roared through him, graying his vision and making the floor pitch beneath him.

"Knock it off," he told himself, his words going slurred. "You're not that guy anymore." He was finished with being weak, finished with fading and giving up when people needed him most. He was a new man now. *So fucking act like it.* Granted, magic burned an enormous amount of energy—he'd seen the magi refueling like marathoners and then crashing hard after major spell casting—but he didn't have access to food right now, so he was just going to have to suck it up and deal. It'd probably be a good idea for him to get going on his research, though. Either that, or figure out how to make the stone jaguar in the corner cough up some grub.

Steadying himself through force of will, he stepped to neutral ground and took a moment to formulate his next question, eventually coming up with: "Can you tell me how the Prophet's magic works?"

Yilaj.

"How?"

No answer.

He stepped off the stone, forced himself to focus through the whirling dizziness, and realized he hadn't asked an actual question. He tried again: "How does the Prophet's magic work?"

This time it wasn't so much of a surprise when his body did an about-face without his input, but it was still damned unsettling to have the scenery passing by him without knowing where he was going. He could feel his muscles interacting as he walked toward the racks, but couldn't tell where the neural inputs governing those actions were coming from. Before, the demon had invaded his skull, pushing him into a corner of his own consciousness and eventually severing his connection with the outside world. Now the magic was somehow controlling his body without pressuring his mind. On one level, that was a relief. On another, it squicked him right the hell out, because if he couldn't sense the invader, he couldn't defend himself against it, either.

Then he passed the first rack and discomfort gave way to some serious gawking. If he'd been moving under his own steam, he would've stopped at a row of carved heads with the smashed-in, crooked noses of pugilists or ballplayers. Or he would've poked through a rack of accordion-folded codices, almost certain to find stories, histories, maybe even poems and songs. Only a tiny fraction of the vibrant culture of the ancient Maya had survived through to modern day on Earth, and at that, most of the info came from versions of oral traditions that had been written down by Spanish missionaries in the fifteen hundreds.

Lucius's soul sang the "Ode to Joy" at the sight of so many codices in one place. His body, though, kept walking until it stopped at the eighth rack in. Unbidden, his hand reached out to touch a stack of fig-bark pages that weren't folded accordion-style, but rather were bound along one side with bark strips that had been soaked and bent, then threaded through holes bored down the left side of each page.

For all that it was made of fig bark, the thing looked like a spiral-bound notebook, jarringly modern in the ancient surroundings. The cover was unadorned, giving no hint to the volume's contents.

A tremor ran through Lucius, though he wasn't sure if it was foreboding or another onslaught of the fatigue he knew he wouldn't be able to ignore for much longer. He was back in control of his body, though; having gotten him where it wanted him to go, the magic had snapped out of existence. Which, given how the human Ouija routine had worked, suggested that the volume he was touching would tell him about the Prophet's power.

"Cool. User's manual." If he was lucky.

Getting a geeky high off the buzz of discovery, he carefully turned back the cover page, wincing as bark grated against bark and the spiral binding stuck. Beneath the cover, the first page held a few lines of text done in black ink. That deep in the stacks, the torchlight was pretty diffuse, making it difficult at first for him to make out the glyphs. Then he realized it wasn't the torchlight that was messing him up; it was his frame of reference. The writing wasn't in Mayan hieroglyphics. It was in English, and it read, *I'm fading, my soul dying here as my body dies back on Earth. So pay attention, because if you're reading this, then you're already in deep shit. What I've written down here could save your life . . . if it's not already too late.*

CHAPTER SEVEN

The barrier

When the disorientation of transition magic cleared, Jade was standing in a sea of gray-green mist that came up to her knees. The fog camouflaged the soft, slightly squishy surface underfoot and stretched in all directions to the distant horizon, where the gray-green mist met the gray-green sky.

She wasn't quite sure how she'd gotten there, but she was definitely in the barrier.

Each Nightkeeper perceived the magic in a slightly different way, depending on how his or her brain worked. Strike saw his teleportation as a thin yellow thread connecting him to his destination. Sasha perceived the life forces of all living beings, their *ch'ul*, as different kinds of music. Jade, being more practical than poetic, thought of the barrier as a big-ass chat room. The gray-green mist was the lobby, and it wasn't all that hard to get in if you knew what time the room would be open—the cardinal solstices and equinoxes, and a few other days of astronomical barrier activity—and what address to type in—the proper spell and blood sacrifice. The chat lobby was moderated by the bloodline *nahwal*, a group of dried-up stick people with apple-doll faces, who harbored the collected wisdom of each bloodline without the attendant personalities. Like god-mods in an exclusive chat room, the *nahwal* were sometimes visible to all of the barrier's visitors at once, like during the Nightkeepers' bloodline ceremonies. Alternatively, they could pull a specific mage into an offshoot room for a private chat, or they could kick users out of the chat entirely, either sending them back to their corporeal bodies or stranding them in limbo.

Jade didn't mind being in the barrier; it was one of the few places she ever truly felt like a mage, and an asset. One of her greatest contributions to the Nightkeepers' cause had been when her ancestral *nahwal* had given her a private message during one of the cardinal-day ceremonies, warning her that the Nightkeepers needed to collect the artifacts bearing the seven demon prophecies. The heads-up had allowed them to defend the barrier against Iago's first major attack and had made Jade, albeit briefly, part of the team.

So yeah, she liked the barrier. And she liked visiting the squishy gray-green place . . . during the cardinal days. But this was only the new moon, and she didn't command the sort of magic it would've taken to punch through the barrier on such a low-power day. None of the surviving Nightkeepers did. Even if she assumed her magic could've piggybacked onto Lucius's library transport somehow, she hadn't invoked the *pasaj och* spell required for a mage to enter the barrier. Which suggested that someone—or some*thing*—had summoned her.

"Hello?" she called into the mist, squinting in search of a wrinkled, desiccated humanoid figure. "Are you there?"

There was no answer. Just mist and more mist.

"Hello?" Frustration kicked through her. "What, you're going to drag me in here, then ignore me? How is that fair?"

"Life's not fair, child." The words came from behind her, in a *nahwal*'s fluting, multitonal voice.

She whirled as the mist coalesced, thickening to reveal a tall, thin figure. As it stepped toward her, she saw the *ch'am* glyph of the harvester bloodline, that of an open, outstretched hand. But while that was as she had expected, the *nahwal* itself looked different than it had before. Instead of shiny, brownish skin stretched over ligament and bone, there seemed to be a thin layer of flesh between, making the *nahwal* look subtly rounded, bordering on feminine. More, its eyes, which before had been flat, featureless black, now bore gradations: There was a suggestion of charcoal-colored whites, with irises and pupils in darker gradations.

Unease tightened Jade's throat. "What's going on here?"

"You—" The *nahwal* started to answer, but broke off as it was gripped by a weird shudder. When it stilled, its face wore the neutral, expressionless mask she'd been expecting. More, its skin seemed to crinkle more tightly over its bones and the brief spark of personality she'd seen disappeared. In a multitonal voice it said, "Hear this, harvester child: You have a duty to your bloodline and your king. Do not seek to be more than you were meant to be. Going against the gods can only end badly."

A hot flush climbed Jade's throat as the *nahwal*'s words echoed the things Shandi had been saying for months now—years. *Your role was defined long ago*, the *winikin* kept insisting. *Don't break with tradition when it's all we have to go on.* And the last, at least, was true; the magi were being forced to rely on legend, routine, and the few scattered artifacts to tell them what they were supposed to do—and how to do it—in the triad years, the last three before the end-time.

But, damn it, she didn't *want* to be a shield bearer.

Choosing her words carefully, all too aware that Rabbit had been attacked and nearly killed by a *nahwal*, she said, "With all due respect to my honored ancestors . . ." Saying it aloud, she realized that, deep down inside, she hadn't really thought before about what, or rather *who*, the *nahwal* embodied. For a second, she was tempted to ask about her mother and father, to check if they were inside the *nahwal* somewhere, if they could talk to her. She didn't, though, because she knew that the only *nahwal* to retain any personal characteristics was that of the jaguars, the royal bloodline. In that regard, the harvesters didn't even come close to ranking. Taking a deep breath, she continued: "With all due respect, there are too few of us left to stand on bloodline tradition; each of us must do what we can for the fight."

The *nahwal* started to say something, then stalled as a second whole-body shiver overtook it. The shellacked skin writhed like there were bugs under it, or worse. Caught between horrified fascination and revulsion, Jade took a step back even as the shivers stopped. When they were gone, the *nahwal* once again had pupils and emotion in its eyes, and a hint of feminine curves. "Yes, you must do all that you can and more," it urged. "Be the most and best you can be, and don't yield your own power to another, particularly a man. Don't let emotion turn you aside from your true ambition, your true purpose. Find your magic, your way to make a difference."

Shock and confusion rattled through Jade at this abrupt one-eighty from the "duty and destiny" rhetoric the *nahwal* had started with. "But I thought the harvesters—"

"Don't just be a harvester," the *nahwal* interrupted. "Be yourself." Abruptly it surged forward and grabbed her wrist, its bony fingers digging into her flesh. "Find your magic," it insisted. The place the *nahwal* was touching began to burn, and the gray-green mists around them roiled.

Through the billowing mist, Jade saw the *nahwal* twitch and shudder, felt it start to yank away, only to grip harder. "What's happening?"

"Go," the creature hissed at her, its eyes neither alive nor dead now, but somewhere in between. It let go of her and staggered back, moving jerkily. *"Go!"*

The gray-green fog began spiraling around Jade, making her think of the funnel clouds several of the others had experienced within the barrier—terrible tornadoes that could suck up a mage and spit him or her into limbo. The others had escaped from their plights, but they were warriors with strong magic. She wasn't. Yet even as panic began to build inside her, something else joined it: a spiky, electric heat that lit her up and blunted the fear. It felt like magic, but it wasn't any sort of power she'd ever touched before. Had the *nahwal* given her a new talent? A glance at her wrist showed the same two marks as before—one hand outstretched as though begging, another clutching a quill. Those were the same bloodline and talent marks she'd worn since her first barrier ceremony. But the hot energy inside her was magic; she was sure of it.

Biting her tongue sharply, she drew a blood sacrifice. Pain flared, the salty tang filled her mouth, and a humming noise kindled at the base of her brain. For a split second, she thought she saw another layer of organization to the mist-laden barrier and the rapidly forming tornado—a layer of angles and structure, the metaphorical computer code beneath the cosmic chat room. Then the perception was gone and there was only the terrible funnel cloud that spun around her, threatening to suck her up. The mists whipped past her, headed for the gaping maw; wind dragged at her, yanking at her clothes and hair as she braced against the pull. Around her, within her, that strange, mad energy continued to whirl and grow. She wasn't sure whether it was a memory or real, but she heard the *nahwal* cry, in what sounded like a lone woman's voice, "*Go!*"

It was the same voice she'd heard before, telling her to beware.

She wanted to stay and demand answers, but didn't dare. She had to get *out* of there. Spitting a mouthful of blood into the whipping wind, she threw back her head and shouted, "*Way!*"

This time, the response was instantaneous. Red-gold magic slashed through her, out of her, twisting the barrier plane in on itself and folding her in with it. Gray-green mist flew past and she had the disorienting sensation of moving at an incredible rate of speed, while also being conscious that she wasn't physically moving at all. The sense of motion stopped with a sickening jolt, and she was lying sprawled on her back, still and chill, bathed in the rusty light from the flat-screen TV that took up most of one wall.

She was back in Lucius's cottage, back in her own body.

And thank the gods for that, she thought, blinking muzzily. She didn't know how long she'd been out-of-body, or what time it was, though it was still full dark outside. The sense of emptiness in the room told her that Lucius wasn't nearby. No doubt he'd made it back from the library and had gone to get Strike and the others, so they could wake her. Except that she'd awakened herself. She'd made it home.

She lay blinking for a moment, then let out a long, exultant breath and sat partway up. "I did it." She'd cast the "*way*" spell by herself, had rescued herself from the barrier. "*I did it!*"

More, the magic was still inside her. It hadn't stayed

behind in the barrier. And it was *showing* her things. Where before the glyphs on the TV screen had only hinted at another layer of meaning, she now saw that the text string wasn't illiterate gibberish at all, but a fragment of a spell . . . or rather a blessing, she realized, though she didn't know what would have been blessed, or why.

I'm a spell caster, she thought, using the alternate meaning of the scribe's talent mark, the one that had never before felt accurate. Her throat tightened with the raw, ragged joy of it. *Or if I'm not now, at least I'm heading in that direction.* The *nahwal* had triggered her talent. It seemed that Lucius wasn't the only one to get a jump start tonight.

Still staring at the screen, as happy laughter bubbled up in her chest and stalled in her throat, she put down her hands, intending to push herself to her feet. Instead of finding the floor, though, she touched cold flesh.

Letting out a shriek, she yanked her hand back and spun, her heart going leaden in her chest. *"Lucius!"*

He lay where he'd been before. Even in the reddish brown light his skin was an unhealthy gray, his lips blue. For a long second, she didn't think he was breathing at all. Then his chest lifted in a slow, sluggishly indrawn breath. After another agonizing wait, it dropped as he breathed out.

"Lucius?" She reached out trembling fingers to check the pulse at his throat, steeling herself against the chill of his flesh. She couldn't detect his heartbeat, but stemmed the rising panic. *If his heart weren't beating, he wouldn't still be breathing.* Instead of settling her, though, the thought brought images of animated corpses with glowing green eyes.

No, she told herself harshly. *The* makol *is gone. Lucius isn't. I won't let him be.*

Heart pounding, she scrabbled around, found the earpiece, and keyed it to transmit. "Hey, guys. Need some help in here." Her voice was two octaves too high.

"Are you okay?" Jox asked immediately, his voice full of a *winikin's* concern.

She tried to keep it factual, tried not to let her voice tremble. "Lucius is out and fading. I think we're going to need Sasha, and maybe Rabbit." Sasha could heal him. Rabbit, with his mind-bender's talent, could follow where Lucius's mind had gone. Maybe. Hopefully. *Please, gods.*

There was a murmur of off-mike conversation, and then the *winikin* said, "Sit tight. Strike and the others are on their way."

"I'm on mike," Strike broke in, the background sounds suggesting he was running. "Where is he stuck?" But they both knew he was really asking, *Did he make it to the library?*

"I don't know." She sketched out a quick report of her and Lucius's out-of-body jaunt to Xibalba. She'd tell the others about her solo trip to the barrier after she'd had a chance to think about it herself. By the writs, it was her right to keep her *nahwal's* messages private, and she didn't think her visit with the *nahwal* was relevant to the library. Beyond that, it had confused her. Some of what the *nahwal* had said made complete sense, and it seemed that the creature had given her the missing piece of her magic. But at the same time, some of what it had said jarred against Jade's own instincts . . . although admittedly those instincts had been ingrained by Shandi, whose loyalty first and foremost was to the harvester bloodline, Jade had long ago decided, not necessarily to the needs and desires of her own charge. Which left her . . . where?

Before she could even begin to answer that, Strike booted the cottage door open and strode through the kitchen with the others in his wake. Instinctively—she couldn't have said why, or where the urge came from— Jade punched the remote to kill the image on the big TV, and clicked on the light beside the sofa instead. The others didn't notice her actions or question them; they were intent on Lucius as, in a flash, the cottage went from being too empty to being too full, jammed with overlarge bodies, gleaming good looks, and expansive personalities.

Michael and Sasha were on the king's heels: He was dark and green-eyed, with jaw-length black hair, wide features, and a big fighter's body that all but oozed pheromones; she was lean and lithe, with flyaway brunette curls and eyes the color of rich milk chocolate. They balanced each other perfectly. More, they were Jade's closest friends at Skywatch. Under other circumstances, in another life, that might have been odd, given that Michael had been her lover for a time. But Jade was a pragmatist. Michael, though a death wielder and their resident mage-assassin, was a good man; and Sasha was a friend. They made it work. More, Sasha was a *ch'ulel*, a master of living energy, and Lucius badly needed an energy infusion. Jade was glad Strike had brought them both.

Behind them came the two other mated mage-pairs in residence, bringing the exponential power boosts of their *jun tan* mated marks. Alexis led the way, a blond Amazon of a warrior whose ambition had gained her the position of king's adviser, as her mother had been for Strike's father. Nate was right behind her, not because he was secondary in their mated power structure, but because he didn't feel any need to jockey for position, with her or with the others. He was the Volatile, a shape-shifter who could turn into a man-size hawk that featured prominently in some of the more obscure end-time prophecies. He was also a loner, brought into the Nightkeepers' tightly knit group—and the royal council—by his and Alexis's rock-solid love match.

The couple following them, in contrast, was far from rock-solid, in Jade's opinion, both professional and personal. Brown-haired, intense Brandt and blond karate instructor Patience had found each other, and the magic of love, more than three years before the barrier reactivated and they all learned they were the last of the Nightkeepers. But for all that they'd been married human-style for nearly five years now, and had twin sons together, they walked apart, not touching. Barely even looking at each other. The problems in their relationship had been going on for some time, but Jade was struck anew by the distance that gaped between two people who, on paper, at least, seemed as though they should be the perfect couple.

Ghosting in behind them came Sven, the lone remaining Nightkeeper bachelor within the training compound. Loose limbed and all-American handsome, with a stubby blond ponytail and a seemingly endless supply of ass-hanging shorts and surf-shop T-shirts, he wore his I-don't-take-anything-seriously attitude like a shield. Jade, though, saw beneath to a man who was deeply bothered that he'd failed the Nightkeepers several times when they'd needed him.

Although simple math and the value added by matings between Nightkeepers would suggest she and Sven should try the couple thing, the suggestion had never been broached in her hearing. While she suspected that was largely because she lacked the warrior's mark, she was grateful it had never come down to that for either of them. Duty would've demanded she at least try to make it work, and that would have been . . . uncomfortable. She liked Sven, but wasn't attracted to him. She liked a man who made her laugh, one who made her think. One who challenged her, teased her, made her a little crazy.

At the thought, she looked down at Lucius's motionless form and heard a multitonal whisper in her mind: *Don't let yourself get distracted by the human.* That wasn't exactly what the *nahwal* had said; she wasn't sure if it was her own reservations talking now, or something else. Still, though, she was acutely aware that Strike's human mate, Leah, wasn't there. For all that they loved each other fiercely, and he'd gone against the gods to claim her as his own, ever since the destruction of the skyroad had severed her Godkeeper connection, Leah had offered little in terms of magic.

Leah wasn't the only one missing, either, Jade realized with a kick of unease. Rabbit wasn't there. Granted, Strike would've had to 'port out to UT for him, but still. Who better than a mind-bender to find a lost soul?

"Let's get him up on the couch," Strike said, not really acknowledging Jade. He glanced at Sasha. "Unless you think we should haul him to the sacred chamber, or even down south to the tomb?"

She shook her head. "Let's see what we're up against before we change too many things at once. Couch first, then triage, then we'll make decisions about moving him." Given that she was their resident healer it was logical for her to take command of the situation. But that didn't stop resentment from kicking through Jade as the others crowded around Lucius's motionless form, putting her on the outside of a solid wall of wide shoulders and too-perfect bodies.

The men lifted Lucius onto the sofa, jostled him until he was wedged in place, then nearly mummified him with the quilt. *Don't trap him like that*, Jade wanted to tell them. *He'd hate it.* But she stayed silent, feeling invisible and unimportant. This wasn't about her; it was about the Nightkeepers doing what they could for Lucius. And even if the *nahwal* actually had unlocked some part of her talent, it wasn't like she could rattle off a spell capable of bringing him back. For now, Lucius was better off with Strike and Sasha taking the lead, with the others lending power to them, and through them into Lucius.

Feeling extraneous, Jade eased back farther.

"Where are you going?" Strike asked. It took Jade a second to realize he was talking to her.

"Sorry. Did you want me to stay for the uplink?"

The king locked eyes with her, his expression unreadable. "Sex forges a connection within the magic. You're his lover, which means you're our best means of finding him."

"I'm not his—" She broke off the instinctive denial, because this wasn't about the "L" word. And she couldn't claim there wasn't a connection. It didn't make sense for her to argue on one hand that sex magic was just about the sex, then on the other hand claim that a magic bond between sex partners required an emotional bond that wasn't relevant to her and Lucius.

"You said you wanted to step up into the fight, even without the warrior's mark. Well, here's a chance for you to do exactly that."

Strike's challenge hung on the air for a moment, seeming to suck all the oxygen from Jade's lungs. She was acutely aware of the others watching her, waiting for her response. Part of her wanted to melt into the woodwork. Another wanted to cut and run. Instead, she took a deep breath and nodded. "Of course. I'm in." She only hoped she was strong enough to make a difference . . . and that the Nightkeepers together could bring Lucius home.

CHAPTER EIGHT

The library

During one of the many roundtable discussions about what might or might not happen once Lucius connected to the library, he remembered Sasha suggesting that even if he managed to make the connection, his energy reserves might be too limited to sustain it. The Night-keepers had high metabolisms and huge appetites, both designed to feed the magic. He didn't. And yeah, as he bent over the notebook he could feel the drain, knew he had to get himself back to Skywatch. Problem was, the notebook's construction and the warning on the first page were its most coherent aspects. The text was a scant three pages of cramped writing done in a strange stream-of-consciousness style. Some of it made sense; most of it didn't.

Scrubbing the heel of his hand between his eyebrows in an effort to recenter his spinning brain, he went back to the beginning and started over.

Within my bloodline—the keepers of the library's secrets—they say that a powerful Prophet will arise as we get close to the end-time. This Prophet will be an outsider, one who has lost his way, but once he finds himself, finds his magic, he'll have the power to avert a terrible tragedy. How could I not think the prophecy was talking about me? Ostracized from my bloodline, stripped of my powers, yet born for so much more than I had become, there couldn't be anybody better for the job.

Did this happen because of my pride? Because I wasn't humble enough before the gods or the magic? Rather than dying and giving my people a Prophet, I'm stuck in here. I've got the answers, but no way to give them to those who once loved me.

That all made sense to a point, Lucius supposed, but he could've used more context. Unfortunately, the next page and a half contained confusing rambles about flames and staring eyes. Then, finally, on the last written page, there was something useful.

Therefore, as the last of my bloodline, the last keeper of the library's secrets, I write this both fearing and hoping that nobody will ever read it. I hope that a true Prophet will arise at the end of the age, one who dies as is meant, leaving his body behind to transmit all that is hidden here. But I fear that this may not happen . . . and if you're reading this, you're like me. The gods didn't take your soul during the spell, and they gave you only this small window into the library. To you, I write the following, some of which was known to my bloodline, some of which I've figured out here:

The way-ya spell will get you back to your body from here, but only twice. If you enter the library a third time, you're staying. Trust me—third time isn't a charm in the library magic.

You're here, so you probably figured out how to get in. Just in case, let me spell it out for you: It's talent-specific, so you're going to have to use your own magic to get back here. When you do, make sure you're bringing the right questions, because you've only got one shot. Don't screw it up, because I can only imagine that you're it. You're the last Prophet. The one who's supposed to help save the world.

Finally—and this isn't about the library so much as what I've figured out sitting here dying, wishing I'd done things differently—magic isn't what's going to save the world. Love is. So find someone to love, and tell them so. Better yet, show them you love them by making them happy rather than miserable. Don't be an idiot like I was.

"Which in my experience is a total contradiction in terms," Lucius muttered. In his experience, using the "L" word to a lover was the very definition of being idiotic. At least it was the way he did it. Granted, all the talk about bloodlines meant the journalist had been a Nightkeeper, and from what he'd seen the magi tended to do a good job in the couples department.

Still, it seemed like an odd thing to say, even odder to write as the very last entry in the strange journal. "And who the hell wrote it, anyway?"

His body jolted, lurched upright, and staggered back toward the stacks. "Whoa! Wait," he said, "I didn't mean—" But he broke off at the realization that he was far, far weaker than he'd comprehended. His legs shook and the stone walls blurred around him as he headed across the room, impelled by the magic. It was all he could do to stay on his feet, but he'd be damned if he crawled.

By the time he reached the other end of the narrow stone room, he was breathing hard, nearly doubled over as he fought not to retch. Then he got a good look at what the magic had brought him to, and he froze inside and out.

A woman's corpse sat in the corner, wrapped in a yellow-edged green robe identical to the one he was wearing.

He had his answer. He'd asked who wrote the journal . . . and the magic showed him. For half a second, the torch flames flickering on the body made it seem to move, even though he knew it wasn't alive. It couldn't be. Not looking like that. She wasn't a mummy in the formal sense of embalming and wraps, but she was mummified all the same, with her skin tight and shiny, stretched over where flesh had wasted from bones. Honey-colored hair hung to her shoulders, and the bone structure of her face seemed oddly elegant despite the hooked-nose, bared-teeth grotesquery of desiccation. The robe had ridden up over her forearm, baring three marks: those of the star bloodline, the warrior, and the *jun tan*.

"Bingo," Lucius slurred. "Now we know that the stars were the keepers of the library." Which was only partially useful, given that none of the living Nightkeepers were members of the star bloodline. But it was information, and he'd always been a fan of info. And, dude, he was punchy. The torchlight seared his eyes, and the stones beneath his feet heaved like the deck of a fishing boat, with the same nausea-inducing consequences he'd suffered on his single lamented attempt at deep-sea fishing. "I've gotta get out of here." He didn't have the answers the Nightkeepers needed about the skyroad or the sun god, but his body was flat-out done. If he collapsed and passed out here, he would probably exhaust the last of his energy reserves while unconscious. And death in the barrier was death nonetheless, which meant it was time to go home.

The journal had talked about the "*way-ya*" spell, not the *way* spell, which was what he'd been assuming he should use. "*Way-ya*" meant "home," but could also mean "spirit" or "portal." Similar but different. Chanting the word over and over in his thick-feeling head, he dragged himself back to the study area, with its carved medallions. His feet seemed very far away when he plonked them on the *way* symbol of the snaggle-toothed dragon. Wetting his gone-dry mouth, he croaked, "*Way-ya.*"

Power instantly slammed into him, swept him up. Everything went dark, and the world around him spun hard and fast. He might've puked but wasn't sure; he lost touch with his body, with his neurons—hell, with every part of himself. Terror slashed as he glimpsed a dusty, barren roadway that came from nowhere, led nowhere. The in-between. His own private hell. Adrenaline slashed, sweeping away the cobwebs. Screaming inwardly, he fought not to go there, fought to go anywhere *but* there, but how could he fight without power, without magic, without training?

As he slid toward that dry, dusty purgatory, he lashed out, reaching invisible thought-hands to grab something, anything that might halt the slide. He caught a flash at the edge of his consciousness, a hint of power that wasn't quite familiar, wasn't entirely strange, but was wholly, utterly compelling. He grabbed for it, touched it for a second, then lost it. But at that brief touch, the in-between winked out and the world went gray-green.

Then that too winked out, and there was nothing but darkness and sick, aching pain.

Panic hammered through him as he sensed boundaries all around him, hemming him into a space that was so much smaller than the vastness he'd just traveled through. He was jailed by the pain, trapped within—*Oh*, he thought as the inner lightbulb went off and he recognized the sensation of being back in his physical self . . . which felt like unholy shit. His head hammered with the rhythm of his stumbling heart, and agony flared in each of his joints, making him feel like he'd been stretched out on a huge cosmic torture rack that had stopped short of actually killing him, but only barely. And who knew the body had so many damned joints? Even his pinkie toes were killing him.

"Ngh," he said, wincing when the word—the grunt?—echoed too loudly, setting off cymbal clashes in his skull. He hadn't felt hangover-crappy like this since the day after Cizin had first entered his soul. The thought brought a spurt of panic, but he beat it back. *It feels like this because you're a human trying to do magic,* he told himself, forcing the logic through the pain. *The library is not a makol; it's not trying to possess you.* Though the ask-and-walk thing was borderline.

"Lucius!" Jade said, her voice seeming to come from far above him. "Can you hear me? Are you okay?"

Jesus Christ, don't shout, he wanted to say, but he caught the worry in her voice and felt the grip of her hand on his. He hated that she was seeing him weak and helpless yet again, but that was his hang-up, not hers, so he made an effort to be polite, even through the hammering inside his skull. "M'fine. Food?"

Okay, so maybe that was still lacking in the politeness department. But he heard paper and then clothing rustle and sensed motion nearby. What was more, he didn't sense a crowd nearby, which was a relief.

"Jox left a carb-and-fat bomb in case . . . for when you came around." Her voice trembled on the words. She took a deep breath, and she sounded steadier when she said, "I'll call the others. We've been watching you in shifts ever since Sasha said you were as stable as she could get you. We've been waiting for . . . well. I'll call them."

" 'N a minute." Lucius slitted his eyes, saw the familiar details of his cottage, and relaxed fractionally at finding that he was on his couch, not locked up in the basement in the main mansion, or worse. Craning his neck, he looked for Jade, and found her in the kitchen, leaning on the counter with her arms braced and her head hanging. She was wearing trim jeans and a soft button-down that clung to her skin as her body curved in a private moment of what might have been relief, but he found himself interpreting more as grief. Regret.

What the hell had he missed? He wanted to go to her, to hold her. Wanted to lean into her and let her lean on him. But that was the weakness talking, he knew. More, he knew that it was a private moment, and one she wouldn't thank him for watching. So he forced himself to look away.

Focusing on the changes that had occurred in his main room while he'd been out of it, he saw that the TV was off, no longer showing the scene that had been so strangely mimicked by what they had seen in Xibalba. The coffee table held a notebook and a couple of volumes he recognized from the archive, primary texts on the legends of the sun god, clueing him in that Jade had caught the Kinich Ahau connection. *Good girl.* There was an IV stand beside the couch, a needle taped at the crook of his arm, and a clear line feeding him the nutrient mix the *winikin* had come up with to offset the postmagic crash experience by a mage—or in this case, a human wannabe—in the aftermath of big magic. Which made him wonder how long he'd been unconscious.

A look out the window showed him that sky was blue-black, but with dusk, not dawn. Had he lost an entire day? More? He cursed under his breath.

As he did, Jade came back into the main room carrying a bowl of pasta mixed with the heavy meat sauce he liked, liberally dosed with cheese. At his colorful language, she raised an eyebrow. "That sounded coherent, if physically impossible. I take it your head is clearing?"

"How many days did I lose?" He took the bowl and held out a hand for the fork she was still holding, just in case she had any idea of trying to feed him.

She passed it over. "About twenty hours. From your perspective, it's tomorrow night." She was wearing what he thought of as her counselor's face, serene to the point of blandness. But he knew her well enough to see strain and nerves beneath, along with an unfamiliar edginess.

"I made it to the library," he said before she asked.

"And?"

There was no simple answer to that, he realized as he tried to come up with something concise and vaguely coherent. He dug into the pasta, buying himself a moment. Finally, he went with: "It's amazing. I wish you could've been there with me."

And it was true, he realized. Of all of the magi, she was the one who would've appreciated the artifacts, the Ouija game, all of it. And he would've liked to have seen it all for the first time with her. Whatever else was—or wasn't—between them, they meshed on that level. Always had.

"I tried to find you," she blurted, locking her fingers together until her knuckles whitened. "Last night we uplinked—Strike, me, everyone. I tried to find your *ch'ul* song for Sasha, tried to follow where you'd gone . . . but I couldn't. Our connection, the sex magic, just wasn't strong enough. *I* wasn't strong enough."

"Oh." Suddenly, her sitting next to his bed, waiting for him to regain consciousness—or die, though neither of them had said it outright—seemed less like the vigil of a friend or lover, and more like self-flagellation.

She continued, though he wasn't sure whether she was talking to him or to herself. "I couldn't find the sex link and pull you home. We thought . . . We weren't sure you were going to make it out."

"But I did," he pointed out in between big bites of cheese-laden pasta, not mentioning that it had been a close call. "And for the record, I don't think the library works the same way the rest of the barrier does. It's possible—even likely—that you wouldn't have been able to follow me even if I were a mage and we were *jun tan* mates." He thought of the corpse's mated mark, wondered if someone had gone looking for her. And if so, what had happened to them. He hated like hell that Jade felt like a failure because of him, but knew she wouldn't thank him for saying it aloud. So instead, he said, "I'm guessing you gave the others a full report on Kinich Ahau and the companions?" She had twenty hours' head start on him—it sure as hell hadn't felt that long when he'd been inside the library, but the barrier was known to fold time oddly in some cases.

She nodded. "I gave them what I could yesterday, and am just about finished filling in the gaps from the archive." She paused before saying softly, "The *Banol Kax* are trying to put Akhenaton in the sun god's place."

"Yeah."

"How are we going to stop them?"

At first he thought it was a rhetorical question. But when she looked at him too expectantly, he realized she was hoping for him to play Prophet. Exhaling, he shook his head. "Sorry. It doesn't work that way. I'm not going to be able to channel info on command."

Worse, now that he had some food in him, he was seeing just how big an *oh, holy shit* of a problem that was going to be. If he needed to use his own talent to get back into the library, as the journalist had said . . . then the magi were going to be waiting a long time, because humans didn't have talents, and he was pure human, do not pass "Go," do not collect two hundred.

She looked at him for a long moment, and something sparked in the air, making him very aware that they were alone again in his cottage, where the magic had begun. All she said, though, was, "Do you feel up to a general meeting?"

"That'd probably be best." He might as well break the bad news en masse.

"I'll go spread the word. But I don't want to see you up at the mansion until you've finished eating, got it?"

"Got it." A quick yank and he had the IV out, then had to fumble to shut the thing off when it peed on his foot. "Yeah. Smooth," he muttered under his breath.

She flashed him a grin that looked far more natural than anything she'd managed up to that point. "Glad to have you back."

Looking up, he met her eyes. "Same goes." They locked gazes for a three-count of heartbeats, and more passed between them than had been said. At least, it did for him, though he couldn't have articulated what, exactly, he took away from the moment beyond a hot pressure in his chest and a more than fleeting thought of locking the door and saying, *Fuck the general meeting; they can wait until tomorrow.* But the problem was, he didn't know if they *could* wait, really. He'd already lost a day, which put them at only eight to go until the summer solstice.

Jade broke the eye lock with a self-conscious head shake, then turned and headed for the door, scooping up the books and papers on her way past the coffee table. She paused at the archway leading to the kitchen, glancing back. "In the pit . . . in Xibalba. You were amazing. I don't think I would've made it out of there if it hadn't been for you." Before he could say anything—not that he had a clue how to respond to something like that; it wasn't like he'd had much practice being amazing—she continued: "I froze. Here I am, trying to tell everyone that I deserve to be in on the action, but when it came down to it, I just stood there. I wouldn't have run if you hadn't dragged me, and I wouldn't have made it out if you hadn't come after me. When that guard started marching me toward the fortress—" She broke off, shuddering, her eyes going stark and hollow in her face. "I panicked. I didn't *do* anything."

He stood, forcing his legs to hold him, and crossed to her. Without a word, he folded her into his arms, hoping that this was one of those times when the right action meant more than finding the right words.

Jade stiffened, and for a moment he thought she was going to push away, but then she let out a long, shaky sigh and melted into him. After a brief hesitation, she slid her arms around his waist and hung on. They stood that way for a long time. Finally, when he felt her coiled muscles ease, he said into her hair, "You couldn't have done anything; neither of us could, unarmed and with no real fighting magic to speak of. We owe our lives to the companions. And besides, it was your magic that warned Kinich Ahau that there was a Nightkeeper nearby, in trouble."

Shifting in his arms, she looked up at him, eyes gone very serious. "Maybe it was my magic at first, but at the end it wasn't my magic that got us out. It was yours."

"Maybe." He didn't know what to think about that yet, or how to process it in light of what the journalist had written about needing to use his talent to get inside the library. He didn't have a clue how he'd gotten there in the first place. "Regardless, we got each other out of there. No apologies, no regrets, okay? Let's just be grateful we're both back where we belong." Those words took on new meaning when he realized he was stroking her from nape to hip, that her hands had migrated from his waist to locked behind his neck. His body awoke, hard and fast, and he saw in her eyes that she'd felt the change. Welcomed it.

He eased down, giving her plenty of time and room to step back if she needed to, as she'd done before. Instead, she rose up on her toes to meet him halfway. *We're okay*, the kiss seemed to say. *We're home now. We're safe.* More, it suggested that their being together hadn't been a one-shot deal designed only to test the effects of sex magic. It said she was into him, that she enjoyed touching him, kissing him. And when the kiss ended and they leaned a little apart to look into each other's eyes, he saw a spark of heat that danced over his skin and made his body hard and ready in an instant.

"We could . . ." He trailed off with a suggestive head nod in the direction of the couch, or better yet, the wide-open floor below.

"We could . . . but we're not going to. You're going to eat, I'm going to collect the others, and we're going to rendezvous up at the mansion for a powwow." But she cocked an eyebrow. "As for the other . . . maybe later, if you're still on your feet."

"Count on it."

She grinned and headed out. And as the door closed at her back, he realized he was smiling. The analytical side of him knew that the day—or rather, the past two days—had to go in the minus column of shit news and more shit news. But the man in him thought the crappy-ass intel was balanced, at least in the short term, by the fact that he and Jade were finally on the same page.

Now he just had to make sure they stayed there.

* * *

The residents of Skywatch met, as was their habit, in the great room of the main mansion. The five in-residence *winikin* sat at the breakfast bar that separated the big marble-and-chrome kitchen from the sunken sitting area, where the Nightkeepers were scattered on chairs and sofas—or in Sven's case a couple of pillows on the floor. Jade had staked out one end of a long couch, and didn't mind in the slightest when Alexis and Nate filled up the rest of it. She wasn't trying to distance herself from Lucius, precisely, but she was hyperaware that the others knew they had slept together. She'd known that would be the case going into things, of course. And it wasn't like she hadn't been there before. Private lives didn't stay private for long around Skywatch, not with sex so integrally connected to the magic. For some reason, though, this time the sidelong looks put a strange shimmy in the pit of her stomach and made her want to squirm.

Then there was Shandi, who frowned down at her from the breakfast bar. The *winikin* was in her late fifties, with silver-threaded dark hair worn straight to her waist and distinctive facial features she'd explained as Navajo heritage out in the human world, but that had really come from her Sumerian ancestors. She was petite, as were all of the *winikin*, and seemed to exist in a perpetual state of Zen-like peaceful calm. Jade knew firsthand that the calm was an illusion, though. In reality, the *winikin* had a cold, biting temper and a low tolerance level.

As a teen, Jade had offset Shandi's regular "proper

deportment and behavior" lectures by coming up with various sets of the three "D"s for her *winikin*. Most often, they were along the lines of "disconnected," "disapproving," and "duty-bound." And while Jade had known she could've wound up in a worse situation growing up—there hadn't been any violence, no neglect; if anything, Shandi had paid too much attention to her, stifling her with rules—she'd often wished for something . . . different. She had dreamed of what it would've been like if her parents hadn't died, if she hadn't been left in the care of her chilly, rigid *winikin*. Her mother would've been tall and serene, with Jade's long, straight hair and sea foam eyes. She would've been unruffled by her daughter's childish pranks and youthful bounciness, maybe even playing along sometimes. Her father's image had been less clear, but his voice had resonated in her imagination; he'd been big and strong, and his arms around her had made her feel safe. They wouldn't have lectured her on duty, decorum, and diligence, or at least not all the time, over and over again until she wanted to scream. But her parents were dead, and she'd known Shandi was a better parent than some, so she had done her best to live up to—or down to?—her guardian's expectations of a quiet, well-behaved child.

As Jade had grown to adulthood, she and Shandi had maintained more of a relationship than she might have expected, in part because Jade had discovered over time that Shandi had been right about a number of things, from the value of a calm facade to the advisability of thinking before acting, which had been a hard lesson for Jade to learn when parts of her had wanted to be rash. In the years before the Nightkeepers' reunion, and even in the first months of life at Skywatch, Jade and Shandi had coexisted peacefully under the terms of their unstated agreement that if Jade didn't act impulsively, the *winikin* wouldn't lecture. Lucius's arrival at Skywatch hadn't immediately changed that, but looking back, Jade could see that it had been the beginning of the renewed strain between her and Shandi. And the split had only worsened as time passed.

Now the *winikin* was subtly ignoring Jade without seeming to. And when Lucius appeared at the sliders leading from the pool deck to the great room, Shandi's face soured with a look of, *Ew, it's the human.*

"Come on in." Strike waved when Lucius stalled at the threshold. "I know you just ate, but Carlos'll hook you up with seconds to keep you going for the meeting. You'll still need some downtime—assuming that your physiology works like ours does—but you won't crash as hard or as long as you would have without the IV."

"Thanks," Lucius said, though it wasn't entirely clear which part the word referred to. Easing away from the sliders as though reluctant to commit too far into the building, he dragged a carved wood chair out from underneath a half-round table near the door, and turned it to face the others, so he sat near but apart from them. Although he was positioned above the magi on the higher level of the two-level great room, it didn't seem as though he sat in judgment, but rather that he was offering himself up to be judged.

As he sat and leaned back in the chair, hooking his hands across his flat stomach, Jade was struck anew by how much he looked like a stranger, yet not. And more, how much he now looked like one of them. He'd showered and changed; his normally tousled brown hair was slicked back, his jaw freshly shaven. Wearing jeans, an unadorned black T-shirt, and a pair of heavy black boots she didn't recognize from before, he would've easily fit into a lineup with Strike, Nate, Michael, and Brandt. All five men were dark haired, big, and built, with strong features and auras of tough capability. They looked like a bunch of honorable bad-asses who would make strong allies, fearsome enemies, and dangerous lovers.

The realization that she could easily lump him in with the mated warrior-males wasn't a comfortable one, nor was the inner tug at the thought of classifyng him as her lover, with its implication of a future . . . or rather the question of how she was supposed to balance that desire—and the banked hum still cours-ing through her from his kisses—with the things the strange *nahwal* had told her, and its whispered warn-ing: *Beware* . . . But what was she supposed to be wary of? Him? Her response to him?

She didn't know, and didn't have time to figure it out just then, because Strike started the meeting and then gestured in her direction. "Jade, how about you run us through anything new you've managed to pull together about the sun god, and give Lucius a chance to get a few more calories on board?"

On cue, Jox dished up another piled plate of food

and handed it over to Nate's *winikin*, Carlos, who walked it over to Lucius. Balancing the plate on his knee, Lucius said, "Before you get started, I need to get something out there." He paused, looking grim. "The moment I saw that firebird, I remembered something from when I was the *makol*, something I'd been blocking, or that got lost in the fucked-up parts of my head." He paused, took a breath. "I don't know whether he meant to or not, but Cizin gave me a glimpse inside him, showing me the plans of the *Banol Kax*. In short, they haven't just captured the true sun god. They're planning to sacrifice it during the solstice, and put Akhenaton in its place."

Seeing half a day's work headed swiftly down the drain, Jade shot him a sour look. "It would've been nice if you'd woken up and shared that little nugget *before* I put six hours into convincing myself that we really saw Kinich Ahau and Akhenaton down there, and that it wasn't a barrier vision like the one Sasha had—you know, the one with the same black dogs in it?"

"That wasn't a vision; that was Xibalba," Lucius said. "And those weren't just any dogs; they were the companions, the sun god's protectors. They meet—or used to meet—Kinich Ahau at the night horizon each dusk, and escort the sun safely through the trials of the underworld to emerge from the dawn horizon each morning, and"—he made a circular, continuing motion—"rinse, repeat."

"Again, thanks for an off-the-cuff summary of info I spent the morning digging up." Jade wasn't annoyed, exactly. Just tired of being redundant. "Question is:

Why were the companions in Sasha's vision? Were the gods or ancestors trying to warn us that the sun god was in trouble even back then?"

"*Oh!*" Sasha's dark brown eyes went stark as the color drained from her face.

"What is it?" Michael asked immediately, tensing. As he often did, he was standing behind her in a relaxed but fight-ready position, always on guard, protecting his own. The sight sent a harmless pang of envy through Jade, because he'd never done that for her.

Sasha twined her fingers together in her lap as she answered, "There's that last part of the triad prophecy, the part I never fulfilled about finding the lost son. . . . What if instead of telling me to 'find the lost son,' spelled 's-o-n,' what if it was really supposed to be 's-u-n'? That could be why I saw the companions in my vision last year. The gods were trying to tell me to look for the lost sun!" She looked stricken. "If I'd figured it out then, we could've been planning a rescue all this time."

The *winikin* and magi were silent for a long moment. Jade started to speak, but caught Shandi's *don't draw attention* look and subsided.

"Jade?" Strike said, glancing at Shandi. "Did you have something to add?"

"I was going to point out that . . . well, if we can free Kinich Ahau from Xibalba, we'll have access to a god again." Jade glanced at Sasha. "And if we're thinking that the triad prophecy foretold a link between the sun and Sasha, we could even gain a Godkeeper."

Sasha went wide-eyed, but didn't knee-jerk a denial. After a moment she said softly, "We don't know that I'd be the god's chosen. The prophecy said I was supposed to find the lost sun, but I didn't."

"You were the first of us to see the companions," Jade countered.

"True. Except that one, they were in a vision; two, they attacked me; and three, Michael killed them, or at least their vision-selves. You and Lucius are the ones they defended. And you're the ones who found the lost sun."

Jade snorted. "Right. I'm a daughter of the gods," she said, referring to the first part of the prophecy. She glanced at Lucius, expecting to see an answering gleam of mirth . . . but he wasn't laughing. None of them were. They were all looking at her speculatively, with an intensity that sent two opposing thoughts shooting through her brain: *Oh, hell no,* coupled with, *What if?*

"What if . . ." Lucius began as though echoing her thoughts, then paused a moment before continuing. "What if the prophecy was, let's say, interrupted? What if the original child of prophecy became unsuitable for the full foretelling?"

Michael shifted and sent him a narrow look. "Don't be a pussy. Say it."

In the past, Lucius might have—probably would have—backed down or turned things aside with a joke. Now he met the other man's glare. "Fine. What if becoming your fiancée—and functionally your mate— has made Sasha unsuitable to be a Godkeeper? You and she balance each other out as the *ch'ulel* and Mict-lan, life versus death. Giving her more power as a Godkeeper could tip that balance . . . or it could increase your magic to an equal degree. It's possible that some power source—if not the sky gods, then maybe even the doctrine of balance itself—doesn't want to put so much power into a single couple."

Jade's throat went tight and strange as her mind jumped from Lucius's hypothesis to its corollary—namely that she might have become the focus of the prophecy when Sasha became unsuitable as a God-keeper. She didn't look at Shandi, didn't need to. She knew what the *winikin* would say: *Don't overreach yourself, Jade. You're just a harvester.*

Swallowing hard, she pointed out, "The doctrine of balance isn't an entity; it doesn't have opinions." As far as they knew, the doctrine, which was routinely mentioned in the archive but never really defined, was more a pattern of thought, the belief among their ancestors that the universe was not only cyclical, but sought balance within those cycles.

"Maybe, maybe not," Lucius replied elliptically, his gaze catching and holding hers, making her, for a moment, feel like they were the only two people in the room. "But it sure seems as though you and I may have inherited the last part of the triad prophecy."

CHAPTER NINE

Lucius found himself on the receiving end of a long, considering look from Strike. After a moment the king said, "Since you don't seem inclined to eat, you ready to tell us about the library?" It wasn't really a question.

Lucius nodded. "To put it bluntly, it's not going to be the resource you'd hoped for. Or rather . . . not the way I can use it."

Strike's face tightened, though he didn't look all that surprised. "Go on."

"When I zapped in, the air was dry, it was pitch-dark, and I was naked. . . ." Lucius told them everything, exactly the way it had happened. He described the library itself, how he figured out the Ouija board deal, and how he used it to find the notebook. He recited as much of the text as he could from memory, including the massive buzz-kill about how he could enter the library only once more safely, and then only if he found his own magic. Which he didn't have. He left out the last little bit, though, the part about love. He figured that had been a message just for him.

As he spoke, he watched the faces around him fall from hope to confusion, and from there to dismay. In Jade's expression, he saw a soft, sad emotion alongside the others, this one directed at him. But where before he would have labeled it pity and resented the hell out of it, now he recognized it as sympathy from someone who knew what it felt like to want to be more than her ancestry suggested she should be, more than the people around her assumed she was capable of being. She knew, or at least could come pretty close to guessing, what it had meant to him to be chosen, albeit accidentally, to be the Prophet. He'd dreamed of the library, of the adventure, of finally being a part of things. And now . . . nothing. He'd glimpsed the library's glory, only to have it taken away from him again, in a cosmic backhanded slap of *you're not good enough.* Apparently, despite his new and improved physique, he was still Runt Hunt at his core. And boy, didn't that just suck?

Continuing, he told them about his strength fading, and his inadvertent discovery of his predecessor entombed at the far corner of the library. "She wore the marks of the star bloodline, a warrior, and a mated woman . . . and based on her use of language and the way she spiral-bound the book like a modern notebook, I'd say she lived in the past few decades." He turned up his palms. "Beyond that, we'll need to do some digging to try to figure out who she was . . . and what happened to her."

He fell silent, aware that he'd been talking for a long

time with no interruptions. The faces that had been hopeful, confused, and dismayed were now slightly glazed, most wearing expressions he recognized from his lectures as the fugue the human brain tended to slide into when given too much information at one time, or being asked to change too many preconceptions all at once. He thought it was a combination of the two in this case. Gods knew he was feeling almost numb from everything that had happened in the past day. Two days. Whatever. He'd been to hell and back, been to the library and back. And he'd been with Jade.

"There's a book about the star bloodline in the archive," Jade said after a moment. "It was in one of the boxes of books Jox had salvaged from the private suites before the big renovation. I just scanned and cataloged it without really reading it because . . . well"—she lifted a shoulder—"it didn't seem all that relevant, since none of us are of the bloodline. I'll go back through and read it, see if there's anything pertinent."

Strike nodded. "While you're at it, run some searches on the star bloodline, the keepers of the library, that sort of thing." He looked from her to Lucius and back. "Tomorrow. Right now, you two both look like you need some major downtime."

Until Strike mentioned it, Lucius hadn't been fully aware of the exhaustion hovering at the edges of his consciousness. The second he noticed the fatigue, though, it was all over: The world grayed out and he suddenly could've napped quite comfortably in the straight-backed chair. *Postmagic crash*, he thought. *Huh.* He was too tired even to worry about looking weak, or to fend off Michael and Brandt when they each took a side of him, got him on his feet, and headed him toward the sliders leading out. It was all he could do to crane his head around, catch Jade's eye, and see that she looked tired and sad, but otherwise okay. He flashed back on what she'd said to him earlier, in his cottage, and the way she'd kissed him. And in the back of his mind, he couldn't help hearing the journalist's words, spoken now in a woman's voice: *Find someone to love . . . and tell them so.* It was tempting . . . and a proven recipe for disaster.

"No, thanks," he muttered under his breath. "Been there, done that, doesn't work for me." For now, and maybe for the long haul, he was far better off alone.

Strike had been right on target, Jade realized. She was seriously strung-out and needed some downtime. But as she pushed through the door into her suite, instead of the place making her feel at home and inviting her to turn it all off for a while, the small apartment made her feel jumpy and out of sorts. Or maybe the problem wasn't with the place. Maybe it was with her.

Like most of the other three-room apartments, hers had a kitchen nook and seating area opening off the mansion hallway, with doors on the far wall leading to a bathroom and bedroom. Unlike the others, though, hers was a corner room and had a bonus: a set of sliders leading to a private balcony that offered a heck of a view of the canyon wall as it rose to meet the horizon beyond. Soon after her arrival at Skywatch, she'd re-decorated the suite from the bland faux-Southwestern nondecor it had started with, to a kitschy blend of colors and styles that appealed to her. The end result was part feng shui, part Zen, part hey-that's-cool impulse buy. The walls were painted a soothing blue-gray, the wall-to-wall had been replaced with eco-friendly bamboo, and the comfy furniture was covered in calm, natural-fiber pastels. A trickling water feature burbled in the corner near the sliders, powered not by electricity, but by sunlight and condensation.

She'd been away at the university for nearly six months, but the suite was spotless and fresh-smelling, and her few plants were bright green and tended to. That was all Shandi's doing, she knew, and was grateful for the *winikin*'s efforts, even if done only out of duty.

All of it looked like she remembered it, but nothing there seemed to explain the restless, edgy energy that ran through her, making her prowl from room to room, looking for something, though she didn't have a clue what.

Finally, unable to stay inside, she unlatched the sliders and pushed through to the balcony. The air surprised her anew with its heavy moisture, and it carried a snap of ozone that hinted at one of the quick summer storms that sometimes swept through the canyon, fierce and loud. Though such storms were normally rare, Sasha had said they were getting more frequent as the microclimate changed. Jade had a feeling things were going to get worse before they got better, too, since their improvement hinged on the Nightkeepers returning Kinich Ahau to the sky. Prophecy or no prophecy, it was one thing to find the lost sun, another to storm the underworld itself. She shivered at the thought of the fearsome firebird and its companions, and at the idea of going back down there. She didn't want to. She couldn't.

Exhaling, she leaned on the railing for a moment and stared out into the night. As she'd sat, watching Lucius breathe and praying he would come back safely, she'd arrived at three important conclusions. Her first was that the gods had gotten it right when they failed to tag her with the warrior's glyph. She wasn't cut out to fight—when the moment had come she'd frozen instead of fighting, and could've gotten her and Lucius both killed. Which meant she was going to have to find some sort of middle ground between shield bearer and warrior, a way to be involved without actually being on the front lines. The knowledge stung, as did the need to let go of that long-held goal.

But that led to her second conclusion, which was that she needed to focus on the talent the gods *had* given her. Problem was, it seemed to have died on her. Since the strange meeting with her *nahwal*, she'd tried over and over again to call up the magic that had so briefly let her see patterns in the power, but she hadn't gotten squat. And when she'd stared at the painting on Lucuis's laptop, she hadn't been able to pick out the blessing she was sure she'd seen in there before. The glyphs had reverted to their original gibberish. Which meant . . . what? Had the magic come from the *nahwal*, lasting only long enough to get her out of the barrier? Or was something blocking her from using her scribe's talent, something the *nahwal* had briefly unlocked so she could feel what it ought to feel like, see what it ought to look like? For the moment she was going with the second option, shifting her goal from becoming a warrior to becoming the magic user she was meant to be. Somehow.

The third and last conclusion was one she'd come to deep in the middle of the night, as she sat and stared at Lucius's face, which had softened with the absence of his now-forceful personality, returning to the younger-looking lines she remembered from before. She didn't prefer the old Lucius, necessarily, but he was far less intimidating. And in seeing her friend in the face of the man he'd grown into over such a short, tumultuous time, she had realized that just as she needed to find a middle ground between being a bookkeeper and a soldier, perhaps she could find a middle ground with him. Maybe their relationship didn't have to be a choice between keeping it friends-only and losing herself to him. If she'd learned anything over the past two years—hell, the past few days—it was that things could change in a blink of magic or fate. Maybe it was time to try putting more of herself into her various relationships now, rather than waiting until it was too late and she was stuck sitting at a friend's bedside, wishing she'd made more of an effort when she'd had the chance.

She'd long attributed her reserve to Shandi, sometimes in gratitude, sometimes in blame. The *winikin* wasn't warm and fuzzy; she was efficient and effective. That upbringing had served Jade well in her career, allowing her to pick through the darkest parts of her patients' lives and emerge relatively untouched. But that same defensive shell had kept her insulated from the outside world. Lucius had called her on it, she remembered with a faint smile. Over and over again, when she'd tried to fob him off with something cool and distant, he'd told her to get out of therapist's mode and *feel*. She'd brushed him off, pretending to laugh, but the comments had stuck. The question was: How did she find *that* middle ground, the one between feeling nothing and feeling too much?

"Watching the stars again?" Shandi said from inside the suite. Jade tensed, but didn't let the *winikin* see her startlement, or the bite of irritation brought on by the question. As a child, she'd often slipped out of bed and sneaked up onto the balcony or roof of wherever they were living at the time, to lie out and watch the stars. Shandi had invariably found her before too long, bringing her back inside with a few cool words about keeping her eyes on the path in front of her.

"There aren't any stars tonight. There's a storm coming." Jade turned slowly and found her *winikin* framed in the sliders, silhouetted against the light coming from the room beyond. To Jade's surprise, an uncanny calm descended over her, one that said she would say what needed to be said and deal with the consequences. Maybe that was going to be part of her new middle-ground theory. "I'm not going to apologize for sleeping with Lucius, or for trying to help the others find him. I may not be a warrior, but I'm sick of being in the background."

Shandi didn't argue the point. She simply said, "Come inside and sit down. We need to talk."

Jade was tempted to tell her that she was too tired and bitchy to talk now, that they'd have to deal with whatever it was in the morning, but the shimmer of nerves—and were those tears?—in the *winikin*'s eyes stopped the words in her throat. She nodded instead. "Okay."

She stepped inside, closed the sliders on the incoming storm, and headed for the couch. Shandi took the chair opposite, so the coffee table formed a wide space between them. Jade didn't offer her anything and the *winikin* didn't ask; they just sat there for a few moments, staring at each other. How could it be, Jade wondered, that she didn't have anything to say to the woman who had saved her from the massacre, raised her, brought her to her birthright, and helped her adjust to being a mage? Why was it that for all they had in common, it sometimes seemed that they didn't share anything?

Finally, Shandi broke the silence. "I think the woman Lucius saw in the library was your mother."

On a scale of one to a million, that ranked pretty high on the *things I didn't expect to hear* scale. Shock hammered through Jade . . . but she didn't jump or run, or shout an instinctive, *What the fuck?* She just sat there, stunned.

The words spaced themselves out in her head: *I . . . think . . . woman . . . library . . . your mother*. Still, though, the sentence refused to make any sort of cohesive sense within the scope of what she knew. "But I'm a harvester," she said, because while that wasn't the most important point, it was the one that defined her. "I'm not a star."

"Your father, Joshua, was a harvester. But your mother, Vennie, was a member of the star bloodline."

"But that's—" *Not how it works*, Jade started to say, then broke off, reeling as the world downshifted around her, took a left-hand turn, and sped off in a new, unexpected direction. One with lots of bumps and potholes.

Among the Nightkeepers, certain bloodlines had tended to interbreed while others hadn't, forming the basis for talent clusters. The bird bloodlines tended to intermingle, concentrating the genetic traits—assuming that was how the magic was inherited—that conferred the talents of flight and levitation; the four-legged-predator bloodlines carried teleportation and telekinesis, among other things; while the reptilian bloodlines tended toward the fire and weather talents, and invisibility. The omnivorous peccaries could have any of the other talents, along with mind-bending, while the talents of the nonanimal bloodlines fell into two camps: low power and high. On the low end of the spectrum was the harvester bloodline. On the high end was the star bloodline, which was the third most powerful bloodline among all the magi, behind only the royal jaguars and the peccaries.

And Jade was apparently fifty percent star.

How had she not known that? How could she not have asked about her mother's bloodline before?

"It was a highly unlikely match," Shandi said. "And, as it turned out, not a good one." She paused as though weighing a decision, then said, "Your mother abandoned you and your father a few days before the Solstice Massacre. We thought she'd run off . . . and when I couldn't find any sign of her afterward, I assumed the *boluntiku* had tracked and killed her as they had so many others."

Shock layered atop shock within Jade. Again, the individual words made sense, but the sum of them seemed to represent a foreign language. "You told me my parents loved each other," she whispered, suffering a spasm of betrayal that was far stronger than the information probably deserved. But these were her *parents* they were talking about: the tall, sleek-haired woman with the soft voice and her strong, sturdy-armed husband. And even as Shandi's stories of their having died in a car crash had morphed into the reality of their dying in the Solstice Massacre, Shandi had always said that they had loved each other, that they had died together.

Apparently not so much, Jade thought as her stomach took a long, sick slide toward her toes.

"They did love each other . . . in the beginning." Shandi held up a hand. "Let me tell it my way, start to finish. Okay?" After a moment, she continued: "Vennie was a good Nightkeeper. She was loyal to her king and her magic, and she was a strong soldier. She wore the warrior's mark and excelled at fireball magic. She was . . ." The *winikin* paused, her expression clouding. "Vennie was like a comet. She burned brightly, moved fast, and rarely looked behind herself to see what sort of mess she'd left trailing behind her. She'd been away from the compound for a few years with her parents, and when she showed back up for the solstice ritual of 'eighty-two, she was sixteen, gorgeous, talented, and reckless. It was easy to see why Joshua took one look at her and fell hard. It wasn't so obvious what she saw in him . . . but before any of us knew what was happening, they were asking formal permission to marry, even though her family objected, saying she was too young to know her own mind."

While the *winikin* was talking, Jade did her level best to drop herself into therapist mode, drawing the analytic thought process tightly around her when emotion failed to make sense and threatened to swamp her. Now, putting things into their historical perspective, she said, "I thought that back then King Scarred-Jaguar and the royal council were encouraging gods-destined pairings and pregnancies between teenagers, on the theory that it was imperative to create as many fighting-age magi as possible before 2012?"

"That's true. And even before that, it was more common than not for young magi to pair up early; the magic is hardwired to seek the other half of itself. But this case wasn't as clear-cut, first because their bloodlines weren't considered inherently compatible, and second because they married without the *jun tan.*"

Whoa. "My parents weren't gods-destined mates?" Even through the counselor's calm, she felt the world take a long, slow roll around her.

Shandi tipped her hand in a *yes-no* gesture. "They eventually got their *jun tan*s, but not until a few months after they were married. That was around the time you were conceived, so there was some question of whether the 'mated' marks appeared because your parents were truly destined mates, or because the pregnancy kicked in a new level of the magic. More than a few people whispered that the gods were affirming your value, not actually sanctifying the marriage."

Dull unease twisted through Jade. "Surely there were pregnancies between unmated magi?" Love affairs and infidelity were, after all, part of the human condition. And although the Nightkeepers had a few skills normal humans didn't, there were far more similarities than differences.

"Of course. In those cases, the children were accepted into either their father's or mother's bloodlines— usually the more powerful of the two, to give the child the greatest chance of growing into the maximum magic they could command. Even in *jun tan*–sanctified marriages, the mother's bloodline could accept the child if the father didn't object. That's how Alexis came to be a member of her mother's stronger bloodline. The same thing probably should have been done in your case, giving you the protection and power of the star bloodline . . . but Vennie refused. And, as usual, she got what she wanted, which was a neat little harvester family. For about six months or so."

On one level, Jade was rapt, with energy humming beneath her skin alongside the sense that finally— *finally*—she was getting some of the information she had lacked all along. On another, she found herself wishing with every fiber of her being that she could fold time. If she could do that, she'd pop back ten minutes or so, to when she'd first come into her suite that evening . . . and tell herself to lock the door. She couldn't deal with this right now, couldn't deal with any of it. Or rather, she could deal with it, but she damn well didn't *want* to. She wanted to shut it all out, turn it all off, go to bed, and pull the covers over her head. Maybe when she woke up, it would be 2013, and the others would have won the war without her. Foolish wishes, all of them. But how else was she supposed to deal with learning that she could've been a star, which pretty much would've guaranteed her the warrior's mark? Only that hadn't happened because her parents had decided against it. Her *teenaged* parents.

Gone was the tall, stately woman she'd imagined singing her to sleep. Gone too was the strong press of her father's arms, the deep rumble of his voice, and the feelings of safety. Now new pictures were forming, especially of her mother. Jade knew the type—simultaneously too young and too old for their ages, wiseasses who thought they knew everything, then took off when they finally figured out they didn't know anything. Jade's heart ached with the change, as though she had lost her parents all over again, when she'd never really had them in the first place.

The *winikin* continued: "Vennie was crazy in love with your father and his family. She insisted on your being accepted into the harvester bloodline, and having a harvester *winikin*." Shandi paused, her expression going unreadable. "I wasn't actually in line to be your *winikin*—or anyone's, really—but during your naming ceremony, the magic bypassed your intended *winikin* and tagged me with the *aj-winikin* mark instead." She turned her palms up to say bitterly, "And who are we to argue with the will of the gods?"

That in itself was a shock to Jade . . . yet at the same time it wasn't, really. From what she'd read, mage-bound *winikin* had been selected through a rigorous process that had been part Nightkeeper foretelling, part psychological profiling, and had been designed to provide the best possible caregiver match. If Shandi hadn't been chosen or trained . . . "What were you supposed to be, if not a *winikin*?" Those of the blood who weren't chosen to wear the *aj-winikin* "I serve" glyph had formed the core of daily life at Skywatch, a layer of support staffers below even the harvesters.

A spasm of pain crossed the other woman's face, but she shook her head. "That doesn't matter anymore. What's done is done." *Conversation closed*. "By the time King Scarred-Jaguar started planning to attack the intersection and seal the barrier, you were six months old, and your parents' marriage had been limping along for about twice that."

"But the *jun tan* is supposed to mark a lifelong bond."

"Love doesn't guarantee a problem-free relationship."

Ouch. How many times had she thought that before? More, how often had she seen a client out the door and stood there after it closed, thinking to herself that she would never fall into the trap of pining after a man, or letting a bad relationship crush her? *Don't be like Edda*, she'd told herself over and over again, using one particular client to proxy for the sum total of the broken hearts—and broken spirits—she'd counseled in her five years of active practice. In that time, she'd gained a reputation as a relationship expert when all she'd really done was help the women—and a few men, but mostly women—learn to be the best *them* they could be, without using a relationship as a value mirror. And while she'd been teaching her clients how to self-actualize, she'd been confirming the value of her own chosen lifestyle, one of casual dates and sex between friends.

"So," she said carefully, feeling her way, "when you used to tell me my parents loved each other, that was a lie?"

Shandi nodded. "They were gone, and I . . . ah, I thought you needed the illusion of parents who loved each other."

"And who loved me?" Jade said softly.

Instead of the knee-jerk, *Of course they loved you*, the question called for, Shandi stayed silent. When she met Jade's eyes, though, her expression was resolute. "If you'd asked me that a few hours ago, my honest answer would have been that your father doted on you. All of your harvester relatives did."

Jade's mouth had gone drier than the too-humid desert outside. "But not my mother or the stars?"

"It wasn't like human society. Once a woman married out of a bloodline, she might still wear her original bloodline mark, but her responsibility and affiliation shifted to her husband's family. Vennie . . . I believe she truly loved your father at first, and came into the marriage fully committed to the harvester bloodline. But once the newness of being a wife wore off and she started to understand what it meant to be a harvester instead of a star, she chafed at the restrictions. More, she began losing her magic."

"But the *jun tan* bond is supposed to increase a Nightkeeper's talent."

"I'm just telling you what she told me—and everyone else within earshot—on a regular basis." Faint discomfort flitted across the *winikin*'s expression, but she kept going. "She was frustrated with the menial roles the harvesters were playing in the weeks leading up to the king's attack. She wanted to fight, not sit in the background. More, she and your father fought over the attack itself. She questioned Scarred-Jaguar's visions, which a harvester would never do. That was one of the few times I could ever remember seeing Joshua truly angry. He was furious with her for questioning the king, though I think a large part of it was a spillover of other, smaller disagreements that had been building up. Add that to the stress of their being young parents with a loud, colicky baby, and things got nasty." Shandi paused. "She took off three days before the attack, and she didn't come back. We assumed she ran off, not wanting to be part of a battle she didn't believe in. Based on Lucius's description, though, I think it's possible she somehow found and enacted the Prophet's spell instead, hoping to find something within the library that would help her convince Scarred-Jaguar not to lead the attack . . . or something that would help him win it. Knowing her, she wouldn't have cared which, as long as she got the credit. Instead, she somehow got caught up inside the library instead of forming the proper conduit. And she died there."

Jade closed her eyes on a wash of emotion. She told herself it didn't matter that her parents hadn't died together, that their love hadn't been the deep, abiding joy Shandi had let her believe. That was twenty-some years ago, and had little influence on her life now. She could only control her own thoughts and actions, not those of others . . . and certainly not the past. The sentiments rang badly hollow, though, and her chest ached. "You said she took off three days before the massacre. Didn't the king and the others go looking for her? Surely, if she'd been lying around somewhere, half jacked into the library, someone could have found her."

But Shandi shook her head. "There wasn't an extensive search because nobody in the council knew she was gone. Neither the harvesters nor the stars wanted to draw attention to her disappearance. Back then, the political situation was volatile. There were . . . I wouldn't call them factions, exactly, but there was definitely dissent within the Nightkeepers. Parents held their teenagers back from their talent ceremonies so they wouldn't have to fight, and a few of the magi even spoke openly about leaving. In the end the king, with the queen at his side, declared that anyone involved in desertion, whether by act or knowledge, was guilty of treason . . . which was—and still is—punishable by death."

"You all thought you were protecting her by covering up her disappearance."

The *winikin* nodded. "Your father was heartbroken that she'd taken off, but he didn't want her being charged with treason."

Love strikes again, Jade thought, knowing that she should feel something but not sure what anymore. She was growing numb to the surprises, to the anguish. "He died thinking she had abandoned him. That she had abandoned both of us." She paused as grief echoed through her. "Didn't anyone stop to think that a woman who was all bent out of shape about being kept out of the action wasn't going to just walk away from a fight?"

"Sure, there were questions, but like I said, she was impulsive . . . and I can't say that motherhood had settled her down. She loved you fiercely when she was in the mood, but then, other times, she wanted to pretend she was the same girl she'd been before—the party girl who was always the center of attention."

My mother, the head cheerleader, Jade thought sourly. But at the same time, the logic didn't totally play. She frowned, trying to think it through in her tired, overloaded brain, knowing that if she stopped thinking, she ran the risk of feeling too much. "The Prophet's spell requires a soul sacrifice. By enacting it, she would have been offering her own life in exchange for the information."

Shandi turned her palms to the sky. "Like I said, she was a comet. That was exactly the sort of 'act first, regret later' move she specialized in. Though it doesn't explain how she wound up in the same situation the human is in now. There's no way she was harboring a *makol* or any other sort of soul link."

"The human's name is Lucius," Jade snapped, annoyance flashing a quick burn through her system.

"Yes, it is, and he's bright and shiny now, and you're hot for him. What do you think is going to happen when all that wears off? Your mother was miserable as a harvester. She hated being on the sidelines. She was a warrior, and she was used to having power—not just magic, but a voice among others her age. When she married your father, whether from love or impulse, or a bit of both, she gave up more than she anticipated. She blamed him for that. And she blamed herself for following her heart, because in doing so, she'd lost the right to fight."

The words tugged at a connection in Jade's brain, but she couldn't make it take shape. She shook her head. "I don't know what to say anymore. What to think."

"That's understandable. You're tired, and that was a lot to take in." Rising, Shandi brushed at her tailored pants, which fell in neat creases as though they didn't dare wrinkle. "Just keep breathing," the *winikin* said pragmatically, "and keep yourself steady. Sometimes, that's all we can do."

Jade wanted to argue, wanted to scream that she was tired of only breathing, tired of being steady. She wanted to be unsteady, irrational; she wanted to *do* something, godsdamn it! But she didn't want to prolong the conversation further; she wanted some time alone to process, or maybe just pull the covers over her head.

"I'll be in my room," Shandi said. "Call if you need me."

"Of course," Jade answered numbly. "I will." But they both knew she wouldn't.

She saw the *winikin* to the door and locked it behind her. Then, drawn by the faintest rumble of thunder, barely detectable as a vibration on the air and in the floor beneath her feet, she moved to the sliders and pushed through to the balcony. Lightning flickered on the horizon and a deep-throated, thrumming thunder boom ran through the soles of her feet and up to her body, where it pressed on her heart.

Closing the sliders behind her, she leaned back against the side of the mansion and slid down to sit balled up on the patio floor, with her chin on her knees and her arms wrapped around her shins, feeling the storm approach . . . and waiting for the rain to come and wash away her tears.

PART II

✳

MIDDAY

The sun reaches apogee

CHAPTER TEN

June 14
Two years, six months, and seven days to the zero date
University of Texas, Austin

"Hey, Pyro. You lost?"

The hail startled Rabbit, who'd been head-down, lost in his thoughts as he'd hiked across campus. Pausing just shy of the cement bridge that led to the front entrance of the squat, bunkerlike structure that ironically housed the art history department, he did a mental eye roll and glanced back over his shoulder at the lanky, brown-haired guy who was waving at him. "Not lost, Smitty. Just slumming."

"Ha! Good one." Anna's newest grad student loped a few strides to catch up, made like he was going to punch Rabbit in the arm, then aborted the motion in a fake-out designed to show anyone watching that the two of them were buds, without actually making contact. Everyone who was anyone in the student social structure knew that Rabbit didn't like to be touched, except by Myrinne. "Ready to come to your senses and give up on that science shit?"

It was a running semijoke among the younger members of the Mayan studies department, who, after seeing Rabbit ace a few grad-level courses, had decided that he was the best naturally intuitive Mayanist the university had seen in forever, and ought to be majoring in their department rather than physics.

What they didn't get, and what he never intended to tell them, was that the whole Mayan thing wasn't intuitive at all. It was the way he'd been raised. Rabbit's old man might not have given much of a crap about his upbringing—Red-Boar had been far more concerned about the memory movies playing inside his own skull—but Jox had taken up the slack, with Strike and Anna helping off and on. Rabbit had learned the legends and histories from them, and had picked up a better than rudimentary understanding of the glyphs and language even before the barrier—and his own magic—had come alive. So really, the Mayan studies shit had been fluff classes for him. Cheating, really. Not that he was going to fess up on that one, though Anna had threatened to flunk him if he didn't stop signing up for her classes.

The mental filters he'd installed in his own skull to prevent himself from talking about—or performing—magic on campus wouldn't let him tell guys like Smitty what was really going on with him. Even if he'd been able to talk about it, though, he wouldn't have. Unlike in high school, where he hadn't dared be good at anything lest he get more of the wrong sort of attention from the Reich High Command that had dominated the student scene, at UT he'd found that a guy got points for being good at shit, not just from the teachers, but from the other students.

Granted, his popularity hadn't really taken off until he'd set Myrinne's dorm room on fire, thereby gaining his all too apt nickname, but still.

"Nah," he said, playing along. "I'm still into the science shit." Which remained a low-grade surprise to him. He'd never seen himself as an egghead, but ever since his first day of the midlevel physics class he'd tested into, when Professor Burns had talked about how fire was nothing more than air molecules breaking the speed limit, he'd been hooked. And the deeper into it he'd gotten, the more he'd felt like he'd found something important, something he'd been looking for without knowing he was looking.

Smitty shook his head. "Wasting your talent, Pyro. Wasting your talent." Then he grinned, his brain shifting lightning-quick—as it often did—to another, unrelated topic. "You here to see your aunt?"

Rabbit nodded. "Yep. She around?"

As a shortcut to explaining his lifelong relationship with the head of the Mayan studies department, and why he checked in with her on a regular basis, he and Anna had decided he'd just pretend she was his aunt and move on. To his surprise, nobody had called him on the absolute lack of familial resemblance. It didn't seem to matter that his eyes were pale blue to her cobalt, that his features were hawk-sharp to her classical beauty, or that his hair, which stood up in a pseudo-military brush cut these days, was blah brown to her chestnut-highlighted sable. When he'd asked Myrinne why that was, she'd given him one of her looks—this one conveying, *You're kind of cute when you're being oblivious*—and said that they gave off similar vibes, and that although the conscious minds of most humans were insensitive to magic per se, their subconscious minds registered those vibes and chunked him and Anna together in the category of "powerful bad-ass; don't piss off."

He liked being in that category almost as much as he liked having a nickname and an open invite to most everything on campus that might interest him. But he wished to hell the same could be said of his status among the Nightkeepers. It seemed that the more functional he got in the outside world, the more Strike wanted to keep him there, away from the magic.

"She's in her office, last I knew." Smitty waved in the direction of Anna's first-floor window, which was closed and blocked off by the curtains she kept drawn most of the time these days.

"Thanks. Catch you later." Rabbit sketched a wave and headed across the causeway, which always made him think of the drawbridge leading to a castle, albeit a short, ugly castle.

Smitty dogged him, apparently headed the same way. "You coming to the thing tomorrow night?"

Rabbit didn't have a frigging clue what thing he was talking about, but lifted a shoulder. "Maybe. Hafta see—family stuff, you know." If he had anything to say about it, he and Myrinne would be back in New Mex by the weekend. Screw Strike's plan for having them stay in Texas through summer school and on into the fall semester. There were more important things than class credits, especially when there was a solid chance that the credits themselves would cease to exist prior to graduation day, 2013.

"You should come," Smitty pressed. "It's going to rock."

"I'll bet." They passed through the main entrance. Rabbit turned and made himself punch the other guy in the shoulder. "Have a good one."

As he headed off, Smitty was standing dead-ass still, looking like someone had just given him a million bucks. Rabbit nearly shook his head, but didn't, because who was he to say the human college set had it wrong? Theirs was a different culture; that was all. One he was learning to live inside, and maybe even to thrive within.

Didn't mean that was where he wanted to be long-term, though.

Pausing at Anna's door, he knocked. "Professor Catori? It's Rabbit. I need five minutes." Maybe before he would've walked right in, or called her by her first name just to show he could. But before, he'd admittedly been an asshole most of the time. These days, he tried to play the little things pretty straight . . . and save up his asshole quota for the big stuff.

"Door's unlocked," Anna called, her voice muffled by the heavy panel separating them. When Rabbit pushed through and closed the door at his back, she looked up from where she was seated behind her desk, working on what looked like e-mail. She was wearing a soft steel gray sweater that blended with the backdrop of bookshelves holding artifacts that he privately thought of as All Forgeries Great and Small. She greeted him with a smile. "Hey, Pyro."

He winced, only half joking. "Great. Now they've got you doing it."

"Fits."

"No shit, huh?" But despite the friendly exchange, he stayed standing, not because he was trying to loom over her—even though he *could* loom if he wanted to these days—but because he was twitchy. Silence stretched between them for a moment . . . and that was enough to give him his answer. "Let me guess. It's a 'hell, no.' "

Anna sighed. "Rabbit . . . you know he's only trying to do what's best."

"He" was Strike, and in the king's world, "what's best" was apparently keeping Rabbit and Myrinne as far away from the action as possible by loading them with classes regardless of the school year. Except, of course, when the magi absolutely, positively needed Rabbit's specific talents, whereupon Strike zapped in, grabbed him for the job, then dumped him back in his dorm room as quickly as humanly—or magely— possible.

"This sucks." Rabbit heard his own tone border on whiny territory as a familiar churning frustration rose within him. Reminding himself that he was better than the anger, he tamped it down to a low simmer, lost the whine, and said, "Sorry. I know it's not your decision. You're not king." Though there were times he'd thought she would've made the better ruler of the two of them, in large part because she wanted nothing to do with the job. Or really, he suspected, with the Nightkeepers.

"You're getting to him, though."

Rabbit narrowed his eyes. "Seriously?"

"Seriously. The longer you keep your nose clean here, kick it in the classroom, and generally behave like someone he'd want to have at his back, the more he's going to forget why he doesn't want you around."

From anyone else, Rabbit would've figured that for a blatant pitch to keep him on the straight and narrow, i.e., attempted bribery with no real commitment to an endpoint. Coming from Anna, though, he was tempted to believe it was for real. She thought she owed his old man a life debt, and upon Red-Boar's death had transferred that owesie to Rabbit. That was why she'd stepped up and gotten in Strike's face over whether Myrinne would be allowed to stay at Skywatch even though she was pure human, not bound to any of the magi, and had a history of dabbling in the occult. More, Anna had, for the most part anyway, tried to be available when Rabbit needed her, and tried to fix the considerable amount of shit he'd screwed up in past years.

All that made him want to believe her, as did his desire to think that life was fair, that he'd be able to work his way into the fighting core of the Nightkeepers by proving that, six months shy of being legal to drink, he was ready to do a man's job as a warrior. But he'd learned early and often that life wasn't fair . . . and when Anna looked at him now, she didn't quite meet his eyes. Maybe it was her vibe, maybe his blunted mind-bending talent, but he suddenly knew she was lying. He wasn't sure about what, but she was definitely hiding something. Maybe not about Strike's opinion or the school stuff, but there was something important going on that she wasn't telling him about, no doubt because Strike-out had decided it was need-to-know and Rabbit wasn't on the list.

"Anything big going on back there?" he asked casually.

She shook her head. "Nothing really. They're gearing up for the solstice. Strike'll pick you and Myrinne up for the day, like we planned."

The lie was still there. Whatever was going on, it wasn't going to wait for the solstice, or else the solstice was part of it, but there were already major plans being made . . . without him. Anger flared, hot and hard and feeling like fire. For a second, he thought about yanking down his mental blocks and getting inside her head, looking for what she'd chosen—or been ordered— not to tell him. *What is it?* he wanted to scream at her. *What's going on? Why doesn't he want me there?* But he held it together. Barely.

She looked at him for real, finally, and he didn't see the lie anymore. It had been there, though. He was sure of it. "Be strong," she said softly. "Your time will come."

"Thanks," he said. But inwardly, he was thinking, *What-the-fuck-ever*.

"Was there something else?"

He didn't know if that was a hint, or if she really wanted to know the answer, but either way, he wasn't in a sharing mood anymore. Maybe he'd hiked over to the ugly castle rather than called because he'd been toying with asking her about the Order of Xibalba and some of the stuff Myrinne had been bringing up lately, sort of get Anna's take. But now? Forget it.

"Nah. Just wanted to check in with some face time, so you can report back to big brother that I'm behaving myself."

She smiled, the expression reaching her eyes. "I'll do that. And, Rabbit?"

"Yeah?"

"I'm proud of you."

Under other circumstances—like if she hadn't just lied to his face—that might've caught him hard. Gods knew he was working his ass off not to fuck up these days. Given the scenario, though, he just faked a smile. "Thanks. Some days, I'm proud of me too."

But as he headed back across campus, he didn't know what the hell he was, other than torn. For a change he was doing his damnedest to think through all the possible outcomes and talk to the right people, rather than going off half-cocked and burning up on impact. Literally. But it wasn't easy to talk things out when he didn't know who the hell to talk to anymore.

Anna had said time and again that she owed him, but he didn't trust her not to blab if she thought it was in his best interest. She wasn't a stickler for the writs, but if it came down to a choice between Rabbit and her brother, Strike was going to win out every time. Same applied to Jox. Michael was a possibility for a go-to guy; he'd gone to the mat for Rabbit the previous winter, when the gods had demanded his execution and Michael had refused. But Rabbit figured he owed the guy big for that one, and wasn't sure it was kosher to dump something on top of that debt. Besides, although Michael had ruthlessly followed his own path in the beginning, now that he and Sasha were together, his path paralleled the party line more often than not. Which left Rabbit . . . where? Who could he go to when his usual go-to girl was the one he needed to talk about?

A name ghosted through his brain, one he'd long ago told himself to forget, at least in that context. Not that he'd ever actually managed to forget her.

Patience. The youngest of the Nightkeepers, she was only six years older than him, and after Red-Boar's horrific death, she'd stepped in as his friend, his sister figure, his mother figure, and his first massive crush, all wrapped into one. She and the twins had let him into their lives, made him feel like he had a family, like someone gave a shit whether he woke up each morning, and whether he descended into the same sort of funk his old man had turned into an art form. Brandt had let him in too, but only because Patience had insisted. And after the twins were sent away and the problems in their marriage had gotten more and more obvious, Brandt had wanted less and less to do with him, until the day the shit finally hit the fan: Rabbit had been on guard duty during an op and got distracted, and Patience had paid for it. Terrified, Rabbit had bolted. By the time he'd made it back to Skywatch, he'd had Myrinne with him. He'd meant to apologize to Patience, but somehow that never happened, and then it got to a point where it was too late to apologize, too late to try to fix things.

"Which is why you shouldn't go there," Rabbit told himself as he crossed a parking lot and sent a couple of waves at guys who "hey, Pyro'd" him.

But deep down inside him, a voice was saying, *Why not go there?* It'd been a while since he and Patience had been tight, but she had an open, generous heart. She might be willing to forgive him for being an ass-hole. More, although she was loyal to the Nightkeeper cause, she wasn't too keen on Strike, who still wouldn't tell her where the twins were hidden. It was for their own good to stay incognito with their *winikin*, it was true. But still . . . not letting her see her kids for going on a year now? That was harsh. Rabbit figured that'd make her likely to keep her own counsel rather than run straight to the king if she thought he was in danger of making yet another Rabbit-size mistake.

In fact, the more he thought about it, the better it sounded. Or was he talking himself into something stupid? Gods knew it wouldn't be the first time. But it wasn't like he could ask Myrinne her opinion. Yeah, that'd be smooth: *Hey, babe. I'm not sure whether I like where you're going with this whole "You should look into the other half of your heritage, because your old man might've been a real son of a bitch, but he doesn't sound like the kind of guy who would've slept with the enemy. So maybe the Xi-balbans aren't inherently bad. Maybe Iago is an outlier with his own agenda, and the Xibalbans themselves could prove to be allies instead of enemies." Which sounds good when you say it, but feels pretty cracked when I think about it on my own . . . so I was wondering what you thought about me hooking back up with Patience to talk about it.* Yeah, Myr would just *love* that. Not only was she big into the idea of him doing his own thing, whether or not it coincided with the Nightkeepers' paradigms, but she and Patience didn't get along. At all.

Still, before he was really aware that he'd made the decision, he had detoured off the track leading off campus to his and Myrinne's summer sublet, and parked his ass on a cement ledge that was part of the so-called landscaping at UT—which, to his largely New England–raised self was more land-pouring than landscaping, and suffered from a definite lack of green. But regardless, it was a place to park ass while he dug out his cell phone. Then, not letting himself think it through any further, because thinking hadn't gotten him real far yet in this particular case, he punched in the number for Patience's private cell.

When it started ringing, he had a fleeting thought that she might've changed the number by now, or ditched the phone entirely. He was so expecting to hear a recorded voice tell him the line was no longer in service that when she answered with a breathless, anticipatory whisper of, "Yes, yes, I'm here," he went mute for a second.

It was a second too long.

"Hello?" she said, her tone going from hushed excitement to dread in an instant. "Hannah? Woody?"

Her words tumbled over one another, the way they did when her brain started bounding ahead, cascading from one thought to the next. "Oh, gods. There's something wrong. What is it? What's wrong? Where *are* you? What—"

"*Stop!*" Rabbit interrupted. "Just stop." *Shit.* She'd kept the phone as a secret line of communication to the *winikin* guarding her sons, and must've forgotten he had the number. Now she was heading toward full-on panic mode.

Before he could get into an explanation, she snapped in a horror-laced voice, "Who are you? How did you get this number? If you've done anything to my babies, I'll—"

"Patience!" He did the interrupting thing again, this time rushing on to say, "It's Rabbit. It's Rabbit. Do you hear me? It's not Hannah or Wood, or one of the rats." He'd called the twins his rug rats, back when they'd been his miniature tagalongs. When she didn't say anything, just gave a strangled sob, he moderated his tone. "It's me. I'm sorry I scared you. I just . . . I need someone to talk to." Now it was his turn to babble a little when there was silence on the other end of the line. "I wanted to . . . Shit. I wanted to talk to you about Myrinne and me, about how she says stuff that makes sense at first, but . . . I don't know. It doesn't always mesh with what Jox and those guys taught me. And how am I supposed to know who to trust, who to believe?" When she still hadn't said anything, to interrupt or otherwise, he started thinking she'd already hung up. "Shit," he said again, in case she was still on the other end of the line. "I'm sorry. I shouldn't have called you like this. And I'm sorry about back then, at the museum. I was a total dickwad, and you got hurt because of it, and then I screwed up by taking off. Now I've made it worse. But I'll hang up now, and I'll lose this number. You don't have to worry about me calling again."

He wasn't really breathing as he lowered the phone, trying not to think of how crappy he'd just made her feel, how terrified she must've been. All because he'd dialed before he thought it through. Another fuckup. Seriously, how could one guy screw things up as consistently as he did? It was a godsdamned talent—that was what it was.

Halfway wondering what the forearm mark for "incurable fuckup" would look like, he moved to end the call and delete the number. Before he got there, though, he heard the thin thread of a tear-laced voice say, "Don't hang up."

The phone shook slightly as he lifted it to his ear again. "I'm—" His throat closed on the words. He had to swallow hard before he could continue. "I'm still here."

"So am I."

The three simple words unlocked a hard, hot torrent of grief. It slapped through him, flailed at him, accused him of all his past sins and more. Then it faded, leaving him clutching the phone, hunching his body around it in full sight of numerous classmates who'd only recently decided he was supercool. He wasn't feeling cool now, though. He was sweating greasily down his spine. "I'm sorry," he said again, and this time he wasn't just talking about scaring her with the call. "I'm so godsdamned sorry."

"Me too."

Only two words this time, but they spun through him like sunlight—real, warm yellow sunlight, not the orange shit currently beating down on him. The crushing pressure on his lungs eased, and he could breathe again. His heart could beat again, when he hadn't been aware of it bumping off rhythm. "How . . . how are you?" He wasn't sure he had the right to ask, but couldn't *not* ask.

"I'm . . ." She blew out a breath. "I'm doing my duty."

"Yeah. I'm starting to figure that one out myself."

"I've heard you're doing a good job of it."

"You're shitting me."

"I shit you not. The word on the street—or at least in the great room and out by the picnic tables—is that our boy has grown up, and he's looking more like a mage and a man than a punk-ass juvie these days."

"Then why am I still here? Why hasn't he—" Hearing the potential for a whine, Rabbit broke off. "Never mind."

But Patience answered, "Because he's got a shit-ton on his plate, and he's had to out-of-sight-out-of-mind a few people and problems that he just can't deal with right now." There was no need to clarify who *he* was. In a way, Strike held both of them hostage.

"Which am I—a person or a problem?"

"A person. Definitely a person. He loves you; don't

think any different. But you scare him too. He isn't sure how powerful you really are, and what you're going to be able to do when your magic matures fully."

I don't blame him, Rabbit thought, but didn't say. Hell, he scared *himself* some days, when he could feel the magic rising up inside him, banging against the filters and demanding to be let out. When that happened, his body temp spiked, his muscles and joints hurt like hell, and he felt somehow *old*. Sometimes it lasted a few minutes, sometimes a few hours. Once, it'd been two days before he'd felt like himself again; he'd stayed in bed, claimed to have the flu, and kind of liked how Myr had fussed over him, saying his aura was all jacked up. When he'd gotten back on his feet, he hadn't much liked what he'd looked like in the mirror—all hollow eyed and drawn—but that'd gone away eventually. Since then, the magic had been quiet. Oddly, that hadn't made him feel any better—which was part of why he was jonesing to get back to Skywatch, where he could get behind the wards, drop his mental shields, and see what was doing with his magic. Not that he'd told Strike any of that; he hadn't told anyone.

As though he'd responded—or maybe she was following her own inner dialogue?—Patience said thoughtfully, "No, you're a person to him, as are the twins. The problem I was talking about is Snake Mendez. . . . He's one of us, but he's not, you know? And Strike's dealing with him by not dealing."

"I guess." Mendez was a full-blood Nightkeeper, but the *winikin* who'd saved and raised him hadn't been the most mentally stable of guardians, and Mendez had gone way off the reservation. More, he'd found the magic on his own, just like Strike and Patience had. Except that Mendez was a hard-ass, and it sounded like he hung way too close to the dark side of the Force. He'd gotten hauled in by some bounty hunter, tossed in the slammer, and had stayed there nearly two years so far: eighteen months on the original sentence, then six more for attacking another inmate. Rabbit was pretty sure that Strike—or, more likely, Jox—had made sure Mendez had stayed put. Out of sight, out of mind, indeed. "He must be thinking that jail's one of the safest places to keep a guy like that, at least until we get into the library and figure out some of what's coming next."

"Don't count on the library. It looks like that's not going to be the answer we'd hoped." She gave him a quick rundown of Lucius's latest attempt to breach the barrier, surprising Rabbit, who hadn't realized Jade had left the university, or that there was any sort of experiment planned. And oh, holy shit on the sun god being trapped in Xibalba, with a rescue needed within T minus seven days and counting. Was that what Anna had been hiding? *Maybe, maybe not*, he thought, trying to keep up as Patience bounced from one thought to the next, more talking *at* him than with him, chattering fast, as though she feared he'd cut her off if she slowed down. "But back to Mendez. I've been thinking—what if Strike's wrong about him? What if we're blindly accepting what the king's telling us because, well, he's the king?"

Rabbit zeroed back in on the convo, as what Patience was saying suddenly started to parallel some of what Myrinne had been telling him for the past few weeks. "The jaguars have a rep for being stubborn," he said carefully.

"Yes!" she said, excited now. "And who's to say there's really only one way to accomplish a goal, right? I'm not saying he's wrong, and I'm not talking treason. I'm just wondering if sometimes maybe we're too quick to follow the writs. This is the third millennium. Maybe it's time to . . . update, I guess."

Rabbit wasn't so sure he was tracking her anymore, and the greasy sweat that had prickled his back only moments earlier had gone cold, sending a chill down his spine. "That's kind of why I wanted to talk to you. Myrinne and I have been . . . I don't know . . . discussing a few things . . . and I wanted a reality check from someone I trust, and who won't—"

"Shit," Patience hissed as an aside. "Damn it!"

He sat bolt upright. "What's wrong?"

"Brandt's coming, and he doesn't know I still have this phone. I've got to go, but I'll call you back later, okay?"

"But—"

"Sorry, sorry. I know you called to talk about you, and I babbled about me. But don't you see? You already know the answer; you're just looking for someone else to say it first. So, okay, I will. If you love her, then you need to trust her, and you've got to put her above everyone else in your life."

"But the writs—"

"Are more than three thousand years old. And

Strike's doing the best he possibly can, but he's a man, not a god. With the skyroad closed, he's feeling his way just like we are. Who's to say he's right about everything?"

"I—"

"Gotta go," she said. "But do yourself a favor, and don't let other people's agendas screw up a good relationship." Her voice descended to a whisper on the last word, and then the line went dead.

Rabbit sat for a few minutes, while the world came back into focus around him. He was dimly surprised to see that he was still at the university, that nothing around him had changed. Students passed him, heading from point A to point B and vice versa with varying degrees of urgency, yet no clue that they were practically on borrowed time unless the Nightkeepers figured out how to get Kinich Ahau back where he belonged, without the promise of help from the library.

Anger stirred again, though more sluggish this time. Why hadn't Anna—and presumably Strike—wanted him to know about what was going on? Why were they distancing him from the fight just when he was starting to prove his commitment to the cause by keeping his nose clean?

"Shit. I don't know." But he couldn't get Patience's parting words out of his head. *Don't let other people's agendas screw up a good relationship.* Was that what he was doing? Maybe. If he hadn't yet, he was definitely in danger of it. Hell, he'd just gone behind Myr's back with Patience, whom he knew she couldn't stand.

Damn it.

"Hey," a voice said from a few feet away. "Everything okay?"

He looked up and for a second wasn't sure if she was really there or if he'd imagined her. Surely he'd projected the perfect symmetry of her face, with those long lashes and big, dark brown eyes, narrow-bridged nose, and full, sassy mouth? Then she raised one dark eyebrow in question, and became a flesh-and-blood fantasy of long legs and toned arms and tanned skin bared beneath boy shorts and a tight tank, even though it wasn't that warm out yet. He was suddenly warm, though, as a flush of mingled unease and lust rattled through him.

"Myrinne." Even after almost a year, he still loved saying her name, loved knowing he had that right. She'd been wearing his promise ring for the past five months. It wasn't an engagement, and it wasn't the *jun tan*, damn it, but it was important to him, a symbol that he loved her, and that she knew and accepted it.

She raised her other eyebrow to join the first. "Was that a 'yes, everything's okay,' or 'no, everything's unexpectedly gone to shit'?"

He snorted. "I always expect things to go to shit. Nothing unexpected there."

"And now he's evading the question," she said, as though to the world at large, though she pitched her sexy contralto voice so it was just between the two of them, not the foot traffic. "Spill it, lover."

"There's no problem," he said, realizing it was true. "Nothing to spill." He was the one seeing complications where they didn't need to exist. Stretching out and hiding the wince when his sore muscles protested, he snagged her hand and pulled her to him.

Laughing, she let herself overbalance and fall against him, so they wound up sprawled together, with her partway in his lap, partway on the cement lip where he'd been sitting. Shifting her with an easy strength that'd seemed to come more and more naturally as time passed, he arranged them more comfortably, so she was sitting in his lap, curled against his chest.

At her prickliest last fall, she never would've allowed the public display. Since the winter solstice, though, when he'd nearly killed himself trying to lose the hell-mark so they could form the *jun tan* bond, she'd been more openly affectionate. Now she curled against him and tucked her head beneath his chin so he could lean on her, and she on him. Her hair smelled of patchouli and vanilla, two scents she was particularly partial to. If he wanted to, he could probably remember what they symbolized in the pseudo-occult structure she'd been raised within. For the moment, though, he just let himself breathe her in, feeling his muscles uncoil one after another, until he was looser and warmer than before, though he hadn't really been aware of being tight or cold.

Maybe cuddling his girlfriend in the middle of campus shouldn't have made him feel like da man, but he hadn't gotten to practice that sort of thing in high school. He was making up for lost time.

She snaked her arms around his waist and snuggled in closer, pressing her cheek to his chest with her face tipped up to his. Her eyes drifted shut, letting him know she was listening to his heartbeat, as she often did, as though she feared that one day it would simply stop. And it would, he supposed. But not for a very, very long time, after they'd both lived out their full lives together. He hoped.

"I've made a decision," he said, realizing that really, he'd made it a while ago. It was just taking some time for the rest of him to catch up.

"Hm?" she said, her voice drowsy, as though she were on the verge of falling asleep, curled up against him in the cool orange sunlight that made the world's palette strange and dim.

"I'm going to try to find my mother."

Myrinne didn't say anything when he dropped that, to him, bombshell. But a slow, sweet smile curved her lips, and her arms tightened around his waist. And as the warmth of her body, her existence, seeped into Rabbit's aching self and made everything seem better, he knew he'd finally made a good decision. He just hoped to hell he could see it through.

CHAPTER ELEVEN

Skywatch

The morning after Shandi upended Jade's childhood dreams of the parents she'd never known, Jade took the new information straight to the king, who called an all-hands-on-deck meeting to discuss the new info and what—if anything—it might mean in terms of accessing the library. Which meant that Jade was yet again going to be the focus of attention, when she would far rather have sat in the back and blended.

Intellectually, she knew it shouldn't matter that she was fifty percent star blood. She wore the mark of a harvester, had the talent of one, and there was no shame in either of those things. Similarly, it wasn't critical that her parents hadn't been the people she'd imagined them to be. That didn't change who she was or what she could do. But as she headed for the great room, the churning in her stomach warned her that the prior night's crying jag might have left her scratchy eyed and headachy, but it had been far from cathartic.

She was still pissed that Shandi had let her believe
a lie for so long, and borderline ashamed of what her
mother had done. Who was to say that Vennie's actions hadn't played a part in what Lucius was dealing
with now? Her death might have upset the balance or
the mechanics of the Prophet's spell somehow, or . . .
Don't, she told herself as she stepped through the
arched doorway that opened from the mages' wing to
the great room. *You'll only make yourself crazy.* So she
pushed her emotions down deep and told herself not
to dwell on the feelings. *Just the facts, ma'am.*

She scanned the room in search of a seat—or at least
that was what she told herself she was doing. But when
her eyes immediately locked on Lucius and a flush
heated her skin, the inner lie was obvious. She'd been
looking for him, had needed to know he was there. Although things were far from settled between them, she
knew he was on her side, in this at least.

He looked well rested and less hollow-cheeked than
the night before, and was wearing jeans, a navy rodeo-
logo tee, and the heavy black boots he seemed to have
started wearing in place of his former choice of rope
sandals or skids. He was sitting down in the conversation pit with the magi; he'd saved her a seat beside
him, like they used to do for each other, back before
things got complicated between them. And although
he'd been deep in conversation with Sasha, he turned
to look at Jade as though he'd felt her eyes on him.

When their gazes connected, the churning in her
stomach went to flutters. Worse, she had to suppress
an urge to tug at the too-large sweatshirt she was wear-

ing over old, worn jeans and a loose tee. They were her comfort clothes, the ones she wore when she was tired, PMSing, or otherwise needed a proxied hug. It had been the only outfit she could stand to drag on that morning, but now she wished she'd dressed with more care . . . and then cursed herself for wishing. She wasn't trying to impress him, damn it.

Covering the scowl that threatened to form, she took the seat beside him on the theory that it was better to sit there than to have to explain why she didn't. She kept a careful distance, though, and told herself that the soft flush of warmth that touched her skin was nothing more than body heat. Physics, not chemistry.

Evidently seeing the dark circles beneath her heavier-than-usual makeup—and apparently not needing to keep his distance in order to maintain his sexual sanity, damn him—he frowned and leaned in to ask in a low rasp, "What's wrong?"

Nothing, she started to say, when the answer was really: *Everything.*

Before she could answer, though, Strike and Leah came through the archway leading to the royal quarters, and the king did the *okay, we're all here; let's get started* thing. When the crowd settled, Strike said, "Before we talk about the possible scenarios for rescuing Kinich Ahau, Jade has some new info for us." He gestured in her direction. "Go ahead. You've got the floor."

If she'd been a different person, she might have found a way to soften the delivery. Since she was who she was, though, she went with the naked truth. "We have good reason to believe that the dead woman in the library was my mother."

A ripple of shock ran through the room. Beside her, Lucius sucked in a breath. She could guess the questions that must be racing through his overactive brain. *Are you sure? Why was she in there? What does it mean?*

"Shandi came to me last night . . ." she began, and repeated what she'd told Strike earlier. Shandi herself wasn't available for questions, or even to nod encouragement; she had locked herself in her suite, pleading a headache. *Wish I could've done that*, Jade thought wistfully, as she finished, "So, for better or worse, it all fits. She would've had access to the Prophet's spell via her bloodline. Thinking that she was supposed to be the last of the Prophets, she enacted the spell. But it misfired somehow, putting her in the same sort of position Lucius is in now." She spread her hands. "I don't know how this will help us, or even if it will. But I thought everyone should know."

There was a long moment of stunned—or perhaps merely thoughtful?—silence. Then Strike said, "Since she wrote about being able to enter the library twice, with the third time being the trap, she must've come back to this plane." He glanced up to the breakfast bar to ask Jox, "You said you don't remember seeing her in those last three days?"

The royal *winikin* shook his head. "None of us did— at least, not that we can remember." The other *winikin* made various apologetic motions as Jox continued. "Not to mention that Vennie wasn't exactly subtle. If she was around, you knew it. And if she had discovered something that would've impacted the attack, she would've made sure everyone heard about it, and knew where it'd come from." He tipped his head in Jade's direction. "No offense."

"None taken," Jade said with absolute sincerity. "I am not my mother, and vice versa. Despite what the writs say about 'what has happened before will happen again,' I'm not the sort of person who acts on impulse. You can count on that."

"Flames and dead, staring eyes," Lucius said abruptly, in a total non sequitur.

A chill touched the back of Jade's neck. She turned to him and found him gaunt faced, his expression turned inward. "What?"

"It was in the middle of the journal, where the handwriting was really tough to read, and what I could read was all jumbled up; she kept talking about flames and dead, staring eyes. She used those same words over and over again. I was assuming she was dazed when she wrote it, maybe confused from the transition." He paused, locking his eyes with hers. "What if she wasn't confused? What if she saw exactly what she described?"

Jade's stomach headed for her toes. "Oh, gods."

Lucius continued. "I felt like I was only in the library for a couple of hours, but I lost most of a day out here. She was a full mage, so she was probably able to stay in there longer than me. Maybe she came out once to rest someplace safe, like you were saying, then went back in, maybe because she hadn't found what she was looking for. By the time she found what she was looking for, came back out of the library, and headed for the mansion . . . What if she was already too late? What if Scarred-Jaguar's attack—and the Solstice Massacre— was already over?"

Flames and dead, staring eyes, Jade thought, and shuddered, her heart twisting in her chest.

When Scarred-Jaguar led the magi to war, hundreds of children and their *winikin* had gathered in the big rec hall. That was where the *Banol Kax* had found them. And killed them. The next day, when Jox had emerged from hiding with Strike and Anna, he had found bodies everywhere: stacked in the rec hall, cut down midflight, some even dead in Jeeps headed away from the compound. Every Nightkeeper child over the age of three, and their attending *winikin*, had been killed, as had all the adults involved in the attack. Only the babies and their *winikin* had survived, a scant two dozen left to fight against the end-time war.

"If she saw the bodies, she must have come back that night," Jox said, his voice ragged, his eyes dark and hollow. "I burned the bodies the next day. I didn't see Vennie." He looked at Jade, stricken. "I would have seen her if she'd still been there. I would've stopped her from going back into the library."

Up at the breakfast bar, silent tears trickled down the cheeks of several of the *winikin*. They had survived because they had fled the scene with infant charges who had been too young to have forged their first connections to the magic, thus rendering them invisible to the minions of the *Banol Kax*. But whereas those children had all—with the exception of Strike and Anna—been too young to remember the carnage, the *winikin* didn't have that luxury.

It struck Jade suddenly that they were a week away from the massacre's twenty-sixth anniversary.

"She must've panicked," Lucius said. "Maybe she ran back to wherever she'd been hiding and put herself into the library because it seemed safer there. Then, once she'd pulled herself together and tried to get out, she realized that she couldn't." He swallowed hard. It was one of the few outward signs of the revulsion Jade knew he had to be feeling. He'd been trapped in his own skull, and in the in-between. She could only imagine what he would do to avoid being trapped permanently in the barrier, library or no library. His voice rasped as he said, "Question is, if she came out of the library to rest, but nobody saw her, where was she?"

Strike's head came up. "You're thinking she may have left some clues wherever she was hiding? Maybe something that could help you get back into the library?"

"I'm not usually that lucky," Lucius observed dryly, "but it's a possibility."

"Too bad Rabbit offed the three-question *nah-wal*," Brandt put in, earning him a sharp look from Patience.

"I'll ask Shandi," Jade said. "Of all of us, she knew Vennie best. Maybe she'll be able to guess where . . ." She trailed off as Brandt's comment struck a chord, resonating against a connection that had almost, but not quite, formed in her brain the previous night. Something about the . . . "Oh," she said dully. "Oh, gods. It was her. Vennie."

Beside her, Lucius stiffened. "Who? Where?"

She closed her eyes, feeling idiotic as the pieces clicked together. She should have figured it out sooner, probably would have if she hadn't been so focused on so many other things. "The other night, as you were being transported into the library, I was pulled along too, only I wound up in the barrier itself. I think the library magic must've weakened the barrier enough that my *nahwal* could call me through, and then boot me again when it was done with me." She held up a hand when Lucius drew breath to interject. "I know, I should've said something sooner. And I would have if I thought it had anything to do with Kinich Ahau or the library. But I didn't. Not until just now, when Brandt mentioned the *nahwal* . . . and I realized what had been bothering me since last night." She paused, shaking her head as the impossible began to seem frighteningly possible. "The *nahwal* was acting very strangely. I didn't understand it at the time. Now, though, I think I do." She looked over at Strike. "It was acting like my mother."

Her thoughts raced as she tried to remember the exchange, word for word, gesture for gesture. She described how the *nahwal* had alternated from a normal form that had transmitted the "duty and diligence" tenets of the harvesters, to a more feminized version that had talked about Jade finding her own path and maximizing her strengths, even if they led her away from the harvesters' paradigm. "It was just what I would expect Vennie to have said, based on what Shandi told me about her resenting the harvesters' limitations. If I'd seen that sort of behavior in a patient, I would've taken a serious look at schizophrenia. But in a *nahwal*?" She turned her palms up. "I know that technically she shouldn't play much of a part in the collective of the harvester *nahwal*, given that she's a married-in, and her priorities weren't aligned with theirs. She should be . . . outvoted, I guess you should say. Except she wasn't. She was *there*."

The more she thought about it, the more convinced she became. And the more confused, not by the logic, but by her own response. She felt . . . numb.

"It's not out of the realm," Strike allowed. "The jaguar *nahwal* wears Scarred-Jaguar's earring and has some of his traits." She noticed he didn't say "my father," and wondered why.

Lucius said slowly, "What if the bloodline *nahwal* are morphing as the end-time gets nearer? The dominant personalities could be moving to the forefront and taking over because they're stronger, have the closest ties to the survivors, or have the most pressing need to speak with their descendants."

Jade imagined more than a few of the others were thinking, *Why her? Why not me?* She didn't have an answer for that one, except that maybe Vennie had urgently needed—wanted—to talk to her.

Why did that feel like too little, too late? She'd never met her mother, didn't have a relationship with her beyond shared DNA. But then again, if she couldn't judge Vennie, who could? Shandi? The king?

Suddenly Lucius sat up, his face reflecting a light-bulb moment. "What if the *nahwal* are gaining personal characteristics in preparation for the Triad spell?"

The room went dead silent.

Legend held that in times of the most acute need, the Nightkeepers would gain the ability to enact a spell that would call on the gods to choose three Nightkeeper magi: the Triad. Once chosen, the three would be given the ability to channel all of their ancestors, not just the wisdom contained within the *nahwal*, but also their personalities, and, most of all, their magical talents. In the space of a single spell, three of the Nightkeepers would become superbeings. But that was the good news. The bad news was that—historically, anyway—the Triad spell had an attrition rate of two-thirds.

Only one Triad had been called previously, back at the end of the first millennium A.D., when a rogue group of Nightkeepers had splintered off, allied themselves with the king of a Mayan city-state that controlled a potent ceremonial site, and called six *Banol Kax* through the barrier to the Earth. The dark magi, who later took to calling themselves the Order of Xibalba, had wanted to control the empire; instead, unable to rein in the creatures they had summoned, they changed civilization forever. Modern archaeologists still puzzled over why the population of the Mayan empire had crashed abruptly in the late ninth century, with entire cities abandoned seemingly overnight. The theories usually touched on plague, drought, and warfare, with the artifactual evidence to back them up. But that told only a small part of the story; in the larger realm, each of those catastrophic breakdowns of civilization had been wrought by the six *Banol Kax*, which had run amok in Mesoamerica while the Nightkeepers fought to force them back to the underworld, where they belonged.

In the end, in the most extreme of exigencies, the gods had sent the Triad spell to King One-Boar, who had searched his soul . . . and enacted it. One-Boar was chosen, along with his brother, Boar Tusk, and One-Boar's only child, a girl barely out of her teens. Boar Tusk died almost instantly; One-Boar went mad from the voices inside his head . . . and the girl survived. Wielding the talents and knowledge of her forebears, she rallied the Nightkeepers and used dire magic to drive the *Banol Kax* back to Xibalba. In the aftermath, with the males of the royal branch of the peccary bloodline gone, One-Boar's daughter married into the jaguars, who became the Nightkeepers' new ruling bloodline. She ruled well, died an old woman, and time passed without a Triad . . . but a single fragmentary codex reference decreed that the Nightkeepers were supposed to call a Triad during the third year prior to the zero date. If they didn't, the end-time was screwed.

They were almost halfway through the year in question. And they didn't have the spell needed to call the Triad.

"Which means," Lucius said, making it sound like he was answering a question, though nobody had spoken, "that we need the Triad spell." He turned to Jade. "But there's a problem."

Only one? she thought, a bubble of half-hysterical laughter lodging in her throat. But she knew what he meant. "If I can reach my *nahwal* and Vennie can take over again, she could tell us how to get you back into the library, or at least where to look for information here on earth. But in order for me to reach my *nahwal*, you need to invoke the library magic so I can follow you into the barrier." Maybe. There were a lot of *if*s there.

"We sure as hell can't wait for the solstice," Strike said bluntly. He wasn't looking at Jade or Lucius, but the message was clear. What wasn't nearly so clear was what Jade's response should be.

Before, she'd volunteered for booty duty because it had seemed like her best chance of contributing, and because, well, it was Lucius they were talking about. But the sex magic had come with an unnerving level of intensity. Then there was the *nahwal*'s words, which too closely paralleled her own experiences. Vennie had urged her not to let emotion weaken her. Should she listen to the *nahwal* and focus on her own magic instead? She didn't know. And because she didn't know, she found herself far too aware of Lucius as the meeting continued. She was acutely sensitive to each of his breaths, to every shift of his body. Her peripheral vision showed the bunch and flow of muscles beneath his jeans and tee, and her mind replayed the sight of him naked against her, atop her, lit by the art of her ancestors. Although she told herself to concentrate on what was being said, she was far more aware of what was going on inside her as desire heated and built, and her body readied itself for something her mind told her she should walk away from.

But which part of her should she listen to? Did she even have a right to make a choice when so much was riding on her and Lucius's getting back into the barrier before the solstice?

The meeting lasted well past afternoon, as the magi and *winikin* brainstormed various plans to get into Xibalba and rescue Kinich Ahau, all of which hinged on the magi finding a way to get into—and, more important, back out of—the underworld. The *winikin*— including Shandi, who reappeared quietly and shook off both questions and concern—dished out pasta and drinks, and the group worked through dinner and up to the late-summer dusk, which turned the sky blood-red. Finally, Strike called it a day and dismissed the meeting, which had covered a great deal and resolved almost nothing.

The story of our lives, Jade thought as the magi and *winikin* dispersed to their rooms and tasks, very carefully not making a big deal of leaving her and Lucius alone.

When they were gone, she braced herself for Lucius's anger; she hadn't missed his tension upon learning that she'd gone into the barrier alone, without sufficient magic to get back out on her own, and hadn't told anyone. But that was her prerogative; it had been her *nah-wal*, her message. And she'd revealed it the moment it became clear that it related to Vennie and the library.

Bracing herself, she turned to him. "I didn't—" She didn't get any further; her words were muffled by his hard, solid shoulder as he hauled her into his arms. For half a second she stiffened, thinking he was presuming far too much, far too publicly. But then she realized it wasn't a sexual overture, not really.

He was, quite simply, holding her.

"I wish you'd woken me up last night and told me what was going on," he said into her hair. "I don't like thinking of you dealing with all that shit alone."

"I—" She had to swallow against an unexpected and inexplicable sob. "I had Shandi."

"Like I said. Dealing with it alone."

Finding too much comfort in the embrace, she tried to push away. "I can handle myself."

He wouldn't let her push. "I know you can. But you shouldn't always have to." He paused. "If you don't want to lean on me as your lover, lean on me as your friend. I've always been that, even when we weren't really talking to each other."

She sagged against him, defeated. "Shit. You played the friend card."

"My mama never called me stupid." He hugged her hard and eased away, so he was looking down at her when he said, "Granted, she babied me, told me I was fragile, and made me carry an inhaler I'm not sure I ever needed. Then, when my dad couldn't figure out what to do with me, sitting inside with my nose in a book, she told him I was lucky I got her brains, because my body wasn't ever going to amount to much."

Jade frowned at him, trying not to notice how right it felt to be in his loose embrace, with her half on his lap as they cuddled together on the couch, the mansion gone conveniently empty and quiet around them. "Your point?"

"Family is the luck of the draw. It might not seem fair that your *winikin* is less than warm and fuzzy, or

that after all this time you find out that your parents
were younger than you thought, and your mother
made some decisions that don't seem compatible with
the responsibilities of a mother, though that might de-
pend on your interpretation of the writs. But fair or
not, that's the family—or at least the family history—
that you've got. Question is, what are you going to do
about it?"

She broke eye contact. "I don't know. Do I have to
do anything? I am who I am, you know? Learning all
that stuff about my mother doesn't change the fact
that I'm a harvester who wears the scribe's mark but
doesn't have the talent to go with it. Except . . ." She
brought her eyes back up to his. "As I came out of the
barrier, it was like I could see the magic, the layers of it,
and the inner structure of the spell. But I haven't been
able to access the power since then. I'm sure the *nahwal*
did something to help me find a piece of my talent . . .
but what if the sex magic was part of it too?"

His eyes darkened. "I hate knowing that you got
pulled into the barrier like that."

"If we can make it happen again, I can ask her about
the library." Though the prospect was more than a little
unnerving. Like meeting her mother again for the first
time. What should she say? What would the *nahwal*
do? Could she even find her way back there? Would
it be worth it?

For the ability to do magic like the glimpse she'd
been shown . . . yes.

"I don't want any of it to happen again," Lucius
rasped, but they both knew that wasn't the right and

proper answer. "Damn it," he muttered. "This should be easier."

"We can make it be," she said firmly, though she wasn't quite so sure about that anymore.

His expression flattened for a moment, but then he nodded and rose to his feet, drawing her up with him and then stepping away. When they were standing facing each other, he held out his hand, turning it so his palm was painted bloodred by the dusk, slashed through with a shadow-scar. "Come home with me tonight?" he asked softly.

On one level, she wanted him to say something about wanting her outside of the magic and the greater good, that what was between them was real and not a by-product of the situation and the need. On another level, she was relieved that he didn't, because she wanted it too much.

She took his hand and said simply, "Yes."

Her blood burned as he led her out into the night, went to flame as they undressed each other in his cottage, staying out in the main room because bedrooms were too intimate. They left the lights off and came together in the red darkness, in a clash of lips and tongues, inciting caresses and hard, hot bodies slicked with sweat.

The sex was fast and greedy, almost animalistic. It left her limp and wrung-out, and filled with inner fire as she clung to him and tried not to need. It was amazing, staggering, mind-blowing . . . but it wasn't magic.

CHAPTER TWELVE

June 15
Two years, six months, and six days to the zero date

Patience didn't hear the king coming. Walking soft-footed on the rope sandals many of the male magi favored for at-home wear, he appeared around the corner, headed full-steam along the hallway leading to the royal quarters.

When he saw her, he stopped. "Were you looking for me?" But although his words were neutral enough, his expression was wary. He knew why she was there, all right. But how could he blame her? She wasn't just a mage. She was a mother too.

"I need to see Harry and Braden," she said without preamble. "I'll take whatever blood vows you demand. I'll make myself invisible; they won't even know I'm there. I just . . . I have to see them."

The king didn't answer for a moment, just stared into her eyes, and she fleetingly wondered whether he'd somehow gained the powers of a mind-bender, because it was almost as if he were trying to see inside her, and find . . . what? She would've given it to him if she knew what he was looking for. She'd give anything to see her babies.

"Why?" he finally asked, then clarified, "I mean, I know why you want to see them: You're their mom, and it's been more than a year, and the situation sucks royal donkey dick. I get that. I mean why now, specifically? Has something happened?"

For a half second, she wondered whether he was asking her to give him an excuse to ignore his better judgment and the council's recommendation. He'd gone against the thirteenth prophecy by taking Leah as his queen rather than sacrificing her to the gods, based on having seen her in his dreams. He believed in the power of visions, even when the mage having them wasn't a seer. If she told him she'd dreamed of the boys, and sold it hard enough, he'd give her what she wanted.

It would be a lie, though. She'd dreamed of them— of course she had; she was their *mother*, damn it. But the dreams were always normal, garden-variety agglomerations of daily experiences, vague fears, and the grind of a life that had seemed so exciting when she'd first arrived at Skywatch, but over time had become rote, routine, and so very lonely. She missed her boys, missed her *winikin*, Hannah. And she missed the man Brandt had been when his *winikin*, Woody, had been around to keep him from taking himself too seriously. Without the boys and *winikin*, she and Brandt had drifted, badly. But none of that, she knew, would be enough to sway the king.

"I'm miserable," she said simply. "I'm not sleeping, I'm not eating, and I feel like crap. Worse, my magic is for shit. I can hardly boost Brandt past a trickle anymore, and vice versa." She paused hopefully, but Strike's face had gone neutral. She continued. "I tried antidepressants, but they killed what was left of my powers, which is no good. I've talked to Jade in therapist mode; I changed my diet, worked out, used the shooting range, practiced a shit-ton of hand-to-hand, had sex with my husband . . . all the tricks she suggested to break out of depression. And maybe they helped for a little bit, but not long. I want, I *need*, to see my boys. Please. I'm begging you. Just tell me where they are, or have Hannah and Woody bring them someplace random, where nobody would think to look. I just want to see them. Then I'll be okay. I'm sure of it."

The king didn't say anything for a long moment. Then he said simply, "Is your own happiness worth their lives?"

The oxygen vacated Patience's lungs, leaving her trying to breathe around an empty space in her chest. She'd thought she'd braced herself for the question. She'd been wrong. Somehow, hearing it in Brandt's too-reasonable, too-serious tones had just put her back up and made her think, *You're wrong; it's not like that. It's not an either/or question.* But somehow, facing her king, she couldn't be so sure.

Still, she pushed onward. "There's been no sign of

Iago in months; he's either dead or he's trying to assimilate Moctezuma's spirit. With him out of commission, the Xibalbans haven't done a damn thing. For all we know, all of the red-robes died in Paxil Mountain when Michael unleashed his death magic. If that's the case, then it's a good bet the gray-robes have disbanded, or at the very least that they're disorganized and blind without their magic users. Given that, don't you think we could come up with a safe way for me to see the twins?" *Or, even better, bring them home*? She didn't say that last part, though. One important lesson she'd learned over the past two years was that in some wars it was possible to fight only one battle at a time. Looking at the whole thing at once was too damned daunting.

"Even if Iago and the Xibalbans are out of the picture for the moment—and I'm not convinced they are—then we still have the *Banol Kax* to consider," Strike pointed out.

Her pulse sped up a notch. "I *am* considering them. That's why I need to do this now. The *Banol Kax* haven't been able to reach the earth plane recently because Iago closed the hellroad and hid it in the barrier, right? That should mean they can't perceive us up here, that they don't know what's going on. If Lucius manages to find the hellroad and we get it open to rescue the sun god, there's no guarantee we'll be able to close it again. So I need to do this now, before we make any sort of move on the hellmouth."

"Damn it, Patience." The angry words came not from the king, but from behind her. In her husband's voice. "I thought we agreed to wait on this . . . and to put it in front of the royal council, officially, and *together*."

She closed her eyes on a spasm of the grinding, wrenching, nausea-inducing pain in her stomach that made her want to cross her arms over herself and moan. She didn't, though, because that would accomplish exactly nothing. Back during the early days of their marriage, Brandt had loved it when she played girl and leaned on him, needed him. These days, though, he took any sign of weakness as an excuse to take over and start making unilateral decisions, pushing her aside.

She didn't know if his Borg-like assimilation into the Nightkeeper ways was what had caused him to put his responsibilities to his family behind his duties to the magi and the end-time war, as demanded by the writs. Maybe the magic itself had changed him, making him harder and uncompromising, or maybe he'd always been that way and she hadn't noticed because their needs had coincided rather than clashed. Whatever the cause, the small disagreements had snowballed, then avalanched, until she barely knew him anymore.

"*You* agreed to that. I just didn't argue," she said softly, still facing away from him. Then, avoiding Strike's eyes because she didn't want to see the sympathy she knew was in his expression, she turned to face her husband. Her heart clutched a little at the frustrated anger in his gorgeous brown eyes and model-perfect face, the lines of tension in his big body.

Despite everything they'd been through lately, she

still felt a gut-deep kick of desire, and heard a faint, egotistical whisper of, *The other girls can eat their hearts out. He's mine.* That was pretty much the first thing she'd said to him six years earlier, when she'd awakened beside him in a Cancún hotel room in the midst of spring break. Her brain had been full of disconnected images of the previous night's hard partying, her bed had been full of gorgeous guy, and both their forearms had been marked with what they had thought at the time were tattoos of Mayan glyphs, but had later proved to be so much more. It was that *more* that was screwing them up now, she thought. Or maybe they'd been doomed from the start, and it'd taken them this long to figure it out.

She waited for his eyes to soften, waited to see some of the old wonder in them, the look that had made her believe he was just as awed as she was by what they'd found. But he stayed annoyed. More than that, he looked hurt, which was ridiculous. He'd been the first one to suggest sending the twins away, after all. She'd initially believed it had been Strike's idea, but Brandt had later confessed that it had been his. He might've thought knowing that would help her resign herself to the separation. He'd been wrong.

Looking past her, he said to Strike, "Sorry. I thought we'd settled this."

"Don't apologize for me," she snapped, anger rising. "You don't own me, and you don't speak for me."

"Clearly." He moved up beside her, still looking at Strike. That forced her to turn, as well, so she and Brandt wound up standing shoulder-to-shoulder, facing their king. But although the shift created an illusion of their joining forces against a common enemy, she knew that was far from the case. She was on her own in this one, not part of a team anymore.

"I want to hook you up and let you visit," Strike said. "And gods know I'd love to bring them back here, not just for you guys, but so Hannah and Woody could come back, too, and because we all enjoyed having the kids around. But at the same time, I'm not willing to bet that the Xibalbans are out of the equation, not the way you're proposing. Similarly, I can't rule out the *Banol Kax*. They don't seem to be able to get through the barrier right now . . . but is that a reality, or is that what they want us to think? Not to mention that they may still be able to punch through the barrier to create an *ajaw-makol*, even if they're unable to pass through themselves."

Patience gave him credit for talking to her rather than Brandt. She probably shouldn't have been mildly surprised—Strike was gender-blind when it came to warrior stuff, assigning duties based on skill rather than sex. And she had a feeling that Leah had likely cured him of any residual chauvinism that might have come from his being raised in the human environment, by a royal *winikin* who was firmly entrenched in the Nightkeepers' patriarchal, male-dominated society. The queen had managed to maintain her individuality without losing her mate's regard. Patience envied that.

"I know it's a risk," she said now, softly, "but aren't we all taking calculated risks these days? And let's be honest—we may not have lost the war yet, but we're not winning it yet, either." She took a deep breath, only to find that the air carried a hint of the aftershave she'd bought her husband for the *wayeb* festival—the Nightkeepers' nod at a Christmas-type holiday. Not letting herself dwell on the scent, or the low churn it brought to her midsection, she said, "I don't know whether we're going to win or lose this war, but either way, I know for certain that I don't want to spend my next— maybe my last—two and a half years separated from my sons. I've already lost a year with them. I'm asking you . . . I'm begging you. Let me at least see them. Just a glimpse. That's all."

She paused. To her astonishment, Brandt reached over and took her hand, squeezing tightly. She thought his fingers might even have trembled a little, letting her know that he cared far more than she'd realized. Tears stung her eyes, but she wouldn't let them fall. She was a warrior, after all.

Sighing heavily, Strike shook his head. "I hope you both know how much I wish I could authorize a visit. The council has brainstormed some options, even, but we just can't see a way to absolutely protect Harry and Braden while giving you access. They don't have their bloodline marks and they're not connected to the barrier. Which means that as long as we don't contact them, and vice versa, there's no way for the Xibalbans or *Banol Kax* to find them. They're absolutely safe." The king paused, looking suddenly far older than his thirtysomething years. "This is one of those times when I have to be the bad guy. As much as I understand how awful this is for you, I have to do what I think is best."

Patience's mouth dried to dust, and dull anger kindled in her chest, making it hard to breathe. "You have *no idea* what I'm going through. None of you do. Or have you lost track of the fact that Brandt and I are the only ones here who are actually married, not just *jun tan* mates, and we're the only ones who are parents?"

"The *winikin*—" Strike began.

"The *winikin* raised us, but they're not our parents. There's a difference."

"Not to some of them, there isn't." But Strike didn't meet her eyes. "I'm sorry. I'm not going to tell you where they are, and I'm not going to arrange a meeting, or even an invisibility-cloaked look-see. I want you to stay away from them. Let Hannah and Woody do their jobs while you do yours." He fixed her with a stern look and reached for his belt, where he wore his father's ceremonial knife. "I want you to swear to me, on your—"

The normal-size door inset into the heavily carved ceremonial panels guarding the royal suite swung open and Leah stuck her head through, interrupting with, "There you are! Hurry up, will you?"

Strike broke off and swung around. "Did you get Anna on the line?"

"Yeah, but she's trying to escape. Better move your fine ass." Leah's attention shifted from Strike to the others. "Unless you're busy?"

"We're done here," Strike said, thoroughly distracted now. Brows furrowed, expression suggesting he viewed the upcoming convo with his sister with both anticipation and dread, he turned back, reached out, and gripped Patience's shoulder. "I'm sorry," he said for the second—or was it the third?—time. "Be strong and do your best. That's all any of us can do." Then, shooting Brandt what she strongly suspected was a mated man's look of commiseration, the king turned on his heel and beat it for the royal suite. Moments later, the door swung shut at his back, leaving Patience and Brandt out in the hall. Together. Alone.

Before, what seemed like an eternity ago but had been only a couple of years, they might have taken the opportunity to sneak a few kisses, maybe more. Now, although Brandt kept hold of her hand, he scowled down at her. "What the hell was that?"

She bristled. "Excuse me?"

"Please. You know damn well you agreed to hold off on talking to the king." But his eyes softened and he caught her other hand, holding her still when she would've shifted away. "We're on the same side here, sweetheart. I want what you want."

I thought you did, once, but I feel like I don't know you anymore. I knew Brandt the man, not the White-Eagle mage. The man had loved their sons to the exclusion of everything else except her. The four of them had been a unit, a family. But he'd changed since their arrival at Skywatch, which had been followed by the revelation that they'd both been hiding their true natures, pretending to be human when their respective godparents—aka *winikin*—had raised them to be more. He was harder now, and had lost the playfulness she'd loved about him. And his sense of humor wasn't the only thing that had disappeared; so had her belief that he put his family first, no matter what.

Even now, as he looked at her, those damned gorgeous brown eyes were pleading with her to play by the rules, to be part of the team. As far as she could tell, that was the deal. If she behaved herself and bought into the king's paradigm, Brandt would be the guy he used to be. She'd seen flashes of that man even recently, though he seemed buried beneath the stifling weight of tradition, responsibility, and Brandt's unwavering belief that the king's word was law . . . to the point that she sometimes wondered whether he was using that paradigm to hide something else. More secrets.

She thought she saw a hint of those secrets now, as she looked into his eyes and tried to find the frat rat she'd met on spring break, the architecture student she'd married, or the man who'd been beside her as she'd given birth to the twins. When she couldn't find any of those safe, familiar incarnations of her husband, she gently drew her hands from his. "I'm sorry I disappointed you." Rising up on her tiptoes, she brushed her lips against his and felt tears sting as the familiar heat rose at the touch, then subsided when she eased away. "I've gotta go . . . you know. Do something." She made a vague gesture in the direction of the main mansion and fled, afraid that if she said what was in her heart, she'd make things between them far worse than they already were.

*   *   *

Jade pushed through the keypadded archive door near midafternoon. Although she had headed for the archive intending to run some additional searches on the star bloodline, once she was there, she found that she wasn't in the mood for research. She was restless and churned up. Edgy. Unsatisfied.

She prowled the outer room of the three-room archive, which boasted book-filled shelves on every available inch of wall space and a trio of computer workstations on one side of the open space. On the other side was a conference table where Jade—or, less frequently now, one of the others—could spread out and work. The color scheme was neutral, and the decor leaned heavily on functionality rather than beauty. The general consensus among the Nightkeepers and *winikin* was that the archive was boring and could use a facelift. Jade, though, had refused to change things around. What the others found boring, she found peaceful.

At least, she usually did. Today she found it annoying.

There wasn't even anything particularly wrong to put her in a snippy mood, either; at least, nothing new. That was the problem, though—she *wanted* to be somewhere new, wanted to do a different job. But what? She didn't want to be stuck in the archive, didn't want to be on the front lines. The work of a spell-casting scribe would be ideal . . . if she could figure out how the heck to use her talent. Sex magic apparently wasn't the answer. So what was?

Scowling, she picked up the spell book she thought of as the *Idiot's Guide to Nightkeeper Magic*: the one the prepubescent mage children had used to learn their magic in the years between their toddler-age bloodline ceremonies and their pubertal talent ceremonies. This particular copy was worn and smudged, and as she unfolded a dog-ear, her heart ached at the thought of the mage child who had marked the page, which was at the end of the last chapter, where the kids got their intro to the most basic of talent-level spells.

Always before, she'd focused her research farther back in time, trying to understand what was happening now based on what had happened hundreds, sometimes thousands of years ago. Now, though, her head filled with thoughts of the generation before hers. Had her mother touched this book? Her father? Had they been in class together, pretended not to look at each other? She could even picture them playing eye tag now, because that morning, when she had walk-of-shamed it—though technically she supposed there was zero shame involved—back to her suite from Lucius's cottage, she had found an envelope slipped beneath her door. She had guessed what it would contain, and had opened it knowing it would only make some things harder than they already were. Sure enough, Shandi had left photographs of her mother and father, both separate and together.

Her father, Joshua, had been tall and broad shouldered, though he hadn't filled out yet to the brawn of the typical full-blood. His face had been soft and sweet, especially in the pictures where he and Vennie had posed together. In those photos, though, he all but disappeared into the background, eclipsed by Vennie's bright, sharp effervescence. Jade had suffered a pang at the thought of that shining, vivid teen reduced to a desiccated corpse in the library, a *nahwal* in the barrier. A second pang had come when she'd reached the bottom of the stack and found several pictures that had included not just Joshua and Vennie, but also a dark-haired, scowling baby who always seemed to be waving clenched fists in the air. Oddly, Jade had felt the least connected to that baby, who looked like she was ready to fight the world.

Now, she traced a finger over the glyph string of the fireball spell and its phonetic translation below, and deliberately turned her mind away from her parents. Instead, she imagined a rawboned, overlarge puppy of a boy, poring over the spell book she held, looking for his first taste of the loud, fiery destruction that fascinated men of all ages. Or maybe it had been a girl of eleven or twelve, a little rash, a little vain, daydreaming about becoming a warrior and making a difference. The children wouldn't have been able to actually enact the spell, of course; fireball magic was reserved for those with the warrior's mark. But they would have practiced, just in case. Talent sometimes broke through on its own schedule, after all.

Telling herself she was just practicing her translations, Jade ignored the phonetics and read the simple spell straight from the glyph string, using the techniques Anna had taught her at the university.

Nothing happened.

It wasn't until disappointment spun through her

that she admitted she'd been hoping for . . . what? She wasn't a warrior. She was a scribe.

"At least, I'm supposed to be," she muttered, dropping the book on the conference table and spinning to pace the suddenly small-feeling room. She forced herself to bypass the keypadded door that led to the second room of the archive, where the more valuable artifacts were tagged and stored under ruthless climate control, and from there to the inner archive, where the writs were displayed on the walls as a tangible reminder of a Nightkeeper's duties and responsibilities. But it wasn't the writs that drew her thoughts to the small sacred room. "Damn it, Lucius." It was his fault she was so edgy, his fault she couldn't settle to the work that usually soothed her.

Okay, that wasn't strictly true either. He hadn't done anything wrong; *she* had, or was in the process of doing so—getting in over her head when she *knew* better, damn it.

"You're sleeping with him."

For half a second, Jade thought that had come from her own subconscious, but her inner monologue had never achieved a tone of such frosty disapproval. Bracing herself against a fleeting wish that she'd locked the door, she turned and nodded to Shandi. "Good morning to you too."

The *winikin* marched in, leaned back against the conference table, folded her arms, and scowled. "Don't change the subject. You're sleeping with him, as in, not just the once. You stayed with him last night."

Jade just stared at her for a second. "Do you seriously want to do this?"

The *winikin* waited her out.

I don't answer to you. You're not my keeper. But that was the human viewpoint, wasn't it? The same wasn't strictly true within the Nightkeeper mores. The *winikin* didn't just serve and protect their Nightkeeper charges; they were also responsible for their morality and service to their bloodline duties. Granted, there wasn't any sort of formal repercussion for a Nightkeeper who ignored, disobeyed, or otherwise pissed off her *winikin* . . . but social pressure could be a real bitch.

Breathing through her nose to stem the knee-jerk irritation that came as much from her own frustration as from Shandi, Jade said, "Last night was an experiment. We needed to see whether the sex would trigger the Prophet's magic." She paused. "Either that wasn't the actual trigger, which doesn't make sense, given the sequence of events, or the sex magic needed the boost of the new moon we had the other night . . . which by extension would mean we can't use sex magic to put him into the library again until the solstice, which will be too late to help Kinich Ahau."

Shandi's frown went from a full-on scowl to a thoughtful expression. "If we've worked out the time line correctly, which I think we have, then Vennie made the transition into and out of the library at least twice over the seventy-two hours leading up to the summer solstice of 'eighty-four. Those weren't days of barrier activity, which means there's got to be another way to trigger the magic."

"She used her mage talent. He's not a mage."

Unfortunately, that brought Shandi full circle and had her eyes narrowing. "No, he's not. Yet you've taken him as your lover again, despite what the *nahwal* told you. Have you thought about what this could do to your magic?"

What magic? Jade wanted to ask, but didn't, because it would disrespect both of them, not to mention the harvester bloodline. It wasn't anybody's fault but her own that she couldn't figure out how to be a true scribe. And besides, that wasn't what this fight was about. "You mean because he's human, and Vennie found that her powers dropped to match those of a harvester after she and Joshua were married." Somehow it was easier to call them by their first names. "But if you're saying that my powers are going to drop to those of a human—i.e., none—then you're assuming that Lucius and I will become a mated pair. Do you really believe that was the gods' intention?"

"I don't believe your parents were destined mates, yet they wound up wearing the *jun tan*, and Vennie believed that her magic had decreased to that of a harvester. Are you willing to risk losing yours entirely?"

"Lucius can't form the *jun tan*; he wears the hell-mark." Which was too easy an answer, given that Sasha and Michael were clearly mates despite their lack of the formal mark. Jade exhaled, shaking her head. "We're not lovers. We're just enjoying each other." But the words caught a little in her throat and she felt a stir of the panic that had driven her to the archive and had her pacing rather than working.

Last night might've started hard and fast on the TV room floor, but after that first time, when it had become clear that the sex magic wasn't theirs to invoke at will, they had transitioned to the bedroom without her even realizing that the decision had been made and acted on. There, the *get off and get gone* sex had morphed to soft touches and sighs, and slow, easy lovemaking that had gone way further than she'd meant to let it go. Then, this morning, she'd woken up curled against him, her hand over his heart, their legs twined together beneath the earth-toned quilt. More, where she'd expected the morning-after conversation to be uncomfortable, as both of them acknowledged they'd gotten in deeper than they'd meant to, and needed to pull it back, he'd been pure relaxed, satisfied male as he burned toast and made bad coffee wearing nothing but jeans and a smile.

She'd kept waiting for him to say something about how intense things had gotten. He didn't. He'd just given her a friendly kiss and a, "Later," on her way out the door, like they were just friends sharing damn good sex.

It was what she had wanted, what she had insisted on. So why did it make her want to scream?

"I've never before seen you 'enjoy yourself' with a man who didn't make sense in the context of your life," Shandi pointed out. "This one doesn't. He's different."

That startled a strangled laugh out of Jade. "*Everything's* different. *I'm* different."

"No, you're not. People don't change, not that way. You're just confused."

"You can say that again." Jade realized she was back to pacing , made herself stop. Leaning back against the conference table beside her *winikin*, she scrubbed both hands across her face and let out a sigh. "It's like there are two different people inside me. One wants to be a good girl, quiet and obedient, the perfect harvester. The other just wants to make noise and blow shit up."

"It wasn't arbitrary that some bloodlines intermingled and some didn't. There are traits that just don't mix well."

"No kidding. I think I'm starting to get an idea of what Rabbit's going through."

"*Don't* say that." Shandi gripped Jade's wrists and yanked her hands down from where she'd been rubbing her eyes, trying to massage the encroaching headache away. "You're a full-blood. Be proud of that if you're proud of nothing else the harvesters have to offer."

Jade stared at the raw, naked emotion on the face of a woman who didn't do emotion, and her inner counselor suddenly spoke up when it had gone silent over the time away from her old world. *Here's the way in*, her instincts chimed. *Follow it if you want to know her inner truth.* She hesitated fractionally, wondering whether she really wanted to know, or if it would be better to let the *winikin* have her privacy. The Skywatch community was too small for everyone to be tangled in one another's business. But then again, this wasn't just business. It was her life. She and Shandi were linked, despite whether either of them was happy with the pairing.

Jade shifted within the *winikin*'s grip, until they were holding hands in a rare moment of physical contact. "Listen to me, and please believe me. I'm proud of being a harvester. That's one of my biggest problems right now. I feel like I should be doing more—my *nahwal* is telling me to be more, for gods' sake—but I know that's not the harvester way. It's because of my respect for the bloodline, and for you, that I'm all screwed up right now." At least in part. Great sex, a guy who was sticking to the friends-with-benefits arrangement she'd demanded, and the threat of her inner Edda weren't helping. But the *winikin*'s stricken expression didn't ease, even with the reassurance. Confused, Jade gave their joined hands a shake. "What is it? What's wrong?"

The *winikin*'s voice broke. "Yesterday . . . all that talk about the day of the massacre brought it back. Not that it's ever far away, but it was suddenly right *there*. They were there again, beside me, inside me. They're why I need . . . I need you to be perfect. I need to know it was worth it."

Jade nearly recoiled from the pleading in the older woman's face. *I can't be perfect. Nobody can!* But the counselor in her set that aside, pushed it deep beneath the shell, and said, "You need to know that *what* was worth it?"

Shandi's eyes were wide and stark, not seeing the archive anymore. "Letting my husband and son die."

"Your—" Jade's breath left her in a rush. "Oh, Shandi." Her heart twisted, shuddering in her chest. "Oh, gods." *Oh, shit.*

The *winikin* chosen for binding to Nightkeeper children typically didn't marry or have children of their own, as their first and foremost priority had to be their charges. There had been exceptions, of course, but those families had, of necessity, been loosely knit, with the children often raised crèche-style in extended networks of relatives. The system had evolved over generations and had been part of the fabric of Nightkeeper-*winikin* life. The chosen *winikin* focused on their charges; the unchosen fell in love, got married, and had families.

Unless an unchosen *winikin* was somehow picked by the gods to serve in a role she hadn't planned for, hadn't been prepared for. *Oh, Shandi.*

"Denis and little Samxel," the *winikin* said, pronouncing the "x" with the "sh" sound it took in the old language. "On the night of the attack, Denny went with the king, along with all the other unchosen adults, the fighting-age magi, and their chosen *winikin*. I stayed behind with you. Samxel was there too, dancing with the other children in the middle of the rec room. He was ten, not old enough to fight, thank the gods. Or so I thought. In the end, it didn't make a difference." A tear tracked down her cheek. "They were playing a Michael Jackson song and trying to moonwalk when the first *boluntiku* broke through the wards and attacked the great hall. Dozens were dead within the first few seconds. There was blood everywhere, children screaming. It was . . . it was chaos. Hell on earth."

You don't have to tell me if it hurts too much, Jade wanted to say, but what she would've really meant was, *I don't want to hear this,* so she said nothing. She just held on to Shandi's hands while the other woman broke into harsh, ugly sobs that rattled in her chest. "You were in one direction, Samxel in the other. I started to go after him; gods help me, I did. But then my marks started burning. I looked down and saw them disappearing, one after the other, doing this crazy vanishing act right in front of my eyes. The harvesters were among the last to die, of course, because they were in the rear guard. But they died. All of them, except you."

Back in the day, each chosen *winikin* had worn, in addition to the *aj-winikin* glyph of service, row upon row of small bloodline marks denoting the individual members of their bound bloodline. The night of the massacre, the loss of those marks had warned the *winikin* that the attack was a disaster, the Nightkeepers dying. That warning had preceded the attack on Skywatch by mere seconds. Now, most of the surviving *winikin* had only the single bloodline glyph of his or her lone charge.

Shandi continued: "When I saw that, I knew Denny was gone too. He would've been right near the harvesters in the ranks with the other unbound *winikin*. I looked for Samxel, but I couldn't see him anymore. The children were screaming, crying. Some of the older boys were trying to get through the doors to fight, and there were *boluntiku* everywhere. I couldn't see him. . . ." Her face shone now with tears. "I tried to get down there, but my legs wouldn't work. My arm was burning. I only had one bloodline mark left, but it was flaring, throbbing, not letting me go get my baby. It was the magic, you see. It wouldn't let me go to Samxel because you were my charge, my first and only priority. It made me go get you first." There was bitterness now in her voice and her eyes. "So I went. You were in the nursery zone, surrounded by a sound barrier that kept the music from disturbing the youngest ones. I grabbed you and started running for the dance floor, screaming Samxel's name. Then the next thing I knew, I was outside, headed for the garage. It was the magic again. It made me get you out rather than go back for him." She stopped and pulled her hands from Jade's, not in an angry gesture, but so she could mop her face with her sleeves. Her words were muffled behind the cloth as she said, "I would've tried to go back in, but I knew. Somehow I knew he was gone." She lifted a shoulder. "A mother's instincts, I guess. Or maybe I needed to believe he was dead so I could do my duty by you."

And that was what she had always been to her *winikin*, Jade realized. Duty, pure and simple. More than even she'd realized, raising her had been Shandi's job. The knowledge bit with sharp, greedy teeth, but she said only, "I'm sorry, Shandi. I'm so sorry."

"We might have gotten away," the *winikin* said softly. "Only the chosen were marked with the *aj-winikin*; the unchosen weren't marked at all. If I hadn't been chosen, the *boluntiku* wouldn't have been able to track us through the magic. Maybe Denny and I would've even taken Samxel and slipped away before the attack; who knows?"

"Did other unchosen do that?" Were there others out there, unmarked and anonymous?

"Maybe. I don't know. I'm not sure I even care at this point—they're gone, just like everyone else." Shandi shook her head, blinking tear-drenched eyes. In their depths, though, Jade saw the *winikin*'s habitual hardness coming back into focus. The starch—bitterness? resentment?—was back in her voice when she said, "That's why I'm not like the other *winikin*, why I couldn't ever love you the way you wanted me to. Loving you would've been giving in to the magic that bound me to you and forced me to save you rather than Denny and Samxel. So there you have it, the truth. Are you happy now?"

It was one thing, Jade found, to think that the woman who raised her had never loved her. It was another to have it confirmed flat-out. Breathing shallowly past the hurt, she said, "It explains some things. But does it make me happy? Hell, no. There's nothing good about that, nothing fair."

Shandi sniffed. "Life's not fair."

Jade found the ghost of a smile. "That was the first thing the Vennie *nahwal* said to me. 'Life's not fair, child,' she said." And then everything had started to change for her. Or had things been shifting around her for weeks before that? Months even? Where did the old Jade end and the new one begin? Or, hell, was she even changing at all? What had happened to the whole "people don't change" thing? What if she was just deluding herself into thinking she'd begun to evolve? *Gods.* This was at once too much for her to bear, and not enough for her to believe in.

Wrenching her mind back to the conversation, she

said, "If life were fair, you wouldn't have been tagged with the *aj-winikin* glyph, and both our lives would've been different." This time, hers was the voice carrying a slash of bitterness. Who would she have been, she wondered, if she'd grown up with a loving, supportive *winikin* like Jox or Izzy?

Shandi made a sour face. "Don't be so sure about that. I deliberately tanked the psych profile."

"You . . ." Jade trailed off, gaping. "During the *winikin* testing? But why? What about the three 'D's?" Being chosen had been the ultimate honor in *winikin* society. She couldn't picture Shandi turning that down. She just couldn't.

The *winikin* smiled with faint wistfulness, and her voice was soft with memory when she said, "I'd only known Denny for a couple of months when I went for testing, but I already knew he was the one. I tanked my chance to become a *winikin* because I wanted to be with him instead. In the end, though, the gods and destiny got their way." She sniffed again, and blotted at her now-dry face with jerky motions. "That was far more than I meant to tell you, but maybe it's good that you know why I've pushed you to be the best harvester you can be. That's . . . It's the only way I can justify what happened, the only way I can see to make their deaths mean something on a personal level. For you to be what you were meant to be, what you were born to be."

Jade sank back against the conference table, staring at the walls of books. Her thoughts coiled around another of those truisms she'd learned over the years:

Love could make a woman defy her own nature. More, the loss of love was a terrible thing. But she said, "You can't put that on me."

"I already did. I've been putting it on you your entire life."

"Okay, then let me rephrase: I won't let you put that on me, not anymore. I want to be a good harvester, but I also want to be the best mage I can be, the mage the Nightkeepers need me to be right now. If that means going beyond the restrictions of a harvester, then so be it."

"But you *are* a harvester."

Thinking of the Vennie *nahwal*, Jade lifted her chin. "I'm half star."

"That's not the way it works."

"Maybe not before. But what if it's time to change the rules?" Strike had said something similar to her the night of the new moon, she remembered. He'd said that the modern magi sometimes had to make their own choices, their own rules.

So then why did it suddenly seem like a revelation?

Shandi pushed away from the table, her face setting once again in the fallback expression of peaceful calm that hid so much. "The rules are the rules. If you try to defy or avoid them, you'll pay for it one way or the other, just like I did." She headed for the door stiff-shouldered, turning back at the threshold to pin Jade with a look. "I lost my entire world because I tried to have a love outside my gods-determined destiny. Your mother lost her life doing the same thing, and your father died thinking she'd abandoned him. Who are you to think you can do better?"

"I don't know who I am," Jade snapped. "All I know is that the person you want me to be isn't all there is."

Shandi bared her teeth. "That sounds like something *she* would have said."

"I—" *Shit.* Jade's stomach roiled. Pressing her lips together, she shook her head. "I don't want to fight with you."

"But you don't want to follow my advice either."

"Which is what, exactly? What would it take to make you happy?"

The *winikin* took a long, hard look at her. Then she just shook her head and walked away, pushing through the door without another word. The message was clear, though: *Nothing you could do would make me love you, because you'll always be second-best.*

CHAPTER THIRTEEN

Shandi's rejection was an almost physical slap, one that left Jade pressing a hand to her lurching stomach as the door swung shut at the *winikin*'s back. Gods, she hated fighting. And if more than once along the line she'd thought she could deal with Shandi if she only knew what the *winikin*'s problem was, she'd been way off on that one. Knowing the *winikin*'s history only made things worse by slapping her upside the head with the reality she'd long avoided: Her *winikin* didn't just not love her; she actively resented her, and blamed her—rightly or not—for the deaths of the people she *had* loved.

And oh, holy hell, that sucked.

"It wasn't my fault," Jade whispered, finding a kernel of frustration amidst the sickening dismay. "I didn't pick her as my *winikin*, and I didn't force her to choose me over them. The magic might have, but I'm not the magic. I shouldn't be blamed for it." Unfortunately, knowing that she had a valid point didn't do anything to smooth over the raw, ragged edges.

The counselor's cool was long gone. Jade took brief satisfaction in imagining a cartoon version of herself, red faced, with steam coming out of her ears, but that was still a woefully inadequate outlet for the churned-up feelings inside her. For the first time since completing the rudimentary firearms training course all the magi had gone through when they had first come to Skywatch, she was tempted to head down to the firing range and shoot the crap out of some targets. She hadn't been all that great a shot, but a pump-action shotgun loaded with jadeshot required approximately the finesse of spray paint. Point and shoot she could do, she thought, as long as she didn't try one of Michael's advanced training runs, which featured moving targets and good guys standing next to bad. Bull's-eyes she could handle. She would go shoot some stationary targets. That'd make her feel better, she thought, or at least allow her to burn off some steam.

Pleased to have a plan of sorts, even one that was uncharacteristically violent, she made a quick circuit of the archive to put away the few things that were out of place. She was suddenly buzzed to get going; she wanted the thud of recoil, the tearing of paper targets. Hurrying now, her skull throbbing with a headache that was rapidly turning to a rattling, humming whine, she reached to grab the *Idiot's Guide*, which lay on the conference table where she had dropped it.

It was still open to the fireball spell. Her eyes skimmed over the glyphs as she moved to shut the book. And she froze.

On the page, the glyphs began to glow, radiating off

the page and drifting toward her, outlined not in ink, but in bright red-gold fluorescence against a sudden backdrop of blurred images. She gaped as two of the glyphs shimmered and morphed, becoming entirely different syllables in the phonetic system. The humming whine became a song, and the buzz of anger in her blood suddenly felt like . . . *magic*.

Abruptly, the red-gold, almost holographic writing flared brightly, then disappeared, but the afterimage stayed imprinted in her brain. The air had gone strangely cold.

She mouthed the syllables and felt something wrench inside her. A tingling sensation flared from her center to her extremities and then reversed course, fleeing back up her arms and into her body, leaving her chilled. Breathing hard, unable to get enough oxygen, she looked around wildly, but nothing had changed in the shelf-lined room. Nothing but the syllables that danced in her mind's eye. Cool heat spun inside her; the spell hovered at the edges of her mind, tempting her. Daring her. Mad euphoria gripped her as something deep inside whispered, *Try it. What have you got to lose?*

Leaving the book where it lay, she held her lightly scarred palms out in front of her, making it look as if she were cupping an imaginary basketball, as she'd seen the warriors do when she'd watched them practice their fighting magic and pretended she didn't mind being on the sidelines. Then, halfway convinced that nothing at all was going to happen, she tipped her head back, closed her eyes, and recited the spell aloud.

Magic detonated within her, ripping a scream from her throat, more from surprise than pain. The air shimmered between her outstretched hands, and then blinding blue-white flashed simultaneously with a crackling roar that was like being inside a clap of thunder. On the heels of the flash-boom, a shock wave hammered away from her, sending her staggering back as the archive door *exploded*. Cold seared across her skin, a frigidity so intense that she couldn't tell if it was fire or ice; she knew only that it burned. She heard crashes and shouts in the hallway and main mansion, then a second huge detonation that rocked the whole damn building, even the reinforced security of the archive.

As quickly as it had come, the magic drained from her in a rush. The noise quieted. Or rather, the noise of the immediate destruction died down, to be replaced with shouts of alarm and tersely snapped orders as the warriors prepared to man a defense.

Oh, shit, Jade thought on a spurt of horrified adrenaline. *They think we're under attack!* She had to get out there and explain, but she couldn't move. She was frozen in place, not by the magic or shock now, but by the sight of the crazy, misplaced winter wonderland that surrounded her.

She hadn't created a fireball. She had summoned ice.

The walls, floor, ceiling, bookcases, and every other damn thing that had been to the sides or behind her when she'd recited the spell were covered in a thick layer of furry white frost, as though the whole room had been stuck in a giant freezer that had missed out

on the past fifty years of frost-free technology. In front
of her, where her inadvertent and out-of-control . . . iceball, she supposed, had exploded away from her, the
door was gone, along with most of the wall. In their
place were sheets of ice and drifts of frosty snow that extended far out into the hallway. The opposite wall was
frost-crazed, the windows cracked from the quick war
between the heat outside and the insta-freeze within.
And, as far as she could tell, the snow and ice kept going on down the hallway. She was pretty sure that last
big detonation had come from the great room.

"Oh, gods," she moaned. What if she had hurt someone? Yanking herself from her paralysis, she bolted
out of the archive, slipped on a wide patch of ice just
outside the door, and went down on her knees. Water
soaked through her jeans almost immediately; the frost
layer was already melting, saturating the walls and
floor and dripping from the ceiling.

"Jade!" It was Sasha's voice, relieved. Armed with
a submachine gun she held with easy familiarity, she
was partway up the hall, slipping and slithering as she
followed the ice trail to its source. "What happened?
Was it Iago?"

Jade's legs gave out on her at that, and she found
herself sitting in a puddle of meltwater, gaping as the
Nightkeepers charged up the hallway toward her, most
of them armed, all of them coming to defend Skywatch
against . . . her. She started to laugh, tried to swallow
it, and ended up emitting a ridiculous hiccup that had
Sasha's expression going to one of pure worry.

Before her friend could go into healer mode, Jade

waved to fend her off. "No, I'm fine, really. Better than fine. I'm sorry about the door, though. And the walls. And the windows." She looked around her at the growing melt, cringing at the destruction, then, when she remembered what the archive had looked like, wailed, "And the books!" They were all scanned into the digital system, but still.

"*Jade!*" Michael gripped her shoulder and gave her a none-too-gentle shake. "Was Iago here? Did something happen with one of the artifacts?"

"No." The hysterical laughter threatened to burble up again. "Something happened with *me*. I did it, all of it. I finally wrote a spell. Or manipulated it, at least." As she watched, a huge blob of slush let go of the ceiling and fell down the back of Michael's neck.

"Gah!" He straightened abruptly, pawing at his nape, then scowled when the others laughed at him. He glared around. "Can we get out of here and continue this someplace *dry*?"

"I'd suggest the great room," a new voice broke in, "but the furniture's gone . . . along with most of the floor, and what looks like part of the gym downstairs." Strike made his way through the crowd. Dressed in full black-on-black combat gear and wearing a loaded weapons belt, he was even more intimidating than usual. He glared around, not immediately locking on Jade. "What in the *hell* is going on here? We have rules about experimenting, you know. As in *fucking don't* unless you're in the training hall, where you can't destroy too much expensive stuff."

Jade closed her eyes as her brief amusement fled.

She was starting to shake now, with a combination of reaction and what she suspected was going to be a hell of a postmagic crash. "I did it. It was all my fault. I was looking at the fireball spell in the *Idiot's Guide*, and it morphed into something else in front of my eyes. I recited what I saw and . . ." She trailed off, opened her eyes, and looked around, seeing a few faces missing. Including Lucius's and Shandi's. Fresh worry clutched at her. "Did I hurt anyone?"

The king shook his head. "We got lucky." From the sudden satisfied glint in his eyes, she got the feeling he wasn't entirely unhappy with what had just happened. He reached down and, before she knew what was happening, he had hauled her vertical and was leading her along the hallway, where their feet squished on the meltwater-soaked runner. "The great room was empty. Jox was in the kitchen, but he ducked behind the breakfast bar when the leading edge hit. The power was dissipating as it came, so by the time it reached the kitchen it was down to a spring frost and a couple inches of snow."

That dry rundown didn't even come close to prepping Jade for the sight that confronted her when she stepped through the arched doorway with the others crowding behind her.

The sitting area was demolished. Jagged, frozen chunks of what might have been the comfy chairs and assorted pillows were scattered across the space, which was draped with sharp-edged splashes of crystalline ice and drifts of snow. The sliders had blown out and snow drifted onto the pool deck, where it melted pretty much the second it hit the sun-baked deck. A large, dark shape lurked in the pool, leviathanesque. She was pretty sure it was the couch.

Holy. Shit.

Jade knotted her fingers together, her stomach churning as it had right before the magic, only more in an I'm-going-to-vomit way. "I'm so sorry." She directed the apology at Jox, who had overseen the renovations and always did his level best to keep the mansion clean and comfortable for everyone. "Gods. I'm sorry."

The *winikin*'s expression bordered on wild. "Ice," he said faintly. "There's no such thing as an ice spell."

"There is now." She glanced at her scribe's mark. "I think I just made it up. Or my talent did."

"Just like that?" Strike snapped his fingers. "No warning?"

At that moment, Lucius appeared from the direction of the cottages, moving fast, his eyes hard and hot. He hesitated at the sight of the melting snowdrifts and the submerged sofa, then strode through into the ruined main room. His eyes swept the crowd and settled on her, then skimmed past. His aggressive stance eased. "I take it we're not under attack?"

"Not an intentional one," Leah answered dryly. "Jade was just about to tell us about when and how her powers started coming online. Because I'm guessing this wasn't the first clue."

Jade winced. "Yes and no. There was one other time, but I convinced myself it was nothing."

"This," Sven said, "is clearly something." Patience elbowed him into silence.

Flushing, Jade sketched a brief summary of what she'd felt when she'd brought herself out of the barrier, and how she'd glanced at a supposedly gibberish text and seen a blessing instead. "I didn't mention it before because I was convinced the magic had come from the Vennie *nahwal*, or that maybe she had tried to jump-start my talent and failed because my magic is simply too weak."

"Apparently that's not the case." Despite the fact that he was standing ankle-deep in the melting mess and most of the living room was gone, Strike's eyes gleamed. "Congratulations, Jade. You're a scribe."

"Yeah." She grinned up at him. "I am." Her smile felt foolish, though, and his image was a little watery around the edges, filtered as it was through unshed tears. "I also think I'm about to pass out."

She didn't, but it was pretty close.

Sasha and Michael propped her up and got her to her suite; she waved off the offer of an IV—she'd far rather pig out, thanks—but nodded floppily when Jox called after them that he'd have Shandi bring food. She would've warned him that Shandi was mad at her, but lacked the strength. Besides, given that Jox was the royal *winikin*, he probably already knew what was going on, and why. He'd already shown, though, that he wouldn't interfere in a *winikin*'s relationship with his or her charge. Each *winikin* was chosen for a reason, even if that reason wasn't immediately obvious. *The gods move in mysterious ways*, Jade thought woozily.

Once she was in bed, Sasha shooed Michael away and

helped Jade undress and drag on an oversize T-shirt. Jade was asleep before Sasha pulled the curtains.

She awoke sometime later to the sight of French toast and OJ on a tray at her bedside table . . . and beyond that, Lucius sitting in the chair where she typically dumped her clean laundry. He was reading.

He didn't realize right away that she was awake, giving her a few seconds to simply watch him. In her mind's eye, the moment kaleidoscoped to the many times they'd read together in the archive, working separately but together, each of them in their old guises. Now, as he frowned down at the text—which was newly water-damaged, she saw with an inner wince—she found his single-minded, almost fanatical concentration arousing, in large part because she now knew that he brought that same level of intensity to lovemaking. *Sex*, she reminded herself. *Sex, not lovemaking. Keep your own rules straight.* Still, the sight heated her blood and tightened her skin despite the tug of lingering fatigue.

"Good book?" she said, drawing his attention before her thought process ran any further aground on itself.

His head came up, though it took him a second to pull himself out of the written world and refocus on her. When he did, his lips curved in a long, slow smile. "Not as useful as I would've liked." He flashed her the cover as he closed the book and set it aside; it was one of the histories of the star bloodline that she had skimmed through earlier and bypassed as being too superficial to be of any real use. "You look better."

"I'm not covered in frost and wearing soaked jeans

and an expression of terror, you mean." Even saying it brought a burst of pride laced with deeper, less sure emotions.

"Something like that." He took her hand, idly turning it so they could both see her forearm, where the scribe's mark was unchanged, even though everything was different. "Big day."

"Yeah." The grin felt like it lit her from the inside out. "I've got magic."

"I never doubted it."

They sat like that for a moment, and Jade found her thoughts going not to the magic, but to what had happened just before she cast the spell. "I talked to Shandi again. She told me more about what happened right before the massacre."

"More about your mother?"

"Not directly." Before she realized she was going to, that she needed to, she was telling him about Shandi's revelation, how it explained so much, yet didn't give her any options. The words spilled out of her, tumbling over one another. "I'm not responsible for the will of the gods," she finished, "and I can't undo the bond between us. Or maybe I could, but to what end? Denny and Samxel are gone, just like my parents are gone. Shandi—" She broke off, frustrated. "I don't know what to say to her. She's been harboring a grudge for twenty-six years. It seems inane somehow to say that I'm sorry for her loss. More, if you ask me what I really think, it's that she needs to grow up and get over it already. It wasn't my fault, and blaming me for it is . . . pointless."

"Shandi's not stupid. I have a feeling she knows that."

Jade looked up at him. "Meaning?"

"Maybe it stopped being about you a long time ago and became the thing that keeps her going from day to day," he suggested. "And maybe she even realizes that herself, but is afraid to let it go, afraid to let herself care for you, knowing what the future might hold for all of us."

"That's . . ." Jade trailed off, thought for a moment, then finished, ". . . not the dumbest thing I've ever heard. Shit. Give me a minute here." Needing to make a mental shift, she pulled herself up to sit cross-legged in the bed, with the sheet pulled over her legs. Pressing her fingertips to her temples, she said, "You're right. She lost her family to war; it's possible that she doesn't want to run the risk of living through that sort of loss again. Although I'd like to point out that unless the Nightkeepers *win* the war, she wouldn't have long to grieve, because we're all going to be wiped out in thirty or so months." Her stomach knotted on the thought, which suddenly seemed far more real than it had before.

His expression went grim. "Even if the Xibalbans and *Banol Kax* are defeated and the cycle of time restarts, there are going to be casualties. It's only natural that we're going to worry about each other more and more as time passes, and that we're going to want to see the people we care about stay safe."

Hope—her own personal demon—stirred to life within her. "Are you saying you'd rather I stay safely back behind the lines?" She didn't want to have that debate . . . but she thought she wouldn't mind hearing him make the pitch.

"We're talking about you and Shandi."

"Right." Her heart took a little slide in her chest, though, warning that her emotions were far too close to the surface. In the space of a few days, she'd taken a lover who threatened to become too important to her. She'd been to hell and back, had her worldview shifted, and met her mother, though she hadn't recognized it at the time. And now she'd found her magic. She supposed it was understandable that her normal defenses would be down. But that didn't mean she was going to cave to the first hint of pressure. She was through being that woman.

She snagged a piece of French toast off the tray and took a bite, both because she was starving and to buy herself a moment before she said, "You think I should . . . what? Stay in the background because it'll make her feel more secure? That'd be an illusion and you know it. Furthermore, it's bullshit." She didn't know when or how, but she suddenly realized she'd come back around to the idea of wanting to fight. Or maybe she did know. Maybe it was the moment she'd accidentally leveled a showroom's worth of furniture with ice magic. If that wasn't a fighter's talent, she didn't know what was.

An image flashed in her mind's eye: that of a dark-haired baby with clenched fists and a scowl on her face.

"That's not what I'm saying at all." Lucius paused,

considering. Finally, he said, "There were a last few lines in the journal, at the very bottom, that I haven't told anyone about. I felt like they were a private message between the journalist and the next Prophet, so I kept them to myself. Now that we know who the journalist was, I think maybe they *were* a message, but not for me. I think she may have meant it for you."

The air trickled out of Jade's lungs. *Oh, Vennie.* "What did it say?"

"I may be flubbing a word or two here, but the gist was: 'Magic isn't what's going to save the world. Love is. So find someone to love, and tell them so. Better yet, show them your love by making them happy rather than miserable. Don't be an idiot like I was.' "

Jade's eyes filled. "She was talking about Joshua."

"And you."

"Maybe. Probably. And I'm sure she meant it at the time." But an aching hollow opened up beneath her diaphragm.

Lucius tilted his head as he looked at her. She halfway expected him to hug her, soothe her. And a large part of her would've welcomed it, for too many reasons. He didn't touch her, though, beyond the hand he still held. Instead, he said, "It wasn't your fault the gods chose Shandi . . . and it wasn't your mother's fault she was seventeen."

"I know that. Of course I know that. It's just . . ." She paused, trying to sort through her thoughts. Finally, she said, "It's like there are two versions of her inside my head now, two different thought chains pertaining to her. On one hand, I pity her. I picture this spoiled, ego-driven kid who wasn't much different from half the teenagers I've ever met. My heart hurts at the thought of her being so alone, isolated from both her own family and her in-laws, convinced that she'd been chosen as the next Prophet but the others couldn't see it. How can I blame her for that? We're doing the same thing now, trying to interpret the will of the gods from old prophecies and and a few scattered clues. When I think of her going through the library spell alone, it makes me so sad for her. And then, when she came back out and tried to go home . . ." She trailed off as the hollowness inside her turned to an ache. "I want to weep for that child. I want to thank her for her sacrifice, and promise her that we won't let her down. But at the same time, I'm so damned *angry* at her. I hate knowing that she took on adult responsibilities—a husband, a baby—and bailed when things stopped being fun. I saw too much of that in the outside world." Exhaling, she stared at her free hand, which had formed a fist. "And I hate that I'm seeing my father as a victim. I don't know him, but I know the type." She had counseled people like him over and over again, albeit mostly women. "I don't . . . Shit, I don't know. I hate being inconsistent when it comes to her, but I can't seem to stop myself from pitying the girl I think of as Vennie while resenting the person who was my mother, when her only sin, really, is not matching up to the image in my head." She glanced at Lucius, expecting him to look baffled— or worse, concerned for her mental health.

Instead, he nodded. "I get that, I think. It's Night-keeper versus human. On one hand, she was following the writs, putting the greater good ahead of her family, and you know you should respect her, maybe even celebrate her, for that sacrifice. But on the other hand, *you're* the family she left behind, which has to hurt. What's more, everything you're being told now suggests that this wasn't a onetime thing; it was another in a long line of grandstanding stunts, which devalues the whole family thing even further. But you know what?"

She met his eyes, feeling somehow chastised yet relieved. "None of it matters worth a damn, because knowing about the past doesn't change who I am. I'm not my mother or father, and I'm not Shandi. I'm me."

"That's right. And you're a strong, wonderful woman anyone should be proud to have as a daughter. . . ."

If she hadn't known him so well, she would've assumed he'd finished his thought. Because she did know him, though, she tipped her head. "And?" *Say it. Tell me you're proud to be with me, that there's more here than just the sex magic.*

But instead, he rose to his feet. "And I'm proud of you for the iceball stunt, regardless of the property damage." He lifted a shoulder. "It looks like we both got what we wanted, doesn't it?"

She tried to see past his guarded expression, but couldn't. Or maybe there wasn't anything more to see? For a moment, she was tempted to ask him point-blank where he saw the two of them going, whether it was more for him than magic and fringe benefits. But she didn't dare. If he'd been the same man as before, she might have, but he was different now, more independent and far harder to read. And what if he didn't share her feelings? Skywatch was a small place, and her running to the university wasn't an option anymore. Not with her talent starting to show itself. So instead of pushing him, or revealing herself, she nodded and found a faint smile. "Yeah. We got what we wanted."

Something flashed across his expression, there and gone too quickly for her to parse. He said only, "Maybe I'll see you later?"

Recognizing that "later" had become their shorthand for "are we still on for sex?" she nodded. "Yeah. See you later." But her throat tightened on the words. And when he was gone, she burrowed back into bed . . . and pulled the covers over her head.

Lucius stalked back to his cottage, telling himself he'd done the right thing. He'd wanted to prod her into reconciling—or at least trying to reconcile—with her *winikin*. What was more, he'd managed to keep the conversation away from their relationship, which had become a suddenly thorny problem, and in a way he never would've anticipated.

He'd sensed the shift in her the previous morning, had known when things had gone from lust-only to tenderness, from "that feels good" to "what are you feeling?" A year ago, maybe even a few months ago, that would've had him doing cartwheels through the busted-up great room. Now, though, he didn't know what to do with it. Did he care about her? Absolutely. But the more time he spent around the mated mage pairs, and the more recent events had forced him to think about family ties, the more he realized that in the past he'd done crushes and affection, occasionally even loyalty, but not love.

He had loved his family growing up, he supposed, in a love-but-not-like sort of way. Or had that been co-existence rather than love? His older brothers had tormented him, his father had cheered them on, his older sisters had put bows in his hair, and his mother had pitted them all against one another in a subtle battle of passive aggression he hadn't recognized as such until he was well away from the whole mess. He'd escaped to UT, floundered a bit, then eventually found his place with Anna. He'd leaned on her, idolized her, and thought for a time that he loved her. But his feelings for her, like the brief flashes of affection from his few lovers, which he'd taken too far, too fast with scant encouragement, hadn't been the sort of bone-deep emotion that had spurred Vennie to sacrifice herself so her husband and child might live, or that had embittered Shandi so deeply that she'd carried the fear and resentment with her for decades. He'd never felt that way. More, he didn't think he wanted to, because wasn't it really another form of possession? He didn't want to have to think of someone else; he was just starting to figure out how to think of himself.

That was why he'd ducked Jade's almost-offer just now. Always before, she had guarded herself so carefully, protected herself so fiercely. The last thing he wanted was to peel those layers back to find the woman within . . . and realize he was incapable of letting himself be equally vulnerable to her.

He wanted her. But he didn't want to be owned by her. And that was what love translated to, wasn't it? Ownership.

They could be friends. They could be friends with benefits. They could even be lovers. But he wasn't interested in falling in love, not anymore. And for a guy who had always thought he was someone who fell too easily, that was a hell of a thing to figure out. Especially when he and Jade were finally lovers. Things were changing too fast around him, inside him, for him to make any sort of commitment. At least, he hoped that was what had happened, because he hated to think he'd been chasing something half his life, only to figure out that once he had it, he didn't really want it after all.

"In a different lifetime," he murmured, but didn't bother continuing, because in another lifetime he and Jade never would have met. And it was this lifetime that they needed to make matter, and not just for their own sakes. Which was why, instead of turning around and heading back to her room, as so much of him was tempted to do, he let himself into his cottage and locked the door behind him, not so much to keep anyone out, but as a symbol, to let himself know he was staying there.

Everything was just as he'd left it when the big boom from the mansion had interrupted him: a garbage-bag tarp was spread in front of the TV, waiting for him to man up and do what needed to be done. *Sacrifice*. There *had* to be magic inside him. He wouldn't have gotten into the library without it, regardless of the sex or the new moon. It was in there somewhere. He just had to get it out. The magi needed Kinich Ahau. They needed the Triad. They needed more from him than he'd given them so far.

Flipping on the TV, he woke his laptop, which projected another of the images he'd been studying. Similar to the one that had been on-screen the other night, this one showed a scene from the ritual ball game of the Maya, with masked, shielded players clustered around the ceremonial rubber ball that symbolized the sun. He hit the "back" arrow a couple of times, returning to the painting that had overseen his and Jade's barrier transitions. He stared at the glyphs coming out of the musician's conch-shell instrument, the ones that were supposed to be gibberish, but that Jade thought were something else.

"A blessing, huh?" He didn't see it, but she'd certainly proven herself with the ice spell, so he'd give it a shot.

Seating himself cross-legged on the plastic, so he wouldn't ruin the rug or upholstery, he palmed the butcher knife he'd lifted from the main kitchen. It was solid in his hand, and far sharper than the steak knife he'd used to offer himself to the *makol* almost exactly two years earlier. Turning his right hand palm up, he set the knife along the gnarled scar that followed his lifeline. Then he closed his fingers around the blade in a fist and yanked the knife free of it. Cool steel burned, then sang to pain as blood welled up, then dripped down. Taking a moment to review the questions he meant to ask if—or rather *when*—he made it back in, he focused on the painting and began to chant the non-sensical words formed by the musician's glyphs, trying different tones and variations, mixing up the order of the symbols, all while seeking the power that had to be inside him somewhere.

Nothing happened.

In fact, nothing happened for long, long into the night. Grimly, he kept going, letting blood from different ceremonial spots on his body and working every spell fragment he'd absorbed during his months at Skywatch, knowing that he had failed at many things in his life, but he couldn't afford to fail now. Jade's mother might have been right about love being a key to winning the war; gods knew the magi drew their powers from one another. But he knew damned well that in this case, it wasn't about love. It was about the magic. All he had to do was find it.

CHAPTER FOURTEEN

June 16
Two years, six months, and five days to the zero date

Jade slept later than she'd intended, but woke more or less refreshed. Trying not to resent that she'd woken alone, in her own suite, when she would've rather been elsewhere, she pulled on jeans and a tight, dark T-shirt, and laced on the boots she'd taken to wearing in place of sandals. Anticipation thrummed low in her gut: She had been banished to the training hall to experiment with her magic. And that felt damned good.

When she headed over to the main mansion to scrounge some breakfast—her appetite had skyrocketed—she found the place nearly empty. Which felt seriously weird. "Hello?" she called, and heard the word echo back to her.

Granted, the compound wasn't actually deserted, but with half the magi out on assignment, it sure felt that way.

After a failed attempt to 'port Lucius himself out to Ecuador—something about Lucius, whether the hellmark, the library connection, or something else, had fouled the magic—Strike had 'ported several of the warriors to Ecuador to search for the hellmouth, in case the *Banol Kax* had somehow returned it to the earth plane in advance of the solstice. Patience and Brandt had gone to Egypt, to the site where Akhenaton's capital city had stood. The city itself had been thoroughly defaced by Akhenaton's successors, who had returned the empire to worshiping their familiar pantheon and done their best to wipe Akhenaton from the historical record. Lucius had put the Nightkeepers in contact with a curator he knew from the 2012 doomsday message boards, in the hopes that Patience and Brandt would get lucky and find an artifact or reference giving a clue as to how Akhenaton thought he might usurp the sun itself . . . and from there, how the magi could stop him.

Jade had been left behind, but not in a business-as-usual way. She had an assignment of her own, and it wasn't in the archive. Which seriously rocked.

Over a breakfast of cold cereal, she wrote down the iceball spell for Strike and the others to try, in the hopes that it wouldn't be specific just to her. Then, refusing to let herself hesitate at the place where the path split off and ran down to the cottages, she headed to the training hall—which was fire-, water-, and freezeproof—to practice her new magic.

She felt a quick, hard jolt of relief when she called up the spell in her mind and got a buzz of power in response. Grinning in solitary triumph, she held out her hands, shaped an invisible, intangible ball, and whispered the iceball spell. Magic detonated, blue-white light flared, and a shock wave exploded away from her, sending a lettuce-size iceball whizzing across the open hall to slam into the far wall. When the light died down, exhilaration roared through her. "I did it!"

The wall was ice crazed and coated with thick frost. It had held, but just barely.

After giving herself a moment to do a booty-shaking solo dance that wasn't the slightest bit dignified or decorous, she pulled herself back to the task at hand, namely figuring out whether she could manage the spell. It didn't take her long to figure out how much energy to put behind the spell in order to create a manageable blast of cold magic that froze whatever it touched and went where she wanted it to. Remembering a scene from *X-Men*, she tried to make an ice-sculpture rose, but wound up with a blob instead, so she decided that wasn't how the magic rolled. But that was okay, because at least it was rolling. Which meant it was time to try morphing another spell.

Jumpy with anticipation, she headed to the temporary archive—aka an unfurnished spare room where the *winikin* had set up laundry racks and hung the worst of the waterlogged books out to dry under fans. There, she hunted up the *Idiot's Guide*, which was boxed up among the other books, the ones that had survived relatively unscathed, with just a little frost damage. Flipping to the last chapter, she paged past the fireball spell to the next standard in the warrior's arsenal: shield magic. *Okay*, she thought, *let's do this!* She focused on the page and opened herself to the magic.

Nothing happened.

The glyphs were there; the translation was there . . . but the shimmer of power wasn't. She stared at the page for a full minute before she was finally forced to admit that whatever magic she'd been jacked into the day before had deserted her. Again.

"Oh, come *on!*" she snapped, disgusted. "This isn't"—*fair*, she didn't say, because it was probably past time to man up and accept it. Life wasn't fair, which sucked, but wasn't something she could change. The magic worked on its own schedule and by its own rules. And more often than not, apparently, it didn't work for her. Resisting the urge to bang her forearm against the table, to see if the same brute-force approach that worked for her TV remote might apply to her talent mark, she flipped back a couple of pages and tried another spell. Still no dice.

Frustration welled up inside her along with the aching drag of imminent failure. *No*, she told herself. *You're not giving up. Not this time.* She was better than that, stronger than that.

"Okay," she said, dropping down cross-legged on the floor. "You're smart; you can think it through. Yesterday you looked at the spell the first time and there wasn't any magic. Then, later, there it was. What changed?" When she put it that way, the answer was obvious: The difference had been *her*. The first time she'd been relatively calm. Then Shandi had shown up and dropped an emotional shitstorm on her, and in the aftermath, she'd had her magic. "So . . . what?" she asked the empty room. "I've got to be pissed off to access my talent?"

Predictably, the damp books didn't have an answer for her. But she had a feeling she already knew at least part of the answer; she just didn't want to go there. Honesty, though, and a certain degree of self-awareness, compelled her to admit that it probably wasn't about being angry, per se. . . . It was about being open to the emotion. Any emotion. Problem was, emotional openness wasn't her forte, not by a long shot. Just the opposite, in fact—she had built a career on teaching others how to distance themselves from drama and guard against upheaval. She had Shandi to thank for that. The *winikin* had closed herself off to affection and emotion in the wake of the massacre, and had taught her charge the value of control for control's sake, making it Jade's automatic fallback when it might not have been her natural inclination.

The more she thought about her mother, the more she realized that her first, wholly negative reaction to Shandi's description of Vennie had come from the fact that Jade had been exactly the same sort of strong-willed, brash, egotistical teenager—or she would have been if it hadn't been for Shandi's iron discipline. Having been told, over and over again, that impulsiveness was a sin against her bloodline and the gods, that she had to control herself or terrible things would happen, how could she not paint her mother with that same brush? But that brought up the question of nature versus nurture. How much of the person she was today was because of her bloodlines and genetics, and how much of it had been created by her upbringing? Gods knew most of her career was based on a single sentence: *Tell me about your childhood.*

What did the gods want from her, really? They had sanctified her parents' marriage, but not until after her conception. Was she, then, a child of the gods? The thought brought a shiver, because that was what the triad prophecy—the one that spoke of finding the lost sun—had called for. But if her parents had been meant on some level to unite the harvester and star bloodlines to create her, why had the gods chosen Shandi as her *winikin*?

"That one's easy," she said aloud. "To teach me to control the impulsiveness that got Vennie killed." Or rather, the impulsiveness that had led her mother to sacrifice herself in vain. If Vennie had been a different, steadier mage, still allied with the star bloodline, maybe they would have listened to her. Maybe they would have tried to make her a true Prophet. And maybe, just maybe, she could have averted the massacre. And oh, holy gods, how different things would have been then.

Which meant . . . what? Was she supposed to be open to her emotions or was she supposed to control them, or was there some ineffable balance she was supposed to find between the two?

"Shit. I don't know." She knew it was ironic that she was a therapist who didn't know how to deal with emotions, but there it was. Or rather, she knew how *not* to deal with them, because Shandi had taught her well:

Turn the emotions off. If you're not having them, they can't hurt you. You're not vulnerable. Now that she understood the reason for those lessons, though, she wasn't sure they played.

Magic isn't the answer. Love is. The words drifted through her brain, bringing a complicated mix of reactions. A warm fuzziness came from Lucius's having brought her the message, keeping it private between the two of them. But countering that warmth was a kick of self-directed anger that she had wanted—needed—to believe he'd meant more than he had, only to have him withdraw when she reached out to him. More, there was the layer of guilt she suspected he'd meant to instill with the message, one that said her *winikin* wasn't the only one to blame for the lack of real friendship between them. As a *winikin*, even a reluctant one, Shandi would have been fully interwoven with the harvester way of life, culturally programmed to support the bloodline's doctrines. It couldn't have been easy for her to see the rebelliousness of the star bloodline surfacing within Jade, when such personality traits had led to heartache and loss of face for the harvesters before. *She should've said something*, Jade thought as anger stirred. *How was I supposed to know? I—*

She broke off the thought train, partly because it wasn't going to get her anywhere, and partly because there had been no change in the spell book she held open on her lap. The glyphs hadn't risen up into the air and danced in front of her, shifting to become something else. The page was just a page, the book just a book. Which suggested that the magic didn't come from anger, and further indicated that the key had to be some sort of emotional openness. *Of course it couldn't be easy*, Jade thought morosely. Pissed off she could have managed these days. It was the other stuff she was going to have trouble with.

Magic. Love.

Shit.

Annoyed, she climbed to her feet and returned the *Idiot's Guide* to its drying rack. Not sure where she was going, just that she needed to be up and moving, she stalked out into the hallway—and nearly slammed into Shandi.

The *winikin* stumbled back, putting up both hands as though warding off an attack. "Whoa, slow down!"

I don't want *to slow down*, Jade wanted to snap at her. *I've* never *wanted to slow down!* But, knowing that her mood was as much about the magic and Lucius as it was the *winikin*, she held in the knee-jerk snarl and tried to smooth herself out. As she did so, she realized that her previously slow-to-boil temper was heading toward becoming vapor-fast. What had happened to peace, serenity, and her counselor's cool? She was off balance and reactive, borderlining on the drama she had so pitied in her patients, keeping herself above and apart from it all.

Which way of dealing was right? Was there even a right or wrong? Gods, this was exhausting.

Consciously exhaling, both her mood and a sigh, Jade said, "I'm sorry. I should've looked where I was going." Shandi hesitated with her mouth partway open, as though she'd planned one response, but Jade's apology called for another. Into that gap, Jade said, "I'm also sorry for how we left things last night. You shared something painful and I made it about me, not you."

The other woman narrowed her eyes. "I don't need therapy."

That's debatable, Jade thought but didn't say, not the least because her own *winikin* was one of the last people she would've taken on as a patient. She might be going a little crazy—to use the woefully unprofessional term—with everything she was dealing with right then, but she wasn't *that* crazy. "I'm not being a therapist right now. I'm apologizing for being insensitive last night, and for not always understanding what you need from me. I'm going to try harder from now on." That much she could promise. And, as she said it, she imagined she felt a faint tingle of magic.

"I—" Shandi broke off and shook her head. "Never mind. We'll talk about it later. You're wanted in the kitchen."

The star inside Jade wanted to ask who wanted her, for what, whether it had to be that exact moment, and what the "never mind" meant. The woman inside her, the one who thought she was starting to understand that the three "D"s were less about never rebelling than they were about carefully picking her rebellions for maximum effect, said only, "Okay, I'm on it. Thanks."

She moved past the *winikin* and headed for the kitchen, but turned back after only a few steps when she realized that the other woman hadn't moved. "I'm sorry. Was there something else?"

"No. I . . . No." Shandi's expression showed a flicker

of surprise, there and gone quickly. "Go on," she said briskly. "The king's waiting."

Jade went. She didn't feel the magic now, didn't see glyphs morphing in her mind's eye, but as she headed down to the main kitchen, she thought the magic might be a little closer than it had been before. Unfortunately, any progress she might've made in that direction was lost the moment she came through the archway and saw Lucius at the breakfast bar, along with Leah, Strike, Michael, Sasha, and Jox.

Her defenses slammed up to buffer the jolt of body memory that came at the sight of how Lucius's faded green T-shirt stretched over his wide shoulders and the strong lines of muscle on either side of his spine, and bared his buffed-out arms. His shirt was untucked at the back of his jeans, slopping out casually, as if to say, *I have more interesting things to think about than the way I'm dressed*. That was purely Lucius, both the old and the new, she thought. And with that thought, she realized that she'd almost stopped thinking about which pieces of him she remembered from before and which were new. He was just . . . himself now. And he was taking up far too much of her attention.

Jerking her eyes away from him, she took a quick look beyond the kitchen to the great room—or what was left of it. She hadn't been in there since the previous day, and to her relief, changes were already evident. The wrecked furniture had been cleared out, the glass sliders had been replaced with their screen counterparts, the couch didn't appear to be lurking in the pool anymore, and tarps were stretched across the conversation pit, where most of the damage had occurred. The atmosphere was damp with a combination of leftover meltwater and the humidity spilling in from the outside. Overall, she thought it looked better than it had right after the iceball incident . . . but not by much.

The odd thing was, though, that she didn't feel all that bad about the destruction. Instead, a bubble of joy tried to push its way into her throat, making her want to do another little victory dance and say, *I did that. I've got magic!*

She channeled her inner harvester and didn't act on the impulse. But she sure as heck thought about it, and did a little inner dance as she turned to the group at the breakfast bar. "Shandi said you wanted to see me?"

Strike nodded. "Grab a seat."

The only empty bar stool was one next to Lucius. She took it without comment and returned his nod of greeting with one of her own.

"Anna called me this morning," Strike began. "She wants to talk to you and Lucius about your encounter with Kinich Ahau. She thinks she might have some ideas."

When he paused, seeming to invite a response, she said carefully, "That's good news, right? I mean, she's the expert." She glanced at Lucius. "No offense."

"Trust me, none taken. She's got almost a decade on me in official fieldwork, and combines her training with knowing the legends backward and forward, thanks to Jox's teachings."

But Jox shook his head. "I can only take part of the

credit. She was good with the stories even before . . . you know. Before." He paused, his voice softening. "She was in the nursery when the *boluntiku* attacked. She'd been telling the little ones about the hero twins traveling to Xibalba to rescue their father from the *Banol Kax*. She was always telling them the stories."

The massacre was very close to the surface for those old enough to remember it, Jade realized, with fragments coming from many different perspectives. Jox's focus had been getting Strike and Anna to the safe room below the mansion. Shandi had been struggling between her two callings. Vennie had arrived in the aftermath. *Flames. Dead, staring eyes.* She shivered as a chill touched the back of her neck, but resisted the urge to shift closer to the warmth beside her. "When is Anna getting here?" she asked instead.

"She wants us to come to UT," Lucius answered.

"More accurately," Leah put in dryly, "she's refusing to return to Skywatch or have the convo by phone or Web conference. She's insisting that you two come to her."

Strike sighed. "As much I'm sorely tempted to 'port out there and drag her home, we don't need just her; we need her talent too. And that's not something I can control by brute force." He turned his scarred palms upward, to the sky and the gods. "She's asked me to give her room. I told her I'd give her as long as I could . . . which means the two of you going out to UT and having a sit-down with her." He paused. "While you're there, I'd like you to check up on Rabbit and Myrinne. Anna swears that they're doing fine, no problems, but

the ki— Rabbit's been ducking my calls. I'd appreciate
it if you could put eyeballs on him, maybe ask around
a little and make sure he's not into something . . . well,
something Rabbit-like."

Which could be anything from vandalism to torch-
ing half of the French Quarter, Jade knew. But beneath
the wry amusement, adrenaline buzzed. She had tried
not to be disappointed when the others were sent off on
assignment and she was left behind. Her talents were
fledgling at best, and the others were better trained and
had field experience. But a trip to the university . . .
it seemed like a nice middle ground. It was a few
hours at most, in familiar territory. "I'm in. When do
we leave?"

"Not so fast," Strike cautioned. "I can't teleport you
there. Or rather, I can't 'port Lucius. So you two are
going to have to get there the old-fashioned way . . .
which is going to exponentially increase your exposure
level."

"It . . . Oh." She'd spent so long at the university
that it hadn't occurred to her that their being outside
the warded confines of the compound would carry
additional risk. But Lucius wore the hellmark, which
meant that once he was outside Skywatch, he could be
tracked through dark magic. More, with the solstice
only five days away, all of the magi had to be on guard
against early moves by the *Banol Kax*. "So, what's the
plan? Airplane?"

"No way," Lucius said immediately. "Bad enough to
stick me inside a small space crammed with bodies . . .
worse if the *Banol Kax* or Xibalbans come after me and

take out a planeful in the process." He shook his head.
"No plane. I'll take one of the Jeeps, load up with jade-
tips, carry a panic button, and take my chances." For
the first time since she had sat down beside him, he
looked at her fully. "I was outvoted on the idea of going alone." His tone suggested that had been less a
case of keeping him safe from dark magic, and more a
case of the Nightkeepers not wanting to let him loose
with the hellmark, a history of debatable loyalty, a vehicle full of antimagic ammo, and intricate knowledge
of Skywatch. "One option is to have Michael and me
do the road trip, while Strike 'ports you straight to the
university for the meeting, then back when it's over."
In other words, Michael and his death magic could
keep a careful eye on Lucius, while she took the easy
way out.

It made logical sense . . . and the rebel inside Jade
thought it sucked. More, she could practically feel Lucius withdrawing from her, even as they sat there only
a few inches apart. If she was right about the emotional
context needed for her magic—and potentially his—
then withdrawing from her wasn't going to help him
get back into the library. Exactly the opposite, in fact.
"What's the other option?"

"For you and Lucius to make the trip together,"
Michael answered. "Obviously, you'd be armed to
the teeth and have all the necessary gadgets, including panic buttons." More than simple buttons, the advanced communication devices not only transmitted
a signal calling Skywatch for help; they also photo-
graphed their immediate vicinity and transmitted the

images so Strike could teleport backup or otherwise decide on a response. "But keep in mind that neither of you has reliable fighting magic, so if it comes down to a fight, you could be badly outgunned until help arrives."

Jade thought about the shield spell she'd tried—and failed—to morph earlier, and couldn't argue the point. Still, though, her instincts said that she and Lucius should travel together. Question was, did that instinct come from actual logic and the slim chance that she might be able to help him regain the Prophet's magic, or was her star DNA urging her to rash action, just for the sake of some excitement?

Knowing she could trust Michael's opinion on any and all strategy, she glanced at him. "What do you think?"

Lucius started to say something, but Michael held up a hand, forestalling him. "We know what you'd prefer. You want her hanging back, safe. And believe me, I can sympathize. But that's not how it's going to work, and you know it." To Jade, he said, "We've talked it over"—by "we" he meant the skeleton royal council gathered there, she knew—"and the decision is that we're not making the decision. It's up to you. There's zero shame in your staying here and continuing to refine your command of the iceball spell and see what other spells you can tweak. Or, hell, even if you can put together one from scratch. That'd be huge." He paused. "But we all know that you've been frustrated with your role here. Before, it didn't seem like a viable option to send you out into the field. Now, though . . .

well, it's not unheard of for a mage to take a little while to grow into his—or her—true talents, which is what you seem to be doing. Add to that the new info that you're half-blood star, which might incline you to more power than if your mother had come from one of the bloodlines that usually intermixed with the harvesters, and it's tempting to think you're on your way to becoming a warrior, with or without the mark. Obviously, we want to encourage that. Under the old training system, your skills would've been developed step by step under the protection of a senior warrior. But those days are gone. Most of us have achieved our full powers by being thrown into situations that were way larger than anything we wanted or expected them to be." He spread his hands. "Here, we're trying to hit a middle ground between the two by putting you into a moderate-risk scenario with a shit-ton of available backup, and a partner who would cut off his left nut before he let anything happen to you."

Lucius looked away at that. Jade nearly corrected the misconception that the two of them were anywhere near that tightly bonded, but she didn't, because what was the point? The others would believe what they believed, regardless of what she said. In a culture that orbited around the concept of destined mates, even the most alpha of males were matchmakers at heart.

"There's a third option," Michael added. "I could go along on the road trip, if you'd prefer. And for the record, if you stay behind, that doesn't mean you won't be allowed out on ops later. Once you've figured out your new limits, done some additional weapons training and hand-to-hand, that sort of thing, we can introduce you to the field in more controlled situations. This isn't a one-shot deal, understand?"

She tipped her hand in a yes/no gesture. "For me, perhaps. But we're getting down to the wire on figuring out how to save Kinich Ahau. Lucius and I were together when he opened the hellroad and then sent himself into the library. Although he hasn't had any luck reproducing that magic so far, his odds are going to be far better if I'm there." She glanced at Michael. "Without a chaperone."

He nodded. "Good point."

"No, it's *not* a good point," Lucius growled. "I—" He broke off. "Shit. It's a good point."

Triumph kicked through Jade, though buffered by nerves and a serious case of *what the hell are you thinking?* "Then it's just me, Lucius, and a tricked-out Jeep. When do we leave?"

CHAPTER FIFTEEN

June 17
Two years, six months, and four days to the zero date
UT Austin

Lucius and Jade left Skywatch midafternoon, spent the night at a chain hotel near the Texas border, had some very satisfying but frustratingly non-magic-summoning "later" in their shared hotel room, and reached the campus around noon the following day.

There had been no sign of pursuit or dark magic, and they had kept the conversation to relatively safe topics like the passing scenery, the sun going supernova, and the end of the world. Jade had floated the idea of them uplinking prior to sex, thinking that the blood link might allow him to lean on her magic to transport himself to the library. When he'd said he'd think about it, she didn't push. And she hadn't even hinted at whatever she'd been about to say the other night, when he'd been pretty sure she was headed in the *what if we decided to be more than friends?* direction before he'd interrupted her.

The fact that she hadn't gone there should've been a relief. Instead, it was pissing him off. Admittedly, that put him straight in the inconsistent-asshole category, at least in his own mind. He shouldn't want her to push him on their relationship when he had no intention of letting things go further than they already had. But still, it chapped him big-time that she seemed to have reached the same conclusion, to the point that he was down to monosyllabic growls by the time they passed the signs indicating they were inside the campus proper.

"We made good time," she commented as he navigated them through light summer on-campus traffic, headed for the visitors' lot closest to the art history building.

He more or less grunted in her direction.

She wore jeans and a cheerful yellow short-sleeved polo shirt that clung to the curves of her breasts and the dip of her waist. Open at the throat, it offered occasional glimpses of the hollow between her collarbones and the soft skin beneath, making him want to touch. And that ticked him off, which didn't make any sense. They were bed buddies, right? He could look; he could even touch. He didn't need to get all weird about it.

He turned into the lot and aimed the Jeep at a decent spot, parking legally because he didn't want to draw attention from the campus security guards, who would have a collective cow if they found the lockbox in the back, which was loaded with weapons, jade-tipped ammo, jade-filled grenades, and a decent array of assorted techware, some of which wasn't exactly legal for civilian use. He and Jade were both wearing semiautomatics inside their waistbands and small-caliber drop pieces in ankle holsters, which worked only because UT hadn't yet installed metal detectors.

Figuring that they were as prepared as they were going to get, he keyed off the Jeep and got out. He hadn't gone more than a step when the air hit him—dry and hot even under the funky sun, and smelling so damned familiar as it brought the sudden gut-punching realization that his pissy mood had nothing really to do with Jade.

He froze in place as memories unfolded around him.

From the moment he'd finally escaped his hometown and come to UT to stay, he'd rarely left campus. He'd found his place at the university, had finally felt like he'd fit somewhere. Granted, he hadn't fit everywhere; he'd still been scrawny and geeky, obsessed with science fiction and adventure role-playing. But he'd found friends. And then, in taking Intro to Maya Studies, he'd found his passion. He'd worked his ass off so he could afford to stay through the summers rather than going home, where, when he did return for the odd holiday, he'd felt even weaker than before, felt himself backsliding into the victim he was damn tired of being. So he'd stayed at the university through four years of undergrad, then slid seamlessly into the grad program, with Anna as his adviser. And, for nearly a decade, he'd immersed himself in the university, in the pieces of it that accepted him as he was, rather than wanting him to be bigger and stronger, more charismatic.

Sure, he'd gone out into the field with Anna, sometimes with colleagues of hers, or even a few times as a team leader in his own right. But those trips had been part of his university life, allowing him to transplant a subset of his stuff, George Carlin–style. And because of that, it hadn't felt as though he'd truly left UT . . . until the demon within him had driven him in search of the Nightkeepers. And oh, holy shit, it felt strange being back.

"How long has it been?" Jade asked softly.

She understood, he realized. She got it. Automatically, he reached for her hand, drew her to his side, and let their fingers twine together as he stared at the students walking from one place to the next, or lying sprawled in the weird sunlight. The faces might change from year to year, but everything else was the same. "Since last spring. Fifteen months or so."

"A very busy fifteen months."

"Except for the part where I was sitting on my ass in the in-between." He tugged on their joined hands, giving himself the luxury of keeping that small connection between them, despite whether he deserved to. "Come on. Let's go see what Anna wants."

Lucius led her in the direction of the art history building. As he did so, a funky shiver crawled down the back of his neck, bringing a serious case of déjà vu. He didn't think he'd ever before walked a date home from that particular parking lot, but he felt as though he'd played out this scene before, but with one major difference: He'd stopped being invisible. Back then he could've walked around the entire campus without getting hassled—which had been a welcome improvement over high school—but also without attracting much in the way of attention. He would've gotten a handful of waves and "hey"s from his few hangout buddies and a wider circle of nodding acquaintances, most of whom he would've met through one of the classes he TA'd. Some would've been girls. Most would've been guys. And the likelihood that he would've been walking beside a woman who looked anything like Jade would've been approximately a zillion to one.

Now, as they walked along, he got five times the nods and "hey"s he would've gotten before, and all from strangers. Women looked him in the eye, actually noticing him. And guys—even big ones with football-thick necks—sketched waves in his direction, gave way on the path, then turned to watch Jade's rear view, glancing quickly away when they saw that he'd noticed. The unreality of it only increased when he finally saw someone he recognized—a friend of one of his former roommates—and the guy walked right past him with a nod, a hint of wariness, and zero recognition.

"Is it everything you thought it would be?" Jade murmured.

He didn't pretend to misunderstand. "It is . . . and it isn't. I can't pretend I haven't thought about what it would be like to come back here, looking the way I do now. And yeah, that part is pretty cool. But at the same time, the campus itself is different. . . . Okay, it's not, but *I* am." He gestured around them. "This used to be my whole world. This and the ruins down south. Now . . ." He trailed off, not sure how to put it into words.

"Now the whole world *is* your world. And not just figuratively."

He exhaled. "Yeah." They walked a moment in silence. Then, as they hooked the last turn heading to the art history building, he said, "Back when I was growing up, I used to picture myself living the adventure, you know? I'd read Tolkein or Bujold or whatnot, and I'd imagine myself in the starring role." He didn't need a former therapist to point out that both authors had often focused on smaller, weaker protagonists who fought with their wits rather than their bodies. That was then; this was now. "I'd think about what I would do if it were my job to save the world, and, of course, I always got everything right, always picked the right battles, fought the right enemies. The harder I fought, the better I did. But now . . . I don't know. I'm doing my best, and I'm still not getting where I need to be."

"Maybe you need to relax and stop trying so hard," she said cryptically. "Besides, to paraphrase Strike, our best is all the gods can ask us to do."

"And if that's not enough?"

"Mankind is fucked."

Her bluntly profane answer startled a laugh out of him. "Such language from a harvester," he chided. He stopped in his tracks, just short of the moat leading to the office that had once been the focus of his life. Tugging on their joined hands, he spun her into his arms.

The sparse foot traffic eddied around them, and the strange orange sun slipped behind an ocher cloud, but he was hardly aware of those peripherals. His entire attention was focused on the woman in his arms, the lover he never could've imagined having when he'd been a part of the UT world.

Their bodies brushed, then pressed together as she slid her arms around his neck and leaned in, her eyes and mouth laughing, but darker shadows lingering beneath. Suddenly wishing he could take those shadows away, that he could make it all go away, he leaned in and kissed her, not a friendly feel-good kiss, or one of the oh-yes-there-more kisses of their lovemaking, but a carnal kiss, a full-on public display of possession. *Mine*, he thought, wanting to snarl it at the other men he sensed watching them, wanting to say it to her. *You're mine.* He spread his hands on either side of her waist, his fingers touching the outline of the nine-millimeter hidden beneath her shirt. If anything, the contrast between soft woman and hard-edged weapon made his blood burn hotter, made him want to wrap himself around her and protect the hell out of her, despite whether she could handle herself as a fighter, a mage, or both. More, he wanted to hear the same things from her, wanted to hear her say she wanted more than he was giving.

Heat flared through him, coiling hard and greedy inside him. His blood buzzed in his veins; colors sparked behind his closed eyelids. He wanted—

He wanted the hot girlfriend he'd dreamed of having on campus, he realized suddenly, the heat and buzz dying in the wake of the realization that he mostly wanted Jade as his arm candy for the next hour or so, wanted to know that the other guys envied the hell out of him. And that had nothing to do with him and Jade, and everything to do with his own stunted-ass psyche and a need to prove that he wasn't still a scrawny, too-tall praying mantis of a dork with a history of *Notting Hill*–like public protestations of love that ended in monstrous flameouts rather than happily-ever-after.

Gods, could he be a bigger asshole?

Jade just stood there watching him, her expression making him wonder just what she saw in his face, what she took away from it. After a moment, she smiled softly and said, "It's this place. It changes our perceptions, I think. Skywatch seems very far away. So does 2012. But at the same time, they both seem very important."

Which totally wasn't what he'd been thinking. It was a relief to know she was oblivious to the fact that he'd almost just imploded the good stuff they had going on, solely from a dorky need to prove a point that nobody but him gave a flying crap about. "Yeah," he said, exhaling. "And we need to keep moving."

Taking her hand once again, he led her across the moat and into the art history building. The heavy layers of reinforced concrete closed around them, swallowing him up. And for a moment, he was kicked back into the past.

The first time he'd visited Anna's office, a little less than a decade earlier, he'd been a sophomore, tall and skinny, and practically quivering in his Reeboks as he'd made the trek, clutching a folder that contained his sacrificial offering: three crumpled pieces of paper that he'd picked up a week earlier, when Professor Catori had first announced that she was looking for an undergrad intern to put in some hours with her group, and she was leaving applications outside her office. The pages asked about the applicant's basic stats . . . and included a glyph translation for them to take a crack at, if they wanted to.

And holy shit, did he ever want to.

He had snagged one of the first sets; they were all gone now. He knew, because he'd come back to get a fresh set when his originals started looking too sad for words. Without a spare, he was going to have to turn in the set he had, even though the last page had a big-ass coffee stain on it from where he'd upended the morning dregs in the process of reaching for a pen. *Dumb ass.* He'd tried to wipe it off, but that had just made things worse. His only hope was that he'd gotten close enough with the translation that she would overlook the fact that he was an almost complete disaster in all other facets of life. He was dying to work with her, to be around her, and maybe get a chance to work with some of the artifacts she'd shown them on PowerPoint slides projected up at the front of the stadium-seating lecture hall.

Those pictures had been too far away. He wanted the real thing. And the more he Web-surfed, soaking up pictures of Mayan ruins and the artifacts that had come from them, the more he wanted to know everything there was to know about a civilization that should have seemed strange and foreign to his modern viewpoint, but instead made *sense* to him. He'd understood their religion as if he were being reminded of it rather than learning it fresh. Human sacrifice might not be part of modern life, but he got where they'd been coming from: They'd been trying to protect themselves against the downfall portended by the stars, and the prophecies that said great white gods would arrive from the east, bringing the end of life as the Maya had known it. *Hello, Cortes.*

And the more he learned, the more he wanted to know.

He wanted to touch the pieces of that past culture, wanted to absorb all the information he could find on them. And when he'd been working on the glyph string she'd handed out, looking up each image in the seminal dictionary put together by Montgomery in the fifties, when archaeologists and linguists had finally cracked the Maya code, he'd gotten a glimmer of something bigger than himself, a kick of excitement when he realized it wasn't just a translation. . . . It was a puzzle. There wasn't much standardization among the glyphs, which had been as much an art form as a language. A given word could be represented by a pictograph or a string of syllables making up the word, or sometimes both. Then the syllables themselves could be represented by many different glyphs, or the same glyphs could look entirely different, depending on the artist who'd rendered them. That very fact had slowed his shit down when he'd gotten to the translation. He still wasn't sure if the third glyph was a hook-nosed god's face with suns where its eyes should be, or a really whacked version of a jaguar's head, but he'd gotten up against deadline day and had to go with what he had.

Walking the halls now, with Jade at his side, Lucius remembered how badly he'd worked himself up by the time he'd headed over to turn in the application, how he'd been practically puking with nerves. Back then, Anna had been less senior, so she'd had an upper-floor office. These days she had a primo ground-floor spot. But despite the difference in location, the clutter stuck to the corkboard hung on her door was much the same. Clippings of journal articles, some hers, some written by colleagues, offered the current state of the art in Mayan epigraphy. They bumped up against a scattering of cartoons and silly slogans, some hung by Anna, others by her coworkers and students. Slapped atop it all was a laminated page printed with her office hours and phone numbers, with a boldfaced note at the bottom: *Knock. What have you got to lose?*

The laminate looked new; the sentiment was an old, familiar friend. One that had been a mantra during certain parts of his life.

That first day, it had taken him nearly two full minutes to work up the courage. Now he just knocked, knowing that wasn't the hard part.

"Come on in," Anna's voice called from within.

He pushed the door open, stuck his head through, and grinned past a sudden spike of nerves. "Damn. And here I was looking forward to climbing in the window again."

Anna looked up, her face reflecting pretty much what he was feeling: a new awkwardness to an old friendship. Sitting behind her big, messy desk, she was dressed informally even for her, in a navy blue UT sweatshirt and collared shirt. He couldn't see her lower half, but was betting on jeans, based on the fact that she had her red-highlighted hair up in a ponytail and was wearing little, if any, makeup. The lack of makeup wasn't why she looked tired, though; the fatigue was real. He knew that because he knew her, and knew she dressed down at the university only when she was feeling crappy. Summer session or no summer session, she liked being put together.

Then again, things changed. People changed. Just look at him.

As if paralleling his thoughts, she glanced at the window he had B and E'd under Cizin's influence. "Ten bucks says you couldn't even *fit* through it anymore." She waved him all the way in. "Come on. Hey, Jade. Glad you could both make it. Any problems getting here?"

Jade shook her head. "None."

"How *are* you?" Anna asked her, the question clearly a *woman to woman, we've got our secrets* deal.

Lucius turned away, giving them a moment to catch up, and to remind himself it was largely his fault that his and Anna's relationship had suffered. He'd stolen from her; he'd betrayed her—albeit inadvertently—with a Xibalban. Because of him, she'd been forced back into her brother's sphere. Because of him, she wore a fourth mark, that of the slave-master, in addition to the jaguar, the royal *ju*, and the seer's mark. He couldn't blame her for not being excited to see him, after all they'd been through together and apart. Nor could he blame her for turning to Jade as a friend. Jade was warm and honest, analytical and near genius-smart. She was, he realized, a little bit like Anna in those ways. But where Anna tended to get caught up in her own emotions and had some drama-queen tendencies, Jade's waters ran still and deep.

As the women did a brief what's-up-how's-it-going, he stuck his hands in his pockets and took a tour of Anna's office, looking for new additions to her rogues' gallery of fakes. She used the hobby as a teaching tool, showing her students—Lucius included—not just how to spot the fakes and haggle in fine old open-market style, but also how to get the so-called antiquities dealers to show them the real stuff they tended to keep under wraps. Her goals were twofold: first, to cooperate with local authorities in blocking the export of national treasures when possible, and second, to potentially track exciting finds back to their sources. Each year, particularly in the less developed areas of the former Mayan empire, new caches of antiquities were discovered and sold off, to the great loss of the archaeologists and the still-scattered knowledge of the two-millennium history of the Maya. At times during his graduate career, Lucius had pictured himself eventually working against the black-market trade in the low country, acting as sort of a reverse treasure hunter, trying to keep the finds in place rather than in museums—or at least making sure that the sites were rigorously documented before the artifacts were split up. He'd cast himself as sort of a geeky Indiana Jones without the fedora, working with some heavily armed locals, maybe even armed himself. In those dreams, he'd been doing his part to save the small corner of the world that he'd claimed as his own.

Now, eyeing the window, which seemed to have shrunk over the past two years, he admitted inwardly that there was no way he'd fit through there now, as he had when he broke in to steal the transition ritual that Cizin had needed to come through the barrier. Lucius's body, like his world, had gotten a whole hell of a lot bigger since he'd left campus.

Anna's voice interrupted his prowl. "Stop pacing and sit, Lucius."

Jade had taken a folding chair off to one side, so he dropped into the visitor's chair, which was an old friend. He'd spent many, many hours working with Anna, their heads bent together as they argued over interpretations. *The good old days*, he thought with a trace of nostalgia and a hint of bitterness. He focused on Anna, realized she was fiddling with her chain, a sure sign of nerves. "Why are we here?" he asked without preamble.

In answer, she lifted the chain from around her neck, pulling the skull effigy from beneath her shirt in the process. In the stark white light coming from the overhead fluorescents, the sacred yellow quartz glittered dully, and the shadowed eye sockets seemed to stare at him. Lucius wasn't sure whether the jolt he felt was magic or awe at the sight of the ancient carving, which had been passed down, mother to daughter, through untold generations of *itza'at* seers.

The legendary crystal skulls were inextricably inter-twined with the mythos of the 2012 doomsday, and had hit the mainstream with the last Indiana Jones movie—unfortunately so, in his opinion, but it wasn't like Spielberg had asked him. And yeah, there were plenty of von Dänikenites who thought the delicately carved skulls that had been found at various Mesoamerican sites were proof of a higher—aka alien—intelligence. But they weren't. They were pure Nightkeeper; always had been . . . going back to the last Great Conjunction, when cataclysmic upheavals had loosed the demons from the underworld and destroyed the crystal cit-ies of the magi, sinking them into the sea. Only a few hundred survivors had been left to drive the *Banol Kax* back to Xibalba and erect the barrier that would contain them for the next twenty-six thousand years. Turning nomadic, the magi had brought with them the few remaining artifacts they had retained from their once-great civilization . . . including thirteen life-size crystal skulls.

The humans had found four of the skulls, all in clear quartz; three were in various museums, the fourth in a private collection. Rigorous science had concluded all four to be nineteenth-century fakes, based on their stone compositions and marks from tools that hadn't been available to the Maya or Aztec to whom they were supposedly ascribed. Which wasn't entirely wrong . . . The timing was just off by two dozen millennia or so. Of the remaining nine skulls, some of yellow quartz, some of pink, six were safely locked in the middle archive at Skywatch, two were missing in action . . . and one had been broken up into thirteen smaller skull effigies that had been given to the *itza'at* seers of the Nightkeepers. Twelve had disappeared the night of the massacre. Only Anna's remained.

Lucius didn't remember reaching out to touch it, but he was suddenly holding it in his hand, feeling the echoed warmth of Anna's body and the unexpected weight of the skull, which looked far lighter than it actually was. Startled, he held it back out to her. "Sorry. Didn't mean to grab. I just . . ." He shrugged. "This is what it's all about, you know? It's one of the skulls. I mean, holy shit!"

"Yeah. I know." She didn't reach for it, instead nodding to Jade.

He passed it over. "Watch out. It's heavier than it looks." When she took it solemnly, he looked back over at Anna, catching on that the effigy was why they had been summoned. "You think the skull might help Jade channel the scribe's talent more reliably?" He tried to remember whether there had been *itza'at*s mentioned in the history he'd read on the star bloodline. He didn't think so.

"No, the effigies are bloodline specific. It'd only work for a jaguar." Anna paused, carefully folding her hands atop her desk blotter. "I need you to take the skull back to Skywatch and give it to Strike."

Jade's soft, "Are you sure?" was quickly drowned out when Lucius held up his hands in protest. "You—" *Oh, no. Hell, no.* "You're kidding."

"Not about this." There was deep regret in her eyes, but behind that was a strange sort of peace. "Never about this."

"But you're our—their only seer!"

"I should have been," she corrected. "Maybe I would have been, if I'd gone through my talent ceremony when I should have. But she said we should wait until after the attack on the intersection, so we could focus on my training."

She was the queen, Lucius knew. Anna's mother. She had been a powerful seer, but loyal to her husband and king. Nobody knew what she had seen, exactly, but her visions had led her to fake a stillbirth and send baby Sasha to be raised in seclusion. More, she had leaned on Anna to pretend she hadn't yet reached menarche, thus ruling her out of her talent ceremony prior to the king's attack on the intersection. Then, the night before the queen marched to battle at her husband's side, she'd given the effigy to fourteen-year-old Anna, even though the teen hadn't known how to use the pendant properly. Lucius had long suspected that some of the *itza'at*'s powers had reached out to young Anna that night, through the effigy's connection to the queen. He had a feeling Anna had seen the massacre firsthand through that uplink . . . and that she'd been running from those memories ever since.

Jade set the pendant carefully on her desk; it made a hollow, echoing noise that seemed to reverberate on more planes than just the audible level. "Don't give up on us. Please."

Anna avoided her eyes. "I'm not. I'm making a

choice. I respect what Strike, you, and the others are doing, but I don't believe in it anymore."

"You don't believe there's going to be a war?" Lucius demanded. The question echoed back to their many debates on the subject of the Nightkeepers and the 2012 doomsday, which Anna had pretended to mock in an effort to keep him from looking too closely at the legends. Had she become convinced by her own arguments? Impossible.

She shook her head. "There's going to be a war, no question about it. But I don't believe that we can stop it. If we had the numbers and the skills . . . maybe. But a dozen magi? No. I'm sorry, but no. So I've decided that if I've only got another two and a half years to live, and there's nothing I can do to change that fact, then I'd far rather spend the next thirty months living my life rather than chasing futile hope."

Dull shock pounded through Lucius, alongside disillusionment. *How could you?* he wanted to demand. Anna had been his superior for the past decade-plus. She'd been his teacher, his mentor, his thesis adviser, his boss, and finally his slave-master. He had looked up to her. He'd harmlessly lusted after her, worried about her, and once he'd learned that she was one of the magi he'd spent a third of his life searching for, he'd practically worshiped her. But now . . . gods, now. How could he respect, never mind revere, someone who would willingly jettison the chance to make a difference?

But he knew her well enough to realize her emotions were already locked into her decision. So he went with logic. "According to the Dresden Codex, the Night-keepers will need a seer during the final battle."

"According to the codex, they'll need Godkeepers and the Triad too. I don't see either of those things happening."

"They might."

"They won't." Her eyes had gone hollow. "I wouldn't do this if I had the faintest hope that we could change what's going to happen. But do the math. There are too few of us. We're cut off from the gods. We don't have the prophecies or the spells we would need to defend the barrier, if we could even muster enough strength in numbers or magic." She shook her head. "No. We can't do it, and we're making ourselves miserable trying."

Low anger kindled in his gut. "You're giving up on yourself."

Her eyes flashed. "I'm making a choice."

"A selfish one. You'd rather be playing house with the Dick than working your ass off like the rest of us." She opened her mouth to fire something back, prob-ably a reaction to his old nickname for her unlikable husband, or an accusation that he was just jealous. But that wasn't why he was pissed. It was that she had the opportunity to be the sort of savior he'd always wanted to be, the mage he was trying to be . . . and she was just walking away from it. So he steamrolled over her response, saying, "Look, I don't know exactly what happened to you the night of the massacre, what you saw in your visions. But think about it. . . . That night, the *Banol Kax* and their *boluntiku* killed—what—a thousand people? Try multiplying it by a million. Ten million. A hundred million. What do you think *that's* going to look like?"

They didn't know exactly what form the end-time would take. The Dresden Codex suggested a flood, while Aztec mythology called for fire. And what about the aftermath? Would there be one? The sixth-century Prophet Chilam Balam had talked about mankind turning away from machines, which suggested a massive technology loss. But would humanity survive or be destroyed entirely? Would the earth itself exist in the aftermath? The Xibalbans seemed to be banking on a shift in world order, with Iago intending to be at the top of the proverbial shitheap when everything settled out. The *Banol Kax*, on the other hand . . . who the hell knew what they were thinking? For all the Nightkeepers could guess, the end-time war would be akin to the Solstice Massacre, only on a global scale.

Anna blanched, but her eyes stayed steady on his. "Screw you."

"Lucius," Jade said in warning.

He ignored her, pressing, "How are you going to feel on that last day, when everything starts to go to shit, and you realize that maybe, just maybe, you could've helped stop it?"

"Then you believe the Nightkeepers are going to fail too."

He bared his teeth. "Don't put words in my mouth. And no, I don't believe we're going to fail." He deliberately included himself in that "we." "I do, however, believe that we've got a far better chance of success with you than without you."

"Bullshit," she said scornfully, choking on a derisive laugh. "How have I helped so far? I've had a couple of visions that have confused things more than they've clarified them, and at that, I haven't had a vision in months."

"Because you're blocking them," he pointed out, taking a guess and seeing the confirmation in her eyes.

She glared. "I forced Strike to let you live, even after you violated my space, stole my property, and generally acted like an asshole. Remember that the next time you want to poke me about my duty to the Nightkeepers and the end-time war. If I'd been adhering to the writs, I would've let them sacrifice you two years ago when you conjured a godsdamned *makol*!"

"Maybe you should have," he said bluntly. "So far I've done more harm than good. But you know what? That just makes me more determined to get it right from here on out."

Anna shook her head. "You've always wanted to be more; both of you have. Can't you understand that I've always wanted to be less?" She addressed the question to Jade, seeking an ally.

Lucius started to answer, but Jade held up a hand. To Anna, she said, "Is that what you're going to tell the gods? How about your ancestors?" When Anna sucked in a breath, Jade pushed harder. "What will you tell your father when you meet him in the spirit world?"

Anna's expression darkened. "Given that I'm the only one of the three royal kids who hasn't had a conversation with the old man's *nahwal*, I'm not sure we'll have much to talk about."

"Your old man," Lucius repeated softly. "Where have I heard that before?"

Her flinch was almost imperceptible, but it was there. And her voice was sharply defensive when she said, "That's not the point. The point is that we can't live for our parents' goals. Sometimes we have to define our own. You guys understand that; I know you do."

Jade nodded. "Sure. But this isn't about your father. It's about you being able to help save the world."

Anna lifted her chin in a gesture he recognized as a member of the jaguar bloodline getting her stubborn on. "Not anymore it's not."

Lucius could see he wasn't going to win this one. But who among them could? *Strike*, he thought. *Maybe Jox.* "We're not going to tell the others that you're quitting." He indicated the polished crystal skull, gleaming softly amber on the desktop. "That's what you're saying by returning this, isn't it? That you're not coming back to Skywatch. Not ever." Leaning in, he dropped his voice. "Think about it for a moment; really think about it. And trust me: From someone who's been on the outside most of his life, it's not a comfortable place to live."

"It is if you've chosen it," she fired back.

"Fine, then. Come back with us and tell them yourself."

Her lips turned up at the corners in an utterly humorless smile, as though they'd finally gotten to the meat of things. Nudging the pendant a few centimeters closer to him on the desk, she said, "You owe me, Lucius."

There it was, he realized. And the bitch of it was that he couldn't say she was wrong. He owed her. Big-time. "You're calling it all in . . . on this?"

"I am. I won't be square with Strike and the others, I know. But I can at least leave things even between the two of us." She rose and moved out from behind the desk, then reached down, grabbed his hands, and hauled him to his feet as she might have done before, in order to kick him back to his own office or out to the lab. Now, though, he towered over her, dwarfed her. And she kept hold of one of his hands once he was up, and stayed standing inside his personal space. Jade remained seated, watching with her counselor's calm wrapped around her and faint panic at the back of her eyes.

Anna palmed a Swiss army knife, seemingly from nowhere. Lucius didn't move, didn't flinch as she scored a sharp stripe across his palm. Pain pinched and blood welled, but he didn't feel any magic. All he felt was failure—his and hers.

"We don't have to swear on blood," he said. The ache spread through him as she blooded her own palm and he got that she really meant it. She wanted to leave the Nightkeepers behind. Or she wanted them to leave her behind; he wasn't sure which was more accurate.

"We're not swearing. I'm doing something I should've done a long time ago." Clasping his bleeding hand in hers, she recited a string of words.

He caught a few, missed a few; he was far more used to working with glyphs than with speaking a language that had been dead for centuries. More, as she spoke, his head started spinning: a mad whirl of thoughts and blurred sight. He heard the words, glimpsed the fake antiquities, but they glommed together, tumbling around one another in a major Auntie Em moment. Pain slashed in his forearm—a wrenching sizzle that started at his marks and zigzagged up to his chest with a ripping, tearing sensation that left him hollow when it ended.

Jade lunged to her feet, reaching for him, but he held her off with an upraised palm, suddenly grokking what was going on. He yanked his hand away from Anna's. "No," he started. "Don't—" But then he stopped, because he knew it was already done. "*Fuck.*" The world settled down around him, his vision coming clear as he flipped his arm and confirmed that the black slave mark was gone. He wasn't bound to her anymore. Technically, he wasn't bound to the Nightkeepers anymore, either. "You didn't have to do that."

"Yes, I did."

His forearm now bore only the red hellmark, startling in its geometry, deadly in its coloration. "The quatrefoil's not balanced anymore." His heart thudded in his chest; his thoughts played demolition derby inside his head. What was this going to mean for his ability to tap the library? Something? Nothing? Was it an entirely moot point?

Jade moved up beside him, so they were facing Anna as a couple. No, he thought, not a couple. As partners. A team. She snapped, "That was a rotten thing to do without talking it through. For all we know, that was his only link to the magic. And you just *took* it." She was so angry she was practically vibrating.

"It was mine to take." Anna turned her palms up, not to indicate the gods, but rather saying, *Not my problem*. In doing that, she bared her right palm, where the sacrificial slice had already closed to a thin scab. Lucius's palm, in contrast, still bled sluggishly.

"That sucks," Jade snapped.

"That's life."

Lucius followed the exchange as if from a distance, through a cool numbness that began where the slave mark had been and spread throughout his body. Anna was a Nightkeeper who didn't want the magic. He was a human who did. "The gods have a strange sense of balance," he muttered.

"The gods are gone." Anna held out her hand to shake, human-style. "And as of today, so am I."

Knowing it was futile to argue further, that he didn't have the strength to shift an entrenched jaguar on his own, he finally nodded. "Okay. Fine. Whatever. Have it your way." He moved to scoop up the effigy.

"No, wait," Anna said. He paused, hopeful. But she gestured to Jade. "That's why I asked you to be here. I want you to wear it back to Skywatch. If it's not being carried by a member of the jaguar bloodline, it's enough that it's being worn by a mage I consider a friend." Her voice caught on the last word.

Lips pressed tightly together, Jade merely scooped up the effigy, draped the chain over her head, and tucked the sacred skull beneath her yellow polo, doing up the lower two buttons to conceal the priceless artifact. Taking her hand, Lucius headed for the door, aching with the knowledge that, unless Strike and Jox worked some major magic, it would probably be the last time he'd see Anna, who'd been a big part of his life for so long. When he had the panel open, his eye caught the laminated sign. *What have you got to lose?* When had the answer become "Everything"?

"Lucius," Anna said.

He glanced back. "Yeah?"

"Good luck." Her eyes shifted to Jade. "And to you. I wish . . . I wish I could be as brave and strong as you're learning to be. Gods keep you both."

Jade didn't answer, but her eyes glittered with unshed tears. Lucius tipped his head. "Good-bye, Professor Catori."

Out in the hallway, he tried to breathe through the numbness and the sense that the squat, dark building was collapsing inward around him. Jade's eyes were stark, her face pale, but she said only, "Do you want to grab any of the stuff from your old office? She boxed most of the things you left behind."

"Leave it," he said curtly. "There's nothing here I need."

"You up for tracking down Rabbit?"

He nodded. "Yeah. Let's do it." In a way, he hoped the kid was up to something. Knowing Rabbit, it'd be guaranteed to take his mind off Anna's defection, and the fact that Jade was wearing the crystal skull.

CHAPTER SIXTEEN

When Jade couldn't get either Rabbit or Myrinne on her cell, she and Lucius headed over to their summer sublet. The apartment proved to be the top floor of a detached garage. The main house was a good-size, brick-faced residential house with freshly painted white trim, ruthlessly shaped shrubs, and a perfectly trimmed lawn.

"Huh," Lucius said. "Doesn't look like either of their styles." It was the first thing he'd said since they left the art history building. He'd just walked beside her, grim faced and stone silent.

Jade slid a glance over at him. The fierce tension that had gripped his body seemed to have eased slightly, but his expression still had all sorts of Keep Out signs plastered across it. She didn't blame him; the past half hour had been a serious shock to her system, and she hadn't had nearly the relationship with Anna that he'd had. Unconsciously, she touched the bulge beneath her shirt made by the skull effigy. She felt a faint hum of power coming from it, but not one that resonated with the way she usually experienced the magic. That confirmed what Anna had said about the skulls being bloodline- and seer-specific. She didn't think it would affect her magic, or Lucius's . . . at least, not directly. Indirectly, though, its presence was a heavy weight between them, as was the bare spot on his forearm where the slave mark had been. She didn't know what Strike and the others were going to think about that. Heck, she didn't know what *she* thought about it. All she knew was that her plan of talking to Lucius about the emotional component of the magic on their drive home wasn't seeming like such a good idea now. He might be standing right next to her, but he'd never seemed farther away.

Hoping he just needed time to work things out in his head, she focused on the task at hand: finding Rabbit. And Lucius had a point on the digs. Although the relative isolation was consistent with Rabbit's fierce need for distance from everyone but Myrinne, the suburban-USA surroundings and soccer-mom minivan in the driveway didn't jibe. If they had just been normal students, Jade would have assumed it was a cost thing, but the Nightkeeper Fund had been set up to support an army of hundreds, if not thousands. It was beyond sufficient for the two dozen survivors. Heck, she'd heard Jox urging the kid to just buy a damn house rather than worry about a sublet. Granted, the *winikin* had followed that by muttering something about getting as much fire insurance as possible, but still.

So why the sublet?

"Can I help you?" A dark-haired woman nudged open the storm door of the main house with one foot. She wore sweats, was jiggling a swaddled baby in one arm, and had a *why the hell did I sign up for this?* look on her face. In the background, an older kid was screaming something about spaghetti.

Jade took a step toward her, smiling. "We're friends of Rabbit's. Are he and Myrinne around, do you know?"

"Sorry, I haven't got a clue if they're home. I saw them headed out this morning; don't know if they came back or not." The woman tilted her head. "They expecting you?"

"Not specifically." Though Rabbit had to know Strike wouldn't put up with being ignored for long, and would have seen her number pop up on caller ID just now.

"You can go up and knock. Be careful on the stairs; a couple of the treads are loose. They'll be fixed by the end of next week, though."

"Thanks." Jade headed toward the garage with Lucius falling in beside her, back in silent mode. Something—instinct, maybe?—told her that the apartment was empty. She figured it couldn't hurt to fake a knock. The woman had retreated back into the main house and shut the door, but Jade would've bet money she was watching through one of the curtained windows. At least Rabbit seemed to have landed in a decent living situation. The surveillance would, however, limit their options in terms of peeking through windows, trying to figure out what, if anything, he and Myrinne were up to.

On the way up, they discovered more than "a few" loose steps; the whole staircase groaned precariously under Lucius's weight. "What do you want to bet they've been on the fix-it list for 'the end of next week' for a while now?" he asked, not seeming particularly worried either way.

"She should ask Rabbit to fix them." Jade grinned. "Might be interesting to see what he'd come up with." Though in all fairness, the in-Skywatch buzz said that the young, powerful mage had cleaned up his act in recent months. When they reached the landing, she motioned him to shield her with his body. "Stand there so she can't see me."

He obliged. "What's your plan?"

"Working on it." She knocked, but wasn't surprised when she didn't get an answer. The place *felt* empty.

"Want me to kick it in?" He paused. "It'd make me feel better."

She grinned, glad he was thawing a little. Wait a minute . . . *thawing.* "Be my lookout, will you? I've got an idea that'll do less damage." *I hope.*

The ice magic came quickly, without even a blood sacrifice. Keeping her inner rheostat turned low, she pushed a small quantity of the magic into the dead bolt and regular door lock, where the forming crystals would expand and create pressure inside the mechanisms. She hoped.

Heat poured through her, lighting her up and bringing a prickle of sweat to her forehead and behind her shoulder blades. The locks clicked in one-two sequence, like she'd planned it that way. *Holy crap, I did it!* She wasted a couple of precious seconds staring at the door as excitement skimmed through her, warming her skin and making her want to dance. She'd actually—*finally!*—used magic for something practical and tangible, something more than just finding a reference that another mage could use instead of her.

Then, aware they were probably still being watched, she called, "It's me. Can I come in?" Pretending she'd gotten an answer from within, she opened up and stepped through. Lucius followed, shaking his hand at the sting from the ice-cold metal doorknob.

"Nice job," he breathed in her ear, sending shimmers through her. For half a second, the world seemed to shift a few degrees on its axis and the air sparked red-gold.

Steeling herself against the tug of lust—or rather, filing it for a "maybe later"—she lifted a shoulder. "I'm not sure I should be proud of my B-and-E skills when we're talking about a teammate." Still, though, personal space was something of a fluid concept among the magi, who lived a lifestyle that landed somewhere between communal and private, with blurred lines separating the two. Shandi came and went freely from Jade's suite, and the magi above her in the power structure could, theoretically, invade her space with impunity. The surviving Nightkeepers had tended to stick closer to the human theory of privacy, but there were exceptions. And this was one of them, she assured herself, even though there was a kernel of fear that Rabbit would come home, realize he had company, and fireball first, ask questions later.

On the theory of better safe than sorry, she reached into her pocket for one of the small, portable motion detectors they had used to secure their hotel room the night before, and set it up on the kitchen counter facing the door.

"We're supposed to make sure he's not in trouble," Lucius said, paraphrasing Strike's order as he scanned the room. "Okay. Where do we start? Or rather, what are the odds that Rabbit and Myrinne, who are both of above-average intelligence and deviousness, would leave something important just lying around?"

"Slim to none," she agreed. "So let's think devious."

The door opened into a kitchen nook that was separated from the main area by a half wall. Doors on the far side of the main room opened into a bedroom on one side, a bathroom on the other. The furniture was upscale box store, the built-in shelves were filled with anatomy and physics texts, and the wall art leaned toward Things I Like to Stare at While I'm Stoned. The few photographs racked on the shelves showed a doughy-looking guy posing with carbon-copy parents and what appeared to be his sister. Or maybe a brother with low testosterone levels? It didn't take a psych expert to guess the place had come furnished, and little—if any—of what they were looking at belonged to Rabbit or Myrinne.

Leaving the main room to Lucius, Jade moved into

the bedroom, feeling seriously uncomfortable to be invading the space of two people she might not consider friends, but who were certainly allies. She found a few fat red candles and some pretty crystals she could easily peg as Myrinne's. She thought she recognized some of the clothes tossed over a chair in the corner as belonging to Rabbit, and the pair of Dark Tower books on the nightstand could've been his. But other than that, there was little for her to go on. It was like the mage and his human girlfriend hadn't left any mark on the space, even though they'd been living there a few weeks already.

Unless . . . "What about magic?" she murmured to herself. Granted, the mental blocks meant that Rabbit theoretically couldn't use his powers outside of Skywatch, but he'd already circumvented those strictures at least once, when Myrinne had talked him into using a pseudo-Wiccan ritual in an effort to call a new three-question *nahwal*. It was possible he'd done something like that again. Or, if she wanted to be cynical about it—which was a good bet when trying to outthink Rabbit—he could've left himself a loophole or two when he'd installed his mental filters. Just in case.

Moving to the edge of the sitting room, which put her in the approximate middle of the apartment's footprint, she turned toward Lucius and crooked a finger. "Come here a minute."

His eyes narrowed. "Why?"

"Humor me. It's an experiment." Under other circumstances she might not have tried it, but she was all too aware that Strike was going to be furious over

Anna's decision. Fortunately for them, he wasn't the sort to shoot the messenger. But the news they were bringing home was going to seriously taint the king's perception of the trip . . . and potentially of her. More, she thought she and Lucius needed the same thing just then, albeit for different reasons.

He moved into her, going toe-to-toe, the spark in his eyes suggesting that he'd guessed her plan. "This close enough?"

"Almost." She closed the last little gap between them and, when his lips curved, moved in for the kiss. But whereas the taste and feel of him might have become familiar, what she put into the kiss now wasn't. She leaned into him, offered herself to him, invited and then demanded a response that he gave readily, sliding his arms around her and crushing her up and into him. She felt deliciously feminine, almost overpowered, yet strong at the same time.

Then, deliberately, she sent her mind back to the previous spring, when he'd disappeared into the desert and they didn't know where he'd gone, whether he was alive or dead. She remembered praying for him at the *chac-mool* altar back at Skywatch, remembered trying to bargain with the gods for his life. When those memories made her feel sad and small, she brought herself forward in time, to when he'd come back to Skywatch, hurt and angry. She thought of how she'd hoped their reunion would be. And in doing so, she fell into the fantasy.

You're back, her kiss said now. *I missed you. I didn't realize how much our time together meant to me until you were gone. And now you're back. Did you miss me? Did you think of me?* He made a noise at the back of his throat, surprise and desire mingled into a low growl that shot straight to her core and left her wet and wanting. His hands stilled on her body; he gripped her hips, holding her against him as he focused on the kiss. The feel of him against her shifted the memory to that of their first night together with him in his new body. Although she had told herself it was just sex, that they were together because of the library, she'd gone to him because of the reunion they had missed out on, and the heat they'd made together before. She'd been nervous and determined not to show it. And he'd been . . . himself. The outer shell might be different, but the man within was largely the same, with impulsivity offset by intelligence, a checkered history but a fierce focus on the future.

It was that man she kissed now.

"Jade." He whispered her name against her mouth as she took him deep again, fisting her hands in his hair and giving herself over to the moment and the sensations. And within her, around her, red-gold sparkled in the air. The world shifted on its axis and stayed shifted.

Easing back, she let her eyes open. And she saw the magic. It was gathered around her, formless red-gold power waiting to be harnessed. She didn't see glyphs now; she saw the raw shape and flow of the energy that could be bound into a spell, just as she'd seen the barrier energy before, the code beneath the chatter.

Lucius said her name again, this time as a question.

"I've got the scribe's magic," she said, keeping her voice low, almost a whisper, as though she might somehow scare it away. "I'm going to check for spell structures."

"You— Oh."

She couldn't read his expression, but couldn't worry about that right now. She didn't know how long the magic would stay with her, and needed to do her duty. They could deal with the rest of it later. Opening herself to the magic, she started moving around the apartment.

"What are you looking for, exactly?" Lucius followed, watching her scan the room.

"I'll know it when I . . . Ah! Gotcha." She ducked into the bedroom. "There's a bright glow here, a place where the power flow is concentrated."

"Power flow?"

"You know how Sasha senses life force? I think I'm doing something similar, only with the energy that can be shaped into a spell. Logically, sensing the magic and its structure is probably a requirement of creating a new spell that works structurally. At least, that's my guess as to why this looks and feels different from the magic I used to tweak the existing fireball spell."

He took a moment to digest that. "And you think there's a spell at work in here? I thought Rabbit wasn't supposed to be able to do magic outside of Skywatch."

"I'm not sure what I'm seeing, exactly. There are two brighter spots under the bed, or maybe one bright spot and an echo? Let's see what we've got." She skirted the bed, got down on her hands and knees, and followed the magic sparks to a long cut slit into the underside of the box spring. Gingerly, she reached inside. Her fingers found a reinforced envelope. She drew it out and stared down at it for a moment, wondering whether she was about to do something she would regret.

"Maybe we should take it straight back to Strike," Lucius suggested.

She was tempted, but shook her head. "I don't want to bring him something that turns out to be nothing." Taking a deep breath, she flipped open the envelope and dumped its contents. And stared at the pictures that landed in her palm, quelling an urge to let them fall to the floor. "Okay. Ew."

She didn't have anything fundamental against porn. But these photographs were . . . unattractive. It wasn't just that the guy in them was pudgy and unfit, and had too much hair in some places and not enough in others, either. Her squick factor came more from the sheer lack of artistry as he posed his way through a variety of odd contortions, all of which managed to aim his startlingly erect member at a camera she thought—hoped?—was on autopilot. Even worse was the scanned printout of a paragraph that came off as so demented, it took her a moment to realize she was looking at a very unfortunate personal ad starring the apartment's primary tenant. The face matched the pics out in the other room.

"He's trying to get a date? With *that*?" Lucius sounded like he was caught between horror and laughter.

"Either that or he's been asked to participate in a

psych thesis on why women are staying single longer and longer as the Internet age progresses," she said dryly. "Okay, that was disturbing." Stuffing the pictures back in the envelope, she filed the whole mess back in the box spring. "Why in the hell did he hide the photos if he intended to put them online? And why is there a power hot spot?"

"Maybe Rabbit found them and had a good laugh?"

"I wouldn't put it past him."

"More likely, the magic was attracted to the highly sexualized resonance of the pictures." He paused, frowning. "Except that the pictures themselves aren't sexual, unless the guy actually looked at them while he—" He held up a hand. "Okay. Not going there."

Jade thought it was more likely that the magic was pulled to things and places that carried a significant emotional charge for the user, but it wasn't the right time for her and Lucius to go *there*, either. She might be buzzed from the magic and excited by the breakthrough, but she was achingly aware of what she'd given up to get there. She was raw and needy, all too conscious of his every move and breath, and the way his raspy-edged voice brought a long, liquid pull of desire regardless of what he was saying.

Even as nerves sparked at the realization that her defenses against him were far too low, the magic dimmed around her.

"What about the second place you saw? The one you said looked like an echo?"

She shook her head. "It's gone now." And so was the

magic, which had disappeared when her inner barriers came back up. That was going to be the trade-off, she suspected, and hoped she could find a way to strike a balance between vulnerability and magic.

"Okay, so we do it the old-fashioned way." They spent the next half hour searching the apartment, focusing on places where her training suggested addicts—and deviants—would hide things they didn't want their friends, parents, and other authority figures to find. They came up with a big fat nothing, which gave them two positive results to report back to Strike. Although they hadn't physically put eyes on Rabbit and Myrinne, the landlady said they were around, and the apartment didn't show any evidence of magic or other misbehavior. And Jade had managed to tap into the scribe's magic and make it useful.

On the theory that the landlady was guaranteed to say something to Rabbit, Jade pulled a blank sheet of paper out of the printer in the main room—which wasn't mated to a computer, suggesting that Rabbit and Myrinne were both schlepping their machines—and scrawled a quick note: *Strike sent me and Lucius to find out WTF is going on with you two. I'd suggest you phone home soonest.* She signed her name, left the note on the kitchen counter, and pocketed the motion detector.

Lucius held the door for her on the way out. As she passed him, he leaned in and whispered, "That was a hell of a kiss. What do you say we get on the road so we can stop sooner than later?"

The heat in his eyes twisted something deep inside her, making her want so much more than he was offering. Self-protection said she should find an excuse, but she was weak enough, wanting enough, that she smiled and hit him with a quick kiss that landed a little off center. "It's a date." Or, more technically, a booty call.

CHAPTER SEVENTEEN

Skywatch

In her twenty-six years on the earth plane, Patience had been a good girl and she'd been bad. She'd been a student and a teacher, a child and a mother, a sweetheart and a bitch. But she'd never considered herself a sneak, a liar, and a thief. Until now. Her pulse thrummed as she paused in the hallway leading to the royal suite. It was empty; had been for the past five minutes. Strike and Leah were out at the firing range, Jox was in the greenhouse, and, given that the magi were largely scattered to their tasks, the coast was as clear as it was going to get. It was now or never. Yet still she hesitated.

"What are you waiting for?" she murmured to herself. "If you're looking for an invitation, it's not coming." Nor was negotiation or any sort of compromise—she'd been waiting for both of those things for nearly a year now, and was finally ready to admit that it wasn't going to happen. She'd begged; she'd bargained; she'd worked her ass off in an effort to earn Strike's confidence, only to learn that it didn't get her as far as she needed to go.

"Be patient," Brandt said every time she brought it up. "Their safety has to be our first priority." Which would've been fine if she'd truly believed that the boys' safety *was* his first priority. Over time, though, she'd come to realize that as much as he loved her and their boys, he was bound to the writs first, with his family coming in a distant second at best.

"Fuck that. I need to see my boys." Having exhausted all her bright ideas for getting what she wanted within the writs, or even within the quasi-human ethics Hannah had raised her with, she was going to have to take it the other way. Sneak. Lie. Steal. *Shit*.

Taking a deep breath and manning up, she crossed the last distance along the hall and let herself into Strike and Leah's quarters. Nausea was a low-grade companion as she shut the door and slipped across the entryway, ninja-style. For all that she'd imagined herself a warrior as she'd trained endless hours in the dojos Hannah had brought her to, she hadn't truly understood what it meant to be a warrior until that first fight against the *Banol Kax*. And now, she realized, she truly understood the other half of her training: stealth. She strongly doubted Hannah had meant for her to use it against her own king, but once she was inside her doubts sloughed away, leaving her determined to achieve the single goal she'd set herself: Find her kids. Strike knew where they were, or at least how to contact them; he was the only one, though. He hadn't even told Jox, because the royal *winikin* had a history with Hannah. Leah might know, but she made Patience more nervous than even the king did. The queen had a *look* that went right through her. Patience wasn't sure if that came from cop work, magic, or something else, but she gave the queen a wide berth. And now, as she crossed the royal couple's sitting room and beelined it for the dining room, where papers were strewn on a dining table turned to office space, she knew she was running a hell of a risk. If she were discovered . . . *You won't be*, she told herself firmly. *Just do it*.

Working fast, she rifled through the papers on the dining table, looking for an address she didn't recognize, a note in Hannah's handwriting. Something. Anything. But no. She pawed through Jade's reports on Kinich Ahau and a bunch of satellite photos of the Ecuadorian cloud forests, but didn't see anything she could connect with Hannah, Woody, or the twins.

"Did you really expect that he was going to leave it lying around?" she murmured. "Maybe with a big arrow highlighting the phone number?"

She'd thought it through often enough, trying to figure out how to find what she sought. She'd never come up with much of a plan beyond a flat-out physical search, though. The Nightkeepers didn't put anything important on the Internet-connected computers. Iago's people had already shown themselves plenty capable of hacking, and a well-made *makol* could command the thoughts and memories of its human host, meaning that the *Banol Kax* could usurp their own hackers. Ergo, the sensitive stuff was kept on non-networked machines. Patience was assuming Strike

and Leah had at least one of them in the suite. But
where was it?

A quick but thorough search of the living space
turned up a big, fat nothing. No paperwork, no computer. She forced herself through the bedroom, which
boasted glass walls on three sides and was dominated
by a big, sybaritic bed that made her decidedly uncomfortable. But not uncomfortable enough to give up the
search. She pressed on, skimmed through the closets
and bathrooms, her nerves notching higher with each
passing minute.

Shit. Shit. Shit. Where could it be? They wouldn't
have taken the safe machine with them to the gun
range. It was in the suite somewhere. Heart pounding,
she checked the doorways leading along a short hallway that didn't seem to have much of a purpose . . .
until she got to a door about halfway down and hit
pay dirt.

As she opened the door, gas torches flared automatically to life, lighting a bathroom-size chamber
lined with stone veneer and holding a *chac-mool* altar.
Adrenaline zinged at the sight of a blond woman looking back at her; it took her a half second to recognize
herself, wild-eyed and nervous, reflected in a highly
polished obsidian disk hung behind the altar. The
king's heavily carved ceremonial bowl sat on the altar,
with an unfamiliar knife beside it, weighing down a
short stack of the heavy parchment that was used for
small blood ceremonies. The room was imbued with
magic, and a weighty sense of history. Under any other
circumstance, Patience would've backed her ass out of

there and pretended she knew nothing about Strike's private place of worship. And she would have done that now . . . if it hadn't been for the laptop case tucked in the corner of the ritual chamber. It was hidden, she suspected, not so much from Leah but from Jox.

Last chance, a little voice whispered inside Patience. *You can still take off. Nobody would know you'd been here.* Which was true . . . except that *she* would know she'd wussed out. And that wasn't an option for her, either as a warrior or a mother.

Her legs shook a little as she knelt; her hands trembled as she fumbled open the case and powered up the little mininotebook. There was no password or security—why would there be? Strike wouldn't have imagined anyone would break into his quarters, into his freaking *shrine*, and fire up his machine.

"Come on, come on!" she chanted under her breath as the stupid thing took precious seconds to boot, longer to bring up the Windows screen, with its reassuring blue background. The desktop was stripped down to the absolute basics, just a couple of folders. She opened one labeled KINGLY CRAPOLA, which was pure Strike.

It contained six subdirectories, none of them obviously what she wanted. She opened each of them and quickly scanned through, discarding anything with last-update codes well before the middle of the prior year, when Strike had 'ported Hannah, Woody, and the twins away from Skywatch. *Nothing. Nothing. Still nothing. Oh, gods . . .*

She struck gold on subfolder number four; she couldn't remember the name, knew only that she was looking at a reference request and credit check on Woodrow Byrd, who was applying to rent a four-room apartment in Seattle. The first name was right. The date was right. And Strike, with the help of the Nightkeepers' tame PI, Carter, had made sure the credit checks all came back fine without linking to anything substantive. More, there was a second file in the subfolder: a lease agreement, signed for a year in Woody's name . . . but in Hannah's handwriting.

A sob caught in Patience's throat and the luminous screen blurred as tears filled her eyes. But when emotion would've put her on her ass, her warrior's talent flared, clicking her over to logic and rationality on one level of her consciousness. That part of her fumbled out her family-only cell phone, punched in the address, and saved the precious information. Then she closed out of the files, powered down the mininotebook, and tucked it back into its case in the corner. Leaving the room as she'd found it, save for being a few degrees warmer, smokier, and lower on oxygen, thanks to the gaslit torches and her own hyperventilation, she slipped out of the shrine and shut the door, pausing to wipe the door handle, not because she thought anyone would be likely to dust for prints, but because . . . well, just because. Then, breathing shallowly through her mouth and moving on cat's-paw feet, she retraced her steps through the royal suite.

Even as her body was going through those motions, though, her heart and mind were focused on her phone, and the treasure within it. An address. She knew where her babies were—or at least where they'd been. Rather than exultation or excitement, she felt numb with the emotional hugeness of it, the prospect that she might soon be watching them walk past as she stood nearby, invisible. Hungry for even the sight of them. Would they sense her? Would they somehow know she was there?

"Don't get ahead of yourself," she warned herself. "One thing at a time." And just then, the one thing was getting out of there unseen. She'd been in the suite far longer than she'd planned, but a quick pause and scan at the main doors showed that the hallway was still empty, the coast still clear.

Once she was out in the hall with the carved door closed behind her, she exhaled a long, deep breath and inhaled its return, the oxygen making her suddenly light-headed. Her blood buzzed in her veins and she could've sworn her feet weren't touching the ground anymore, though it was joy rather than magic making her feel that way. Laughter bubbled in her chest as she spun a full circle, her hands spread away from her body and her hair flaring out.

"Bullshit," the king's deep voice said, faint with distance. "I had you beat until the last set of targets. And you cheated."

Patience froze, her smile turning to an "O" of horror.

"Gods, could you be any more of a sore loser?" Leah's voice was light and teasing as the two of them continued their long-standing debate over who rocked the gun range. "I took out one more target with half a clip fewer jade-tips. And you shot one of the good guys; that's an automatic forfeit."

"I still say she looks like a shifty bitch," he said of one of the new false-alarm targets Michael had installed in an effort to train the warriors to avoid collateral damage.

"She's eighty if she's a day, and she's using a walker."

"Not anymore she's not," Strike said with dry satisfaction. "Bitch is dead."

Leah's laughter burbled, but Patience felt only dread at the happy sound. *Oh, shit.* What was she going to do? The hallway dead-ended at the royal suite; the only other doorway along it led to the royal *winikin*'s rooms. Both of the suites had exterior doors, but if she could hear the royal couple's footsteps, they'd be able to hear a door shutting—the heavy panels weren't quiet, and it'd be far worse to be caught trying to escape versus bluffing it through. Going invisible wasn't an option because the other magi could see right through the illusion; the magic worked only on non-Nightkeepers. So it was bluff time.

You can do this, she told herself. *You've prepared for this.* She'd run through the scenario in her head a hundred times, thought of a dozen excuses for why she was in the royal wing univited. But as Strike and Leah rounded the corner and caught sight of her, their steps hesitating nearly in unison, her mind went completely and utterly blank.

"I'm—" *Sorry*, she stopped herself from saying, because that hadn't been in any of the scripts. A hot flush climbed her cheeks and flop sweat spiked its way down her spine. "Uh—"

"Oh, good, there you are," a new voice said from behind the royal couple. Patience boggled as Brandt rounded the corner, moving full steam ahead and looking purposeful. He nodded to her. "I was coming to tell you they weren't still out at the gun range, but I see you found them."

Leah sent Patience a sharp glance; Patience tried to replace the look of panic with one of purpose. "Well, technically I'd say they found me." She hoped to hell they couldn't see her hands shaking.

Strike seemed to buy it. He refocused on Brandt. "You need us for something?"

"It's just an idea I've been kicking around. Pretty preliminary stuff, but I wanted to get your take on it." He nodded toward the royal suite. "Do you have a few minutes now?"

The king nodded. "Sure thing."

The three of them moved past Patience, but then Brandt paused very near her, letting the others get ahead. As she stared up at him, he looked almost like a stranger, all hard eyed and angry . . . until he leaned in and brushed a kiss across her cheek and whispered, "One of these days you'll start believing we're on the same side."

Then he straightened and walked away, motions stiff and angry. But instead of dismay at his anger, or the irritation she'd so often turned to recently, she felt warmth unfurl in her chest. And as she headed back toward their apartment with her phone clutched to her chest in an unconscious hug, she felt, for the first time in a long, long time, that maybe she wasn't so far away from putting her family back together, after all.

Texas

Lucius and Jade made a quick stop at a drive-through for calories, after which she dozed off in the passenger seat, recovering, Lucius assumed, from the scribe's magic. When they'd left the sublet, he'd been strung tight and jonesing for the sex her kiss had promised, but it was probably better this way. He'd been raw from the scene in Anna's office and the knowledge that he was leaving his old life behind once and for all, making him more vulnerable to her than he'd wanted. He'd been shaken by the makeout session, loose kneed and knocked off-kilter by the intensity of his own response and the sudden, almost overwhelming urge to sweep her up, lose himself in her, promise her things he had no intention of promising.

That was the old Lucius, the one who'd charged headlong into flawed relationships, only to pancake hard. That wasn't him. Not anymore. Still, though, the need for sex rode his blood. He would've liked to think it was magic, that he was close to breaking through whatever barrier kept him locked on the earth plane, but he knew it wasn't the magic. It was Jade.

He kept glancing over at her as he drove. She was partway curled on her side facing him, with one hand under her cheek, the other fisted loosely in her lap. Her forearm marks were a dark contrast to her pale skin;

he wanted to kiss her there, wanted to kiss her all over, until she felt desired. Cherished.

Let her sleep, he told himself. *There's time yet.*

But how much time? They were down to less than four days to the solstice. If the *Banol Kax* managed to put Akhenaton into the sun god's place, there was no telling what would happen. Would the pharaoh come after his ancient enemies once again? For all they knew, Skywatch would be a damned crater by the twenty-second, unless he found a way to get his ass back in the library to pull out the info they so badly needed. But, short of offering himself up for a soul sacrifice and hoping to hell his body would become the receptacle for a true Prophet, he didn't know what he could do to help. More, he and Jade were bringing back news of Anna's defection, which was going to have ripples beyond the cow Strike was going to have. But at the same time, Lucius couldn't help wondering whether Anna might not have a point. The Nightkeepers needed a super-Prophet but didn't have one. They needed Godkeepers, a seer, the library . . . hell, more manpower. None of those things seemed imminent. Some didn't even seem possible.

"The magic has to be the answer, for my part of things, at least," he said, thinking aloud as the miles unfolded beneath the Jeep's off-road treads. "I'm human, so therefore shouldn't have magic, but Cizin was attracted to me. There had to have been nastier dudes than me on campus, and they would've been an easier sell on the *ajaw-makol* possession. So why me?" It was tempting to think that there was some reason the demon had been able to reach through the barrier and influence him the way it had. Although the Nightkeepers guarded their bloodlines and had strict mores against producing half-bloods, the fact that those mores even existed suggested there had been some strays over the years. So he supposed it was possible he could have a Nightkeeper descendant way back . . . but that didn't play, given that his only real connection to Nightkeeper magic had been through the slave mark. Glancing at his forearm, he suppressed a shudder at the thought that he could just as easily be part Xibalban. Regardless, the library spell was Nightkeeper magic, suggesting that he could access either light or dark magic. "But how the hell am I supposed to do that?"

A mildly irritated *beep-beep* from his left warned him that he'd better concentrate on driving; he'd gotten so caught up in his thought process that he'd wandered into the fast lane. A pickup truck zoomed past going a solid ninety, and pulled away, leaving him alone to wander the lanes. Startled from his mull-and-ponder, Lucius realized that he'd gotten farther than he'd thought; the city and suburbs were gone, leaving him on a long, straight stretch of highway with not much to see in all directions. It was also later than he'd realized; the orange sun was dying behind scrub-covered, rolling hill silhouettes. A few more miles down the road, when he passed a small sign for lodging, he pulled off the highway and followed three more arrowed signs that claimed to be leading him to the Weeping Willow Inn. It was farther off the highway than he really wanted to be, but just as he was getting ready to turn back, he saw the turnoff leading to the inn.

The place had probably been a working ranch in the past; the driveway wound through the middle of sparsely covered grassland. Lucius didn't see any livestock, though, and the lane was marked off with neat split-rail fencing rather than the more common barbed wire or electric used for working rangeland. That and the relative newness of the signage kept him from turning around, thinking the place would probably be way too sketchy for an overnight. Then he topped a low hill, got a look at the Weeping Willow Inn, and let the Jeep roll to a stop, not because the inn was sketchy at all, but because it wasn't.

Nestled in a small, scrub-furred valley, a half dozen bunkhouselike cottages were scattered behind a main ranch house that was fronted by a wide, welcoming porch. In the fading light, he saw that all of the buildings were done in earth-toned clapboards and rough-cut wood, and dressed up with fanciful touches of gingerbread molding that gave the buildings a distinctively feminine air. Window boxes and whiskey barrels bloomed with flowers, and stones marked winding paths from each cottage to the main house, which a discreet sign identified as both the office and the kitchen. Two vehicles sat in a fenced-off parking area: a dusty SUV with a cargo clamshell strapped to its roof, and a pickup with WEEPING WILLOW INN painted on the side. *So there's probably room for us*, he thought wryly. More, he liked the cottage idea. He'd dealt with the high-rise hotel the night before, but even leaving the balcony door open to its screen hadn't totally taken away his sense of being boxed in. He'd sleep better in a place like this.

In fact, the inn was pretty much perfect . . . if he'd been planning a honeymoon. It was way more intimate than he'd been expecting, though. The generic hotel room they'd stayed in the prior night had been a way station. This was more like a spot for lovers. The man he'd been before would've rocked a place like this, buying into the kitsch in the hopes that the ambience would make up for his own shortcomings. The man he'd grown into since leaving UT told himself to do a one-eighty and find a Motel 6. A woman couldn't possibly misinterpret a Motel 6.

At the sound of a soft sigh, he looked over at Jade. She'd tucked her other hand beneath her cheek and was trying to snuggle into the hard foam seat, her neck crooking in a position that had to be getting uncomfortable. *She's tired*, he told himself. Not to mention that he was tired too, or at least sick of driving. He wanted some downtime, some space to reset his brain. And the pretty little cottages made him think of Skywatch.

"Fine. The Weeping Willow Inn it is." He eased his foot off the brake and let the Jeep coast down the hill toward the parking area. As he did so, he was aware of a low-grade churning of nerves, one warning him that he was making a mistake. He ignored it, though. He had enough troubles already; he didn't need to borrow more.

CHAPTER EIGHTEEN

Jade awakened warm and rested, tucked into a sinfully soft bed that smelled faintly of minty sage. She was feeling deliciously loose and proud of herself, and that latter emotion was so unusual for her, she took a moment to track the pride to its source. Memory came flooding back in a flash: She'd found her magic through a kiss, and she'd had to give only part of herself to get it. More, she'd proved her second theory correct: She couldn't touch the magic unless she was emotionally available. It wasn't a comfortable discovery for a woman who'd spent years teaching others—and herself—how to self-protect, but there it was. What was it that Scarred-Jaguar was supposed to have said time and again? *Sacrifice isn't supposed to be easy.* Well, this one wasn't, but she thought she could learn to live with it, so long as she kept a firm grip on reality.

Remembering another aspect of her present reality, she shifted under the bedcovers, reaching a hand to reassure herself that she was still wearing Anna's skull effigy. She wasn't looking forward to telling Strike what had happened, but she *really* didn't want to follow it up by admitting she'd lost the irreplaceable pendant. She went still when she found she was wearing only her bra. No shirt . . . and no pendant.

"Don't freak," Lucius's now-familiar raspy voice said. "It's on the nightstand."

Exhaling a long, relieved breath, she opened her eyes to mock-glare at him. "Way to give me heart failure." Then her eyes widened as she caught her first glimpse of their surroundings.

She had assumed he would've checked them into another no-tell motel while she'd been sleeping off her postmagic crash, but the rough-finished wood beams and pristine white plaster of the bedroom she found herself in were a far cry from the average offering of a highwayside chain. The sky was the blue-black of nightfall, visible through a pair of French doors and framed by gauzy white curtains that were repeated in the filmy swags that roped the huge canopy bed. A bedside lamp was on, sending soft light through a cut-glass dome to gleam on the yellow quartz skull, which sat safely on the nightstand, its chain neatly coiled beside it. The bedclothes were white; the whole room was white, except where splashes of violet and navy blue were picked out in framed watercolors on the walls and boxy accent pillows on the long couch along one wall. An open door offered a glimpse into a bathroom done in navy tile with violet edging and pristine white towels, with a Jacuzzi-jet tub big enough for two.

Lucius stood in a wood-framed doorway; beyond him she glimpsed a sitting area of natural wood and emerald green, but it was only a glimpse before her eyes locked onto him. Arms folded, he leaned against the door frame, watching her with a familiar intensity that sent shimmers of heat washing through her in an instant, and took her straight back to the kiss they had shared in Rabbit's sublet. That might have been hours ago, but as their eyes met it might have been no more than a few minutes. She was instantly back there, with need coursing through her body alongside a poignant ache beneath her heart.

His gesture encompassed the room. "Not bad, huh?"

"Nicer than last night's generica America, by a long shot." It was a room made for romance. For love. It had probably been his only non-truck-stop option for a hundred miles, she told herself. The choice had been expediency, not seduction. Unfortunately, she had started the evening already halfway seduced, though that had been her own doing—and the magic.

"We're at an inn called the Weeping Willow," he said by way of explanation. "Willow is our proprietress. The weeping, I gather, occurred when her fiancé died in Vietnam. Her parents both passed soon after, leaving her family money from oil rights, along with the ranch, which she turned into an inn because she likes having the occasional guest." He paused, the corners of his mouth kicking upward. "Or so I learned after I made the mistake of commenting to the lady checking me in that there aren't many weeping willows out in west Texas."

"Ah," Jade said, matching his smile. "I take it the lady behind the desk was Willow?"

"Got it in one. It's just her, a road-tripping family in the cottage closest to the house, and us out here on the edge of it all." His gesture encompassed what she imagined was a whole lot of nothingness in the night beyond the French doors. "And yes, I set the motion detectors around our perimeter and made it clear to Willow that she shouldn't come knocking."

Jade's brain hadn't yet gotten around to worrying about security. She was still stuck on the bedroom ambience and the man standing in her doorway. He'd showered and changed into a fresh tee and jeans; he was barefoot, his hair still slightly damp. She couldn't decipher his expression, and badly wanted to. Although he was keeping the conversation light, there was nothing light in the hazel depths of his eyes or the hard, hungry set to his jaw.

"Well, then. Since you've taken care of the possibility of interruptions . . ." She let the comment trail off on a suggestive purr, acutely aware that she was wearing only her bra and panties beneath the bedclothes, which meant he'd already had his hands on her once that night. Her body tingled at the phantom memory, and in anticipation of what was to come. "I believe that earlier today, you voted for sooner rather than later?"

He hesitated longer than she would have expected. She said nothing, though, did nothing. Although she thought he was almost ready to embrace the magic, to open himself up to it and to her, she wasn't going to trap or trick him into it. Finally, he exhaled a long, shuddering breath, crossed to her in three strides, and eased onto the bed beside her. "I can't not do this," he said in an undertone rasp, and she got the feeling he wasn't totally talking to her. "I want this. I want *you*."

The scent of sage and mint intensified as he kissed her openmouthed, with the blatant possessiveness that had sparked between them back in Rabbit's sublet. She kissed him back, helpless to do otherwise, but deep down inside her, panic kindled at the realization that she didn't know the rules anymore.

Her heart shuddered in her chest. *Be careful*, she told herself. *Be very careful*. Because the man kissing her now wasn't the Lucius she'd come to know over the past week. Or rather, he was, but he was also the Lucius she'd known before, the one who had been so much more open with himself, and with her. The man kissing her now was the man she'd been with in the archive, the one who had sparked feelings strong enough to frighten her and make her shut him down. Back then, she'd shoved him into the friends-with-benefits zone, afraid that he might tempt her into the trap she had seen so often in her practice, the love that caused an otherwise strong, capable woman to disintegrate when her lover turned on her, spurned her. *He wouldn't do that*, she told herself. *He's different from the others. He's Lucius.* But at the same time, she imagined Shandi's voice—or was it the *nahwal*'s voice?—cautioning, *He's just a man. He'll distract you, weaken you, make you forget what's important.*

Which might be true . . . except that Jade was almost certain that *this* was the important part. She'd been wrong before when she'd said sex magic was about the act. It wasn't about the sex, after all. It was all about finding the connection . . . and it was up to her to show Lucius how.

Drugged with desire, with the romance he'd brought her to, intentionally or not, she kicked free of the bed-clothes and came back to him, pressing her near nudity to his fully clothed, fully aroused body. He groaned encouragement and cupped her ass, his fingers splaying wide beneath the lace of her panties as he urged her toward him, rolled partway over her, pinning her with his good, solid weight. Their legs wrapped together, threading in a four-way braid. Her feet rubbed against the strong, lean muscles of his calves, and she thrilled to the strength of every part of him.

Whispering his approval against her mouth, he dragged a hand up from her hip to her ribs, then higher, to shape the outside of one breast. Then he popped the clasp of her bra, freeing her to his touch. Arching into his hand, she grabbed the hem of his tee and pulled it up, rucking it high between their bodies, and then off over his head, so they were skin-to-skin.

"Lucius," she said, his name a sigh. Then, so she couldn't say anything more, she nipped his lower lip and slid into his kiss, moaning when it went suddenly dark and wild, matching what she'd felt before when she'd called her magic. She sensed the power hovering nearby, felt it flowing through her and reverberating with the burn of heat as he hooked a hand around the crook of her knee and drew her leg high against his hip. He surged against her, setting a rhythm that thrummed through her body and made her neurons sing, *Yes, oh, yes.* Or maybe those were her words, urging him on as they kissed and rocked together, rolling so he was fully above her, wholly pressing into her, holding her nearly helpless beneath his big bulk. He kissed her deeply, demanding a raw, primal response that she felt with her entire body.

He pulled away and looked down at her, his eyes dark and nearly wild. "You're so godsdamned beautiful," he rasped. It was the first time he'd said something like that to her, and the small compliment brought starbursts to her bloodstream. Before she could say anything in return, though, he shifted to cup a breast in his wide, scarred palm and lowered his head to taste her, taking the tight, sensitive tip in his mouth. He worked one breast and then the other, concentrating on each action separately, with the intensity he brought to the things he deemed important.

Helpless to do otherwise, Jade arched into him, her mouth opening on a silent cry. She buried her hands in his hair, holding him there for a long, glorious moment. A faint warning sounded at the back of her consciousness, a spark of panic that kindled as heat and want flared through her and she lost track of herself. Her whole world concentrated itself down to Lucius, and the ways he was touching her, the things he was making her feel.

Was this, then, what other women found with their lovers? Was this the path to madness? If so, she needed to back off, gear down, let things level. But even as she was aware of the fear and the thought, both were lost to the pressure growing within her, the need to have her hands and mouth on every part of him, to make him feel the same obsessive need that gripped her. Before she could make the move, though, he moved to kiss his way down her body, leaving her no choice but to caress whatever part of him she could reach, and absorb the feelings detonating within. Pleasure slammed into her, through her, great waves of it building and growing, holding her hostage to each new sensation. Then he moved back up her body and she was surprised to realize that he was naked now, that they both were.

The glide of skin against skin was viciously erotic as he slid up her body to kiss her mouth once again. She tasted the faint salt from her own skin, the sharp tang of his arousal, and the combination of the two. Sinking into him, letting the rest of the world fall away, she gave herself over to the gossamer pleasure he'd brought her, and the sharp need to have him inside her. Wrapping her legs around him, she opened to him, shifting until they were almost, but not quite, joined male to female, hard to soft.

He went still above her, in her arms. But he didn't thrust home. Instead he stayed there, poised and unmoving.

Jade opened her eyes to find him staring down at her, his hazel eyes hot and borderline wild. But when their gazes met, his expression eased. He touched her face, drawing a finger down her cheek to her chin, then tipping her mouth up to meet his in a kiss. When the kiss ended, he whispered, "There you are."

Then, before she could respond—if she'd even

known *how* to respond—he shifted, aligning their bodies more surely, leaned in to kiss her long and deep . . . and slid into her. And as he did so, she understood what he'd been waiting for. Not for her to give in or give up, but for her to return to him and be in the moment, with him. With them.

No longer lost in the layers of pleasure, she acutely felt his penetration, felt her inner channel stretching to accept him, tightening around him in a squeeze of welcome that wrung a groan from deep within his chest. The sound of it vibrated through her, making her neurons hum and spark, and making her intensely aware of his size within and without, and the carefully leashed strength that pulsed through him as he hooked his arms behind her, loosely gripped her shoulders, and used the leverage to hold her in place when he began to move.

She should protest, she knew, should assert herself as a partner in their sex, giving back equally rather than allowing herself to be dominated, pinned down, *taken*. And she *would* protest, she assured herself. In a minute. But one minute turned to several, then to time untold as he moved over her, inside her, giving her pleasure and taking it in return. Sweat slicked his spine and sides, causing her hands to slip as she touched him, stroked him, her hips pistoning in aching counterpoint to his strokes as heat built to a roar. His tempo increased; she clung to him, buried her face in the crook of his neck, and *took*. She wasn't giving anymore, wasn't thinking about his pleasure; she was beyond that, gone past herself to a mindless place that beat with an ungrammatical chant of, "More, harder, yes, oh, yes, *there!*" Gods. She didn't know her own name, didn't care about anything happening beyond the hard grasp of his arms and the expanding sphere of her own pleasure, which had gone sharp, growing teeth, needs, and demands. "Yes, like that. *Please.*"

She was begging and didn't care. He was saying things too, but she could barely hear him over the hammering pounding of the blood in her veins and his body into hers, and the broken gasps of pleasure that streamed from her. *Ohyesohyesohyes!* Clinging to him, hanging on to him with the knowledge that she'd be lost if she let go, she cried out as the first orgasmic contraction seized her, making her whole body rigid and vising her inner muscles around his thick, heavy length.

He gave a guttural roar that brought her even higher as he thrust and thrust again. Then he seated himself to the hilt within her, pressing hard against her most sensitive spots within and without, bowed his head, and let himself go. His muscles locked rigor-tight as he bowed into her, held her against him, and shuddered his release. Hips flexing, he pressed himself into her harder still, once and again, in an automatic reflex that protracted the echoes of her pleasure.

They stayed locked together, holding hard on to each other, for a long, long time.

Eventually, though, the heat faded to languor and reality returned. And that reality had Jade's hands staying locked onto his shoulders, and her face remaining pressed against his throat . . . because she didn't have a clue what to do next, what to say. She would've liked to keep things light and playful, as she'd meant to in the very beginning, but somewhere between desire and domination, things had turned serious.

Lucius let out a long, satisfied breath, muttered something about crushing her, and sort of flopped off to one side. Part of her would've been relieved if he'd landed facedown and fallen immediately unconscious, as one of her unlamented exes had habitually done after far more lukewarm sex than the room rocking that had just occurred. Lucius, though, propped himself up on one elbow and gazed at her, his expression far more intense than she would've preferred. She wasn't sure what he read there; his expression was guarded and his voice gave away nothing of his inner thoughts when he said, "You okay?"

It was the sort of thing lovers said to each other when they didn't know what else to say. In this case, though, she knew he meant it, that he truly wanted to know where her head was at in the aftermath of . . . well, in the aftermath. But she didn't know where her head was at, wasn't really sure if she was okay or not. The sex had been . . . amazing. They'd connected, pleased each other. But whereas her magic had kindled, flowing within her, his magic hadn't. There had been no hint of the whirling, tugging sensation she'd experienced right before their transition to Xibalba, and again when she'd been swept into the barrier in his wake. He'd given no sign of sensing anything beyond very, very good sex. *Which means that was all it was for him*, she thought on a long, slow twist of disappointment.

"I'm—" She broke off, gut icing at what sounded like a cry of pain from outside. "Did you hear that?"

Seconds later it came again, and this time there was no mistaking the sound of a woman's scream. It was muffled by distance, but carried terror and pain. Adrenaline jolted through Jade. She was moving even before the motion sensors guarding their perimeter went off with a loud *whoop* of alarm.

"*Shit!*" Lucius scrambled off the bed and hit the floor hard, yanking on his clothes as he ran. He grabbed her folded clothes from a chair and chucked the shirt and jeans in her direction. "*Hurry.*" He disappeared into the sitting room; moments later, she heard the snick of the lockbox latches and the metallic clicks of clips being slapped home into autopistols.

Dragging on her jeans first, Jade pulled the panic button out of her pocket and activated it as she shoved her feet into her sneakers. She dropped the handheld unit in the process of jerking her shirt on over her head. Just as she bent to retrieve it, the French doors exploded inward and the chatter of machine-gun fire split the night. The bullets cut through the air where she'd just been, slicing the white canopy swags to tatters and pulping plaster to dust as she threw herself flat behind the bed.

"*Jade!*" Lucius appeared in the doorway, carrying a double-barreled shotgun with deadly menace. He was wearing black body armor over his T-shirt and a black utility belt slung low across his hips over his jeans. The belt was loaded with spare clips and guns, and a military-style combat knife hung where the magi wore their bloodline blades. The combination of warrior's gear and human casual should have jarred. Instead, it made him look deadly and capable.

"I'm here! I'm okay." She scrabbled partway up, grabbed the skull effigy off the bedside table, and then lunged toward him while he laid down cover fire with double loads of jadeshot, spraying the night outside the ruined glass doors. The booms of the shotgun were deafening in the close quarters, but it was viscerally satisfying when they cut through the higher-toned chatter of automatic fire. It was even better when the guns outside went silent. She wasn't willing to bet that would last for long, though.

"Hurry." He was right behind her. "We've got to get out of here."

"No shit." She yanked on the body armor Jox had found for her, and grabbed the second shotgun while Lucius loaded up on grenades. Her heartbeat drummed loudly in her ears, and she was shaking with a combination of nerves and adrenaline, but her head was clear; she was thinking, not just reacting. And she hadn't frozen. Not yet, anyway. *Not this time*, she told herself. Which reminded her of the magic: not the spells, but the ice. "I could—"

Something flashed outside, luminous green. "Down!" Lucius shouted, and lunged for her. He hit her with his shoulder and knocked her off her feet and into the sofa, but somehow managed to get his arms around her and turn himself so he partway shielded her from the impact.

They tumbled to the floor as the sitting room windows shattered inward under a hail of gunfire. Curs-

ing, Lucius rolled them to the sofa, flipped it over atop
them, and held her so tightly she could barely breathe.
The furniture was scant protection against the heavy-
caliber weapons; the bullets had wasted the window
glass and the curtains, and were doing a damned good
job of chewing through the walls themselves, coming
from all directions at once.

"We're surrounded," she yelled into Lucius's broad
chest, barely able to hear herself over the thump of
gunfire and destruction.

"Did you hit the panic button?"

She nodded into his chest. "They're on their way."
She'd left the device in the bedroom, but if Strike
couldn't get a good 'port fix off the images from the
built-in camera, there was a similar unit mounted atop
the Jeep. More important, the magi could use the view
from the Jeep to assess the situation, and figure out the
safest place to materialize.

"We can't wait for them here." His voice rumbled
against her cheek, carrying a grim sort of finality.
"Whoever's out there might decide to just fuck it and
crater the cottage. We're safer out in the open than
pinned down here." *Though not by much*, was the unspoken end to that statement.

"Use the grenades to get their heads down," Jade
ordered. "Then we run. I'll shield us."

"You've got shield magic?"

"No, but I've got ice. It'll have to be enough."

He nodded, his jaw tight, his expression set in lines
of concentration. "It will be. I believe in you." Leaning
in, he kissed her hard and fast, and when he pulled

back, there was something new in his eyes, something that made her heart lurch in her chest. "I'll cover you."

For a crazy moment, those three words rearranged themselves in her head to become something else entirely. So she merely gaped when he heaved against her, overturning the sofa and in the same motion yanking the pins from three jade-loaded grenades. He counted, "One . . . two . . ." On "three" he heaved the grenades through the blown-out windows. They landed on "four."

On "five," there was a rending, tearing explosion outside, followed by screams of agony as jade shrapnel tore into their attackers.

"Come on!" Lucius grabbed her and dragged her up, and then they were running for the door. As they ran, Jade yanked the combat knife from his belt, used it to nick her palm, and called the ice magic. Power formed around her, coalescing to include Lucius in a circular swirl of cold air convecting with hot. She had originally intended to put an actual shield of ice around them, but saw the better option immediately. Instead of casting the iceball magic, she built it around them. Ahead of them it was clear. Everywhere else around them, sleet whipped in a twenty-foot whirl, obscuring them as Lucius flung open the cottage door and they ran out into the night.

CHAPTER NINETEEN

Lucius's heart rattled in his ears, sounding like machine-gun fire, but that was the only *rat-tat-tat* he heard as they fled through where he thought the enemy lines had been laid. The grenades had done their work. In the low-lying solar lights planted on either side of the pathway, he saw a hand, a foot, a dark smear he thought was blood, and his gorge rose at the knowledge that *he* had done that. Not Cizin this time. Him.

But he'd do all that and more if that was what it took to keep Jade safe. Dull rage pounded through him, hatred for the bastards that had come after them, and— *Not now*, he told himself. He couldn't think about that right now, just as he couldn't think about the crazy intensity of their lovemaking, or the clutch of his heart when the first salvo of bullets had ripped through the French doors and he'd seen her go down.

Without warning, a machine gun chattered from nearby, sweeping a wide arc that glanced off the icy shield. The bullets passed through the sleet. Jade gasped and the magic winked out.

"Jade!" Lucius grabbed her and dragged her into the lee of the next cottage over. "Are you hurt?"

"I couldn't hold it any longer." Her face was bloodless; she was shaking. But she hadn't been shot. *Yet.*

They needed to buy more time. But how? Between the dim illumination from the solar walkway lights and the bright, welcoming porch lights up at the main house, he could see back to the shattered windows of what had been their cottage, and in the other direction to the cottage where the road-tripping family was—had been?—staying. Everywhere he looked there were dark, slinking shadows and the flash of luminous green eyes. "*Makol,*" he hissed, the word coming out as a curse.

A few of the figures came clear; he saw a pudgy guy in a cheap suit, another in coveralls, a third in insignia-less fatigues. Their eyes were pure *makol* but their motions were jerky and uncoordinated.

Trying to look in every direction at once, Lucius nudged her in the direction of the parking area. "We've got to keep moving. Head for the Jeep. Strike and the others should be—"

A whistle split the air and their cottage exploded.

"Go!" Lucius put himself between her and the blast, feeling shrapnel ping off the body armor. He shoved her toward the Jeep, then jerked her back when the next missile—RPG? fireball?—hit the ground in front of them. *Shitshitshit.* He pushed her back into their scant shelter, trying to think of a way out, trying not to think about what would happen if they couldn't escape.

Adrenaline and denial roared through him. He wouldn't let them have her, wouldn't let her become what he had been. His body flared hot and cold; his head spun; his vision narrowed to pinpoint focus as six *makol* stepped into the light. He took out the first with a blast from his shotgun, nailed the second before the first had finished falling, then ducked a spray of gunfire that chewed up the corner of their hiding spot. He locked onto the third, finger tightening on the trigger—

And the bastard burst into flame. As did the *makol* next to him, and the next, the fire leaping one to the next in a mad, destructive dance. In an instant, the night was lit day-bright with flames that gouted twenty feet into the air.

Lucius stared, transfixed with horror as the *makol* screamed in agony, reeling and pinwheeling, trying to douse the inexorable flames, which burned their clothes away, melted their skin and flesh. They were still linked in a napalm chain; he followed it back into the shadows, just in time to see a man step into the light.

The newcomer was tall and built, his hair trimmed into a military brush cut. Sharp featured, looking to be somewhere in his twenties, he was wearing ass-hanging, ripped-up jeans and a tight wife-beater, and bore the hellmark on his inner forearm along with three Nightkeeper glyphs in black: the peccary, the warrior, and the pyrokine.

It was Rabbit, Lucius realized with a hard, hot jolt of relief. Their backup had arrived.

The young man's face was set, his eyes hot and hard, and flames laced from his outstretched hands as he fed power to the fire magic, driving it higher and higher still while the *makol* folded, slumped to the ground, and broke apart into dark, hard lumps of char.

Then, abruptly, Rabbit dropped his hands and the magic winked out.

The afterimage burned into Lucius's retinas left him momentarily blinded, blinking. By the time his vision cleared, it was all over. The *makol* were briquettes and he and Jade were surrounded by heavily armed Nightkeepers. With a few terse orders, Strike sent Nate and Alexis—apparently back from Ecuador, just as Rabbit seemed to have reappeared—to sweep the perimeter and set a watch.

The abrupt shift from threat to rescue left Lucius feeling badly off balance. Or was that the aftereffects of the strange sensation he'd felt just before Rabbit showed up and played human blowtorch? Had he been on the verge of breaking through to magic of his own? Had he sensed the incoming teleport? Or had it been some sort of entirely human altered consciousness associated with imminent death?

"What the fuck happened here?" Strike demanded.

The question seemed evenly divided between him and Jade, who had moved up to stand beside him. When she didn't answer right away, Lucius said, "Your guess is as good as mine right now. We heard the—"

He broke off when it registered. "Willow. The inn-keeper. We heard her scream."

Michael nodded as he joined the group. "I count five human casualties in the other buildings, a family in one cottage, an older woman in the main house. The *makol* were—" He broke off. "Let's just say I've seen a lot of shit in my life. This was pretty bad."

Gods. Lucius didn't let himself close his eyes, though he very badly wanted to. His stomach pitched with the knowledge that Willow and the road-tripping family of four would've been snoozing in safe oblivion if he hadn't turned off the highway and followed the arrows.

"After the scream," Jade said, picking up his report, "the *makol* breached our perimeter." She sketched out the attack, her voice impassive, her mien gone counselor-cool.

Lucius told himself it was a good thing she could pull herself together so quickly and thoroughly, that he shouldn't resent her recovery. But he was still reeling, and the blood ran hot in his veins. He wanted to shoot something, wanted to tear into someone and let off some steam. Crazy impulses pounded through him, strange and unfamiliar.

Forcing himself to focus, he grated, "The *makol* were new, and they were locals."

The magi zeroed in on him. Strike ordered, "Keep going."

"Their movements were slow and jerky, like the *makol* controlling the bodies weren't used to all the synapses yet. Which was lucky for us, as it made them inaccurate, if well armed. There wasn't any continuity of clothing, so they weren't an assembled fighting unit. There was a mechanic, a guy in a suit, a soldier-wannabe type in military surplus. I bet we'll find a bunch of cars parked down the road." He looked at the charred lumps, wondering if the magi had known Rabbit's magic didn't require the head-and-heart spell to nuke *makol*. From the looks the kid was getting, he suspected that would be a "not."

Michael nodded grimly. "I took down four of them in the main house. One was wearing a T-shirt from a gun shop with a local address. The other three were in military surplus. What do you want to bet there's a private militia quartered somewhere in these hills?" He paused. "It'd be a good hunting ground for someone looking for bad guys."

"Like an *ajaw-makol*," Strike agreed. He looked back at Lucius. "That's what you're thinking, right?"

"It plays," Jade said, her voice strong, even if her color wasn't. "We've suspected there might be an *ajaw-makol* on the earth plane. Either the *Banol Kax* sensed that Lucius and I were outside the Skywatch wards and sent the demon after us, or the thing sensed us and came on its own."

"I'd guess the latter," Lucius said. When the others looked at him, he lifted a shoulder. "My impression—and that's all it is—was that *makol* are similar to the magi in that they have different skill sets. I didn't get the sense that Cizin was in constant contact with its masters, more that it phoned home now and then, probably during the cardinal days."

"What was in your demon's toolbox?" Michael challenged.

Lucius bared his teeth. "How about the ability to reach through the barrier and compel an otherwise decent guy to steal from someone he respected?" But that brought his thoughts circling back to what he'd been thinking on the drive, about birthrights and tendencies. Shelving that for the moment, he continued. "Regardless of who or what gave the order, my guess is that the *ajaw-makol* got here and recruited a couple of dozen locals, pulling the gnarliest and nastiest, and handpicking a couple of specifics, like the gun store owner and the militants, both of whom came with access to firepower."

Strike considered that for a few seconds before nodding. "It plays. Now for the million-dollar question: How did they track you? Or, more important, what changed between last night and tonight? Was it just a question of timing, or was there something more?"

Lucius didn't say anything about the whirling buzz that might or might not have been his magic, because that had happened after the attack began.

Jade, though, said, "I think I know." She loosened her hastily applied body armor, reached in, and lifted Anna's pendant from around her neck. Letting the chain flow through her fingers, she held it out to him. "On the way home, I was carrying this."

The king stared at the skull effigy, which glinted in the

porch lights of the main house. His face ran through a range of emotions, none of them comfortable. In the end, he settled not on the fury that Lucius had anticipated, but on a sharp grief of the sort Lucius had seen before at the gravesides of loved ones cut down unexpectedly. Leah touched Strike's arm and murmured something in his ear. The king blinked, his face went to stone, and he took the pendant from Jade with an almost violent swipe.

"I'm sor—" Jade began, but Leah cut her off with a lifted finger that said, *Not now*, and Jade subsided.

Strike folded the chain carefully and slipped the pendant into his pocket before refocusing on the others, his cobalt eyes gone hollow. "That probably explains it. She should've brought it back to Skywatch herself. It's not safe to separate these sorts of things from their bound bloodlines."

Lucius didn't have an answer to that, so he stayed silent. Inwardly, though, he cursed Anna. Bad enough that she'd given up on the Nightkeepers; worse that she'd endangered Jade in her cowardice.

Four dark shadows melted from the darkness: the sweep teams reporting back that the site was clear. Strike nodded. "Okay. Michael, you and Lucius wait for Rabbit and take the Jeep. I'll 'port everyone else back with me." He moved away to an open space, and he and the others started forming the palm-to-palm link he typically used for group 'ports.

Neither Jade nor Lucius argued against their separation. As far as he was concerned, if there was a demon out there hunting Nightkeepers and their relics, he wanted her safely back at Skywatch ASAP.

When they were gone, Michael tapped his shoulder. "Come on. Let's get the Jeep." The mage claimed the driver's position and waved Lucius to shotgun.

"Isn't Rabbit coming with us?"

"In a minute." Michael burned rubber out of the parking area and didn't stop until they'd hit the top of the hill. Then he spun a quick one-eighty and parked, leaving the vehicle idling as he looked down at the Weeping Willow Inn.

The first lick of flames came from an upper floor of the main house. The second came from one of the cottages. Then it was hard to keep track of where the fire was tracking as it danced back and forth, lighting the buildings, consuming them. Rabbit stood at the edge of the visitor's parking lot, visible in silhouette against the firelight, as he conducted the destruction with wide sweeps of his arms, a maestro of fire.

"Oh," Lucius said as understanding dawned.

"I did my best with the bodies," Michael said quietly. "If their families ask questions, the sort of investigation there's likely to be out here will conclude that they died quickly in their beds, with no suffering."

"Which is a lie," Lucius said hollowly. "They suffered."

"Yeah, they did. But it won't help for the people left behind to know it."

Lucius thought of what he'd yelled at Anna, sanctimoniously bitching at her to think about how she would feel to know that people were dying and she could have done something to stop it. *Well, now you know, asshole. How does it feel?*

The ranch was fully involved now, the fire tongues reaching up to the sky where the deaf gods lived. He pressed his forehead against the now-warm glass of the Jeep's window and watched the flames, how they swirled and slashed, almost but not quite making pictures that seemed they should have meaning. In them he saw the garrulous innkeeper, not as she'd been that evening, but as the young woman in the framed picture that had sat on the front desk. In it, she'd had her arms wrapped around a smiling GI, neither of them knowing they would both die under enemy fire, some fifty years apart.

She'd never remarried, she'd told him; had never really even dated. Her Bobby had been her man, her one true love. She might not have died for him, as Jade's mother had done for her family, but in a way, Willow had given her life just as surely to love.

Gods, how do people do it? Lucius wondered, making himself watch as Rabbit conducted events down below. *Why do they do it?* What was the upside of love, when there seemed to be so many downsides?

"You kept Jade safe," Michael said suddenly, unexpectedly. "You got her out of the cottage."

"We should've kept driving."

"Then they would've hit the Jeep and you probably wouldn't have made it out." Michael paused. "Look, I know the math doesn't work on that one: two people if they hit the Jeep versus five people at the ranch. I'm sorry, but not all of the 'we the people' are actually created equal. Jade is valuable, potentially vital. You're . . . well, we're not sure what you are. But you're something. So, yeah, I'll trade the two of you safe for the lives of five noncombatants."

"Is that the sort of math they taught you in assassin school?" Lucius asked bitterly. "Or is that more of an us-versus-them Nightkeeper thing? How many humans would you trade for a single Nightkeeper's life and still consider it a fair trade? Fifty? A hundred? A thousand?"

Although Michael's temper had mellowed since his engagement, he still had a hell of a glare. He used it now. "Honestly? However many it took. There are eleven of us and however many billion of you. If our survival now means that you all get to see Christmas Day 2012, then fuck the math and protect the magi." He sent a sidelong look in Lucius's direction. "Same goes for the woman you love, mage or not. You do what it takes, whatever the sacrifice."

Lucius let that one pass and returned to staring down at the ranch, where Rabbit was concentrating his fire white-hot on a couple of key locations. "Doesn't he ever get tired?"

"Apparently not this week," Michael said cryptically.

It was another ten minutes before Rabbit, satisfied with his work, doused the flames and trudged up the hill to the Jeep. Michael dug through Jade and Lucius's road supplies and pulled out a gallon of water and Lucius's spare clothes, and made the soot-covered, sweat-soaked mage wash and change before he let him in the Jeep. Still, the smell of smoke was thick and cloying.

Rabbit opened the passenger-side door and jerked his thumb at Lucius. "Out. I've got shotgun."

Lucius bristled. "Why? Mage's prerogative?"

"No, asshole. You grubbed through my apartment. Not that there was anything to see there other than Pervy Doughboy's wiener pics, but still. It's the principle."

Discovering that he didn't have a comeback for that, Lucius climbed into the cramped rear deck, collapsed across the bench seat, and found a semicomfortable position as Michael sent the Jeep back along the narrow secondary roads and out onto the highway. They passed a couple of fire trucks headed the other way, sirens going. Lucius didn't know why that made him feel a little better about leaving. After that, he didn't fall asleep so much as his brain simply shut off, unable to process anything more. It didn't turn off all the way, though; instead it sent him dreams of dead eyes and flames, and a wall of stone that looked solid, but wasn't.

PART III

✳

DUSK

*The sun descends, light is lost, the world darkens, and
secrets grow in the shadows*

CHAPTER TWENTY

June 18
Two years, six months, and three days until the zero date
Skywatch

Jade awoke groggy; for a few moments, she stared at the ceiling of her suite, seeing a gauzy white canopy that wasn't there.

As she dragged her ass out of bed and into the shower, she ached, not physically, but mentally and spiritually. There had been too many highs and lows lately; she just wanted a few hours of peace, maybe with a mindless project that would occupy her brain just enough that she wouldn't have to think about the five dead strangers, or the fact that she would've sworn on her soul that she and Lucius had been simpatico when they'd made love in the cabin. That had been lovemaking, damn it, not fuck-buddy sex. Only his magic hadn't kicked in. Which meant the emotions hadn't been there for him— or at least, not the way they were for her.

Worse, she was becoming the thing she feared, falling prey to the pattern she despised. As she made herself coffee, she was practically counting the hours until the Jeep rolled in, even though she wasn't sure where things stood between them now; wasn't sure where she wanted them to stand.

"Gah!" She threw up her hands, unable to stand herself. "Go . . . do something."

If it hadn't been three days until the solstice, with the whole of Skywatch locked in a state of tense expectation, waiting for something to break with regard to Kinich Ahau, she might have headed out to the greenhouse. The gardens were mostly Jox and Sasha's territory, with Michael's *winikin*, Tomas, doing the lion's share of the manual labor—because, he said, it kept him too tired to bust Michael's chops nearly as much as he used to. But even so, Jade occasionally stopped in for an hour or so of dirt work, which she'd always considered damn good therapy.

Under the circumstances, though, hitting the greenhouse would've seemed self-indulgent. Considering that just yesterday—gods, it seemed like forever ago—she'd finally called the scribe's magic on command, she figured she was duty-bound to hit the *Idiot's Guide* again and see what she could do with some of the other spells.

To her surprise, she found Patience in the temporary archive, frowning at one of the computer workstations, which the *winikin* had moved into the room while the reno crews worked on repairing the archive.

Pushing aside an inner stab of frustration that she'd

done more damage to Skywatch than to the enemy so far, Jade dredged up a smile. "Can I help you with something?"

The power button is the big one with the circle on it, she thought with uncharacteristic bitchiness. But then again, she and Patience weren't exactly tight. Even though Jade had given her a number of tips on beating depression in the weeks and months after the twins had been sent away, the other woman had ducked hard whenever Jade needed help with data entry or any of the other grunt tasks the archive occasionally required. Jade had let Patience get away with the mommy excuse while it was relevant, and the depression excuse after that, but Jade didn't think she was the only one losing patience with the pretty blonde.

Patience looked up from the computer—which was already powered up, so at least she'd gotten that far—and smiled so warmly that Jade promptly felt like a bitch. "Yes, thanks. I'm looking for the ongoing file. Strike asked me to update it with a rundown of the Egypt trip, for good or bad."

"Sure. That's no problem." Unusual, yes, but not a problem. Jade clicked her way through a couple of levels of the computer desktop and pulled up the metafile that was part of Strike's efforts to ensure that the current Nightkeepers' experiences would be transmitted to subsequent generations—assuming that, gods willing, there *were* future generations—far more smoothly than had been done previously.

Given that the Nightkeepers had found themselves fighting a rearguard action against things they quite often should have known about, but didn't, the king had made a point of asking each of the magi, *winikin*, and humans in residence to chronicle his or her experiences, thought processes, strategies, and action plans as they went along. In theory that sounded great. In practice, Jade often found herself transcribing the quick vignettes that the warriors tossed off to her in passing, or patching together fragmentary e-mail missives from off-site ops. Less frequently, the others would write their own stories longhand for her to transcribe. The others almost never came to the archive to type into the raw file . . . as in, she could manually count the number of times that had happened without using her toes.

More, Jade realized as she ran through those few incidents in her head, each of those times had been less about the mage in question wanting some hands-on writing time, and more about their wanting to hide out in the archive, needing some productive-feeling peace. A glance over at Patience suggested that was the case here, as well. The other woman's face was etched with stress and fatigue, and she toyed with the hilt of the ceremonial dagger she wore on her belt.

I can relate, Jade thought sourly. She pushed back from the computer. "You're good to go."

"Thanks." Patience got to work; within moments, her fingers were flying across the keyboard with a clatter that sounded like machine-gun fire.

Breathing past the adrenaline kick brought by the comparison, Jade snagged the *Idiot's Guide* and carried it over to the other workstation. She found herself sneaking looks over at Patience, though. It was strange seeing her at the computer, even stranger that she didn't look out of place. The image jarred Jade's perception of her teammates and the way they fit together . . . or didn't, as the case might be.

"Go ahead, say it." Patience stopped typing and glanced over at her, eyes lit with faint challenge.

Caught out, Jade fell back on counselor mode. "What is it you think I want to say?"

"That I should get over myself, stop whining about being separated from my boys, make up with my husband, and do whatever else I possibly can to strengthen the Nightkeepers and make sure Harry and Braden have a world to live in—and lives to lead—in 2013." Patience lifted her chin, blue eyes defiant, yet wary.

Jade grinned, comforted to find that she wasn't the only one having a pissy morning. "Honestly? I was thinking that you type way faster than I would've expected. What was that, seventy words a minute? Closer to eighty?"

Patience just stared at her for a second. Then she burst out laughing, though the laughter carried an edge. "Why? Because I come off more like a fluffy ex-cheerleader than anything? Are you wondering if I took touch typing as part of an admin course?"

"Is that how you think other people see you?" The question came from both parts of Jade; the therapist framed it, but the woman saw the pain and wanted the answer.

"Don't you?"

Questions and more questions, classic defensiveness. *This isn't therapy.* Patience was a teammate, though perhaps not a close friend. The two women were acquaintances at best, not just because of Patience's lack of interest in academics, but also because she had come to Skywatch with her life already fully formed. She and Brandt had both known all along that they were the Nightkeepers of legend, that they might one day be called upon to serve. Granted, they hadn't told each other about their true natures, leading to a hell of a surprise when they'd arrived separately at Skywatch, but still, they seemed to have gotten past that, seemed to have made a family unit within the Nightkeepers. Or was that only the surface of things? Jade wondered suddenly. She'd known there was trouble in the relationship, but had thought it was strong enough to withstand the bumps. What if she'd been wrong?

"I can't say the word 'cheerleader' has ever come to mind," she answered. "I see you as a woman who was a warrior even before she came here. You started your own dojo and made it a success, even as a young mother, which means you're focused and driven, and you've got good business sense." She turned her palms upward. "I don't know why the typing was a surprise, except that you've always been so much more focused on the physical than I am. You spend most of your day in the gym, on the range, in the training hall . . . so maybe I pegged you as a girl jock, and not someone who would keep her touch typing up to speed."

A slow, almost shy smile had crept onto Patience's face as Jade was speaking. Now the blonde stretched her long, elegant fingers and looked at them. Nine nails were shaped and painted a pale, pearlescent pink. One, the left pinkie, was snapped off near the quick, leaving a ragged edge. "Typing's physical . . . it's really just hand-eye coordination, after all. In fact, it's almost a sport." She paused. "But thanks for seeing me as capable. Sometimes I forget that I used to be that person. Here . . ." She looked around the plain auxiliary room, though Jade suspected she was seeing all of Skywatch and the responsibilities it symbolized. "Here, I feel like a misfit cog in the calendar wheel. I'm a day that's just slightly out of step. A week with too many hours in it, or too few."

"I think we've all felt that way, some more than others." Jade lifted a shoulder. "We just lose track that we're not the only ones feeling it."

Patience glanced at the computer screen, though Jade wasn't sure what she saw there. "It just sucks, you know? There are enough of us here that it shouldn't feel like we're all alone."

"Welcome to my world," Jade said emphatically.

Patience frowned. "But I thought you and Lucius—"

"Are having sex. Great sex, mind you, but that's it."

"Don't knock it," the blonde said dryly. "Sometimes the love part really stinks."

"There's a song in there somewhere."

"Very funny."

After that surprising exchange, the women fell companionably silent. As Patience once again started her rapid-fire typing, Jade steeled herself, closed her eyes, and thought back to the night before—not the attack, but the lovemaking. She tried to remember only her own thoughts and feelings, but instead found herself locked on the look in Lucius's eyes as he'd taken her, possessed her, branded her. Her skin heated as the magic came; her body tightened and throbbed as she remembered his hands on her, his mouth, his fingers—

Jerking herself out of the memory, she opened her eyes. But instead of the spell book, she found her attention drawn inexorably to the man who was standing in the doorway as he had the night before, leaning on the door frame, watching her.

"Lucius!" she exclaimed, hoping he didn't see from her face how open she was to him at that moment, how much her senses lit at the sight of him, and how much she wished they were alone.

Patience's head snapped up. "Oh!" She did something with the mouse, then very deliberately looked back at the screen and started typing again. "Just pretend I'm not here. Or tell me to get lost if you need to."

"You're fine," Jade said, but her attention was locked on Lucius. "I'm not sure I can say the same about you," she told him. "What happened?" He looked tired and run-down, and although his hair was slightly damp and he was wearing clean clothes, he smelled inexplicably of wood smoke.

"Rabbit sterilized the scene," he said when she wrinkled her nose. He held out his hand to her. "Let's take a walk. I need your help with something."

"Is that a euphemism?" Patience asked without looking up.

Lucius grinned. "I thought we were pretending you had turned yourself invisible."

Her head came up and she glanced speculatively at him. "Given that she would be able to see me but you wouldn't, that thought has potential. Weird potential, granted, but potential nonetheless."

Jade snorted. "Glad to see you're feeling better."

"I haven't been feeling good for way too long," the blonde answered bluntly. "I've decided it's time for me to get over myself."

"Fair enough." Jade set aside the *Idiot's Guide,* let the magic dissipate, and stood. To Patience, she said, "After the solstice, you, Sasha, and I should have a chick date."

A shadow crossed the younger woman's face. Jade was familiar with the look, having seen it plenty in her practice. It was one part excitement at the thought of making plans, one part, *Oh, no, I couldn't; I need to spend time with my child/boyfriend/husband,* and one part dismay at realizing that number two wasn't true anymore, whether because of a divorce, a breakup, or a death. Patience rallied quickly, though with a smile nowhere near the wattage of the others. "I'd like that."

To Lucius, Jade said, "A walk, huh? Anywhere in particular?"

"Humor me. I have an idea."

Jade and Lucius left hand in hand. Patience watched them go and felt a twist of envy, not just for the great sex they were apparently having, but for the uncertainty and excitement of a new relationship. New love was supposed to be simultaneously wonderful and awful; that was okay. If it was tearing you up inside, you were doing it right. When that sort of thing started happening for the first time at year six . . . that was a different story.

"Just get through this and you'll be fine," she told herself for the hundredth time. After checking to make sure nobody else was coming to hang in the book room—since when was the archive party central?—she returned to the computer and the two files she had open.

She saved and closed the first one, a quick rundown of her and Brandt's trip to Egypt that she'd named "Camel butter, Cairo, and nothing new on the pharaoh." That left the one she'd really been after, a doc Strike had entitled simply "Finding Mendez."

Patience had been afraid to read it openly with Jade in the room, because she knew that pretending interest in recent history wasn't going to fly with the archivist. So she'd waited the other woman out—and had enjoyed the process far more than she had expected to.

Now, though, she focused on her objective, skimming through the story of how, as a new-made king, Strike had gone personally to collect two of the holdouts who hadn't answered the messages informing them of their true Nightkeeper natures and calling them to Skywatch. The first had been Nate, who had initially resisted, but had eventually come around. The

second had been Snake Mendez, and that was where
things had gotten complicated. Strike had walked into
the middle of the mage's apprehension on an outstand-
ing warrant for several all-too-human crimes. Raised
by a less than sane *winikin*, Mendez had found the
magic on his own, and potentially had access to one of
the lost spell books. He also had an impressive list of
arrests. Amid the chaos of trying to re-create the Nightkeepers out of a dozen human-raised magi, Strike had
decided to let Mendez stay in jail rather than orches-
trating anything.

But Patience wasn't interested in Mendez; she
wanted the person who'd taken him down. The address she'd stolen off Strike's laptop had been six
months too old. A call to their landlord had revealed
that Woody, Hannah, and the boys had moved on. Patience couldn't ask Carter to look into it; he was the
king's PI. Nor was she interested in picking someone
out of a phone book. She wanted the best.

Halfway down the screen, Patience's eyes locked on
the name Reese Montana. "Bingo."

Who better than a bounty hunter to find a couple
of *winikin* who were doing their blood-bound best to
stay lost?

Lucius elected to walk himself and Jade out to the back
of the box canyon on the theory that, one, he was sick
of the Jeep, two, they could return for wheels later if
necessary, and three, he didn't want to make a big deal
out of the expedition, in case his hunch didn't pan out.
So they walked hand in hand along the canyon floor,

breathing the strangely humid air and passing ragged clumps of the algaelike plants that were growing throughout the canyon now. They didn't talk about the plants, though, or the way the dim sunlight made the humidity feel ten times stickier than it might have otherwise. In fact, they didn't talk at all, which he thought was probably best, because he couldn't think about much of anything other than what he hoped they were about to find . . . and how much he dreaded finding it. But at the same time, he was aware of walking in sync with her, breathing in sync with her. She was someone he could share silence with.

When they reached the back wall of the canyon, Jade started automatically for the shallow staircase leading up to the pueblo ruins.

Lucius tugged her back. "Wait. Not up there."

She turned back. "No? Where are we going, then, and what do you need my help with? I'm assuming that wasn't, as Patience suggested, a euphemism."

"I need your magic."

Her brows snapped together. "Okay, that's not what I expected you to say to me." She paused. "For that matter, it's the first time *anyone* has said that to me." But she was intrigued. "Go on. What are you—or rather, what am *I* looking for? Are you thinking buried treasure?"

"Not exactly." He turned her so she was looking off at an angle. "See that curvy rock over there, the one that makes sort of an 'S' shape? And see how next to it there's a round hole that looks man-made?"

"I see them. What do you want me to do?"

"I need you to look for energy patterns, the way you did in Rabbit's apartment. Do you need a boost?"

"Nope, I've got it covered." That shouldn't have irritated him, but it did. Beneath the irritation, though, his worry persisted as she took a couple of calming breaths and faced the rock formation he'd seen in his mind's eye as the burning inn had receded in the distance.

Was there a better way to do this? He'd thought to have her look for a hidden door first, then—

"I see it," she said.

He exhaled in a rush. "Okay. I have to warn you, though—"

"It's a spell I'm not familiar with," she interrupted. "I think it might be like the one that the ancients used to hide the First Father's tomb, not just a visual illusion but a physical one as well. Michael said that one was very old magic, but he figured out how to turn it off and on. Let me see if I can remember the spell he used. It didn't work for me back then, but it might now." She headed toward the spot.

He snagged her arm, shaking it. "*Jade!* Wait up and listen for a second. This is important."

She looked up at him; her eyes were sleepy and blurred, and very, very sexy. She blinked at him, her eyes clearing with a final whole-body shudder. "Whoa." She rubbed her face with both hands. "I went deep under the magic there." She shook her head, seeming more like herself once again. "Okay. What's up? Are you expecting there to be booby traps behind that fake wall?"

"Gods, I hadn't even thought of that. Maybe doing this on the sly wasn't the best idea."

Her eyes sharpened. "Why *are* we out here by ourselves? If you've figured out something, then you should—" She broke off, her color draining as her eyes locked onto the rock formation he'd walked and jogged past a hundred times before, never once suspecting that it marked a concealed entrance until a nightmare showed him the way. "Flames," she said, her voice gone dull with shock as she moved to touch the sinuous, flamelike rock and stare at the empty socket behind it. "Staring eyes."

"Yeah." His voice rasped more than usual on the word. "I don't think she was talking about just what she saw up at the mansion. I think she was talking about where she performed the ritual. If we ever find some in-depth info on the star bloodline—like the stuff they didn't tell outsiders—I think we'll find that this was a sacred chamber that was reserved for them alone, probably connected with the library."

"Assuming there's anything behind the illusion spell."

"Why would it be there at all if not to hide something important?" He knew she wasn't asking about the logic, though. Going on instinct, he gripped her shoulder, more a gesture of support from a teammate than an overture from a lover. But he suspected that was what she needed him to be right then: an almost-warrior who had her back.

"We should go get the others." She didn't move, though. Just stood there touching what he supposed wasn't really a rock at all, but rather a solid-seeming illusory rock.

"It's your call."

She hesitated, hand pressed to the stone. Finally, she said, "I'm going to try the on/off spell. If it doesn't work, we'll go get the others. If it does . . . I need to see. I want to be the first."

He nodded. "Then go for it."

"I'm too scattered to concentrate on finding the magic." With that scant warning, she turned toward him, grabbed him by the front of his T-shirt, and kissed him, hard.

The kiss vibrated with nerves and need, and hit him with a sledgehammer of lust that slammed him right back to where he'd been the night before in that gossamer white canopy bed, fresh from her body and wanting to promise her impossible things. When she pulled away, he had to stop himself from tugging her back and kissing her again, touching her. It wasn't just about sex either. He wanted to wrap himself around her, shield her from whatever bad stuff was on the other side of the illusory wall, giving her the good stuff and taking the rest onto himself. The need was hard, hot, and sharp, and it made him take a big step back, wrestling for control.

He cleared his throat. "Glad to help."

"Shh." She pulled what proved to be a butterfly knife out of her pocket, flipped it open, and used it to score her palm. She didn't explain about the knife and he didn't ask; she wasn't the only one going armed after what had happened the day before. With the blood sacrifice made, she pressed her bleeding hand flat to the fake stone surface and whispered a few words he didn't catch.

For a moment, nothing happened. Then the wall shimmered. And disappeared.

CHAPTER TWENTY-ONE

Breathe, Jade told herself as she stared into the dark entrance of a tunnel leading into the canyon wall. *Just keep breathing*. She was glad she had someone with her, though, and she was glad it was Lucius, who was letting her take it slow when she knew he had to be dying to get in there, not just for discovery for discovery's sake, but because he was hoping that the members of the star bloodline—or maybe even Vennie herself—might have left behind some additional clues that might, gods willing, get him back into the library. It seemed that love—or at least great sex—wasn't the answer. It was all about the magic, after all.

"Dumb ass," he said suddenly. When she turned to him, he made a dope-slap motion. "I didn't bring a flashlight."

"Let me try." She held out her hand and kindled a foxfire. The magic shone brightly and didn't sap her strength nearly as much as it had before. Was she actually getting stronger? It seemed so. She took a deep, steadying breath and didn't let herself lean back into him. "Here we go." Then, remembering the claustrophobia, she asked, "Are you going to be okay with this?"

His grin was that of the overgrown boy he'd first seemed, in the body of the man he'd become. "Just try and stop me."

The tunnel was wide enough for the two of them to walk side by side, so they did. Unlike most of the Mayan-era Nightkeeper temples, it was tall enough that Lucius didn't have to duck. At first, Jade thought that was because it was a natural fissure. As they moved inward, though, she saw smoothed-out areas, and one or two spots where narrow places had been widened by hand. In the absence of the close-fitted stonework and stylized carvings she'd grown used to in ritual settings, the tunnel almost didn't feel Nightkeeper in origin. It rounded a gentle curve, cutting out the daylight and leaving them to rely entirely on the foxfire, but the magic stayed true, with little strain on her reserves.

"I wonder how far—" She broke off when the tunnel widened to a cavern and she had an answer to how far it went.

More, she couldn't breathe, couldn't move, couldn't speak or think as her entire consciousness logjammed on a rapid-fire kaleidoscope of images that she couldn't process all at once.

"Oh," she said. That was all she could manage, really, because the breath backed up in her lungs and her throat closed until only a stingy trickle of oxygen got through.

The budding symbologist in her locked on the spiral designs on the floor and ceiling, recognizing the multirayed galactic symbol of the Chacoans, who had appeared suddenly in the first few centuries A.D., flourished in the canyons of New Mexico, and then disappeared just as suddenly, leaving behind intricate stone cities built entirely for the dead. The scribe in her noted a small carved box of the sort the ancient Maya and Nightkeepers had used to store their most precious possessions.

The daughter in her, though, focused on the dry, desiccated corpse slumped up against the far wall.

Vennie's corpse was much as Lucius had described its spiritual representation in the library, with a hooked nose and protruding teeth that bore little resemblance to the bright, laughing girl from the photos. Oddly, Jade found she could look at her mother's death-ravaged face and hands without any real queasiness; on some level she'd been prepared for that. What she hadn't been entirely prepared for, though, was for the body to be wearing the remains of high-top Reeboks, acid-washed jeans, a faded hot-pink sweatshirt, and a denim jacket that was two shades darker than the pants, and carefully decorated with iron-on patches for bands that now played on classic-rock radio.

The clothes didn't just date the corpse; they drove home the child her mother had been, somehow uniting the two inside Jade. Yes, Vennie had been a wife and a mother, and had been torn between the responsibilities of the bloodline she'd been born into and the strictures of the one she'd chosen. But at the same time, her life had just been beginning. If it hadn't been for the massacre, she would have been in her early forties now. She would've been at her prime as a mage, whatever form that magic might have taken.

"She barely even got a chance to know herself," Jade murmured.

Lucius gave her a one-armed hug and pressed a kiss to the top of her head. Then he stepped away, giving her some space she wasn't sure she needed. "Are you okay with me checking out the box?"

"Go for it." She stayed with the body, though. It seemed like the right thing to do.

Sooner than she'd expected, he made a satisfied noise and held out something to her. "I think you should open this one."

It was a hot-pink spiral-bound notebook with glitter stars stuck to the cover. To Jade's surprise, she felt her lips curve in a smile as she took the small volume. "She wasn't subtle, was she?"

"She was seventeen," he said, which more or less said it all.

She met Lucius's eyes. "Thank you. Not just for the notebook, but for all of it. For being here with me, for letting me see her first . . . For all of it."

He tipped his head, but didn't quite meet her eyes. "That's what friends are for."

Telling herself not to read too much into that—or too little—she nodded and cracked open the notebook. The lined pages were brittle and yellow; the first half of the book appeared to be class notes, full of cryptic scribbles about the hero twins and the end-time interspersed with doodles of the spiral pattern that was echoed on the floor and ceiling of the cavern, along with two repeated symbols: the star and the warrior's glyph. "A little full of ourselves, were we?" Jade commented, though more fondly than anything. She thought she was getting a handle on her feelings where it came to Vennie, slotting her—for the moment, anyway—in a mental position she thought was someplace between sister and mother.

"Again, she was seventeen." Lucius grinned, but lines of tension bracketed his eyes and mouth as he read over her shoulder. "Is there anything in there besides class notes?"

She flipped a few more pages, then stopped. Everything stopped—her voice, her breath, even her heart—as she stared down at the single page filled with looping writing.

It began: *Dear Jade.*

"Oh," she said, a single syllable of pained longing.

Lucius read the top line over her shoulder, then simply touched his temple to hers in support. "Read it to me," he suggested, his voice barely more than a whisper of breath in her ear. "More, read it to *her*. Let her know you got it, that she's been found after all these years." Then he moved away, giving her the room to make her own decision.

She nodded, swallowing to clear the huge lump in her throat. " 'Dear Jade,' " she began, and had to start over when her voice cracked. " 'Dear Jade, please forgive me for what I'm about to do. And please ask the stars to forgive me too. I know I don't belong here anymore. But I don't really belong anywhere, do I? I'm an outsider, soon to become a Prophet. Please ask them to use my voice to help the king with his decisions. If it's to be an attack, use me to win. If not, use me to plan the 2012 war, though that's still so far away. Either way, please know that I am satisfied so long as the magi don't march to their deaths the day after tomorrow, which is what I'm scared will happen if I don't do this. And finally, please tell your father, tell Josh, that it wasn't always easy loving him, but I never stopped. I love you both. Your mother, Venus.' "

When Jade fell silent, the cave seemed to hum with the echoes of her voice, the sound becoming, for a moment, multitonal.

"Vennie must've been a nickname for Venus," Lucius observed. "Venus is one of the most visible stars in the sky, and its patterns form a cornerstone of the entire calendric system."

Jade found a ghost of a smile. "Venus. Yeah. That fits." She sighed. "She must've written this part before she tried the soul spell. She was assuming that the Prophet's magic would take her soul and she wouldn't get another chance to say good-bye." Something nudged at the edge of her brain—a question she hadn't asked, a connection she was missing.

" 'This part'?" Lucius said. "There's more?"

She nodded, skimming ahead, not sure what she was feeling, what she was supposed to feel. "The next one is another 'Dear Jade' letter. I think she was expecting the members of the star bloodline to find her once she became the Prophet—maybe there was some sort of magic signal to announce its arrival?—and wanted them to have this info, but couldn't bring herself to write it directly to the family members who had turned away from her. So she wrote them to a six-month-old baby instead."

"Or else she wanted you to know she was, in her own way, a hero."

Nodding, Jade began reading again: " 'Dear Jade . . . Gods . . . oh, gods, how do I say this? How can it be true? I said the spell right, made the sacrifice, but the magic didn't take me. Instead, it took *her*, took someone I didn't even know about, but loved with all my heart—' " She broke off, her blood chilling as she made the connection that had been bothering her. "That's why she ended up like you. She wasn't possessed by a *makol*. She was pregnant, and she didn't figure it out until it was already too late."

Gods.

How was it that they had missed asking that question? Jade wondered. Or had it been asked and she skimmed over it, somehow guessing this might be the answer and not wanting to add it to the mix? Nausea pressed hot and thick against the back of her throat. A baby. A sister. Her mother had sacrificed her unborn baby to the Prophet's spell. And being a soul spell, it wouldn't have freed the child's essence to enter the afterlife. The baby's soul would've been completely and utterly destroyed. *Poof, gone.*

Lucius made a move to reach for her, but she shook her head and held him off. "No. I need to finish this." If she didn't keep going, she might lose it entirely.

"If you're sure."

She nodded and read: " 'Tell the harvesters they lost one of their own because of me, because I was too proud, too vain, too sure that the elders of the star bloodline were wrong when they said it wasn't yet time for the last Prophet, that he wouldn't be made until just before the triad years. They were wrong, I thought, when really *I* was the one who was wrong, and an innocent paid the ultimate price. Her soul isn't in the sky. It's just *gone*, destroyed in order to propel me between the worlds. I still need to go back into the library again, gain what knowledge I can, and hope to hell it's enough to convince the king not to march. I didn't get any answers the first time because it took me too long to figure out the yes/no bullshit, which doesn't work exactly like the stories said it would. I'm starving, but I ate all the bread, and the fountain ran dry, and . . . and I'm whining. I'll stop now and rest so I can keep going. Sometimes it seems that all you *can* do is keep going. I love you. Your mother, Venus.' "

"Now she's starting to sound more like she did in the other journal," Lucius noted. "Less like she's writing a thank-you note—or rather, an apology—to an elderly relative, and more like a strung-out, confused kid."

"There's one more line. Just a sentence scribbled at the bottom." Jade scanned the sentence, and went still.

"What is it?"

"Information."

He took a step toward her, his eyes lighting. "Does it say how to get me back into the library?"

"No." She took a deep, shuddering breath. "It says: 'To reach the lost sun, play his game on the cardinal day.'"

"Oh," Lucius said. "Oh, wow. Oh, *shit*. I know what that means." Their eyes met, and they said, nearly in unison, "We need to get this back to the mansion."

With the great room in the middle of being renovated, the residents of Skywatch gathered at the picnic tables beneath the big ceiba tree, mopping at sticky-humid sweat and bitching about the gnats that had made a sudden appearance in the normally bug-free canyon. Strike, who'd already been briefed on the discoveries, opened the meeting, then turned things over to Jade and Lucius.

Jade was pale and withdrawn, so Lucius did most of the talking. He described the clues that had led him to the hidden chamber, and summarized what they had found inside it. He finished by reading Vennie's words verbatim from the pink notebook, ending with what sure as hell sounded to him like a prophecy: "To reach the lost sun, play his game on the cardinal day."

When he finished, it seemed that the world itself had gone silent, save for the whine of gnat wings.

After a moment, he said, "That's random enough that I'm willing to bet it's a snippet from the library, especially given how well it lines up with both the triad prophecy and what we're going through now. If she asked the library, for example, what information the

Nightkeepers needed most from her, that might have been the answer."

"Was there anything else in the box?" Nate asked.

"It was empty except for the notebook. My guess is that the stars may have removed their sacred texts from it, maybe in preparation for the attack. But there's more." He lifted the box from where he'd left it sitting on the table, and turned it in his hands, so the orange daylight made the shadows dip and move across the carved wooden surface. "I translated the glyphs on the outside of the box. It's another prophecy, this one about the library, and presumably the über-Prophet who is supposed to arise during the triad years. Paraphrasing to modernize the grammar and clean up the end, where the grammar gets a little wonky, it reads: 'In the triad years, a mage-born Prophet can wield the library's might.'" He shook his head. "By becoming the non-Prophet, I must have blocked the true Prophet from being formed at the end of last year. So I think we can consider that a prophecy of the null-and-void variety."

"Is there such a thing as a voided prophecy?" Sasha asked. "It seems to me that all of the prophecies the ancients have left us have factored into things in some way or another. Maybe not the way we've expected them to, but they've factored."

"I don't see how this one could," Lucius answered. "I'm not mage-born, and there's no mistaking that part of the translation."

Sasha looked thoughtful. "Maybe that's not all of the prophecy."

"Gee. Why don't I go to the library and check? Oh, that's right. Because I fucking *can't*." He exhaled. "Sorry. It's just . . . Shit. Sorry." Sasha hadn't done anything to deserve his mood. "You're right; it's certainly possible that there was another box that continued the saying. That might account for the funky way this one ends, glyph-wise. But that's pure speculation, and we're running out of time. I don't think we dare waste the time searching for something that might be a figment of our imaginations." He paused. "Besides, there's another option. Something we can try relatively easily, right from our own backyard." Lucius hooked a thumb over his shoulder, past the training hall to the high parallel walls that had been built back when Skywatch was originally constructed in the twenties. "I hope you're all up for a game."

" 'Play his game,' " Michael repeated. "You think the prophecy is talking about the Mayan ball game?"

"I know it is," Lucius said with bone-deep certainty. "The entire game was one big metaphor for the sun's daily journey, first across the sky, then through the underworld. It stands to reason that it would be a way to reach Kinich Ahau." *I hope.* Because if this didn't work, they were pretty much screwed.

"It's like volleyball, right?" Sven asked. "Bounce the ball back and forth, no holding, and keep the ball off the ground using the nonhand bodypart of your choice." He paused. "But I thought the point of the game was to sacrifice the winners. Are we sure that's a good idea?"

"We'll do whatever it takes if it means gaining ac-

cess to the only god not currently trapped in the sky,"
Strike said implacably. "We need the gods—or at least
a god—to form the Triad. No god, no Triad. No Triad,
no hope in the war. Are you following?"

Yeah, Lucius thought inwardly, *I'm following.* Because
they didn't just need at least one god; they needed the
damned Triad spell, and they didn't have a clue where
to look for it. They had exhausted all the possible
searches on earth. Which left them with "not on earth"
as their last option.

Aloud, he said, "Although sacrifice was sometimes
part of the game, it wasn't necessarily the winners who
died. Sometimes it was the losers, and sometimes there
weren't any deaths at all. It depended on who was
playing, and why. But that's getting ahead of things.
Strike asked me to give you guys the quick four-one-
one on the ball game, so here it goes: First, to understand the game, you've got to keep in mind that it's
the progenitor of almost all modern ball games. Before
its evolution, game balls were always made of wood
or leather, and fell dead when they hit. That changed
when the Olmec figured out the trick of mixing the sap
from latex trees and morning glory vines to create a
bouncy, elastic rubber polymer." He paused. "For the
record, that was good old human ingenuity, circa 1600
B.C., not something you guys taught us."

He got a couple of snorts for that, a couple of nods.

"Anyway, because rubber seemed to have a life and
mind of its own when it bounced but was otherwise
inanimate, it was considered spiritual, sacred. It was
used in medicines, burned with sacred incense as a

sacrificial offering, made into human-shaped effigies, and poured into spherical wood or stone molds and turned into balls." He held his hands a little less than a foot apart. "We're not talking hollow basketballs, either. They were heavy as hell, though sometimes their makers lightened them up by using a sacrificial victim's skull as a hollow center, and layering rubber around it. Regardless, these things could do some serious damage, which is why body armor evolved along with the game."

He passed out a couple of pictures he'd printed off his laptop; they showed photos of various ball game scenes. "Here are some pics to give you an idea. Some were painted on slipware." Including the scene that had been showing on-screen when he'd brought Jade back to his cottage. Their eyes met when he sent that one around; her cheeks pinkened. "Others are from the actual ball court walls." These included the famous scene from the great court at Chichén Itzá: that of a kneeling ballplayer being ritually decapitated, the blood spurting from his neck turning into snakes. "Finally, here are some some three-D models that were made of clay." He sent around the last of the printouts, showing replica "I"-shaped courts, with armored teams facing off over the ball, referees keeping an eye on out-of-bounds, and fans sitting up on top of the high walls. "In a couple of them, you can even see piles of fabric and other trade goods, sort of the A.D. 1000 version of a stadium concourse."

"Huh." Michael flipped through the pictures. "It was really a ball game, the way we think of it."

"Definitely. But like so much of life in the Mayan-Nightkeeper culture, it also had a strong set of symbolic elements. Although the game itself existed before the Nightkeepers arrived, things got far more organized after 1300 B.C., when you guys showed up. The Egyptians had formalized games with rules and scoring, amphitheaters, and such. Odds are, those came from the Nightkeepers, and the First Father brought them along for the ride to this continent."

"Including the sun connection?" Nate asked without looking up from the pictures.

"Yep. On one level, the ball itself represents the sun, the ball court the underworld. You've got two teams—or sometimes just two opposing players—competing to control the sun." Lucius paused, trying to decide whether the parallel with their current situation was creepy, prophetic, or both. "Different versions of the game had different ways for players to gain or lose points, depending on how they returned, or failed to return, the sun ball to the other team, up to a match point of fifteen or so. Because teams could lose points as well as gain them, evenly matched games could last for days. But in a twist that's more billiards than volleyball, if a player got the sun ball through a vertical-set hoop high up on the ball court wall, it was an instant win. Eight ball, corner pocket. Game over; hit the showers."

Sudden understanding lit Jade's face. "The hoop represents the dark spot in the center of the Milky Way galaxy, which they thought was the entrance to Xibalba."

"Exactly, which makes the symbolism twofold. In the context of the sun passing through the entrance to Xibalba, the game reenacts Kinich Ahau's daily journey into and out of Xibalba, even as the arc of the ball itself symbolizes the sun traveling across the sky. From the perspective of the dark center of the Milky Way, putting the ball through the hoop represents the sun traveling through that dark center, which is the astronomical event that's going to coincide with the winter solstice of 2012, precipitating the barrier's collapse."

There was a moment of silence before Brandt said sourly, "When you put it that way, seems kind of dumb we haven't been playing the game all along."

Lucius tipped his hand in a yes/no gesture. "I'm distilling out the points that relate to Kinich Ahau, but there are a ton of other connections within the game: to reptiles and birds, to harvest festivals, different gods and events, even to the class system itself. Chichén Itzá had seven ball courts located at various positions relative to the different temples and neighborhoods, which were stratified by socioeconomic status. If you give me enough time, I could probably make an argument for tying the game to almost any god or prophecy you cared to throw at me."

Brandt pressed, "But you think this connection is solid?"

He nodded. "I do. In fact, I think my subconscious has been trying to tell me about the connection for a while now. I kept gravitating toward ball game artifacts, when the game had never been that big a deal for me before. So, yeah. The connection is solid."

The other man nodded. "Then I guess we're playing. What are the rules?"

"In the ancient versions of the game, serves were typically made with the hands or forearms, returns with the hips, legs, and feet, which were protected with light armor, some of which got pretty elaborate. In addition to the shin and body protectors, there were hand stones, which worked on the same principle as brass knuckles, adding weight and force to the return hit, and yokes, which covered the hips, lowered the player's center of gravity, and increased the power of a body hit." Lucius sketched in the air as he spoke. "There were face masks and helmets, of course, because the balls were heavy enough to do some major damage. And there were other pieces that were largely decorative, which the players wore for the opening ceremonies and then stripped off for the actual game."

Michael grinned. "Sounds like a cross between a WWF grudge match and the Super Bowl."

"Mix in some major religious overtones, and you're not far off," Lucius agreed. "The ballplayers were the rock stars of their day. Even after retirement, they were revered for their wins, and some became the boon companions of their kings. To be buried with your ballplayers' gear was a huge sign of power and respect."

"How much of these raiments survived into modern day?"

"Of the original stuff, very little. Most of it was made of wood and leather, some of rubber itself. None of that lasted long, given the climate. The artifacts we've got now are mostly pottery replicas, like the ones in the pictures I passed around." He paused, grinning. "However, rumor has it that there's a pile of modernized equipment in the back of one of the storerooms, along with a couple of experts who are going to show us how it's done."

That got him a few confused looks, until Jox, Carlos, and Shandi all rose from their places at the far end of the table and came around to its head. Carlos was carrying a banged-up cardboard box. All three *winikin*, it turned out, had played seriously before the massacre, and had been among those responsible for teaching the younger generation the moves of the ritual game. *What has happened before will happen again*, Lucius thought. Circles within circles, past, present, and future.

Jox stepped forward, with the other two behind him, looking grim, efficient, and suddenly very coach-like. "Everyone ready for the rules of the game the way your parents played it?"

Almost in synchrony, the magi turned and looked at the tall parallel walls of the ball court. "I guess I always thought of it as another artifact," Brandt said. "It's just always *there*, you know? Like it's watching over us."

"And now maybe it's going to do more." Jox nodded to the other two *winikin*; they dug into the box and started handing out thin booklets that were heavy on diagrams, light on text, and laid out the basics. Lucius had snagged one earlier and already had it memorized. He'd even run through some of the moves, which had come back to him with an ease that had surprised him. He'd never been much into sports before. Then again, that was before.

"We're just going to study pictures?" Rabbit asked from the far end of the table. Lucius glanced over, surprised to see him and Myrinne at the outskirts of the group. He hadn't noticed the young couple's arrival, and he wasn't used to Strike letting the girl sit in on meetings. More, it seemed, had changed than just Rabbit's level of pyrokinesis.

"Only briefly." The corners of Jox's mouth kicked up. "Then we're going to practice."

CHAPTER TWENTY-TWO

June 20
Two years, six months, and one day to the zero date

Jox's idea of practice turned out to be two days of sweaty, hard-hitting, brutal play, without the benefit of helmets or arm and wrist guards, which he claimed were only for ceremonial use anyway. By the time the *winikin* declared them competent enough not to embarrass themselves in front of the gods, Rabbit's nose was sore and swollen, and his knees and elbows were skinned to shit. They hurt badly enough to remind him of when he and his old man had lived briefly in a cheap apartment that would've been more of the same old, except that there had been a half-pipe down the street, and a couple of kids who'd taught him a few tricks on their boards. That had lasted until his old man had shown up in his penitent's robes, with his head shaved and his eyes crazy-wild; that had been the end of Rabbit's half-pipe friends, and they'd moved on soon after.

This isn't about the old man, Rabbit reminded himself

as he trailed after Jox, heading out of the ball court. *Not directly, anyway.*

He and Myrinne had done some digging on their own, but hadn't come up with much info on the Order of Xibalba that wasn't already common knowledge. Rabbit had negged the idea of hiring a PI, first because he'd thrown money in that direction once before with minimal results, and second because he might not agree with all of Strike's tenets, but he had to believe it was better for the magi to stay well under the human radar. With his luck, he'd hire a PI, the guy would find something on the Xibalbans, and the next thing he knew, the *Enquirer* would have a headline like: *Mayan Doomsday Cult Implicated in Black Magic Slaying!* or some such shit. No freaking way. He was trying to be smart these days.

It seemed to be paying off too. Despite the knee-jerk piss-off of having Jade and Lucius break into his place and sniff around—*hello, personal space*—when he'd called Strike to bitch, the king had actually been pretty conciliatory about it. He'd even gone back on his *keep Rabbit and Myrinne at UT through the solstice* decree, and zapped out to get them. Then, when Jade's panic button went off, Rabbit hadn't just gotten to come along for the ride; he'd been front and center of the rescue when he'd said he thought he could crisp the *makol* without doing the head-and-heart thing. Strike hadn't been too keen on his doing so much killing, but it wasn't like they were people anymore. Once a *makol* was fully bound, the human host was dead one way or the other. Rabbit had just sped things up.

In the aftermath of the op he'd been pumped, even after the drag of twelve hours in the Jeep with Michael and Lucius, who weren't bad guys, but had both been in pissy moods and had argued about every stop. Didn't matter, though, because when he'd gotten back to Skywatch, Myrinne had been there, waiting for him with a smile and the bright idea to ask Jox about his mother. Not in so many words, of course, but that was the basic plan. If anyone living knew anything, it would be the *winikin*.

Subtle, Rabbit reminded himself as he lengthened his strides to catch up. *You're going for subtle.*

Doing the eyes-in-the-back-of-his-head thing he'd perfected over more than four decades of in loco parenthood, Jox stopped at the edge of the narrow, rectangular playing field, right on the out-of-bounds line. He raised an eyebrow. "Did you need something, or are we just headed in the same direction?" There was no asperity in the question; it was just a question. Jox was like that—a straight shooter who tried to do his best by everyone and, as far as Rabbit was concerned, didn't take nearly enough for himself.

"I thought you might want some help digging the stuff out of storage for tomorrow." Rabbit didn't quite stick his hands in his pockets and whistle innocently, but he sure imagined it.

A year ago, Jox probably would've busted out laughing. Now he nodded, looking pleased. "Sure. Come on. These days, a *winikin* can't afford to turn down free labor under the age of fifty."

They headed for the mansion, bypassed the construction crews by going in through the garage, and turned down a seldom-used hallway that had doorways marching down it on either side, numbered in sequence starting with one hundred. "These are more residences, right?"

"They used to be," Jox answered grimly. "Three floors of one-room studios for the unchosen *winikin*, single nonranking magi, out-of-town visitors, that sort of thing. Now it's fucking storage space."

Rabbit held his hands up. "Sor-ry."

"Damn it." Jox shook his head. "I'm the one who's sorry. I really, really hate this part." Stopping in front of door 121, he checked the number against a spreadsheet on his iPhone screen, muttering, "And I really don't want to have to paw through any more boxes than absolutely necessary." Pushing open the door, he flipped on the lights and waved Rabbit through.

Jox had been in charge of the massive renovation and updating of Skywatch almost exactly two years earlier, when the barrier reactivated and the magi returned to their abandoned home. At the time, Rabbit had been sulking up in the pueblo, listening to tunes and hating the world. When his old man had bothered to hunt him down and nag about him pitching in and helping Jox with the cleanup, he'd sneered and done a fast fade.

Now, looking at row upon row of moving boxes, stacked on floor-to-ceiling racks set with minimal aisles between, like something out of the closing credits of *Cold Case*, for the first time, Rabbit thought, really *thought* about what the *winikin* had been facing. Some boxes were marked with content lists, some with bloodlines, others with names. They were all carefully stored, cataloged, and cross-reffed in Jox's database. And he'd done most of the work himself. He'd sorted through the residences of dead men, women, and children—family members, teammates, friends— and although he'd had a hired cleanup crew come in and strip the place of nearly a thousand people's worth of daily living crap, he'd had to pull out the Nightkeeper-specific stuff first so it wouldn't hit the mainstream via Goodwill. He'd done it mostly alone too, wanting the rooms pristine, with no sign of their former inhabitants or their slaughter, before the other Nightkeepers and *winikin* arrived.

Diverted from his stealth mission, Rabbit swallowed. "Shit. I'm sorry. I should've helped with this."

"You were too busy planting your head up your own ass at the time."

"No kidding."

The mild response earned him a longer look from the *winikin*, and a faint, approving nod. "So the rumors are true. You're growing up."

"Doing my best."

"Glad to have you." The *winikin* turned away before shit could get mushy, consulting his phone once again. "Back corner, six boxes here, another ten a couple of rooms down. We won't need everything, but we'll pull them all out and pick and choose." He paused with a sidelong grin. "You get to carry the ones with all the five-pound hand stones."

"Screw you," Rabbit agreed good-naturedly.

They found the boxes. Jox tensed up when Rabbit popped the first one, then relaxed when it proved to be full of the promised shin guards and a couple of crazy-looking headpieces adorned with brittle parrot feathers. At Rabbit's look, the *winikin* lifted a shoulder. "Let's just say I was working fast back then, and was more than a little stressed. When I came looking for Gray-Smoke's battle gear, to give to Alexis, I opened up what I thought was the right box and saw—" He broke off, jerked his shoulders irritably. "Ghosts. Not important now; let's get these boxes back out into the light of day."

After that, Rabbit almost didn't ask him about Red-Boar. The *winikin* was already dealing with massacre flashbacks. Didn't seem fair to pile on another set of memories. But as they schlepped the boxes out of the first room and moved on to the next, and the boxes didn't yield any surprises, the *winikin* unwound by degrees. What was more, Rabbit started hearing Myrinne's voice in his head, telling him he had to look out for himself and not worry so much about other people's opinions. Eventually, he said, "I've been thinking about my old man lately."

The *winikin* didn't look up from his iPhone. "What sort of thinking?" He seemed okay with the question.

Rabbit shrugged. "Trying to figure him out, I guess. The more distance I get, the more I realize that not everything he did or said was bullshit. It's just tough deciding which is which." And that was the gods' honest truth. The more he and Myrinne had tried to figure out where Red-Boar had been during the years after the massacre, when he'd disappeared into the jungle and eventually came back out with a tagalong half-blood toddler he'd refused to give a proper name, the more Rabbit had started remembering his old man without the anger those memories usually brought. Granted, the useful shit Red-Boar had taught him had been pretty sparse when weighed against the me-me-me shit, but still.

"Good luck," Jox said dryly. "I couldn't always tell the difference, and I knew him his entire life." But after a minute of silent schlepping, he said, "Anything you want to know in particular?"

"Well . . . Anna's told me a bit about what he was like, you know, before." He almost hadn't bothered asking her, but had figured, *What the hell?* To his surprise, she'd talked for nearly an hour, making Red-Boar sound like the local big man on campus, his first wife the homecoming queen. Rabbit hadn't known what to make of the picture she painted, couldn't reconcile it with the stubborn, zonked-out asshole he'd grown up with. When Jade turned up with the skull effigy a few days later, though, he'd thought he understood. Anna had been saying good-bye to the memories. No wonder she'd made them sound better than they probably were. He continued. "And Strike's filled in most of what I was too young to remember about growing up. So I was hoping maybe you could tell me about when the old man went missing . . . and what happened when he came back." Even as he said it he felt like a total shit. Nothing like putting the guy right back where he didn't want to go.

At first he thought Jox was going to give him a well-deserved, *Ask me that some other time . . . like never.* But after a moment, the *winikin* said, "It happened a few years after the massacre. Every cardinal day, your father and I would hop a plane down to the Yucatán and sneak into Chichén Itzá, and he would try to jack in, to see if the barrier was still blocked. This one time, as we came out of the tunnel, he just . . . I don't know. Snapped. I knew he was having trouble dealing—we all were. But this . . . It came out of nowhere. One minute he was treating me like furniture, like usual, and the next he was coming after me." The *winikin*'s voice dropped. "Three times in my life now, I've thought I was going to die. Once was during the massacre. Once was when the *makol* took over Lucius and got loose inside the compound. And once was when Red-Boar came after me that day."

A shiver crawled down the back of Rabbit's neck. "I thought he just up and disappeared."

"He did. But he beat the shit out of me first." Jox clenched and unclenched one fist, staring at it as if remembering pain, or perhaps broken bones. "I don't know what was going on inside his head, or what specifically triggered it. All I know is that I was surprised as hell when I woke up and found myself alive—more or less—and him long gone. I dragged myself to our bolt-hole in the village—remember that place?—doctored myself up, and managed to make my flight home, barely. I remember sitting there with his spot empty beside me, hoping to hell he wouldn't show up."

"He . . . Fuck." Rabbit gave up any pretense of hauling the next-to-last box and just stared at the *winikin.* "I'm so fucking sorry."

"Don't be. Those were his fists, not yours. I consider it damned lucky he didn't use his knife on me. If he had, we'd all be living very different lives right now."

"Whoa." Rabbit's brain tripped over the sequence of what-ifs. If Jox had died back then, Strike and Anna would've gone into the foster system. Anna had blocked out most of her memories from before the massacre, and Strike's had been those of an average, if doted-on, nine-year-old boy. What would they have done when the barrier reactivated? Where would they have gone? They wouldn't have known about Skywatch, wouldn't have known there were other survivors. More, Rabbit didn't even want to think what his own childhood would have been like without Jox in it, and Strike and Anna as his unofficial siblings. Granted, Jox had been able to buffer his old man only to a point, but without that leveling influence . . . Hell, he probably would've ended up in the system too. If he'd been lucky.

"Your father came back three years later. I had taken Strike and Anna down to Chichén Itzá for the cardinal day—with Red-Boar gone, it was up to them to try the magic. We were just coming out of the tunnel when he stepped out of the rain forest. I pulled a gun on him," Jox said matter-of-factly. "I'd been carrying a piece the whole time he was gone, afraid that he'd show up and go after one of the kids instead of just me. But he didn't try to hurt us. He put his hands in the air. A few seconds later, you came out of the underbrush and stood beside him. I looked at you for a moment and you looked back, and I put the gun away." The *winikin* paused. "He never apologized, and I never asked him to, just like I never asked him where he'd been or what he'd been doing."

Rabbit's throat had gone dry. "You let him come back because of me?"

"Because of you . . . and because it was bad enough living through what happened at Skywatch. He was the only one who survived being ambushed by the *Banol Kax* at the intersection. I had to believe the gods kept him alive for a reason."

"Do you still believe that?"

Jox sent Rabbit a long look. "I do. I hope you'll do your best to prove me right."

"I . . . Shit." When his chest got tight and funny at the idea that his old man might have lived solely so he could be born, and the pressure that idea put on him, Rabbit grabbed his box. "Weren't we supposed to be schlepping this crap somewhere?"

"That was the general theory." Jox seemed willing to let the topic drop. But as they were heading along what Rabbit had started to think of as the Hall of Ghosts, the *winikin* said, "The only time he ever mentioned those missing years, he said something about a village called Ox Ajal, up in the highlands." Jox looked sidelong at Rabbit. "But keep in mind that sometimes when you go looking for answers, you don't get the ones you're expecting, or particularly want."

Rabbit lifted a shoulder. "Nah. I appreciate your telling me about the old man. It . . . it helps to know it wasn't just me, you know?" It wasn't an evasion, precisely. But he still felt like shit, given how cool Jox had been to him just now, and what he'd revealed about the past.

"After what's been going on with Jade's mother and the *nahwal*, I think most of us are thinking about our families, particularly our mothers. But do me a favor and keep it in perspective, okay? You're doing a good job building your own life. Don't fuck it up trying to prove something to a dead man."

Rabbit didn't know what to say to that, so he said nothing. Part of him knew Jox was right, that he should let it go and concentrate on his role within the magi. He was making headway finally, and it felt good. But he already knew what Myrinne was going to say, because he was thinking it: The name of the village—his mother's village?—couldn't be a coincidence.

In the old tongue, *ox ajal* meant "thrice manifested," and its strange, double-skull glyph was used to represent the Triad.

June 21
Summer solstice
Two years and six months to the zero date

After the grueling *winikin*-led practice finally ended at midafternoon the day before the solstice, Jade had dragged herself to her suite, curled up in her bed, and pulled the covers over her head to shut out the rest of the world. She had slept a solid ten hours and awoke well past midnight; the sky was dark and lovely beyond the balcony, with a sliver of moon providing pale blue light. She felt good; heck, she felt better than good, riding on the early buzz of barrier magic that would build exponentially in the hours leading up to the solstice. Driven by the magic-wrought urgency, she showered and dressed in jeans, a tight black tee, and her boots. It wasn't until she was pulling on a long-sleeved shirt against the cool night air that she acknowledged she was headed outside. To Lucius. They hadn't spoken more than a few words to each other in the past three days, but although the whirlwind of game practice, rescue plans, and magical preparations had left her with little in the way of time or energy, she'd never stopped being aware of him on an intimate, visceral level.

Don't be an Edda, she told herself, but the warning fell flat because she might be a mage, but on another level she was only human. And having spent the past two days watching Lucius practice the gracefully violent moves of the ancient ball game . . . wow. Just wow.

After the first few times one of the *winikin* had demonstrated a move to have Lucius not only pick it up immediately, but sometimes even improve upon it with his greater mass and strength, his ability to instinctively shift his center of gravity lower to get a knee or a hip under the heavy ball to keep it aloft or in play, Jox had called him on it, and he'd admitted to having played some pickup games while out in the field, albeit with the smaller, lighter balls used in the modern era. It had startled Jade—and, she suspected, some of the others—to realize that the game was still played as pure entertainment among the Mayan villages, and not just as the tourist-focused reenactments they had found on YouTube. Indeed, it seemed to Jade like an unfortunate statement on humanity that the ball game, which had religion at its center, had survived the conquistadors while the Mayan writing system and codices were systematically destroyed as heathen tools. The game itself had evolved over time, but its core was largely unchanged, and Lucius's experience with the moves put him at a substantial advantage.

Watching him move lightly over the ground, completely at home in his body, entirely in control of his movements and reflexes, Jade had found herself brutally aroused despite her fatigue. Now, with the fatigue gone, the arousal remained, a sharp ache that drove her out of the mansion in search of Lucius.

She found him sitting atop one of the ball court walls, staring into the night.

She climbed up the steep stone staircase and sat beside him, so their arms brushed lightly as their legs dangled over the sheer twenty-foot drop of one of two parallel stone walls. To her right, she could just make out the moon shadow of the high-set stone ring that was the game's ultimate goal. From down below, it had looked impossibly small in relation to the size of the game ball. From up atop the wall, it still looked damn tiny. No wonder there was also a point system of body hits and out-of-bounds penalties; the hoop seemed an impossible target.

Without preamble, he held out his right hand and flipped his palm up to reveal the quatrefoil hellmark, which looked black in the moonlight, though she knew it was the bloodred of dark magic. "Do you think it's possible that I'm part Xibalban?"

"You— Oh." She rocked back in startlement and fumbled for a few seconds, trying to redirect her brain from the sex buzz in the air to his question.

"Is that an 'oh' as in, 'I'm thinking,' or as in, 'Where the fuck are my jade-tips'?"

"That was 'oh' as in, 'I'd like to say you're crazy, but it would explain a few things.' More than a few." She paused, thinking that, unfortunately, it wasn't the dumbest thing she'd heard lately. "One of the questions we've had about you from the beginning is: Why you? Why did the *makol* reach through the barrier to you, when you're a fundamentally decent guy? Impulsive, maybe. Stubborn, definitely. Occasionally self-serving, check. But on balance, there never seemed a compelling reason why a demon would go after you, and more, why you'd be susceptible to it. What if the connection and susceptibility come from a few drops of Xibalban blood, but your makeup, your essential *you*ness, runs counter to the darkness? That could explain why the *makol* was able to come through the barrier into you, but couldn't integrate your soul with its own . . . thus making it possible for you to survive the Prophet's spell."

Instead of looking appeased by the thought that his inner good guy had saved his life, he seemed pensive. "That would imply that I've got a part in the gods' plan. That they intended for me to go through everything I've been through. For me to do the things I've done." He scrubbed both hands over his face. "Hell,

I just don't know. I can't think about it anymore or I'll drive myself up a wall."

"Newsflash: You've already done that." What was more, his vibe had gone dark and sad, his expression closed. Which was high on the *not good* scale if openness was the key to his magic. *Leave it alone*, her cautious self said. *You came looking for him, not the other way around.* But there was another voice now, a stronger, more adventurous one that said, *Do it. I dare you.* Her heart hammered against her ribs as the moment gained meaning and importance. Then, taking the risk, the leap of faith, she shifted to straddle him suddenly, so they were aligned center-to-center in an instant. Heat fired in her blood. Magic. Desire. He went stiff and still and his hands came up to grip her hips. Before he could pull her close or push her away, she leaned in so her face was very close to his and their breath mingled as she asked, "Question is: Now that you're up the wall, what are you going to do there?"

CHAPTER TWENTY-THREE

Gods. Lucius's blood drained from his head to his lap and he went hard at the spot where they were pressed together, where she rode him unexpectedly. He didn't answer her with words, didn't think he could form a coherent sentence as a roar of heat came close to obliterating the train of thought he'd been locked into for too long. Intellectually, he knew that the question wasn't whether he had mageblood a few generations back; it was whether he would give in again to the weakness that had given the *makol* its toehold. But as Jade's taste exploded across his senses and heat roared within him, he knew the answer wasn't as simple as the instinctive *hell, no* inside him, because if he didn't know what the chink in his armor looked or felt like, how could he be sure of staying strong? That was what had kept him studying the paintings and prophecies long into the night, looking for an answer. That and struggling with thoughts of Jade, and the knowledge that he couldn't go to her until he had his fucking head screwed on right. Except he hadn't gone to her; she'd come to him, propositioned him with the glitter of solstice magic in her eyes. And what the hell was he supposed to do about that?

She broke the kiss to whisper against his lips, "Stop brooding. It's a cardinal day."

Wry amusement had his mouth curving despite his mood. "That doesn't exactly equate to party time around here. In fact, it seems like the perfect time to brood. We're pinning everything on a damned ball game. If this doesn't work, we're screwed."

"And your sitting out here alone is going to change that?" When he didn't respond, she nodded as though he'd answered. "Exactly." She took his hand in hers; their scars rubbed together in an inciting echo of being blood-linked. "This doesn't have to be complicated. Right now, for today, it can just be about the solstice."

Deep inside, he knew he shouldn't let it be that easy. But at the same time, there was nothing easy about the electricity that crackled between them, nothing simple about the roar of heat and need that pounded through him, or the frustration that had ridden him for the past three days. But then, unbidden, his hand rose to cup her cheek. He felt the softness of her skin, saw the wary heat in her eye, and he was lost. "Fuck it. Happy summer to me."

Throwing thought and caution aside with almost giddy relief, he kissed her, deep and dark, and he filled his palms with her curves. Her hands fisted in his hair and she whimpered at the back of her throat, her body molding to his, her breasts pressing against his chest.

On a surge, he swung around and rose to his feet with her legs around his waist, her arms around his neck.

"Lucius!" She grabbed on convulsively.

"I've got you." He carried her down the steep stairs like that, their mouths fused. The man he'd been wouldn't have dared try it. The man he'd become reveled in how easy the move was for him now, just like the ball game had been. Whereas in the past he'd struggled with his own body, now he was in total control.

When they reached his cottage, he carried her across the TV room to the bedroom, this time cradled close to his heart. In some atavistic corner of himself, he was aware of the danger, but just then he didn't care. It was the solstice, a time for sex and magic. He set her on her feet just inside the bedroom door, sliding her against him inch by torturous inch. In unspoken agreement they shed their clothing with glorious abandon, not stopping until they were both naked. The earth-toned light reflected from the ball game scene on the TV screen limned the dip of her waist, the curve of her breast, and the long lines of her arms and legs. He reached for her, thinking to carry her Rhett-like to the bed, but she held him off with an upraised hand. "Wait. Let me."

Before the ridiculous image of *her* carrying *him* to the bed could form, she knelt down and closed her mouth over him almost in a single move. His vision grayed and he forgot what the hell he'd been thinking, damn near forgot his own name. All he could do was lock his knees, bury his hands in her hair, and hang on for the ride.

She drained him, left him weak legged and shuddering, wholly at her mercy. At some point they collapsed together on the bed with her astride him, driving him up again as he filled his hands, his mouth, with her breasts, her lips, her tongue. He talked to her, slipping from English to Yucatec and back, saying her name, lacing it with praise and pleas, urging her up and over, saying more perhaps than he'd said to anyone since he'd nearly lost the option to say anything ever again. She shuddered against him, small climaxes building to the whole, as she rode him, drove him onward, controlled him, until finally she clenched around him, shuddering, his name seeming ripped from her throat as she came.

He followed her over, kept her going, grinding against her, pulsing into her as she said his name again, this time on a moan. Then on a whisper. Until, finally, she sagged against him, pressed her cheek to his, and went still. In fact, he was pretty sure the whole world went still for a long, drawn-out moment that laid him bare, stripped him raw. And in that moment, he thought that he would do anything to keep her with him, anything *for* her.

He lay there drained, reveling in the languor of an orgasm that had devastated him, seeming akin to an apocalypse in its own right. Unable to move, he lay sprawled and satiated while his senses spun and a faint breeze seemed to come from nowhere to tug at him.

It took him a few precious heartbeats to recognize the sensation through the postcoital haze. Then exultation slammed through him. *Magic!* It was there; *he* was there. He reached for it, grabbed on to it, opened himself to it—

And the world hazed luminous green around him.

"No!" He lunged upright, pawing at the night. "Godsdamn it, *no*!"

He saw Jade's face swim into his vision, saw her mouth moving but couldn't hear the words; he couldn't hear anything over the hammer of his heartbeat. His vision flickered back to normal and the world lurched, or maybe he was the one moving. Jade's voice cut in, soothing: "It's okay, it's—"

"It is godsdamned well *not* okay," he snarled, then froze when the words came out instead of being trapped inside his skull, and he snapped back to awareness of his own body. The world solidified around him. "Fuck. Oh, fuck." He doubled over, leaning against her. "I'm going to be sick."

"Up," she ordered. "Into the shower."

"Yeah." His voice was thick; his mouth tasted like shit. He staggered to the bathroom, got the shower on, and stuck his head under the fiery spray. Nauseated and shaking, he stayed under the stream, heat on max, until his skin was red and he was back under control.

Then he stayed another couple of minutes as his brain came back online and things started making sense, and not in a good way. He toweled off, found clean jeans and a tee waiting for him, and dragged them on, his heart pinching at the expectation of things to come.

Jade had gotten dressed and was waiting for him in the main room. She'd shut off the TV and turned on a light. When he appeared in the doorway, she looked up at him, her eyes huge in her face. "Why did you fight the magic?"

"I wasn't fighting the magic. I was fighting the *makol*."

She paled. "You weren't."

"Trust me, I'd know that green eye slime anywhere, anytime. The bastard is still inside me. If I hadn't yanked myself out of there, I might have—" He broke off, had to swallow hard so he wouldn't gag on his own bile. It was like before, only worse, because this time he'd thought he was finished being a slave. "I can't go back there. I fucking *won't*."

She stood to face him. "You're not going anywhere, Lucius. The *makol* is dead; its soul was destroyed during the spell, just like my sister's was. There's no way it's still connected to you. *It doesn't exist anymore.* If it did, you wouldn't have been able to access the library even the first time. Get it? The only place that demon still lives on is in your memories."

He went very still. "You think I'm making this up?"

"I think . . ." She blew out a breath. "How about we sit down?"

Eyeing the sofa, he said softly, "Would you rather I lie down while you pull the chair around? I've told you I don't want to be your patient, Jade. Don't try to therapize me."

"There's no such word as 'therapize.' And another word for therapy is a two-way conversation, Lucius." But the way she said his name, he knew she was thinking "asshole."

Deciding she was probably right about that, he sat on the damn couch, and he didn't move away when she sat beside him and took both of his hands in hers. In fact, he was tempted to lean into her, lean *on* her. He compromised by tipping his head to rest lightly atop hers. "The sex was fabulous. Sorry about the postcoital girlie screaming."

Her fingers tightened fractionally on his. "That was more than sex. And there's no *makol*. Whatever you felt just now was your psyche's way of warning you away from the powerlessness and lack of control that comes from caring for another person. You're not afraid of the *makol*. You're afraid of what's happening between the two of us."

For a second he thought he'd misheard. When he went over the words and they didn't change in his head, he bared his teeth. "In what way?"

She seemed to miss the danger signs, instead rolling on: "I accessed my magic by opening myself up to my feelings for you; I was hoping you'd eventually come around to the point of doing the same thing on your own. You finally did just now, and the Prophet's magic started to come back online, but—and here I am therapizing a little, to use your word for it, but bear with me, because it plays—I think the magic triggered some of the fears you carry from your experiences with the *makol*, namely those of being trapped and out of your own control. Your psyche knee-jerked that into a signal it knew you'd react to, namely the green glow of *makol* possession."

He ground out, "Back up to the part about hoping

I'd come around, will you? Exactly how long have you been working on this theory?"

Her encouraging smile—her counselor's smile—faltered. "Since I started being able to access the scribe's talent by thinking about you."

If he hadn't been so shaken by the *makol's* reappearance, the fear that it would block him from getting back to the library, and, yes, the intensity of the sex, he might have appreciated the irony. Here he was, facing down a lover who was looking up at him as if he were the answer to her freaking prayers, and all he could think about was escaping. From his own damn house.

Hello, shoe on the other foot.

He hadn't gone into this looking for a relationship. He'd been looking to grow up and move on, and stop getting caught up in old patterns. He'd gotten caught, though, in reverse. And with a woman he cared about, one he hadn't meant to hurt. *Bullshit*, a voice said inside him, sounding like Cizin all of a sudden. *If you really didn't want to hurt her, you would've cooled things off days ago. You knew she was falling, but you kept coming back. Hell, you carried her over the damn threshold. What the fuck was she supposed to think?*

He was suddenly chilled, both by the familiar mental tone of a creature that logic said was dead, and by the realization that whatever the source, the inner bitch-slap had a point. He'd been telling himself one thing while doing what felt good. Those weren't the actions of the nice guy she'd painted him as. It was the sort of thing *makol* bait would do.

There was a flicker of nerves in Jade's eyes now, but

she continued. "What just happened is good news, really, because it means that the next time, if you ignore the green and let the magic take over, you'll wind up in the library."

"Maybe," he said coldly. "Or maybe you'll wind up with another *ajaw-makol* loose inside Skywatch. And maybe this time I won't be strong enough to stop it."

She paled. "There's no *makol* here right now. It's your way of processing the fear of being vulnerable."

His anger drained, leaving a hollow ache behind. "Damn it, Jade, they were your rules. Just friends, you said. I was the one who started off wanting more, back before, and you let me down easy." He shook his head. "Now I guess it's my turn, for the first time ever, to try to do this right. So I'll start off with the cliché: It's not you; it's me. If I've learned anything over the past nine days, it's that love means putting the other person first, even over your own safety and life, and despite what the writs say about loyalty to the king and the war." He paused, trying to get it right, and trying not to falter as her face fell. In the end, he said simply: "I can't put you first."

Her eyes flared for a second and she snapped, "That's—" Then she clicked her teeth shut on whatever she was about to say, and shook her head. "Forget it. Just forget it. I guess I misread what I thought I was seeing. I thought we were on the same page."

"So did I." He was going to feel like unholy ravening shit in a few minutes, he thought. For the moment, he just felt numb and gray. Like all the color and life had leeched out of him. Was this what it felt like to

break up with someone you liked but didn't love?
Gods. He'd thought it sucked to be on the other end.
This was ten times worse. A hundred. He felt as if a
piece of his world were suddenly out of joint.

"I . . . I guess I'll go. It'll be morning soon."

Reminded that it was the cardinal day, Lucius fleetingly wondered whether he should have let the magic
take him, on the chance that he'd been wrong somehow about the green. No, he knew that had been *makol*
green. No question about it. He'd done the right thing,
just as he was doing the right thing now. He didn't
know how to love as people like Shandi or Willow did.
He had no basis for it, and didn't want to learn. Jade
had been right in the first place when she'd said that
love destroyed lives. Love wasn't the answer. Inner
strength was.

He watched in silence as she crossed the TV room
and turned back at the kitchen threshold he'd carried
her across less than an hour before. Her face was calm,
composed, but he could see the strain beneath. "I'm
sorry things got messy. I'll see you on the ball court in
a few hours. We've got a game to play."

She turned and left. He didn't call her back.

When her family-only cell phone rang, Patience nearly
dropped a plate of eggs in her husband's lap.

Brandt's head came up at the unfamiliar ringtone.
"Who's that?"

The accusatory edge to the question assuaged her
guilt when she flipped open the phone and blithely
lied, "Kristie, at the dojo. I know I'm not an official

owner anymore, but I gave her my private number in case there were any questions we didn't go over during the transfer." *Don't overexplain.* She placed the plate in front of him at the dining table they hardly used anymore. "Dig in. I'll take this in the bedroom while I finish getting ready for today."

Alone, she pressed the phone to her ear. "Ms. Montana?"

"Nope. Apparently today my name is Kristie and I own a dojo. I'm betting I dot the 'i' in my name with a little smiley face. Or am I a Kristy-with-a-'y'?"

Having already discovered that the bounty hunter had a high retainer, a killer hourly rate for nonbounty work, a smart mouth, and little interest in making friends or even being polite, Patience didn't bother responding to the dig. "Did you find something?"

"Not just something. I found your sons."

"You—" Patience's voice broke on a surge of emotion.

The other woman rattled off a quick summary about facial recognition and driver's licenses, blah, blah, followed by an address.

"Wait! Let me write this down."

"I'll text it."

"Thanks." Her heart was going rapid-fire and her palms were damp; it'd been months since she'd last felt this good. A year. "Do that."

The phone clicked. It took her a few seconds to realize the bounty hunter had hung up on her. Moments later, the text came through. She stared at the address, memorizing it. Then she pressed her lips together and made herself delete the info, just as she'd deleted all the other small nuggets of info as soon as she'd committed them to memory, just in case. All the while, her head spun with a litany of *She found them! She found them! I can't believe she found them!*

Dropping the phone back into her pocket, she headed back out into the kitchen to scare up some cereal for herself while Brandt finished his cholesterol bomb. He gave her a fork wave as she passed. "Everything okay?"

She smiled. "Everything's fine now. Just a few details we need to nail down." *And then, after that? Clear sailing.*

Within the first hour of playing Kinich Ahau's game, Lucius discovered that being a jock wasn't nearly as cool as he'd imagined it would be. Or rather, it was fun being one of the cool kids, but it was also damned hard work. By the second hour, he'd come to understand the game on a cellular level; his body seemed to know where to put itself to return each serve with a forearm, shin, or hip. By the third hour, he'd become almost prescient within the confines of the ball court, always placing himself at the point of maximum impact, maximum play.

The heavy ball, made of natural rubber and infused with some sort of magic that had kept it resilient despite the years, was heavy and irregular, meaning that it bounced erratically, often confounding lifelong athletes Strike, Michael, and Alexis, as well as more analytical players like Nate, Brandt, and Leah. Sven flung himself through the game with wild abandon, usually winding up out-of-bounds, while Rabbit played with vicious glee and lots of knees and elbows. By that time, the others had rotated out and were watching from above.

The points stayed grimly even, rising and falling together, never hitting the magic thirteen. The hoop, eighteen feet in the air and mere inches larger than the ball of play, could've been an illusion; the ball passed by it, banged off it, arched over it, but never went through.

By hour four, when the strange orange sun hit the apex of the sky and began its descent toward dark and destiny, Lucius had entered a glazed, numb-feeling zone where he was down to physical action without internal reaction, sport without soul. He'd even ceased being aware of Jade sitting up above, carefully not watching him with cool, hurt eyes.

A finger tapped him on his unarmored shoulder and a voice said, "It's over."

Anger surged through him, hard and hot and searching for an outlet. Blood hitting fever pitch in an instant, he whirled on his enemy, lifting his stone-weighted hand. "Fuck you."

Jox stood there in a referee's robe, with the conch-shell pipe that acted as a time-out whistle, his eyes going wide and scared as the hand stone descended. Lucius's vision flickered green, then normal; he didn't pull the punch.

"Son of a bitch!" A heavy blow slammed into him from the side, sending him to his knees; he lost his grip

on the hand stone and came up swinging with his fists,
dully surprised that it was Rabbit who had knocked
him aside, Rabbit who protected Jox with his body and
shouted, "Leave him alone, asshole; he's just doing his
job!"

"He—" Lucius stopped dead, aware that the others had stopped playing, were ready to step in. "Shit.
Fuck. Sorry, I— Sorry. I got caught up." Was that all it
had been? He hoped to hell so.

"Understood." Jox nodded, accepting the apology,
though he stayed behind Rabbit's bigger bulk. "But
like I said, play is over for right now. We're breaking
for an hour. You might want to take two."

"I'll take an hour," Lucius grated. "I don't have time
to be tired today."

He grabbed food at random from the overloaded
picnic tables that had been moved to just outside the
court, found a spot far away from all the others, and
sat on the steps of the ball court alone. He ate mechani-
cally but didn't make any headway against the hollowness inside.

"I'm disappointed in you." The censure came from
slightly above him, in Jox's voice.

He glanced back and saw the *winikin* set down his
plate and take a seat one step up and a few feet over,
out of his immediate reach. Lucius shook his head. "I
don't have anything against you personally. You just
seem to be the guy in my way when I lose it."

The *winikin* bit into a hot dog. "That wasn't what I
was talking about. You're wimping out."

"The old me was the wimp. Try again."

"The old you might not have been able to bench-press a Hummer, but he wasn't afraid to go after what he wanted."

"You're talking about Jade." Appetite gone, Lucius shoved aside his plate. "You're off on that one; she didn't want the old guy. Besides, he was terrified of being alone, and spent most of his time wishing, not doing. He . . . Shit. I don't want to talk about it."

"You don't need to talk to me anyway. Talk to her."

Lucius looked over to where Jade sat between Sasha and Patience, chatting. She was wearing a pale peach-colored shirt and had a matching scarf tied around her loose ponytail, its color nearly washed out in the funky sunlight. The others might think nothing had changed. Her face was smooth, her eyes clear, her tone light. Lucius, though, saw the hurt beneath the calm surface. "I can't. I'm not ready to. She's the one who says that people don't change, not at their core, and I think that's true to a point. I'm bigger and stronger now, better co-ordinated. I've made choices not to repeat old patterns. But deep inside, I'm still me."

"You're the one distinguishing between the old version of you and the new one," the *winikin* observed mildly. "The rest of us aren't."

"She is. She gave the old me the 'let's just be fuck buddies' speech. The new me got a watered-down version of the same speech at first. Then, the next thing I know, she changed the rules on me and tried to manipulate me into falling for her. How is a guy supposed to deal with that?"

"Let me see. . . ." The *winikin* paused, considering.

"A beautiful, talented woman you've been panting after decides she wants to be more than bed partners. . . . How should you feel? I'm thinking flattered would be a good start. Maybe grateful. How about overjoyed?"

"She changed the rules."

"She changed herself. And she did it because of how she feels about you."

That brought Lucius's head up. He turned to face the *winikin* more fully, but scowled. "Not until I got buff." He didn't know the resentment was there until he'd said it aloud.

"Reality check. You don't get to talk down about the old you and then get pissed when you think she likes the new-and-improved version better. And besides, I wasn't talking about the past few weeks, or even the past few months. Think about it. When did she start standing up to Shandi and the others?"

"While I was gone."

"It was *because* you were gone, dipshit. Anna had more or less checked out, and everyone else was concentrating on their own problems. Jade was the one who kept your name out there. Why do you think Michael put his own life on the line to get you out of the in-between?"

"Because it distracted the *boluntiku* and bought him enough time to cast the spell he needed to free himself of the Mictlan's magic."

"Screw that. He did it because he knew Jade wanted you back, and he owed her one. He did it for her. Because he knew how much she cared about you, even if she wasn't ready to admit it at the time."

A dull rushing noise built in the back of Lucius's head, and a heavy weight settled on his chest. "I thought about her all the time. It was the only thing that kept me going."

"So why are you pissed at her now?"

Lucius looked up at her, catching her eye. She glanced away, her chin high and her features tight. "I'm not. I'm . . . Shit, I don't know. I think it was easy for us to care for each other when we were apart; we could remember the good stuff and forget the rest. How can I be sure we won't go through the same pattern over and over? What if chemistry and friendship aren't enough? She's the one who says people don't change, but I think they do. I mean, just look at her. She's getting stronger every damn day, whether she realizes it or not. How do people make it work when they can't control what they're going to get from day to day?" He thought of his parents, locked in a thirty-year stalemate between football and Tupperware, thought of his brothers and their interchangeable, silent girlfriends, and his sisters and their husbands and lovers, who could have been swapped out for his brothers without anyone noticing or caring. Who the hell wanted to live like that?

"If two people truly want to stay together, then they grow in the same direction. Not accidentally, but because they work at it." The *winikin* gestured at the picnic tables, where the mated pairs sat close together, sharing intimate looks and private smiles. "Doesn't that look like people making it work?"

"Those are magi, not people. The gods care for humans, but they don't give them destinies."

Jox tapped Lucius's wrist, right above the hellmark. "Don't be so sure of that." The *winikin* collected his plate and rose to his feet. "Break's almost over, but like I said, go ahead and sit out the first shift if you want to."

Lucius dumped his leftovers and headed toward the playing field, where the teams were assembling, the players looking steely eyed and rested, determined that one side or the other was going to get the upper hand. But when he reached the edge of the playing field, he paused and looked back to the tables, where Jade was helping Shandi clean up. As though she felt his eyes on her, Jade looked up, their gazes connecting.

He saw the hurt beneath the calm. More, he saw her determination, her refusal to give up on the people who needed her, even though she might have preferred to be somewhere else, doing something else. Duty, dignity, decorum; she'd said it was the harvester way, and she had all of those qualities. But she was also brave and intelligent, quietly fierce and loyal. And none of those things, he realized, jibed with her being shallow or manipulative. She was a kind person, a healer, not of the body like Sasha, but of the mind and spirit. She hadn't been trying to trap him into anything; she'd been trying to do what she thought was right, trying to let him find his own way rather than control him, because she knew he needed to not be boxed in.

Which left them . . . where? Hell, he didn't know, but he suddenly knew one thing for certain: They weren't over. Not by a long shot.

He tried to convey that in a look, but her face went blank and confused at first, and then gained an edge of anger beneath. That anger reminded him too strongly of his own, of the green flash and the echo of the *makol*'s voice inside his skull. He couldn't go to her, not yet. He needed to deal with the darkness inside him first . . . and pray to the gods it was possible to break free, finally, from his past mistakes.

Then Jox blew the conch shell and tossed the heavy rubber ball to Nate for the first serve, and Lucius told himself to get the hell on the field.

He crossed to the picnic table instead.

When he drew Jade aside, her eyes went stormy. "No," she said firmly. "You don't get to apologize. You were right about some of it, and so was I, but what's said is said; what's done is done. I don't—" Her voice broke; she looked away, visibly trying to hold it together. "I don't like feeling this way. I want my peace and quiet back."

"Too late." Not sure what possessed him, he tugged the scarf from her hair. Looping it around his arm, he tied it above where the ballplayers' asymmetrical armor attached. Leaning in, he dropped a quick, hard kiss on her lips. "We'll talk later."

He retreated before she could respond, before she could insist that no, damn it, they were going to talk now. He didn't know what he wanted to say to her, didn't know what he wanted from her, but he knew it wasn't what they had right then, and it wasn't for them to go back to where they'd been before. They needed to go forward.

Moving fast, impelled by a sudden, fierce sense of urgency, he raced onto the playing field. Now, as he spun and pivoted, throwing hips and elbows, feet and shoulders as the scrum boiled from one side of the narrow pavilion to the other, there was nothing rote or mechanical in his actions. He was entirely there, entirely in the moment and the game.

He instinctively knew when Jade climbed the stairs and joined the audience, knew when she saw him, locked her eyes on him and didn't look away. He played for her, trying to make his case without the words he couldn't find just then. A faint note hummed on the air, high and sweet. It sounded like it might have come from Jox's referee's pipe, but the *winikin* stood off to the side, arms folded.

"Nightkeepers onto the field! Everyone, *now*!" Strike bellowed suddenly, and Jade and the others raced to join the game. The pace shifted, grew frenzied as the high, sweet note intensified and the orange light coming from up above seemed, for a moment, to brighten and turn white and warm.

Lucius was barely aware of these peripherals, though; his whole focus was on the ball and the play. Sven served to Nate, who returned to Alexis, who bumped back to Sven. Action and reaction, arc and flow. *Over there*, Lucius knew, and headed for a clear spot at the edge of the action. Seconds later, the ball flew straight toward him. So did Strike and Michael, their eyes locked on the arcing sphere.

Michael crouched; the ball hit his shoulder guard and deflected straight upward, when all physics said it should have ricocheted to Strike in the pass they had undoubtedly intended. Lucius didn't slow or swerve; he barreled straight at Michael. He saw the other man's eyes go wide, saw him brace for impact.

Only Lucius didn't hit him—he jumped, springboarded off the other man's shoulder, and went vertical.

The ball reached its apogee and descended, hurtling toward a ball court that represented imprisonment in the underworld. Lucius flew up to meet the sun ball, slammed his armored forearm into its yielding irregularity, and sent it hurtling through the heavy air. The ball shot sideways, not toward the underworld court now, but toward the sacred stone ring. Toward the future.

Gravity grabbed Lucius, yanking him earthbound as though pissed that he'd broken free for a brief and glorious moment. He slammed into the ground and rolled to lie flat, staring up, as the sun ball passed through the sacred ring without touching the sides. For a moment, the earth went still, and he imagined he could hear the cosmic swish of his sideways slam dunk.

Then the sweet note went to a scream, a brilliant red-gold flash split the air, and the world lurched around Lucius. Adrenaline slashed through him. This wasn't his magic, whatever that was. There was no green haze, no feeling of inward pressure; this was entirely external, a greater force taking him somewhere. Then he was moving, accelerating, the world whipping sideways past him and going to a gray-green blur.

Air detonated around him, drier than the rank humidity of Skywatch. He had only a moment to register tall tree trunks covered in dry, dead moss and wilted vines before gravity yanked at him again—he could almost hear it snarl, *Stay* down *there, will you?* He landed on his feet, bent kneed and not alone. The other magi were all around him, with Jade at the edge of the group, near a thick stand of brownish vegetation. He caught an impression of a blighted rain forest, with tall tree giants forming an overhead canopy protecting wilted air plants, with their long, ropy roots. Vines hung in limp tangles, and sad-sounding parrots called desultorily from up above.

Climate change, he thought. *The cloud forests are dying*. But even as that clicked in his brain, he saw the brittle ferns sway with the passing of a large creature. Then another. "Jade," he shouted as adrenaline spiked. *"Behind you!"*

As she spun, the greenery parted beneath paws the size of a man's palm, and a big, black shape emerged, joined seconds later by another. The fur bristled between their shoulder blades; their hackles were raised.

The companions of Kinich Ahau had come to earth!

Michael shouted and the magi converged on the creatures. Lucius lunged in front of Jade, and lifted his hand stone. Then he hesitated, because the companions weren't attacking. The creatures were just standing there, with their eyes locked on Jade. "Don't move," he said out of the corner of his mouth. "Don't even breathe."

She touched his arm. "I think it's okay. Remember, they defended me before."

"Now *I'm* defending you."

"I know."

He glanced back at her, saw the decision in her eyes, and grabbed her arm before she could do something impulsive. "Oh, no, you don't."

"They came from Xibalba," she pointed out. "They must have come through the hellmouth. Maybe they can lead us back there. If it's still closed, I might be able to manipulate the magic hiding it, like I did with Vennie's cave."

The other magi were gathered close in support, but he saw only her, feared only for her. "Jade—" he began.

She touched his mouth, silencing him. "Shh. We'll talk about it later," she said. And this time, the "later" was a promise.

Lucius knew he didn't have a choice. She was a warrior, with or without the mark, and she needed to do what the gods intended, both for the Nightkeepers and for herself. He stepped slowly back and gestured for her to do her thing.

The moment she started forward, the dogs whirled and plunged into the undergrowth. Without looking back or hesitating, she plunged after them, with Lucius right on her heels. If anything bad wanted to get at her, it was going to have to go through him to do it.

CHAPTER TWENTY-FOUR

Jade's nerves revved high as she followed the companions, who were moving fast through the dying cloud forest, their heads and tails low as though they were on a mission. Which she supposed they were: Save Kinich Ahau, and get him back in the sky where he belonged.

One thing at a time, she reminded herself. *First we need to find the hellmouth*. As she chased after the long-legged black hellhounds, she sought the magic, called it to her, but nothing happened. Panic flickered. *Don't you dare quit on me now*.

But it wasn't that the magic had quit on her, she knew. She'd quit on it. Or rather, she was blocking the hell out of it.

Damn it, Lucius, she thought, but even as she did, she knew it wasn't entirely his fault, or hers. They had both screwed things up the night before. She should've told him about her theory of the connection between their emotions and their magic, and she should've come clean to him that she was falling hard and fast for him despite all her best intentions. Even admitting it to her inner self brought a lick of panic. He'd turned her down, said that wasn't what he wanted, *she* wasn't what he wanted.

Granted, his behavior on the ball court and the way he'd worn her scarf as a knight's Dark Age favor suggested he'd been doing some rethinking too, and the way he was following close behind her now had all the hallmarks of a male warrior-mage protecting his mate. But they hadn't said the words, hadn't had the conversation.

More talking? she asked herself, irritation spiking. Therapy might be a two-way conversation, but she was getting sick of it. She was tired of talking herself into trouble; she wanted to *act*, to react, to make a difference, damn it.

Up ahead, the big black creatures crossed a wide clearing and then stopped dead, standing shoulder-to-shoulder, facing nothing in particular. Then they sat, still staring at that same nothingness. Only it wasn't nothing, Jade knew. It was the hellmouth . . . or it would be if she could figure out the magic.

Lucius moved up beside her while the other magi fanned out, waiting for her to do her thing. None of their talents was compatible with the task—fire could level the forest but it couldn't uncover what had been hidden; a shape-shifted hawk could fly a search pattern, but the Volatile could see only what was visible. Mind-bending wouldn't help; Strike couldn't 'port blind; and invisibility wasn't their problem—visibility was.

"It's all yours," Lucius said, his thoughts paralleling hers. He took her hand, squeezed it. "You can do it. I have faith in you."

That jarred against his recent behavior. "Maybe," she said softly, "but what if I'm not strong enough?"

He looked down at her, his eyes intense. "The harvesters believed in the importance of their work; Shandi believed in the value of the harvesters. The stars believed in the prophecies, Vennie in her own brilliance. You're a part of each of them. What do you believe in?"

She didn't answer right away. She knew that the clock was ticking, that everyone was waiting for her. But she was stuck on Lucius's question. What did she believe in? She believed in the magic, in the Nightkeepers and the war. She believed that she was stronger than she used to think she was, and that she and Lucius . . . what? Did she believe they could make each other happy in the long run?

That was the problem, she realized suddenly, or one of them. She'd seen the end of so many relationships that she entered each new affair preparing for its end, creating a self-fulfilling prophecy that made it easier, safer, and less dramatic to not bother trying to keep it going. What would happen if she threw herself into it heart and soul?

She might be crushed, she realized. But she might also succeed.

"I believe," she said slowly, "that inner peace is highly overrated." While he was trying to puzzle that one out, she stepped into him and kissed him, hard.

What was more, she opened herself fully to her own emotions and damned the consequences.

The magic shimmered within her, in the air around them, and a hidden door opened inside her, letting in the power of the solstice, and the power that was hers alone. She stepped away from Lucius, taking her place directly between the companions, facing nothing.

Only it wasn't nothing, she saw now. It was everything.

The bright sparks she'd seen as part of the shifting pattern of power in Rabbit's sublet had come from sex or emotion, maybe both; the fluid magic she'd sensed covering the hidden tunnel at Skywatch had been an ancient spell imbued with modern hopes and fears. But seeing those things was just half of her magic. The other half was in the spell words themselves, and her ability to morph them from one thing to another. She had created ice magic, it was true, but she hadn't been able to use that part of her talent since.

Now, as she laid herself open to the magic, to the possibilities, she saw it. In front of her, rising from the dried-up cloud forest floor to the wilted canopy above, stretching the width of the clearing in either direction, was a wall of magic. It was bright sparks and flowing power. It was the code beneath the chatter, the structure underlying the fabric of the earth. At the same time, glyph strings crawled across the undulating surface of the spell, morphing and mutating as she watched. How in the hell was she supposed to alter a spell that was altering almost faster than she could follow it?

Gods, she thought, stomach twisting. It was too complex, too mutable. She could see the structure but she couldn't get a grip on it. The spell was a slippery ball of power, sliding through her grasp each time she thought she had it.

She stared at the nothingness, sweat prickling on her brow.

"Jade." It was Lucius's voice, low in warning. On either side of her, the companions were growling, their shoulder fur ruffling.

"They won't hurt me. I think they're worried. The magic of the game brought them through, and now they can't get back to him. Unless . . ." She trailed off as a glyph glinted in the flowing string. It glowed, floated off the spell surface, and locked itself into a single pictograph. As she watched, a second followed. Then another. Her magic churned and spun, but she wasn't quite there yet. The magic wasn't quite there.

Without another thought or hesitation, she opened herself to the task, to the power and the potential for failure and drama. *Take what you need.* Something shifted inside her, a sharp lurch beneath her heart, and she gasped. Then it was there: The counterspell flared in front of her, burning itself into her mind's eye.

She reached back for Lucius's hand, felt their fingers twine and link. Whispering a small prayer in her heart, she recited the counterspell.

The shimmering curtain of power and spell words disappeared as though it had never existed. There was no explosion, no power surge. One moment all she saw in front of her were more trees, more dying vines. In the next, she was staring at a mountainside with a terrible skull carved into it, jaw gaping wide so it screamed the dark, ominous entrance to a cave. Just inside its mouth, a skeleton hung skewered to the cave wall, still wearing the remains of what had been a purple velour tracksuit.

Overhead, heretofore silent monkeys screamed in fear, and parrots took wing in a thunder of brittle feathers. For a second, nobody moved. Then, without warning, an unearthly shriek split the air and terrible creatures with twisted, humanoid bodies and the heads of animals boiled out of the blackness of the tunnel. Snakes, jaguars, eagles, hawks, crocodiles, every sacred creature was mocked in twisted Egyptian parodies arising from dark magic. Their human parts were gnarled and gray skinned, with some parts grown too large, others shrunk to vestiges.

Jade screamed; she couldn't help it. These were the creatures that had captured her and Lucius before, only now they were damaged even worse and pissed about it. She could feel their rage as a palpable force against her magic, and instinctively tamped down her power, her vulnerability.

Strike roared an order and the warriors let fly with a fireball salvo that detonated against the front line of animal-heads, sending body parts flying in a spray of blood, fire, and flame. Their screams were terrible; the smell was worse. Gagging, Jade reeled against Lucius. He grabbed her. "Back to the trees!" he yelled over a roar of fire as flames napalmed from Rabbit's outstretched palms, turning the second rank of attackers to a pyre. "We need to take cover!"

Jade was turning to comply when sharp teeth seized her arm and dug in, pulling her the other way.

She screamed and swung out with her cudgel; it slammed into the shoulder of one of the big black dogs. For a second, she thought she was dead, that it was going to tear her throat out then and there. But it simply glared at her and bore down on her hand, almost—but not quite—breaking the skin. Its legs were braced, its ruff standing straight up in a vicious line along its spine, making it look like some prehistoric, spiked creature.

Lucius cursed and rounded on the companion, but she waved him off as understanding dawned. "We have to fight through," she said urgently. "Kinich Ahau needs our help!"

At her shout, the warriors knotted together in a defensive formation. "We can't help shit if we're dead," Michael said, then spun to unleash a stream of deadly silver *muk* into the horde; the death magic cut a swath as animal-heads crumbled to dust. Sasha stood behind him, her hand on his waist, her eyes closed as she fed him her lifegiving magic, balancing out the danger of using the ancestral magic that melded both light and dark halves.

The animal-heads kept coming, their ranks swelling to overrun the clearing. Some of the creatures climbed over their own dead, uncaring, while others stopped to feed on the bodies with a ferocity that made Jade's gorge rise.

"The whole world is going to die if we don't rescue Kinich Ahau," Strike countered. "If Akhenaton's ascension doesn't spell the beginning of the end, our failure to rescue the last god remaining outside the sky plane might." He looked from the companions to the cave mouth and back again, and Jade could see his anguish. His father had ordered the Nightkeepers to their deaths under far better odds. He didn't hesitate long, though. Sweeping his cudgel in a high arc, he pointed to the tunnel mouth and shouted, "Go!"

The big dog released Jade's hand, spun, and bolted away, with its twin right behind.

The other warriors picked up the cry and charged, clearing the way with fireballs and Rabbit's human-flamethrower routine. Jade found herself screaming, "Kinich Ahau!" and running with them. Ice magic raced through her veins but she held it in, not sure whether it would douse the flames. Lucius was right with her, solid at her side, his fierce loyalty not up for question, even if their relationship remained hazy and uncertain.

The Nightkeepers' charge carried them to the cave mouth before the animal-heads rallied. A huge creature with a crocodile's head rose above the others, snarling something in that strange, guttural tongue she had heard before, in Xibalba. At their leader's orders, the animal-heads reoriented and charged, surrounding the magi and killing the momentum of their charge.

"I've got it!" Michael shouted. He called a thick, sturdy shield spell and slapped it across the point where the cave mouth narrowed into a tunnel leading into the mountainside. A hundred animal-heads, maybe more, were trapped outside the shield, cutting the immediate threat in half. "Go!"

"Good man," Strike said shortly as he and the others faced forward, to where a seemingly endless stream of animal-heads poured up through the tunnel. Under the next fireball onslaught, the narrow space filled quickly with burning bodies, their stench turning the air thick with an oily, choking smoke that made Jade gag. She reached for Lucius, who caught her against him, holding on tightly.

Sasha moved to her mate's side to boost his magic and keep him leveled off. She glanced at Jade and the friends—a former chef and an ex-therapist—shared a quick *how the hell did we end up here?* look, and then returned to their tasks.

Jade and Lucius followed Strike and the others as the small fighting force slaughtered its way deeper into the tunnel, winning forward one bloody foot at a time. Jade focused on the companions; they always seemed to know where to twist and turn in order to find their way through the surging melee. Lucius cracked his cudgel to his left and right, his jaw tight, his eyes reflecting the same sharp horror that rattled through her. In the underworld, the animal-headed warriors had regenerated quickly. Up on the earth plane, they just flat-out died. And although they resembled the ancient Egyptian gods, each of the head-types was also a species that had—or used to have—a corresponding Nightkeeper bloodline. Had Akhenaton harnessed the Nightkeepers' ancestors as an army? Was that who the magi were killing?

"Don't think about it," Lucius rasped against her temple. He was still holding her close, using his body to shield her as they forced their way through. "Not now. Just go."

So she went, following in the companions' wake. They outdistanced the fireball-wielding magi, so she lashed out with bursts of ice magic that froze some of the animal-heads, slowed others by dumping drifts of snow. Time lost meaning, becoming a cycle of spell casting and advancing, with Lucius staying strong at her back. Then the tunnel opened up around them and they were standing in a ceremonial chamber with ritually carved walls and a wide altar. Jade didn't process the details, though. Her attention was immediately commanded by the liquid shimmer of the far wall, which bent and flexed, seeming alive.

The companions bolted toward it.

"The barrier!" She surged after them, but Lucius yanked her back. "What—" She spun on him and broke off on a gasp. The tunnel was blocked with animal-heads and the Nightkeepers were nowhere in sight.

"They're cut off," Lucius reported grimly. "And this is a dead end."

"No, it's not. It's the beginning of the hellroad. It's open because of the solstice, or maybe because of the hellhounds and the ball game. Who knows? All I know is that we need to get through there."

"We can't—" He began, but then broke off when a jaguar-head started barking orders. "Fuck. Come on."

They ran together to the back wall, which looked like stone but wasn't. The companions had waited for them, and the four rescuers dove through together. As she passed through the barrier, Jade felt power ripple across her skin. Then she was caught up, sucked down, spun around. Her hand was torn from Lucius's grip and she screamed. She heard him shout her name; then even that was lost to the roar of acceleration as the world whipped past her. She felt the same wrenching, sliding sensation as before, when she and Lucius had traveled to Xibalba. Only this time it was ten times worse, because she was experiencing it fully. Her physical self wasn't safely at Skywatch anymore. She was traveling, body and soul, into hell.

Xibalba

This time, when Lucius and Jade blinked into existence within the dry, angular canyon, he immediately recognized it as a giant, "I"-shaped ball court, with the out-of-bounds lines marked by the faint shadow of dark shield magic. Then again, the association was a hell of a lot more obvious: The pyramid and its surrounding columns were gone, small vertical stone hoops protruded from halfway down each of the long sides of the canyon . . . and there was a game in progress.

His mind snapshotted the scene. Akhenaton's ghostly form was on one side with his guards and five animal-heads. The *makol* was a dark shadow. The other nine, decked out in full armor, held spiked cudgels and wore knives on their belts. Kinich Ahau stood alone on the other side in the guise of a horned, plumed man, not the firebird. The god wore a feathered robe with hints of glistening armor beneath but held no weapon. There were stone shackles on the god's wrists and ankles; heavy sinew-threaded ropes stretched from the cuffs to a stone ring set low on one wall. A man's head lay on the ground between the two teams, wide-eyed and staring, with fluid leaking from the stump. Lucius thought it might have belonged to the musician, who was nowhere in sight.

Oh, he thought. *Of course.*

He must've said it aloud, because as he and Jade scrambled to their feet, she whispered, "What is it?"

The players, locked in a preplay stare-down, seemed oblivious to the newcomers, but Lucius figured he didn't dare count on how long that would last. Keeping his voice low, he said, "One of the creation stories in the Popol Vuh describes how the Hero Twins journeyed to the underworld and played ball against the *Banol Kax* themselves. If the dark lords won, the twins would be stuck forever in Xibalba. But if the twins won, their father would be reincarnated on Earth and they would be free to return with him. Akhenaton must not be able to rule the sky in his *makol* form. In order to take his place in the sky, he has to defeat Kinich Ahau and be reincarnated on Earth."

A soul-curdling fanfare sounded from all around them, and the players scrambled to gain control of the game ball. The sun god lunged and hit the end of his tether, which stopped him several paces shy of the ball. The horned god shrieked with rage, the firebird's cry coming from the man's mouth as a snake-headed warrior snagged the ball.

Jade whispered, "Does that mean that if Kinich Ahau wins, he automatically returns to Earth?"

"That'd be consistent with the legend. Not much

chance of that, though, unless—" Lucuis broke off as transport magic surged again, the air rippled nearby, and the sun god's companions materialized midlunge. The big hellhounds hit the ground running, baying the attack. And all hell broke loose.

Akhenaton whirled toward the threat. His fury laced the air as he split his team, sending the guards after Kinich Ahau, the animal-heads toward Jade and Lucius, who had landed maybe thirty yards farther down the playing field, on the sun god's side. The companions bolted toward Kinich Ahau; the sun god jerked its plumed head toward Jade and Lucius. Its eyes were anguished.

The animal-heads closed quickly; there were two snakes and three caimans, reptilian jaws gaping wide. Lucius stepped in front of Jade, suddenly feeling very human. But they'd damn well have to go through him to get to her.

"Down!" she yelled from behind him.

When a chill touched the back of his neck, he didn't waste time asking questions or arguing; he pancaked it.

The air snapped freezing cold and a deep-throated roar of power sizzled through the space he'd just been occupying. An iceball the size of a MINI Cooper flashed at the animal-heads; it hit with a big *whump*, the ground heaved, and sand shot in the air. When the debris came back down, there was an ice-lined crater where the animal-heads had been.

Lucius flipped to his feet, mouth hanging open. "Holy shit."

Jade was pale, her eyes huge in her face, but her expression was resolute. "We need to use the tools we're given, right?" She sagged a little, and when he took her arm, she leaned into him. The iceball had drained her more than he liked, but she was up and moving, and ready to fight.

The gods got it wrong, he thought. *She's a warrior. Always has been.*

Motion on the field of play caught his attention; two of the guards were heading for them, leveling those damned long pikes as dark magic rattled low at the threshold of hearing. The remaining guards were passing the decapitated head as they ran toward the sun god, aiming for the hoop high on the wall.

If they made the basket, it was all over.

"You've got to block that shot!" Jade shoved him toward the field. "Go. I'll be right behind you!"

Lucius wanted to stay with her, to hold her close and shield her, but he couldn't. Not right now. *She's a fighter*, he reminded himself. *She's got your back*. It was strange to realize that he'd never thought that about her before. He'd seen her as his friend and his lover, his adversary and his ideal, but never before as a teammate. Locking eyes with her, he said, "You can do this."

"Don't worry about me. I'm tougher than I look."

"About time you figured that out." He flashed her a smile. And took off running.

Head down, he barreled into the first of Akhenaton's guards, taking the brunt of the blow on his armored shoulder. It was like running into a side of beef mounted on a house. His shoulder sang with pain, while the other guy barely blinked, just raised his spiked cudgel and swung for his head.

Jade screamed his name. Then, inexplicably, she whistled a short, sharp burst, as though calling a taxi.

Lucius ducked, cursing when dark magic dug bloody furrows across his bare shoulder. A second guard arrived as the first raised his weapon for the killing blow. But before the guard could let loose with the magic, a growling black blur slammed into him from the side. Moments later a second snarling creature joined the fray. The companions! Summoned by Jade's whistle, the big black creatures drove the guards away, giving Lucius time to scramble to his feet.

He looked for her and his blood froze in his veins when he saw that she was headed straight into the scrum, where Kinich Ahau was down, wrestling with one of the guards. The remaining player and Jade were both zeroing in on the head-ball, which lay inert on the nearby sand.

One of Lucius's attackers had dropped his pike when the dogs showed up; it had returned to its shorter form and no longer shimmered with dark magic. Instead it looked like a short, wickedly spiked club. Lucius grabbed the heavy weapon and bolted toward the field of play as Jade grabbed the head. The guardsmen of the other team converged on her as Lucius shouted, "*Jade!*"

Her head whipped around; she saw him and yelled, not his name or for help, but, "Here!" She threw him the head. A split second later, one of the guards tackled her, taking her down.

Lucius caught the head on the fly; the thing weighed more than he would've expected, and was slippery. He wound up grabbing it by the hair. Then he hesitated. The hoop on the opposite side of the court was unguarded. It was far above him, an almost impossible shot.

If he made it, he would return Kinich Ahau to Earth. But in doing so, he would lose Jade. Gods, *Jade.*

The writs told him to save the world. His heart told him to save his woman.

"Fuck it. *Catch!*" He hurled the head to the sun god, aware that the game was fixed, that the god's bonds wouldn't allow it close enough to score the vital point, barely allowed it to guard its own hoop. "Don't let them have it. I'll be right back." He hoped the god understood English, or at least his intent.

Without looking to see if Kinich Ahau had gotten the head—or the message—Lucius spun and lunged toward Jade—

And stopped dead. The guards held her immobilized as Akhenaton's dark shadow drifted toward her. The ghost soul lost its form as it approached, becoming amorphous, insidious. Lucius flashed hard on the memory of a dark shadow entering him, filling him up, making the world go green.

"*No!*" he shouted, his voice cracking on a howl that was echoed in the companions' voices. Behind him chaos erupted as the animal-heads finished regenerating from whatever molecules had been left after the ice explosion, and rejoined the fray.

Duty, ambition, and his need to make a difference

in the world said he needed to play the game, needed to save the sun. Duty, he decided, could go fuck itself. Turning his back on the game, on the god, Lucius gripped the spiked cudgel, though he knew it wouldn't do any good against a shadow. He could think of only one thing that could go up against a demon on its own turf.

Another demon.

The shadow touched Jade, moved up her body. Her eyes locked on Lucius's, wide and scared. His heart pounded, not with dread, but with an all-important realization that came far too late. "I love you," he said to her. Then, when the words were lost beneath the animal roars from the game and the god, he raised his voice and shouted, "*I love you!*"

Her face went blank, then flooded with emotion, followed by quick understanding. Horror. "Don't—" she began.

But he did. He lifted the cudgel and used one of the spikes to lay his palm open in a quick slash. Pain bit. Blood welled. Then, closing his eyes, he opened himself to her—not to her magic, but to the things he felt about her, the things he felt when he was with her. He threw himself wide, remembering their first night together, their last. He filled his senses with the image of her face, the soft brush of her hair, the taste of her when they made love. His love for her entered him, filled him, completed him. And as he invited the heat and wonder and awe inside him when he'd held it away before, power stirred and his vision flickered from normal to green hued and back again. He didn't know whether it was Cizin or another *makol*, and didn't think he cared. He needed a demon's power, and this was the only way to get it.

Yes, he thought. *That's it, you bastard. Come into me.*

Opening his eyes, he threw his arms wide and shouted, so it echoed across the canyon: "I love her! I love Jade." In that moment, he put her above everything else inside him and gave over control to the magic, letting it have him in exchange for her safety. The air detonated around him, whipped past him. Power surged and crackled; motion caught his eye, and he turned to see that a few feet away the canyon wall had suddenly gone liquid and strange. Inside him, the place that had been empty for the past half year flared with bright, brilliant agony and began to fill up.

"Lucius!" Jade screamed.

He couldn't answer, couldn't look at her, could only drop to his knees in agony as an alien presence entered him, invaded him, became him. *Come on, come on, hurry up!* He had to get the demon inside him, had to gain control somehow and pit it against Akhenaton before the bastard took Jade.

The shimmering nearby grew more distinct, then flared bright white with a boom of detonation. When it cleared, the other Nightkeepers stood on the canyon floor, bloody and bedraggled, staring around in themselves in shock.

Gods. Lucius sagged as greasy brown vapor wisps surrounded him, but he managed to make his mouth work enough that he could croak, "Win the game. Free the god."

Then his vision washed green and he wasn't just himself anymore. He was Akhenaton too.

Akhenaton?

It didn't make any sense, but it was true. He could see the pharaoh's thoughts, his history, his greed— everything that made him the monomaniacal murderer he had been. The *makol* seemed equally shocked to find itself inside the human male rather than the mage woman; Lucius caught the demon's thought-pictures, though no language was transmitted. Then Akhenaton saw the Nightkeepers: Michael and Sasha were freeing Jade from the guard, while the others raced toward Kinich Ahau, who still had control of the ball but was under siege by the five animal-heads. Seeing its plans crumbling, its opportunity to rule the sun sliding into jeopardy, and fearing the wrath of its *Banol Kax* masters, Akhenaton's demon spirit thrust itself brutally into Lucius's psyche, grabbing for control of their shared body.

No! Lucius roared inwardly. *Never again!* Using every iota of mental discipline he had learned from Cizin, he slammed mental shields around Akhenaton's essence and forced the damned soul *away*. Power surged and magic swirled, forming a vortex Lucius remembered from the Prophet's spell. Added to that now was the power he'd felt before, that hollow, rushing sensation of a connection forming between worlds. He caught a glimpse of black nothingness, and pushed the demon's soul toward it.

Akhenaton howled in outraged protest. Too used to commanding through fear, the demon didn't know how to dominate someone who wasn't afraid.

Die, Lucius grated. *Die!*

The pharaoh's spirit scrabbled for purchase, lost its grip, and tore away, pinwheeling. A terrible, thin scream trailed off as the *makol*'s incorporeal soul was sucked into the void.

There was a flash of luminous green. Then the pharaoh was gone.

For a moment, there was only emptiness inside Lucius. Then fierce triumph roared through him. He'd done it. He'd defeated a *makol*! He wanted to scream victory, wanted to pump his fists, wanted to snatch Jade up and spin her in a circle, kissing her until she admitted that she loved him too, that they would muddle through, make mistakes, and make it work.

But Lucius's eyes wouldn't open. His body wouldn't move. In fact, he was looking *down* on his body, which was lax and slack-muscled. He saw Jade racing toward him, bending over him. And, strangely, he seemed to be floating up to the pale brown sky.

Jade crouched down beside Lucius. Tears stung her eyes when she couldn't find his pulse. Akhenaton was gone; she'd seen its shadow leave Lucius. But then she'd seen another, glowing mist rise from his beloved body. The faint shimmer was gone now, but she thought she knew what it meant.

He'd sacrificed himself for her, in all possible ways. And she'd be damned if she would let that be the end of things for them.

Leaning in close, she whispered in his ear, "I love you, so stay the hell alive." Then, nearly blinded by

unshed tears, she scrambled up and lunged toward the
field of play, where the magi were jockeying for position as the pharaoh's guards and animal-headed minions passed the ball among them, heading for the sun
god's goal. For a moment, she didn't understand what
was going on; Akhenaton was gone, so who were they
playing for? Then she saw that beast-shadows lined the
high walls of the ball court. The *Banol Kax* had come to
watch, lending their weight to the play.

If the Nightkeepers' team won, they would be free
and Kinich Ahau would return to Earth. If not, they
would all remain trapped in Xibalba. Forever.

Habit and instinct told Jade to hide on the sidelines.
Instead, she bolted straight for the action. Her breath
whistled in her throat as she dodged a spiked club,
spun past a snake-head that snapped and hissed at her,
and lunged for Sasha. Tapping her on the shoulder,
which had been their signal for a player to rotate out
of the game, Jade shouted over the game noise, "Go
help Lucius. He's hurt." She pointed toward where he
lay, steeling herself against the sight of his motionless
form.

Sasha nodded and took off, leaving Jade to play her
position. When she was just barely clear of the field,
the sun god screeched an avian war cry. Holding the
head-ball under one arm, it raced across the canyon
floor, headed for the opposite team's goal. The slack
whipped out of the sinew ropes, which snapped tight
and yanked the god to a roaring, thrashing standstill.
The animal-heads boiled in pursuit, regenerating as
quickly as the Nightkeepers cut them down. Kinich

Ahau fought the bonds, which stretched but didn't give.

They're too pliable! Jade thought suddenly. Heart pounding, she summoned the last dregs of her magic and shaped it into the now-familiar iceball spell. Cold touched the air and raced through her veins as she let the ice magic fly. It hit the ropes, which froze with a hissing, crackling noise. And turned brittle.

With an exultant howl, Kinich Ahau snapped free, tossed the head-ball into the air, and leaped after it. As if the bonds themselves had contained the god's magic, the man-form became the firebird, morphing midair to the fierce flame-clad creature. It flapped its wings once, twice, and on the third sweep, it caught the head-ball in its beak. Banking, the god swept past the hell-team's goal, and flung the head through the hoop with a shriek of triumph. As the ball passed through, white light lit the sky and a soundless detonation rocked the firmament. The animal-heads and the last of the pharaoh's guards dropped where they stood and lay, unmoving. Atop the high walls on either side of the ball court, shadows rippled and the *Banol Kax* disappeared, beaten by a game that was part of the fabric of the planes themselves.

Drained of the last of her magic, Jade collapsed to the canyon floor and buried her face in her hands. She didn't weep, not yet. Not until Sasha told her Lucius was gone. But somehow she knew, she *knew* that had been his soul leaving his body and heading for the sky, where warriors went after they died in battle.

"Gods, please, no," she whispered behind her hands.

The pain was incredible, overwhelming, impossible to bear. But she didn't wish it gone. She embraced it, wallowed in it, held it to her. And if that put her on the level of the most heartbroken patient she'd ever counseled, then it was a good level to be on, because she had finally taken the risk. She had loved. She had *lived*.

"Jade." It was Strike's voice, oddly hushed. "Look up."

"I know," she said, sighing as she let her hands fall. "He's—" She broke off on a gasp.

The firebird stood in front of her, flanked on either side by the big black dogs that guarded it. The flames that had wreathed it before had turned to soft red-gold feathers. It looked like a giant eagle with the plumage of a parrot, and it towered over her, dwarfed her as it stretched out one wing, unfurled its long flight feathers, and brushed them across her face and down her right arm. The touch tingled; it burned, but not unpleasantly . . . and in a familiar way.

Pulse suddenly hammering, she looked down at her forearm. There she wore a new glyph, a third mark. It wasn't static, though; as she watched, it morphed from one glyph to another and back again, oscillating between the two.

The god was offering her a choice, she realized: the sun or the *jun tan*? Godkeeper or mate?

She looked up at the firebird, her eyes blurring with tears. Even knowing that her choice might cost them a Godkeeper, she said without hesitation, "I choose to be his mate. Magic isn't the answer. Love is." And although he might already be gone, the sudden warmth that curled around her heart told her that it was the right answer for her.

"Ho-ly shit," someone said from behind her. She didn't know who.

The firebird dipped its head—in acknowledgment, she thought. It touched her again with its wing, and the *jun tan* firmed in place, stark and black on her forearm. Then the god swept its opposite wing toward Lucius's motionless body. Sasha knelt beside him, trying to keep his body going in the absence of its soul.

Jade's heart shuddered as a white shimmer coalesced from the sky and drifted down toward him. She told herself not to hope, but she couldn't stop the hot, hard anticipation from forming as the vapor settled over him, sank into him.

For a moment, nothing happened. Her world contracted, started to crumble around her.

And then he began to breathe.

CHAPTER TWENTY-FIVE

Joy exploded through Jade. Hardly daring to hope, to believe, she lunged up and ran to Lucius, choking on her sobs. He groaned and rolled toward her, then sat partway up and reached for her. She dropped to her knees, her tears finally breaking free as his arms closed around her, strong and sure. "I love you," she said, the words muffled against the side of his face. "Gods, I love you." Then he was kissing her, and she was kissing him back, and the world settled into a new, better shape around her.

When they parted, Lucius looked past her, and his eyes went wide. And it was his turn to say, "Ho-ly shit."

The firebird was bowing down in front of Sasha. Michael stood at her side.

Another hot wave flashed through Jade, this time one of relief. She hadn't cost the magi a Godkeeper, after all. "She was meant to be Godkeeper to Kinich Ahau all along," she said softly, although she suspected that when she and Sasha had jointly fulfilled the triad prophecy, they had both become equal candidates for the honor.

Lucius seemed to follow her thoughts, because he lined up his forearm next to hers. On his inner wrist he wore a *jun tan* to match hers . . . and the quatrefoil hellmark had turned black. "Thank you," he rasped, in a voice that had started out that of a stranger and become that of her mate.

She looked at their marks. Despite the hot, hard joy that raced through her at the sight of the *jun tan*, she shook her head in pretend rue. "Shandi is going to kick my ass."

"First she'll thank the gods that you made it home safely. Then, yeah, she might kick your ass." They grinned at each other. He stood, his strength returning quickly, and helped her up. As they headed toward the others, hand in hand, power flashed red-gold, there was a thunder-loud clap, and the firebird sprang aloft as Sasha and Michael embraced, leaning into each other.

Kinich Ahau gained altitude, winging into the sky. As the god rose higher and higher, flames limned the red feathers and trailed from the beat of its wings. Then, suddenly, white-hot light flashed. And the god was gone.

"We did it," Jade said, not quite ready to believe, though Lucius's fingers were tightly threaded through hers. But then she stared up at the sky in dismay. "I thought winning the game would send us home. Why are we still here?"

"Because it's my job to get us home," Lucius said.

"The magic inside me originally belonged to Cizin. When its soul was torn away from mine, I somehow kept hold of that one piece of the demon's power. You know how we've theorized that different *makol* have different skill sets? Well, I think Cizin was capable of forming temporary roads through the barrier. But you were right that I couldn't touch the power until I got to the point where nothing else mattered . . . which happened when Akhenaton tried to possess you." He caressed her cheek. "I'd rather live forever in the in-between than have you go through that."

She wanted to close her eyes and lean into his touch. Instead, she poked him in the stomach. He let out a surprised "oof" as she got in his face. "You'd better consider yourself lucky you fought off Akhenaton. If you hadn't, I would've had to find a way to get to the in-between myself, because, starting now, I don't intend to live without you."

His lips tipped up. "Yeah. I got that." He turned to Strike. "I think this is going to take both of us. That first night, I think I called the road magic without really specifying a destination; at first Kinich Ahau's need drew us to Xibalba. Then I called the magic a second time to get us out of there, but I still didn't have a real destination in mind. In the absence of Cizin's magic, I suspect the library magic would have drawn me straight to the library. As it is"—he turned his palms up—"if we can combine your 'port targeting with my ability to form a conduit through the barrier, we may have gained more than just a new Godkeeper and two new mated pairs just now."

Startled, Jade looked at Sasha's wrist, where she too wore a new *jun tan*. Curious, Jade craned to pick out Rabbit in the crowd. Face set and angry, he deliberately looked away, but turned his forearm toward her. He wore no *jun tan*, and his hellmark remained bloodred. Her heart ached for him.

"When I used the road magic previously," Lucius said, "Jade's and my bodies stayed safely back at Skywatch. This time we all came down here body and soul, via the hellroad. Problem is, the solstice is past and the hellroad is sealed, or close to it."

Sven glanced at his heavy-duty diver's watch. "Shit. He's right."

Lucius held out his still-bleeding palm to Strike. "You can move bodies on earth. I can move spirits between planes. You want to see if between the two of us we can get our collective asses home?"

"Fuck, yeah."

The men linked hands as the others nicked their palms and joined up in a circle, linked by blood and magic. Jade kept hold of Lucius's hand, with Michael on her other side, which seemed fitting somehow.

"Everyone think about Skywatch," Lucius said. "The magic needs a destination."

"We should"—*all think of the same spot*, Jade started to say, but she was cut off midword when the magic triggered unexpectedly, the power leaping from zero to ninety in no time flat. She heard Lucius yell something but missed what he said; his magic roared in her head, masculine and commanding, blending now with Strike's red-gold teleporter's talent. The power grabbed them, snatching them out of the canyon in an instant. She saw a flash of dark, ominous shadows moving toward the "I"-shaped ball court; then it was gone. Xibalba was gone. And still they moved up, accelerating, the universe moving past them in a blur that wasn't gray-green, wasn't black, wasn't any real color at all. Then, in the blur, she saw an image: a teenager's face, smiling at her. *"You're so much smarter than I was,"* the *nahwal*'s voice said. *"So much braver than I. You fought for him."*

Jade gaped even as truth and joy sang through her. "You died trying to save us. That's as brave as it gets."

"If I had truly been brave, I wouldn't have gone into the library that last time. I would have stayed. I would have found you . . . somehow."

Jade's heart took a long, slow roll in her chest. What would it have been like to have her mother with her growing up? To have another senior mage alive when they returned to Skywatch? But she shook her head. "I don't blame you."

"Maybe you should."

"I don't," Jade said firmly. "I forgive you. I hope you'll forgive yourself." She paused. "I'm okay now . . . Mom."

As if that had been what the *nahwal*—ghost?—had been waiting for, despite whether she knew it herself, Vennie's lips turned up in a smile that Jade knew from seeing her own face in the mirror. Then the vision wavered and went thin. In the instant before it disappeared, though, Jade saw another shadow: that of a tall, broad-shouldered young man waiting for Vennie in the mist.

Tears blinded Jade alongside a thought of, *Thank you, gods*. Then the air detonated around her and the magi materialized, their feet firmly planted on the floor for a change. Only they weren't at Skywatch.

They were in the library.

Lucius's hand tightened on hers and his face drained of color. "Oh, gods. Oh, *shit*!"

Jade's heart stuttered in her chest. They stood in the study area Lucius had described: There were the racks and robes, the tables, the yes/no stones, and the *way* glyph. Beyond, shelves stretched into the distance. The fountain was just as he had described it, with one difference: It was working now. Water spilled from the wall spigot, filled the bowl, and trickled down the back of the stone jaguar's gaping throat. Between its paws, the bowl was filled with flat, irregular rounds of corn bread.

A disbelieving laugh caught in her throat and emerged sounding like a moan. "At least we won't starve right away." But could they get out again? Had she found love, inner strength, and a new sort of peace, only to lose it too quickly? More, had they just doomed the earth to—

"*That's* new." Lucius's eyes were locked on a plain wooden door that was inset beside the jaguar. Tugging on their joined hands to bring her with him, he crossed to the door. Seeing no latch, he pushed on it.

The panel opened easily. Sunlight spilled in, blinding Jade. She squinted into the light, which was too bright, too white, too hot. . . . Her eyes were slow to adjust. When they did, she found herself blinking at canyon walls and a worn pathway leading to a small cluster of buildings in the middle distance.

Skywatch. Oh, holy shit.

"We're home," Lucius said. "And I think we brought the whole fucking library with us." He let out a long, shuddering breath as the others clustered behind them, and they poured through the door as a team. The sky was very blue, the sun very white. The air felt drier than it had the day before, and the encroaching algae slime was already turning black and dying beneath the might of Kinich Ahau.

Turning back to look at where they had come from, Jade let out a long breath of her own. "No," she said softly. "*We* didn't bring the library home. *You* did."

The plain wooden doorway had appeared in the spot where the hidden tunnel mouth had been, flanked by the flame-shaped stones on one side, the staring eyes on the other. She imagined that when they went back inside, all the way to the rear of the chamber, they would find that the place where Vennie's skeleton had sat in the star bloodline's secret room would match up precisely with the metaphysical version of her corpse Lucius had seen within the barrier. Or maybe they would both be gone, vanished now that her soul was where it belonged. Either one would be fine, Jade thought. She knew her parents now.

Above the door, blazoned into the canyon wall in glyph writing, was the prophecy Lucius had translated from the carved wooden box.

"Fuck me," he said on a sharp bark of disbelief. "It was a true prophecy after all, but Sasha guessed right. It was a damned fragment." He read aloud, translating: "'In the triad years, a mage-born Prophet can wield the library's might, but it will take a human's love to bring it back to Earth.'" He turned to Jade, pulled her into his arms, and kissed her deeply. When they came up for air, he finished the translation: "'Magic isn't the answer. Love is.'"

GLOSSARY

Like much of the Nightkeepers' culture, their language comes from the people they have lived with throughout their history. Or if we want to chicken-and-egg things, it's more likely that the other cultures took the words from the Nightkeepers and incorporated them into their developing languages just as they did their science and religions. The following is a brief glossary of some of the most common (or uncommon) terms and their meanings. Pronunciation-wise, most of these words sound the way they're spelled, with two tricks: First, the letter "x" takes the "sh" sound. Second, the letter "i" should be read as the "ee" sound. Thus, for example, Xibalba becomes "Shee-bal-buh."

For more information on the Nightkeepers' world, excerpts, deleted scenes, and more, please visit www.JessicaAndersen.com.

Entities

Akhenaton—More than three thousand years ago, this pharaoh forcibly converted the Egyptian empire to monotheistic worship of the sun god, Aten, and proclaimed himself a god-king. As part of converting his subjects to the new god, he had all priests of the old religion slaughtered . . . including the Nightkeepers who had guided ancient Egypt up to that point.

Banol Kax—The lords of the underworld, Xibalba. Driven from the earth by the many-times-great-ancestors of the modern Nightkeepers, the *Banol Kax* seek to return and subjugate mankind on the foretold day: December 21, 2012.

Godkeeper—A female Nightkeeper who has bonded with one of the sky gods. The Godkeepers are prophesied to form the core of the Nightkeepers' fighting force in the years leading up to the 2012 doomsday.

itza'at—A female Nightkeeper with visionary powers; a seer. The *itza'at* talent is often associated with depression, mental instability, and suicide, because the seer can envision the future but not change it.

Kinich Ahau—The sun god of the ancient Maya. Each night at sunset, Kinich Ahau enters Xibalba. With the aid of two huge black dogs called companions, the god must fight through the underworld to reach the dawn horizon each morning, beginning a new day.

makol (ajaw-makol)—These demon souls are capable of reaching through the barrier to possess evil-natured human hosts. Recognized by his luminous green eyes, a *makol*-bound human retains his own thoughts and actions in direct proportion to the amount of evil in his soul. An *ajaw-makol*, which is a ruling *makol* created through direct spell casting, can create lesser *makol* through blood sacrifice.

nahwal—Humanoid spirit entities that exist in the barrier and hold within them all of the accumulated wisdom of each Nightkeeper bloodline. They can be asked for information, but cannot be trusted.

Nightkeeper—A member of an ancient race sworn to protect mankind from annihilation in the years leading up to December 21, 2012, when the barrier separating the earth and the underworld will fall and the *Banol Kax* will seek to precipitate the apocalypse.

Order of Xibalba—Formed by renegade Nightkeepers, the order was believed to have been destroyed in the 1520s. However, the Order of Xibalba survives, and is now led by a powerful mage named Iago, who seeks to bind his soul to that of the long-dead Aztec god-king, Moctezuma.

Prophet—An oracle created when a magic user's soul is destroyed but the body is magically preserved, becoming an animate shell that relays information from the barrier-bound library to the Nightkeepers on earth.

scribe—A mage who holds a powerful but fickle talent among the Nightkeepers: the ability to create spells.

winikin—Descended from the conquered Sumerian warriors who served the Nightkeepers back in ancient Egypt, the *winikin* are blood-bound to act as the servants, protectors, and counselors of the magi.

Places

hellmouth—Formerly found in the cloud forests of Ecuador, this underworld access point, which opens only on the cardinal solstices and equinoxes, has vanished from the face of the earth.

Skywatch—The Nightkeepers' training compound is located in a box canyon in the Chaco Canyon region of New Mexico, and is protected by magical wards.

Xibalba—The nine-layer underworld, home to the *Banol Kax* and *makol.*

Things (spells, glyphs, prophecies, etc.)

archive—This three-room stronghold at Skywatch contains the writings and artifacts collected by the Nightkeepers since they escaped Spanish conquest in the fifteen hundreds and migrated north to what became the United States. Although impressive in its scope, the archive contains very few prophecies focused on the 2012 doomsday and end-time war, as these were addressed in far older texts.

barrier—A force field of psi energy that separates the earth, sky, and underworld, and forms the energy source that powers the Nightkeepers' magic. The strength of the barrier fluctuates with the positions of the stars and planets, and weakens as the 12/21/2012 end date approaches.

jun tan—The "beloved" glyph that signifies a Nightkeeper's mated status.

library—Created by far-seeing Nightkeeper leaders, this repository contains all the ancient artifacts and information the magi need to arm themselves for the end-time war. Once housed in a sacred cavern on earth, the library is now hidden deep within the barrier, and may be accessed only by the Prophet.

Solstice Massacre—Following a series of prophetic dreams, the Nightkeepers' king led them to battle against the *Banol Kax* in the mid-eighties. The magi were slaughtered; only a scant dozen children survived to be raised in hiding by their *winikin*. These are the Nightkeepers of today.

skyroad—This celestial avenue connected the earth and sky planes, allowing contact between the Nightkeepers and the gods. Since Iago's destruction of the skyroad, the gods have been unable to influence events on earth, giving sway to the demons and tipping humanity's balance dangerously toward the underworld.

Triad—The last three years prior to December 21, 2012, are known as the triad years. During this time, the

Nightkeepers are prophesied to need the help of the Triad, a trio of über-powerful magi created through a powerful spell . . . one that the Nightkeepers cannot locate. Their only hope is that the spell is contained within the library . . . and that their Prophet can find it.

writs—Written by the First Father, these rules delineate the duties and codes of the Nightkeepers. Not all of them translate well into present day.

The Nightkeepers and their *winikin*

Coyote bloodline—The most mystical of the bloodlines. Coyote-Seven, known as Sven, can move objects with his mind and wears the warrior's mark, but he is the least mature of the magi. His *winikin*, the senior statesman, Carlos, has been reassigned to Nate Blackhawk, whose *winikin* died when Nate was a baby. Carlos's daughter, Cara Liu, is supposed to be serving Sven. Instead, she has returned to the human world.

Eagle bloodline—A bird bloodline, and therefore connected with the air and flight. The current members of this bloodline include Brandt, his wife, Patience (who has the talent of invisibility), and their twin full-blood sons, Harry and Braden. On the king's order, Brandt and Patience's *winikin*, Woody and Hannah, have taken the twins into hiding for their own protection, dividing the family unit.

Harvester bloodline—The harvesters most often worked behind the scenes, and were the most passive magi. The bloodline's last remaining *winikin*, Shandi, has raised its sole surviving member, Jade, to be the prototypical harvester . . . but Jade chafes against the restrictions of her heritage.

Hawk bloodline—Also connected with air and flight, this bloodline can be aloof and unpredictable. Nate Blackhawk, the surviving member of this bloodline, was orphaned young and trusts few. He is a shape-shifter whose potentially destructive power is kept in check by his love for his mate, Alexis, and the steady guidance of his *winikin*, Carlos.

Jaguar bloodline—The royal house of the Nightkeepers. The members of this bloodline tend to be loyal and fair-minded, but can be stubborn and often struggle between duty and their own personal desires. The current members of the jaguar bloodline include the Nightkeepers' king, Strike, and his sisters, Anna and Sasha. Strike is a teleporter, Anna a seer who denies her talents, and Sasha a wielder of the lifegiving *ch'ul* magic. They are protected and guided by the royal *winikin*, Jox. Strike's mate and queen, Leah Daniels, is full human, a former Miami-Dade detective who now leads Strike's royal council.

Peccary bloodline—The boar bloodline is old and powerful; its members ruled the Nightkeepers before the jaguars came to power. Red-Boar was the only adult mage to survive the Solstice Massacre; he lost his wife and twin sons, and never forgave himself for living.

He was killed by a *makol* during the reunited Night-keepers' first battle against the dark forces. Red-Boar's teenage son, Rabbit, lives with the stigma of being a half-blood, and commands wildly powerful magic.

Serpent bloodline—The masters of trickery. Snake Mendez is serving the tail end of a jail sentence and is apart from the Nightkeepers, yet he already has some of his powers. His *winikin* is locked up in a secure psychiatric facility, driven there by despair at what his charge has become.

Smoke bloodline—Often seers and prophets. However, the surviving member of this bloodline, Alexis Gray, has shown neither talent. Instead, she once wielded the power of the goddess Ixchel, patron of weaving, fertility, and rainbows. With the destruction of the skyroad, she has lost her Godkeeper connection but remains a fierce warrior.

Stone bloodline—The keepers of secrets. The members of this bloodline are known as great warriors, although the last surviving bloodline member, Michael, is a master of the protective shield spell as well as the killing silver magic called *muk*. His *winikin*, Tomas, and his mate, Sasha, combine to keep him balanced when the deadly magic threatens to tip him toward darkness.

Earthly allies

Lucius Hunt—A longing for adventure and recognition rendered Lucius vulnerable to seduction by one of the demon *makol*. Under its influence, he found and nearly betrayed the Nightkeepers, and then defected to the Order of Xibalba. Newly returned to the Nightkeepers, with the demon exorcised, he should wield the power of a Nightkeeper Prophet.

Leah Ann Daniels—The former detective is now Strike's mate and the Nightkeepers' queen.

Myrinne—Raised by a witch who told fortunes in the French Quarter and was sacrificed by Iago at the hell-mouth, this young, ambitious beauty is Rabbit's lover.

Earthly enemies

Iago—The leader of the Order of Xibalba, Iago is a mage of extraordinary power, capable of "borrowing" the talents of other magi. Iago hopes to gain additional power by allying himself with the might of the bloodthirsty Aztec through the soul of their god-king, Moctezuma.

Don't miss the thrill ride of the next paranormal romance in Jessica Andersen's Final Prophecy series. With the two-year threshold to the 2012 doomsday on the horizon and an earthquake demon wreaking havoc worldwide, Patience and Brandt must race to rescue their kidnapped twin sons. But in order to do so, they must reveal long-hidden, deadly secrets that threaten their marriage . . . and their lives.

December 15
Two years and six days to the zero date

Deep underground, as the robed Nightkeepers formed a circle around the First Father's sarcophagus, Patience badly wanted to blurt, *Call off the ceremony. The omens suck!*

She didn't, though, because the others didn't give a crap about the omens or the Mayan astronomy that had become her thing in recent months. Besides, when the First Father's recently rediscovered end-time prophecies said "on this day, you will jump," the surviving magi freaking jumped. And when he said they had to enact the Triad spell on the Day of Ancestors in the third year before the end date, lest the dark lords release a brutally destructive demon from the Xibalban underworld . . . well, there didn't seem to be much point in her suggesting that they should wait for a day that was governed by a more propitious sun or sacred number.

It was now-or-never, do-or-die time . . . or potentially "do-*and*-die" given that the Triad spell had a two-thirds attrition rate.

Patience suppressed a shiver at the thought. The air in the tomb was cool and faintly damp, and the flickering torchlight made the carved stone images surrounding her seem to move in the shadows, morphing from Egyptian to Mayan and back again, as though echoing an earlier chapter of the Nightkeepers' evolution. Sweat prickled from her back beneath the lightweight black-on-black combat gear she wore to go with the warrior's mark on her inner wrist. She was heavily armed—they all were—though it was questionable whether jade-tipped bullets and ceremonial knives would do a damn thing to improve their odds. They weren't going up against a physical enemy; they were offering themselves to the sun god, which would choose three of them to receive the Triad powers. At least that was the theory. Problem was, the theory also said that the entire pantheon would choose the Triad, not just the sole god that currently had access to the earthly plane. Which meant . . . well, they didn't know what it meant, and the uncertainty intensified the *not good* vibe that had first lodged in Patience's stomach early that morning when she'd charted the day's sun, sacred numbers, and light pulses, and got what amounted to a cosmic suggestion that she should stay the hell in bed with the covers pulled up over her head until tomorrow.

Not that anyone wanted to hear *that* particular opinion at the moment.

Across the circle from her, Strike began the ceremony by ritually inviting the gods and ancestors to listen up; he spoke in the old tongue, having memorized the spell phonetically. Beside him, Jade joined in to smooth over his occasional fumbled syllable, as she was the only one there who was even passingly fluent. Granted, Lucius and Anna were experts in ancient Mayan, but this was a Nightkeepers-only ceremony, which meant no Lucius, and Anna was incommunicado. With Leah also excluded for general humanness, the circle consisted of a whopping ten magi who were eligible for the Triad spell, when the legends said there should be hundreds, even thousands of them for the dozens of gods to choose from.

Yeah. Not so much.

But as Strike and Jade finished the first of three repetitions of the spell, a faint hum touched the air, beginning at the very edges of hearing, and gaining depth and voice as the magic began to gather. More than just red-gold Nightkeeper power, it was laced through with a white-light crackle that smelled faintly of ozone. Would being chosen feel like electrocution? Patience wondered. One second, everything normal, then the next . . . *zzzzap*?

Don't pick me or Brandt, she whispered inwardly. *Please.* Even that much of not-quite-a-prayer went against the writs, but it wouldn't be the first time she'd been guilty of the sin. How could she avoid it, when the rules set down by the First Father himself said she had to put the needs of the gods, her king, her teammates, and mankind ahead of those of her husband

and children? Then again, Brandt hadn't found it at all difficult. He'd just pushed her and the twins into a mental box called "family" . . . and nail gunned the shit out of the lid.

Don't go there, she thought fiercely. *This is about the magic, not us.*

Keeping her head down, focusing on the process rather than the flickering torchlight and the buzz of magic, she waited for the king's signal. When it came, she—along with all the others—palmed the ceremonial stone knife from her belt and used it to slash her right palm along the lifeline. Pain bit, bringing magic to bubble a champagne fizz in her bloodstream. It beckoned with hints of power and pageantry, and made her wish for a moment that she were solely a warrior rather than a tripartite of warrior, wife, and mother. As a warrior, it would've been easy to answer the call to duty, maybe even hope she'd be tapped as one of the three super magi prophesied to tip the balance.

But then again, that would mean undoing the past six years. It would mean her not meeting Brandt on spring break, nor marrying him months later. She would've missed the good years with him, when they'd lived as humans, neither of them knowing that they were both under the shadow of the same secret heritage, that their crossing paths had been more destiny than chance. In the altered reality of her warrior self, they wouldn't have met until two and a half years earlier when the magic reactivated and Strike summoned the surviving magi to Skywatch. They would have met as strangers, probably would've become lovers, but without the complications of all the secrets and lies, and the heavy weight of the love they shared for their twin sons, Harry and Braden.

Would it have been easier that way? Probably. But even on the worst of the bad days, she'd never, *ever* wished she could go back and not have the twins. Granted, she hadn't seen them in almost two years; she had missed out on so many firsts, and longed to see them with an intensity that was a physical constant, an ache beneath her heart. But even without seeing them, she still knew they were out there, safe with Hannah and Woody. And the knowledge kept her going.

I'm doing this for you, she whispered to them, although she knew that, without their bloodline marks and the accompanying connection to the barrier, they couldn't hear her. They were far safer off the grid than on it. But knowing that they couldn't hear her didn't stop her from talking to them in her head, even if that sometimes made her wonder whether, in marrying Brandt, she had taken on some of the madness rumored to linger in his eagle bloodline, along with the depression she'd battled for the past two years. That didn't really matter, though. She'd beaten the depression, or at least learned to manage it. She could do the same with the other impulses too. Most of them, anyway.

Switching hands, her grip going slippery, she cut her other palm, then wiped the blade on her robe and returned it to her belt. Then, unable to delay any longer, she held out her hands to the men on either side of her so they could uplink, joining blood-to-blood in order to call on a deeper, collective wellspring of magic.

On her left side, Sven took her hand immediately. The contact brought a flare of heat and magic, amping the champagne fizz to Alka Seltzer foam as he squeezed her hand in support, or maybe nerves—it was hard to tell with him.

To her right, though . . .

When her hand hovered midair, unclaimed, ice frosted the hard knot in her stomach. *Don't do it. Not here. Not now.* It was her darkest unvoiced fear, that one day Brandt would decide that with the twins gone and the two of them living mostly separate lives, he didn't want to bother with the thin veneer of a shared suite and matching rings anymore. He wasn't big on public displays of anything, but gods knew he was more obsessed by the concepts of duty and destiny than even the *winikin* who'd raised him. He might think he was doing the right thing by severing the last of their ties before the ceremony, leaving either or both of them free to enter the Triad if chosen, without fearing that the mated bond would transfer some of the magic and risks. And those risks had to be on his mind, she knew. Of the three members of the previous Triad, one had survived, one had died outright . . . and one had gone insane.

Don't you dare break it off, she thought fiercely. *What we've got left is still better than what most people ever get.* Or so she kept telling herself.

Once, their mated bond had been so strong that he might've caught a whisper of those words in his head even without the bloody hand clasp of an uplink. That wasn't the case anymore, though, which forced her to look at him, an action she'd been avoiding ever since he'd taken his place beside her. As she turned her head, she swore she heard her vertebrae creak, as if she'd grown old at twenty-six.

Their eyes locked, her sky blue to his gold-spangled brown. She took in the details without wanting to, seeing how his bronzed skin stretched across his high cheekbones, aquiline nose, and wide brow, drawn tight by stress and the sleepless nights that were reflected in the shadow smudges beneath his eyes. His sable hair was as neat as ever, his shave smooth, his eyebrows the matched curves of a gliding eagle's wings. He was physical perfection even under the weight of duty and the threat of death or madness, and his cool calm made her feel sweaty and desperate in comparison.

"Don't." She thought she whispered it aloud, a single word of an unvoiced prayer to the gods he refused to call on. The room was silent around them, as the others waited for her and Brandt to complete the circle.

"What's wrong?" Unlike his smooth looks, his voice was slightly rough, edged with a sensual rasp that, even now, shot straight to her core and made her remember warm sheets and lazy mornings spent in bed, sometimes cuddling with the boys, other times just the two of them.

She looked away as a spike of anger flattened the magic fizz. What the hell kind of question was that? *Everything's wrong*, she wanted to say, but that was the answer of the woman she'd been for too long, the one who had turned inward and self-pitying. She had pulled herself out of that place and didn't intend to go back, which meant the easy answer wasn't an option anymore. But what could she say instead? The woman inside her—the one who still loved the memory of the man she had thought she'd married—that part of her wanted to tell him to be careful, to stay strong, and, even, gods forgive her, reject the Triad power if it was offered to him, knowing the added risk his heritage would bring. She wanted to tell him to think of the twins, of her, of the shared future they had once imagined, even though it seemed to grow more distant by the day. The warrior inside her, though, couldn't let those words come. The ritual they were about to enter wasn't about being careful; it was about fulfilling a three-thousand-year-old prophecy. It was about ascending to the next stage of the end-time countdown, and maybe—hopefully—gaining the power the Nightkeepers needed to defend the increasingly volatile barrier against the *Banol Kax* during the upcoming winter solstice.

Knowing it was the right answer, the only answer, the woman let the warrior take over, blunting her emotions and quickening her blood with determination and the hot, hard throb of magic. She stretched out her hand, palm up, so the blood track glistened dark in the torchlight. "Right now the only thing that matters is calling the Triad."

It was the proper answer, the dutiful one. And the warrior within her meant every word of it, even as the woman would've given almost anything to turn back the clock to safer, easier times.

"We need to—"

"Uplink," she interrupted.

He exhaled. "Patience . . ." he began, but then trailed off, as though he didn't know what else there was to say anymore, either. Magic curled between them, hazing the air red-gold and making it sparkle in the flickering light. The hum within her changed pitch, inching upward as their eyes locked once again, and she felt the click of the connection that had been absent for far too long.

Heat pooled in her midsection, forming a hard pressure on her diaphragm before it dripped down, warm and liquid, making her ache with longing for another time, an earlier version of the man he'd become. The need came from the inextricable link between Nightkeeper magic and sex, she knew. That and the power of the *jun tan*s, the mated marks they both wore on their inner wrists, joining their flesh and souls through the power of the barrier even though the connection of their minds and hearts had waned.

"We're running out of time," she said, not quite sure where the words had come from. Was that the warrior's sentiment or something else?

His eyes flared, going hard and hot, more like those of the intense young architect she'd married than the reserved, withdrawn mage he'd become. He opened his mouth to say something, but the words didn't come. Instead, he growled, "Fuck it."

Leaning in, he closed the distance between them. His mouth covered hers before she could brace or even comprehend. He swallowed her gasp, smothered her half-formed protest, and took her under with a kiss. He wasn't holding her, wasn't touching her anywhere but her mouth, but his kiss held her shackled as shock collided with a roar of magic-amplified lust that had her opening to him before she could call back the impulse. Their tongues touched and slid; his flavor caromed through her, lighting neurons that had been dim for months now. Years. She felt the vibration of his groan, though the sound was lost beneath the escalating hum that surrounded them, bound them together.

Heat raced through her veins. Magic. Power. *Love.* Then he took her hand, pressed their bleeding palms together, and completed the circle of ten. The red-gold buzz went to a bloodred scream, the world lurched, and suddenly Patience was moving while standing still as her spirit-self peeled out of her corporeal body and lurched sideways into the energy curtain that separated the earth, sky, and underworld. Gray-green mist raced past her, laced with lightning and the smell of ozone and desperation. Then the Triad spell took them . . . and there was no going back.